Let The Swine
Go Forth

Auriel Roe

To James Bloom, who was there when it all happened.

1

And there was a good way off from them an herd of many swine. So the devils besought him saying, "If thou cast us out, suffer us to go away into that herd of swine." And he said unto them "Go" and when they were come out, they went into the swine: and behold, the whole herd ran violently down a steep place into the sea and perished in the waters.

Matthew 8:30-32, KJV1

A diavola red Aston Martin DB5 rounded the corner of the street below and reversed smoothly into the VIP parking space. The driver's door opened and there emerged from the incomparable sports car a long pair of legs swathed in Black Watch tartan and terminating in what Randolph suspected from a distance to be a pair of Manolo Blahnik court shoes. The rest of the woman followed a moment later. The trousers were part of a perfectly fitted suit and the heels elevated her to a full six feet. Her face was partly obscured by sunglasses and a fringe of dusky blonde hair but he could tell she was striking. As she swept up toward the hotel entrance, pulling off her leather driving gloves, there was a flurry of servility. The doorman stood to attention. A bell boy rushed out, although her only luggage was a handbag resembling a vintage school satchel. And the two uniformed security police officers either side of the door saluted and, he could have sworn, clicked their heels.

'I must be dreaming,' Randolph murmured to himself, looking from car to woman, woman to car. He still had his Aston Martin DB5 Corgi model with ejecting James Bond, a birthday present from his parents some forty-five years ago, but this was the first time he'd seen the real McCoy. He dabbed his lips with a paper napkin, hurriedly deposited his breakfast tray on the floor outside his room, opened the wardrobe and removed his sheepskin driving jacket for the selfie he was planning to take in front of the DB5. What a brilliant idea it had been to bring it along in case of a springtime Central Asian chill. Thankfully, he already happened to have on his tapered taupe suede trousers and fitted Liberty of London paisley shirt. He smiled at his reflection in the full-length mirror as he pulled on his Chelsea boots, feeling particularly enamored with his new head of flaxen hair, painstakingly restored to its former youthful glory over the past six months by one of the best clinics in the country, courtesy of his parents' largesse.

He trotted through the lobby and out into the street, his dilute blue eyes blinking in the sunlight. As he approached the divine automobile, two men in dark suits and sunglasses appeared. He asked one of them if he wouldn't mind taking his photograph standing beside the car, which question had to be largely in mime as neither of them spoke any English. The men demonstrated a mixture of confusion and suspicion in response. When the taller of the two finally cottoned on, he gave a negative hand gesture, faintly edged with menace. Randolph backed away deprecatingly and returned to the hotel lobby. He took a complimentary copy of *The Financial Times* from the newspaper rack, sat down in a leather and chrome armchair from which he could see the parking area and began pretending to read whilst he waited to have another go at getting the photograph once the sentinels moved on.

Randolph was attending the annual International School Drama Immersion Conference (ISDIC), which was held in a different capital city each year and offered significant perks for accompanying teachers, in that there was a full programme of workshops led by visiting professionals. This allowed the teachers, the of majority of whom were of the single, divorced or unhappily married variety, to mingle with one another, whilst their young charges were otherwise occupied. Admittedly, there was a modicum of extra work prior to departure, in so far as each group had to produce a dramatic offering of no more than ten minutes duration on an annual theme, which entries were then judged by a locally illustrious patron of the dramatic arts who had subsidized the cost of the contest and duly awarded a trophy. Randolph's school, Swineforth Hospital, had yet to win even an honourable mention, a fact that Swineforth's chronically choleric and 'overdue-to-retire' bursar, Nigel Dare, would repeatedly bring up by way of a veiled threat in his eagerness to cut the funding for this annual term-time jolly of Randolph's.

This year's theme was 'Master and Servant' and the conference was being held in the curiously named city of Diskebapisbad, which was a new one on Randolph, as was the oil and mineral rich nation of Kebapistan. He had been assured though that it was fundamentally safe, ruled as it was by a 'president for life' with an iron fist, who had been in power since Soviet days, and of whom it was said that merely looking askance at his omnipresent portrait was an offence punished with draconian severity.

He found himself wondering whether there might be a lady from the conference in the vast and ornate lobby who'd care to pop outside with him for the photograph once the coast was clear. He scanned the room over his pale pink newspaper. Perhaps, if she were well enough turned-out, she might accompany him on his meanderings about town. This had proven useful in the past as he could never quite manage to manipulate his selfie stick on his own. There had even been one occasion, a couple of years back in Reykjavik, when such

3

meanderings had provided the entree to a romantic turn in a hot spring, which liaison had continued for the duration of the conference. The lobby, however, was deserted, apart from the Aston Martin goddess, sitting behind a Turkish coffee, absorbed in her phone, her hair swept over in a luxuriant wave at the top, the lapel of her tartan suit adorned by a fine gold stick pin of a dragon with ruby eyes, complemented by matching earrings of the creature's head. Assuming the ensemble was real gold, it must, Randolph deduced, be worth a mint.

A woman like this was, he reflected, probably just that bit beyond his reach but, if nothing else, he could at least ask if she would grant him her permission to take a photograph of himself with her car. Fittingly, she was seated near a rotating columnar display case of 'Gemstones of Kebapistan'. He determined to stroll over, pretend to take a closer look at the display and try his luck.

'What absolutely gorgeous rocks!' he mused aloud after a moment or two.

She looked up, albeit without smiling, and said in a cut glass English accent, 'Yes, Kebapistan is blessed with many beautiful natural treasures.'

'Are you here for the conference, by any chance?'

'Yes, you too?'

'I am indeed, along with my young protégés from the West Country. And have you also brought over a group?'

'No, I'm only having a tour of the conference today but I will be returning on Friday to do the judging.'

'Oh, goodness me!' Randolph gasped, performing a kind of mock kowtow, 'Then I hope you won't mind giving me a few pointers on what you're looking for. My school has never even had an Honourable Mention during the ten years we've been attending.' He was feeling terribly bold with his luxuriant new mane and gestured to request her consent to sit down with her.

However, the two dark suited men from outside were suddenly in front of him again blocking his way. It was all Randolph could do to babble a nervously jovial, 'Oh, whoops, I do beg your pardon, chaps, I don't think we've been introduced.'

The woman's violet eyes scanned over him for a few seconds, working their way up his smart casual attire, from his Chelsea boots to his well-groomed head. Then she said something in a language he presumed was Kebapi and the suits withdrew.

'Gosh! Do the competition judges get minders these days to protect them from corrupting influences such as myself?' Randolph smiled, showing off the whitening treatment he'd had done at the dentist the week before and reflected that, upon closer inspection, her face revealed that she had hit 'the Naughty Forty', which he thought might improve his chances a smidgen.

She returned the smile and a Turkish coffee was immediately placed in front of him by a timid waiter. 'I am Zara Zoran, pleased to meet you.' Her hand was proffered regally, revealing a heavy gold bracelet in the same dragon motif and a substantial ring to match on her index finger. Randolph gingerly took it for a few seconds, which seemed to be the expected length of time.

'Tristram Randolph, charmed, I'm sure...I do believe you're attired in the Black Watch tartan of Inverness,' he ventured; he prided himself upon being a man who possessed an intricate knowledge of the Scottish weaves.

'Am I?' she raised her eyebrows impressed. 'I wasn't aware of that and, you know, there's not much even a British man can teach me about my favourite country in the world after Kebapistan. I am an Anglophile through and through! I try to get over to my townhouse in Chelsea every summer.'

'Oh, really? My parents live in London,' Randolph chimed in, deciding not to add at this juncture that they lived in Twickenham, where he had been born and bred.

'So, a Drama teacher from London? How

marvellous! I love the West End theatres.'

'Ah, I *was* a drama teacher....and I reside in the West Country these days, which is miles from the West End, I fear. I only do this annual trip because it always crops up at a busy time for our drama teacher. I'm Head of the International Stream at Swineforth Hospital, a premier English public school, to which the Asian market is increasingly turning for a top notch boarding education.'

Zara Zoran's eyes widened at this. What Randolph failed to elaborate on was that Swineforth Hospital currently boasted a grand total of a dozen international pupils, mainly over-privileged tearaways who had stampeded through, and been thrown out of, a score of private schools across the United Kingdom. A couple of handfuls of international pupils per year was the most the school had been able muster with Randolph at the helm. He had never swelled the ranks of the programme as he'd promised to do at interview a decade ago. Due to the shambolic nature of the school, however, he'd kept the job as no one else could face attempting to contain 'the foreign tykes', a feat Randolph barely managed even with his weekly wheedling over cream cakes at the town 'tea shoppe'. His role at the school was a perpetual bone of contention between himself and Nigel Dare, the Bursar, who so despised paying Randolph for his 'bloody Mickey Mouse job' that his left eye would twitch uncontrollably each month when he saw the man's name when was signing off the salaries.

'Now, to answer your earlier question...' Ms Zoran confided, 'While it would be unfair of me to tell you exactly what I'm looking for as a judge, I think it can do no harm to say 'Nothing too radical, *please!*' I didn't choose the rather dystopian sounding theme. It is not interesting to me this agitprop theatre. I like to see something traditional that supports the status quo.'

'Oh, yes, my sentiments exactly, I'm all for convention,' Randolph had now resolved to meet with his group that evening and tone down their avant garde approach to this year's theme of Master and Servant. He'd seen a pattern among the winning pieces at these conforonoon nupronninnist, physical theatre pieces, laden with ambiguous symbolism-- and had, this year, put together a cutting edge tour de force, which he had been hoping would sweep away the competition and the judges. Should he finally return with the trophy, Dare would have to eat his hat. With his new, insider knowledge on the predilection of the judge, he saw he'd have to change tack fast if he wanted to win and safely continue with his annual term time holiday.

The television screen that took up most of the far wall had been showing a documentary on the Kebapistan Official State Marching Band (KOSMB) earlier. Randolph hadn't been paying much attention since it seemed dull, as marching bands inevitably did on the telly. Now though, a drama feature had popped up that caught his eye. 'The Kebapistan Unified National Theatre (KUNT),' Ms Zoran pointed out, 'our example to the world of excellence in drama. This is the award-winning *Annals of Kebapistan*, a four-hour extravaganza. The director received the Rhombus of Honour, our highest state decoration, from the President himself. Last year's sell out premier was filmed and will be aired annually across Kebapistan and neighbouring countries for the foreseeable future.'

The spectacle before them at this point in the epic farrago was the episode of the attempted Roman invasion, which had apparently been thwarted by the Romans' inability to survive the alternately freezing and searing desert plain conditions of the country, putting them at the mercy of nomadic Kebapi tribesmen with Queen Saltanat at their helm, riding bareback upon a milk white mare. She was played by a strikingly curvaceous woman in metallic tribal makeup, clad Lady Godiva style in little more than long silvery blonde locks and a minimal leather and bronze tunic. There was a close-up while she delivered what Randolph surmised was a stirring speech to her warriors, whereupon the tribes charged at the Romans who, as they fled, revealed boxer shorts of various hues and patterns beneath their flapping tunics.

'Didn't know they had boxer shorts back in the day,' Randolph tittered.

'What do you mean?' Zara Zoran asked, puzzled.

'Well, of course, they have to wear something or the show might get a bit rude,' he reassured her.

Seeming not to catch his drift, she asked him what he thought of the lead actress who was, at that moment, having another close-up atop the milky mare, accompanied by a pontificating voice-over from a narrator who sounded like a motivational speaker.

'Well, I don't know what she's actually saying, as it's not in English so I can't really judge her acting, but possibly she's a tad on the melodramatic side, what with those wooden poses and rigid arm gestures. That being said, all can be forgiven as she's absolutely bewitching of face and, well, everything.'

'She's my younger sister, Zina,' Zara Zoran seemed to be rebuking him, possibly because, at the ripe old age of 53, he shouldn't be ogling a woman nigh on 20 years his junior in this manner.

'Ah, really? Right-ho, gosh!'

'Of course, her hair is dyed; it is naturally my colour,' Ms Zoran clarified. 'It was meant to be she judging here this week, as she is Kebapistan's most famous actress, but she is touring with the National Theatre. They are in Montenegro at present.'

'And are you also an actress?'

'No, not at all, I am a business woman, but I see my guide is here so I must have my workshop tour,' she rose and genially held out her silken hand again. 'I wish you and your pupils a most pleasant stay in our country and look forward to seeing your performance at the end of the week.' Randolph gushed about what an honour it had been to meet her, then turned his attention to the feature demonstrating what Kebaps evidently regarded as the apogee of theatrical excellence, making copious mental notes on how to reshape Swineforth's offering accordingly.

That evening, the Swineforth pupils were surprised to see Mr Randolph at their dinner table, rather than holding forth among the other drama teachers, as usual. He'd booked one of the function rooms, he told them, in order that they might 'iron out a few kinks' in their competition entry as he had 'got in with the judge' and sussed out the winning formula. Little did they guess that the ironing session was going to take them through to midnight, and that their fiery experimental offering would be toned down to something barely lukewarm. The resulting production was scrubbed clean of expressionism. Out went the choral chanting, the tableaux, the flashbacks, the screaming catharsis and in came a slice of melodramatic realism– a simple tale based on a Kebapi parable of the development, through hard times, of mutual respect between a farmer and his stable boy.

'There can only be one winner,' Zara Zoran opined into the microphone, dressed in a charcoal grey, pinstripe suit-dress, pleasingly cut just above the knee. Randolph knew it would be him because he had watched her wincing at the other entries, all of which had contained the elements that usually won, which he had so recently and deftly excised for erring on the revolutionary side.

Randolph was seated betwixt two drama teachers whom he'd fallen in with somewhat during the conference. On his left sat a Dutch lady with piano key teeth whose name sounded something like 'March On'. She was dressed in a sort of tie-dye tent, that served to emphasize her enormous rump, which was, at that moment, oozing onto the edge of Randolph's own chair. Fortunately, being a slender-hipped English gentleman, he was out of range of the creeping flesh. On his right sat Scottish Steve, or 'Stiv' as he styled himself, a weathered-looking fellow who sported an unkempt goatee and was never seen out of his distressed leather jacket, even at mealtimes. Randolph had quickly learnt to avert his head when Stiv spoke as his breath smelt of caffeine, nicotine and Stilton cheese. Marjon and Stiv, both of them previous winners, were each plainly thinking they had the trophy in the bag again. They'd been mystified by Randolph's Soviet Realist style interpretation of the theme and he'd heard them whisper behind his back 'lame', 'lacklustre' and the dreaded 'non-experimental'.

'So, I would like to present this year's International School Drama Immersion Conference trophy to...' Zara Zoran paused, toying with the tension in the room. Randolph noticed that Marjon and Stiv had both uncrossed their legs in readiness to stand up and come forward, each presuming their name would be announced as the winner. Ms Zoran caught his eye in the auditorium and smiled as she declaimed, 'The pupils of Swineforth Hospital and their teacher, Mr Tristram Randolph.' The multitude raised its eyebrows and watery applause trickled. Randolph strode forward jauntily. His pupils were jumping up and down on the stage and he shared a chuckle over this with Zara Zoran.

'Congratulations on a subtle and moving piece with humility at its heart,' she intoned into the microphone, after which she handed it over to Randolph who made the customary speech thanking his pupils and praising all the hard work of the other competitors before returning to his seat. As he passed Ms Zoran, she handed him an envelope and he wondered excitedly whether he was receiving a cash prize.

'Vaat did zee give you?' Marjon nodded toward the envelope as he sat back down. He duly opened it to find a card with an invitation written in immaculate sloping script, only he couldn't read it as he'd left his glasses in his room since he didn't like to wear them in public. Marjon had her glasses on a day-glo green string around her neck and had them up on her nose in no time. 'Zee's asking you on a date! Luncheon tomorrow!' she blurted out for everyone around them to hear, as if the sole reason for his winning was that Zara Zoran fancied him. She leered at him obscenely, showing off salmon-coloured gums.

'Don't be silly,' he scoffed, 'it's just a congratulatory lunch; it doesn't mean a thing.'

'I'd be careful if I were you!' Marjon warned.

'Whatever for?' sniffed Randolph.

'You'll find out sooner or later!' was all she said before stalking off to commiserate with her group.

2

Randolph spent most of the following morning choosing an outfit for his lunch date. He had risen early and padded out into the hotel corridor in his silk fleur-de-lys dressing gown and aubergine Moroccan mule slippers to see off his young charges for the final activity of the conference, a desert hike culminating in an outdoor workshop with the Kebapistan Folk Acrobatic Troupe (KFAT). He was going to be collected in front of the hotel at noon by Zara Zoran in the DB5 and felt he had to look the part for the moment when he was whisked off in the automobile of his dreams. Perhaps, he thought, he would turn out to be the man of her dreams, and dashed on a few extra splashes of Clive Christian Cologne after his long soak in the tub. He finally settled on a brass-buttoned, double-breasted navy blazer with grey flannel slacks, a pair of boating shoes and a cream cashmere turtleneck, hearkening back to Roger Moore's younger days as a knitwear model.

While he was waiting on the pavement outside, Marjon and Stiv walked past sniggering.

'Off on yer li'l date, are ya?' Stiv jeered.

'Aw look, he's got all drezzed up,' Marjon mocked.

Randolph smiled tartly and turned away. Teachers, he'd found during his long career, were frequently worse bullies than the most obnoxious pupils, only Stiv and Marjon didn't have the excuse of youth and inexperience. They were probably heading back to the Irish pub, the limit of their interest in the city, whither he had, regrettably, accompanied them almost every day. He suspected that they were consumed with jealousy that he would soon be having a no doubt splendid lunch with a beautiful woman, whereas they would be sipping watered down Guinness accompanied by a poor imitation of meat and potato pie flecked with a congealing gravy.

The diavola red DB5 drew up and Randolph clicked a quick selfie before, with a flutter in his heart, placing his hand on the polished chrome handle, carefully avoiding contact with the glossy paintwork so as not to sully it in any way. On opening the door, he found himself taking an involuntary intake of breath for the interior was as miraculous as the exterior: glistening walnut trim, plump red leather upholstery and Ms Zoran herself in an exquisitely tailored jumpsuit of heather-coloured tweed, mauve driving gloves, gold-rimmed sunglasses and vermilion lipstick.

Could this really be happening to him? he wondered as he lowered himself onto the passenger seat, allowing the welcoming upholstery to caress and then engulf him. He closed the door so gently there might have been a sleeping baby in the back, and ran his fingers over that sleek walnut veneer, which gave him goose pimples on the back of his neck. He turned his rapturous face to Zara Zoran's and she smiled and nodded, understanding his euphoria. Without a word, they sped off and he imagined himself in the company of Honor Blackman as Pussy Galore on his way to a little sparring in the hay at a conveniently situated roadside barn.

'We're going to have lunch with my father, Mr Randolph,' she said as they slid down the long, smooth, straight street.

'Your father?' he repeated, 'Oh, right-ho, and please call me Tristram.'

'Then you must call me Zara...and I have a proposition for you.'

'Really?' Randolph's heart skipped a beat.

'As I told you, I am a businesswoman and my latest

venture is setting up a brand new school here in Diskebapisbad. It will be the first of its kind in Kebapistan– a school with a British curriculum, British style uniform, British teachers, British accents, all the trimmings, and I want you to be headmaster.'

Randolph almost choked on his own tongue, 'Seriously?!'

'Yes, Tristram. And I want to call it Swineforth Hospital International. Many famous British schools are doing this nowadays, setting up outposts abroad to spread the gospel of Anglophilia.'

'Mmm, yes, I've heard about that, but why me as headmaster?' he inquired diplomatically, already thinking that it was about time that his talent as an educator was finally being recognised.

'Well, to be honest, Tristram, we did have a team in place from Saint Nicholas Bilberry, Norfolk, but they fell short in many ways. One of the aspects that left a lot to be desired was their uniform which was just plain silly. What parent wants to see their child wearing pillar box red corduroy knickerbockers? Your Swineforth Hospital uniform is far more tasteful. As you know I am a great fan of tartan. Anyway, I have decided to change tack and find new blood. You have the leadership experience required for this job in that you are Head of the International Streak at Swineforth Hospital: it is a logical step that your next post should be as headmaster of an international school. You can break your teeth as a headmaster here in Kebapistan. The school buildings are basically finished and all will be operational by September. What do you say?'

'Gosh, it's a bit of a quantum leap from the West Country to Kebapistan but I'm certainly interested.'

'I have in mind a school that is going to be like *a family* for children and teachers alike. In fact, when you recruit a teacher, I want you to tell them, 'Welcome to the Swineforth *family*', I think this will help people to feel secure and comfortable. Will you do that?'

'Oh, yes, that's rather good, isn't it?'

'Well, I believe so. And I'd like the school in England to be known as 'the sister school' to extend the metaphor. How does that sound?'

'It sounds great.'

'Excellent, so now you will be presented to my father. He's the principal donor, you know.'

'So does that make him a 'Donor Kebab'?' Randolph punned, striving to imitate the wit of James Bond.

Zara glanced over at him and frowned slightly, 'My father adores English humour but that is *not* a joke he would appreciate. His country is everything to him and he can sometimes take offence at something that even hints at mockery of it. It is essential that you understand this if we are to work together.'

They drove down one long gently curving stretch road after another, Zara handling her machine beautifully, quite unhindered in that theirs was the only vehicle on the road. In fact, the streets were quite empty of pedestrians. Between mirrored glass mid-rises clad in gleaming white marble, Randolph occasionally caught glimpses of the desert beyond, greyish-coloured sand with occasional scrubby, thorny looking bushes. Sand was accumulating at the edges of the pavements and every mile or so a gaggle of sweepers dressed in white overalls, and all, men and women, wearing their hair in the same close-cropped style, could be seen moving along hypnotically, removing any trace of the grey dust with broad, long-handled sweeping brushes. Beside each group, an armed guard rode along slowly on an electric moped.

'Sweeping is a kind of therapy for them,' Zara explained when she saw Randolph staring. 'Citizens may be prescribed a certain number of weeks, months or years of sweeping therapy, if they have issues with their mental health. There is an eminent Kebapi psychiatrist who has proven that this monotonous, repetitive action can, so to speak, help sweep away their negative thoughts and feelings. The guard is there to assist them in case they start to go astray but they are given medication so this rarely happens.'

They had arrived at a pair of soaring wrought iron gates, which promptly swung open allowing them entry without having to slow down. Each decorative stave in the gate and railings was in the shape of a spear tipped with gold. Randolph noticed that on each side of the gate was affixed a sizeable boss bearing an image of the same dragon-like creature that had featured on Zara's jewelry. As they drove on, he took in the vast gardens, sprinklers going full pelt to maintain the sumptuous lushness. Where could all that water be coming from in this desert land? It was a manicured oasis with a legion of uniformed gardeners snipping at anything that was the tiniest bit out of place, whether a blade of grass or a leaf of topiary. They passed under a long canopy dripping with honeysuckle then, on their right, there was a dovecote stocked with an abundance of white plumaged specimens, all of whom somehow seemed to be making eye contact with him with an expression of admonitory concern.

On their left there arose a sort of pagoda in an orchard of cherry blossom. 'My father had that built as a playhouse for my sister and I,' Zara waved a gloved hand, 'We used to dress up as girls from Tamerlane's harem and have tea parties there-- Ah, 'In Xanadu did Kubla Khan a stately pleasure dome decree,' as one of your English poets wrote.'

'Gosh!' Randolph shook his head, amazed, 'I never did anything like that when I was a boy.'

'Tristram, these gardens are a testament to my father's international outlook. There are miniature representations of eighteen different lands, one for each of the other fourteen former republics of the Soviet Union, plus four more. Can you guess what they are?'

Randolph shook his head, at a loss.

'Why England, Scotland, Wales and Ireland, of

course! We have a garden of daffodils displayed in planters shaped and coloured like different Welsh cheeses. I will give you the full tour one day in the golf cart. Oh, and we have a nine hole Scottish-style links beyond the English oak and beech grove.'

'Remarkable!' Randolph realized he had entered the realm of serious money and was glad he'd put on his best blazer.

Zara parked the DB5 around the side of a vast edifice that resembled some fortified caravanserai on the Silk Road. As they walked up the steps, two men in livery sprang up from gold-painted footstools and opened its double doors in perfect unison. Randolph smiled and thanked them, though Zara didn't appear even to notice them. They walked through the showpiece hallway with a sweeping marble staircase lined with oil paintings– mainly portraits of Tartar looking fellows, but still including one of Zara and her sister in their teens sitting under a rose arch in ball gowns. They went through a banqueting hall and into an antechamber at the rear of the building. Five men and women were hard at work at their desks but when Zara entered, they dropped everything and stood to attention.

'The brain of Kebapistan, Tristram, is held within these rooms,' Zara gestured for them to continue with what they were doing. 'These people are closest to my father and are his advisors. They are experts in what keeps our country ticking, with oil at the heart of it all, of course, lubricating the works.'

The man nearest the door spoke on the phone then told them, in perfect English, that the President was ready for them now and they may go in.

Randolph realized with a start that Zara's father must be the president of Zoran Oil & Minerals (ZOM), the corporation that held the monopoly on oil and mining in the country– he'd read about it in the KebapAir in-flight magazine and seen billboards for it at the airport. He'd never rubbed shoulders with wealth like this before and, frankly, he thought it was long overdue.

Zara went in first and they greeted each other. Mr Zoran was a powerfully built man approaching seventy with a full head of dyed wavy black hair. He wore a grey flannel suit and a tie emblazoned with the national colours, purple, yellow and black. Holding the tie in place was a smaller version of the pin Zara had been wearing when they met. A large beige dog of a breed that Randolph had never seen before, snarled at him from its repose under the desk, its jowly mouth glinting with sharp shards in an evil grin. It appeared to consist of velvety folds, which concertinaed down its body, rather like a tardigrade that had been shot with a magnifying ray gun and endowed with fangs.

'Toz, is that the way we greet our guests?' Mr Zoran asked the dog who had suddenly changed tack and, wagging the stump of its docked tailed, hurled itself at Randolph, shoving its snout into his crotch and leaving a dreadful string of slobber there which Randolph attempted feebly to cover with his blazer.

'Ha, ha, what a cute fellow!' Randolph chortled, joining in with the laughter of Zara and her father and masking his annoyance at the mess it had left on his smart trousers.

The dog suddenly returned to its place under the desk, reclined, blinked its pinprick eyes three times under its drooping eyelids and it lay its head back down on the floor.

'Tristram Randolph from England, I believe? Anomaly Zoran—' Mr Zoran shook Randolph's hand with steely strength.

'Anomaly, that's an interesting name; it means 'peculiarity' in English, you know—' Randolph realized he may have given offence and engaged in rapid damage repair, 'Peculiar in a good way, of course, as in standing out from all the rest.'

'Well, Father certainly stands out,' Zara concurred, 'How else could he have accomplished so much in his life?'

'Ah, I see you are admiring my barometers,' Mr Zoran declared, although Randolph was more puzzling than admiring, for there must have been over a hundred of them in widely differing styles all showing exactly the same weather outlook– sunny but with oncoming storms. 'My friend and associate, Mr Edwin Sneed, retired bank manager of Nether Wallop in Hampshire, who happens to own the second largest private collection of barometers in the world– mine is the largest– visits me here often to ensure the accuracy of these fine pieces. He also acquires for me any unique new pieces that come onto the antique barometer market. I trust him, and only him, to transport them with the care they require. Let us say it is a small obsession of mine. I have often said that my friend Mr Sneed has done more for international relations between Britain and Kebapistan than anyone else since the days of The Great Game. A shrewd and loyal man. I hope to introduce you to him someday. Now, let us have some lunch, Mr Randolph.'

Mr Zoran gesticulated broadly and sallied forth toward the next room. Randolph followed Zara's lead in walking behind her father, 'We have prepared a creamed tea in your honour. Zara loves raspberry jam, you know. It is one of her few little foibles. I hope that is the correct word for it. But she rarely indulges. She watches her figure. This is the right expression, I think. Her younger sister, Zina, on the other hand loves cream. She will have it three times a day, when the mood takes her.'

In the centre of the room stood a long, oval polished mahogany table, laden with a cornucopia of carefully prepared finger foods. The emphasis on British cuisine was demonstrated in tiered cake stands of halved scones topped with jam and cream, china platters of triangular sandwiches and tea served in Royal Doulton. Three footmen in livery eased in their chairs as they sat down and then poured their tea. Mr Zoran sat at the head of the table and asked Randolph how he liked it all.

'Just like being back at home!' Randolph jested as he surreptitiously attempted to wipe the dog slobber off his crotch under the table with his linen napkin, only it was gelatinous somehow and merely smudged making matters worse.

The view to the rear was breathtaking– Randolph had been expecting some ornamental ponds but here was a sizable lake with clusters of papyrus and water lilies, with an artificial geyser at its center.

'Ah, you are admiring our lake, Mr Randolph,' Mr Zoran said in that tone he had that suggested *'I always know what you're thinking'.*

'I most certainly am,' Randolph presented his best awe-filled face.

'There is an old Kebapi riddle which asks, 'When does the papyrus speak?' Can you solve it, Mr Randolph?'

'Umm, when the wind blows through it?' Randolph guessed confidently.

'No, when it is cut down, shredded and pressed into paper,' Mr Zoran corrected, tapping the tip of his nose. Then he took a gulp of his tea, the teacup too dainty for his broad and ruddy face, dabbed his mouth with his napkin and laid his huge hands flat upon the tablecloth importantly. 'So, we are to put you into a position of great importance, Mr Randolph, one in which you will be tested at every turn. My two grandchildren, will attend this school, as will several of my great nephews and nieces, in addition to children and grandchildren of Kebapistan's Ministers of State and its most prominent business families. You must hand-pick the best of British educators, develop a rigorous programme of learning and, most importantly, ensure that every child develops an English accent. Are you ready to meet this challenge?'

'Well, to tell you the truth, Mr Zoran, Zara's only just sprung all of this on me but I'll certainly give it my best shot. Will I be able to have a tour around the campus before I go back tomorrow?'

At this point, Zara stepped in, adopting something of a peremptory tone, 'I'm so sorry, Tristram, but that won't be possible as it is still under construction. Finishing touches only, of course. But I will email you our publicity video, along with the contract that you will need to present to your headmaster, giving us permission to use your school's name and uniform, etcetera, in exchange for which Swineforth will receive what I am certain they will find to be excellent compensation.'

'Now that's something I wanted to talk to you about, Mr Randolph,' Mr Zoran looked slightly pained, 'The name.'

'The name? Ah, I see, something about the swine part– does Kebapistan have an aversion to– dare I say it– our little pink trottered friends?'

Mr Zoran looked to Zara for clarification but she shrugged, 'Pardon me, I do not know any friends in possession of trotters– isn't that a kind of animal hoof?'

'You know, the P word,' Randolph continued.

'The P word? You mean Please?' Mr Zoran chuckled remembering something from the past, 'My daughters had a wonderful English speaking governess who used to say that if they ever forgot their manners... 'Don't forget the P word', I even have used it with them myself when they're being demanding.'

'No, *pigs*, I mean pigs. Swine is an old fashioned word for a pig or group of pigs,' Randolph clarified.

'Pigs? No, not a problem at all!' Mr Zoran reassured him, 'We like pigs here– some of these sandwiches have ham filling-- the very best Iberian, forest fed on acorns in the Extremadura. No, it is not the pig we have an aversion to, not at all! If there is any animal we collectively condemn in Kebapistan, it is...the turkey!'

'Good grief, really?' Randolph was intrigued, 'Is it against your religion in some way?'

'Ha! Religion!' Mr Zoran scoffed, 'There is no religion in Kebapistan, other than that citizens must honour their country...and their leader. Still, the turkey is very problematic for us– it is a proud, vain bird. It struts about, thinking it owns the whole farm yard. In this sense, it is the perfect symbol of American Imperialism. It is a bad example for the people of Kebapistan, who need to work hard to succeed and not develop such pretensions of grandeur.'

'So, I'm guessing you don't have turkey for Christmas dinner?' Randolph took a tentative bite of his cucumber sandwich.

'The turkey cannot set its scaly foot into Kebapistan! Moreover, its flesh has a vile texture and odour!' Mr Zoran put down his knife gravely. 'Our border guards had to arrest an Englishman two years ago who had the nerves to arrive at Diskebapisbad airport drunk with a rubber turkey hat on his head. Amnesty continues to campaign for him but it is futile; the insult was made, and made knowingly.'

'Flipping heck!' Randolph coughed, 'I'd better make a mental note to destroy all my rubber turkey hats lest one surreptitiously finds its way into my suitcase when I return!'

'What? You own turkey hats? Are there *many* hats like this?' Mr Zoran was glowering.

'Oh, gosh, no, that's just me having a little joke– eccentric British humour and all that,' Randolph thought it best to move out of the danger zone and return to the previous point under discussion. 'So, putting the T topic in a box, locking it up and throwing away the key, what actually concerns you about the name of my school, Mr Zoran?'

'Ah, yes, it is the Hospital part– I am not really understanding this. It is a school, not a hospital.'

'Yes, that's a tricky notion. A couple of older schools in Britain still have the title. It goes back centuries. It's connected to their past as charitable institutes, although they're generally far from being that today. It's all about bringing in enough money to stay afloat.'

'Very well, I am still not really understanding this but if it is an old English tradition, I will accept it,' Mr Zoran said and popped a whole sandwich into his mouth. 'Ah, my favourite– egg and cress.'

Zara had been writing something on her phone and now turned to Randolph with an announcement, 'Tristram, I have just enrolled you in the Hunt Associates recruiting fair next month and the advertisements for teachers are now live so you must expect to receive enquiries very soon. When you interview a teacher whom you think is a good fit for our school, sign them up without delay. I have just attached the contract in English for you. There is no need for one in Kebapi. You will see that the salary scale follows that of your government, only there will be no tax payable and luxury accommodations will be provided, along with medical insurances and annual flight home. This, combined with your enthusiastic presentation of life in Kebapistan, will ensure that our school will be attractive to the best candidates.'

Mr Zoran stood up and Randolph followed Zara's lead in doing the same. This was clearly the symbolic motion marking the end of the luncheon. The three footmen rushed forward and drew back the chairs, then one of them came forward with a slim box which he presented to Randolph.

'A small gift, Mr Randolph, a tie emblazoned with the colours of our beloved flag,' Mr Zoran said.

Randolph lifted off the lid to find the same tie his host was wearing...alas without the gold dragon pin.

'Oh, that's very stylish, thank you so much,' Randolph inclined his head in a mini bow.

'It has been a pleasure meeting you, Mr Randolph. I

trust that this is going to be the start of a fruitful working relationship,' Mr Zoran held out his hand and Randolph reluctantly accepted it for another painful clamp, masking his wince with a white-toothed smile.

Randolph scampered after Zara through a reception room with yet more barometers on show. High French windows opened onto a quadrant shaded with palm trees and pools stocked with huge ornamental koi. Sitting alone at a table, absorbed in playing a game of chess with himself, was a large pale man dressed in a dreadful pastel blue velour leisure suit that served to emphasize his ballooning form. He was bald on top, which immediately made Randolph recoil, with the rest of his hair curling out giving the impression he was wearing a clown wig.

'Who on earth is that?' Randolph was unable to mask his disdain.

'That?' Zara hadn't registered he was there until that moment, 'Oh, that is Max, my ex-husband.'

'What?' Randolph was astonished.

'He didn't always look like that. When I married him sixteen years ago, he had a full head of blonde hair like your own and was as fit as a fiddle. He held a position high up in our intelligence service but something happened to him after our marriage. He gradually...softened, let us say, melted like butter, his waistline spilling over, his skin losing its vigorous glow. He was second to none; now he's second from nothing. He's only here because my father took a shine to him long before we ever met. He's quite clever, though he makes no use of it any longer, except for chess. He's Father's chess partner in the evenings. We are thinking to try to find a role for him at the new school. Nothing too demanding, office boy or suchlike.'

As they walked on, Randolph noticed Max, who had been stooped over the table, transfixed by the game before him, suddenly squint up in their direction, watching them intently until they were out of sight.

3

Within a week of his return, Randolph found himself
sitting around the conference table in the headmaster's
study with the key members of the board of Swineforth
Hospital, who had been hastily convened to discuss the
surprising proposal that they establish an outpost in
Kebapistan.

'I think we are unanimous, Tristram, in finding this
an interesting idea,' the new headmaster, Hastings
Culpepper, affirmed in his usual buoyant tones. He'd
come to his current position via the usual route:
attended a solid private school, followed by a place at
Cambridge, straight back to his old school as an
Economics master, before moving into a Head of
Humanities and House Master position in a top private
school, and now to Swineforth, a second division
boarding establishment, to cut his teeth as a head. He'd
hang around for five years or so before returning to the
premier league as a deputy and finally, before he hit his
half century, he would be a headmaster at one of the
most exclusive schools where he would linger on until he
was bowled out by infirmity.

'Yes, it *is* very intriguing indeed,' Harold
Pettistone's voice quavered in avouchment of his
youthful successor. Headmaster of Swineforth Hospital
for nearly four decades, Pettistone had finally agreed to
step down last year when his general frailty rendered a
second hip replacement no longer feasible, sentencing
him to a life reliant on a Zimmer frame. His position on
the board meant everything to him, and he attended

meetings with as much gusto as any late octogenarian with a walking aid could ever be expected to muster. 'And what a wonderful franchising fee they are offering! Equivalent to ten full boarding places per year. Swineforth could really do with an annual cash injection like that.'

'I must say, the headmaster post was rather sprung on me,' Randolph smiled, 'But I'm keen to give it a go, given that they're firmly convinced I'm the right man for the job.'

Roger Swainson, retired headmaster of Randolph's former workplace, Blindefellows, the more successful private school in the next town, now seized the moment to deliver his two penn'orth, 'I have to say that I am not *entirely* at ease with this idea.' Swainson didn't have a lot of faith in Randolph. At Blindefellows, the sum of Randolph's teaching had been one 'pupil empowerment project' after another, which had ultimately meant that his role in the classroom virtually evaporated. He was often to be spotted in beer gardens, or rumoured to be coming back from some university alumni gathering in Lincoln, when he should have been teaching a Drama class. In order to sympathetically dispose of the fellow, Swainson had sent him across to Swineforth Hospital with the lure of the international stream post, which Swainson had talked Harold Pettistone into setting up.

Swainson had served on the board at Swineforth for over a decade. They were often in need of advice, while Blindefellows was often in want of sporting competitor. Hence, with Swineforth being the nearest school for miles around, the arrangement was mutually beneficial. Swainson's advice had, on a couple of occasions, saved them from going under when imminent closure loomed, thus ensuring Blindefellows maintained a handy sporting competitor. Swainson liked to tell himself, nevertheless, that it wasn't entirely for his school's sake that he helped keep Swineforth afloat, there was also a modicum of beneficence.

'Well, I can go one better than that, Roger,' Nigel Dare, Swineforth's bursar piped up in reedy tones, 'I think it's bloody outrageous.' Nigel Dare had a gaunt countenance with bulbous eyes in deep sockets. 'It beggars belief' was one of his stock phrases and Randolph was waiting for him to utter it at any moment. 'It beggars belief that we're considering doing business with a country that has such a shoddy human rights record. One of the worst in the world, in fact. And to become the 'sister school' as they're asking to call us, of an institution being set up out there! Doesn't any of the company here assembled recall 'the turkey incident' a couple of years back?!'

'But surely, Nigel, you can see the advantage of all those extra coppers in Swineforth's coffers just for extending the privilege of their making use of the school's uniform, crest, and the erstwhile leader of its erstwhile international stream,' Swainson winked.

'Yes, I like the aspect of the extra money, Roger, but I've worked here for twenty-odd years and have a sentimental attachment the place: I want to safeguard Swineforth's good name and, with a man like Anomaly Zoran involved in this new school, I am more than a little worried.'

'Anomaly Zoran? President of Zoran Oil and Minerals? *I know him*. I had lunch with him. A very pleasant chap,' Randolph declared.

'That's not all he's president of, Randolph,' Swainson chuckled.

'Look,' Hastings Culpepper interrupted, reining them in, 'Agreed, it's not the best country on the map but maybe we can make a positive difference with Tristram out there as our representative.'

'My sentiments exactly,' Harold Pettistone nodded, 'We have the power to lead an errant nation into righteousness by showing its future leaders the way. Direct your eyes, if you would, to that fine carving above the mantelpiece, the heraldic shield of Swineforth

Hospital: seven boars sable upon a field argent, tierced in pale, the six in the two peripheral pales passant toward the inner one, where a far larger boar stands rampant in Phrygian cap. That same shield was carried forth to eastern lands by Sir Hubert Swineforth during the Fourth Crusade just over 8 centuries ago. He didn't get as far as the Holy Land but what did he return home with? Enough pillaged riches to found this fine school. Now it is our turn to bring something back to those desert planes, to give them a taste of the fine education descended from their gold, their silver and their baubles.'

Randolph suddenly beheld a marvellous image of himself in his golden years as a renowned headmaster, who had made major breakthroughs in the field of international education and fostered friendships across nations, for which he had received from Her Majesty an OBE, at the very least.

'That's all well and good but are you sure we're sending out the right man?' asked Dare, 'Sorry not to mince words but Randolph is about a much use as a chocolate teapot. Having said that, he does have a few basic duties here at 'the sister school' and who else have we got to do them at such short notice? I mean, who's going to shepherd our crew of Eastern tearaways? Not that that amount of work is in any way deserving of a full time wage, as you've all heard me mention many times before, so I'll not harp on about it.'

Dare had, by this point, raised his rangy frame out from its chair, and was pacing, something he always did when he became extremely agitated, which was a frequent occurrence. After he'd loped around the table once, he hitched up his trousers, which was another of his tics, and completely unnecessary since his waistband was always cinched tight with a plaited leather belt worn just below his rib cage. The tearaways referred to him, aptly enough, as 'High Trousers Man', which always made Randolph smirk.

'I've already thought about that, Nigel,' Culpepper soothed, walking over to him and laying a hand upon his bony shoulder, '*I* will manage the international stream.'

Nigel Dare sunk back down in his chair and contemplated this prospect, stroking his beard as he did so. It seemed to have a stupefying effect upon him and he often did it when he was coming down from one of his diatribes, 'So we won't have to pay a wage any longer for this international job?'

Culpepper, Pettistone and Swainson shook their heads in unison.

'And I can take Randolph off my books?'

The three now nodded, smiling.

'And we can be sure than the good name of our school will be respected?'

Here the three could gesture neither in the affirmative nor the negative. After an awkward interval, Randolph jumped in with 'Of course it will! I will guard Swineforth's reputation with my life!'

'I think you have been reassured on most counts, Nigel,' Swainson concluded, 'but regarding this element of uncertainty, I have a solution, which I would like to broach today. I thought that perhaps *I* could go out to Kebapistan each half-term to see how things are progressing, and to assist Randolph with any hiccups.'

'That would be awfully generous of you, Roger,' Culpepper remarked with evident relief, 'But can Ms von Ravensbrück spare you, being as she is, in only her second year as Head of Blindefellows?'

'It was Diana who suggested it, Hastings, as she has a particular interest in this project. She has already established herself as one of the most capable heads in the history of Blindefellows, and she was an outstanding deputy to me. She has no real need of my assistance.' Swainson thought it wise not to mention von Ravensbrück's premonition about this venture most likely being 'all over by Christmas', although she hadn't let on exactly why she had these reservations. All she had been willing to say was that she knew 'the Stans' well, having travelled in them extensively following the dissolution of the Soviet Union, and that they were, like her own dear Latin America, a region of the world in which, all too often, things were not quite as they seemed.

'So, gentlemen, does that conclude our business for the day?' Culpepper enquired amiably.

'One further point, with the unease Nigel has demonstrated today, I'd like to invite him along to be my assistant.'

'Oh, I say, I think that's a capital idea, don't you, Hastings?' Pettistone chirped.

'Yes, splendid,' the younger man agreed, 'Are you content with that arrangement, Tristram?'

'Oh, yes, certainly, all hands on deck and that sort of thing!' was all Randolph could manage.

Pettistone then arose, trundled around the table, leaned heavily on Randolph's shoulders, and suddenly grotesquely animated, performed a jerky rendition of the school rugger cheer, 'To the East...To the West...To the South...To the North....Baffle the de-fence...Nobble the of-fence...Let the Swine go forth!' Culpepper and Swainson cheered with a hearty 'Hear...Hear!' and Randolph felt himself blush.

4

Sitting on the train on his way to the Hunt Associates fair in London, Randolph leafed through the CVs of the attending teachers, making little notes on them with the fountain pen he'd dug out of the back of a drawer which, he felt, would help him look the part. A further accessory that he thought gave him a headmasterly air was his new pair of gold-rimmed half-moon reading glasses. Admittedly, they didn't exactly peel the years off but there were going to have to be some sacrifices if he were to assume the position of pedagogical sage. With it being May, most teachers were sorted on the job front for next year so there wasn't a lot to choose from. In fact, there were, by and large, only two or three candidates per job.

Fortunately, Swineforth Hospital International was to start small, with just two year groups in the opening year– 7 and 9. It hadn't occurred to him to ask Zara Zoran why she'd decided to run two school classes a couple of years apart. Not so many teachers were needed as Zara wanted each to take on two related subjects and she was filling a couple of posts with local hires who were considerably cheaper. The humanities teacher would be a Kebapi since the government prescribed the content of history lessons. Said teacher would also run the Kebapi language and literature classes. One of Zara's acquaintances, a retired Olympic athlete, would be taking on Sport and a government required subject ambiguously termed 'Citizenship'.

Randolph had decided to travel first class, as

befitted his new status as a head and his complimentary muffin sat before him on the table. He'd worn a khaki worsted suit, which he felt gave him an air of old fashioned colonial officialdom, complemented by the Kebapi national tie with which Anomaly Zoran had presented to him. Zara had also given him a gift, a badge of Kebapistan's flag in enamel on silver, which he now sported on his left lapel. He would stay two nights at the hiring fair venue, the Undershaft Hotel in Whitechapel. This evening there was to be a reception with drinks, where candidates and recruiters were given the opportunity to rub shoulders, and sometimes more, an opportunity to which he was quite looking forward as the majority of candidates attending were women of a certain age.

At the hotel, he checked in and took the lift up to the sixth floor. His room was down a featureless labyrinth of thickly carpeted corridors that greatly hindered his wheel along suitcase. When he arrived at his room, he was disappointed to find it was on the cubicular side and looked out into the hideous central air shaft with a couple of decades' worth of rubbish accumulating at ground level. Dusty air conditioning units, almost certainly harbouring Legionnaires disease, lined the walls. It was rather awkward that he'd have to conduct his interviews in such a pokey little room—there was only one chair so the candidates would have to perch on the bed!

He went into the bathroom to style his hair, which he did gently with a wide-toothed comb for fear of upsetting his hair replacement surgery. Having his hair again had renewed his confidence to its former glory and he felt ready to dip his toe etcetera in a relationship again, perhaps even with Zara Zoran, if he played his cards right. He practiced a few headmasterly nods in the mirror-tile above the child-sized sink, reeling off some of the phrases he'd selected from an online educational jargon generator. He'd memorised them and they would be peppering his dialogue this weekend... 'It is our aim to maximize meaning-centered strategies within the zone of proximity' and 'We plan to unpack subject explicit direct instruction through the collaborative process' were his two favourites. He was banking on no one's asking him to clarify what he was talking about. He imagined they wouldn't dare, or they'd appear out of touch with current trends and scupper their chances.

One of the amiable young ladies at the Hunt Associates welcome desk in the foyer presented him with a nylon bag with drawstring emblazoned with the Hunt Associates logo (HA!) and the motto... *The Hunt is on! Tally-Ho!* Within the bag, were the programme of events, two HA! biros, a HA! notepad, a HA! Undershaft, London 'Recruiter' identity badge clipped to a HA! neck lanyard and a print-out of the slim list of candidates who had confirmed their attendance. He ambled into the hotel bar where the drinks reception was soon to commence and noticed other recruiters posted around the periphery. A few of them were sporting his type of gold-rimmed half-moon spectacles so he could see he was on the right lines.

Almost all the heads were male, middle-aged, around the 6 foot mark and sporting a good head of hair. Randolph didn't feel a bit out of place and fancied that it was like casting a school play, all about typecasting first, with performing skills hopefully falling into place later. To judge from the intensity with which the recruiters were eyeing up the competition and scrutinizing the few candidates scattered about, he wondered whether this drinks reception was the bona fide start of the selection process, rather than the interview sign up session tomorrow morning. He sat down at an empty table and a waiter immediately offered him a glass of wine. He took out his fountain pen and notepad and tried to look busy but, in reality, he was feeling as furtive as his fellow recruiters seemed to be, slyly glancing up at every new person who walked in. By the time Terry Pactman, the silver haired and tongued CEO of Hunt Associates appeared, there were still so few candidates dotted around the bar that Randolph felt some of recruiters might resolve to rugby tackling to fill their quotas.

Pactman was the embodiment of a distinguished older educator, apart from his glasses which were a throwback to the 1960s with their thick black rectangular rims Randolph could forgive him this fashion faux-pas, however, as it was he who had started the craze for these international hiring fairs and he had become a very rich man out of it. There were now a couple of smaller competing fairs but Hunt Associates still claimed they attracted la crème de la crème. Wine glass in one hand, Pactman strode to the centre of the room, bearing a superfluous microphone in the other hand, which he now raised to his lips, putting Randolph in mind of a Dean Martin impersonator.

'Welcome candidates, welcome recruiters,' he bantered with a trace of a Zimbabwean accent. 'Welcome to our final Hunt Associates fair of the year! This fair is always the tricky one– it's the smallest, for one thing, and the choice is limited, but don't give up hope as you look around this sparsely populated room. There will be many more candidates and recruiters here tomorrow morning for the sign-up session. I would like to reassure candidates new to the international circuit that at Hunt Associates every school we host is scrutinized to ensure that our candidates are moving to a safe and supportive environment. We have over 500 schools on our books and today it is my pleasure to introduce a few new ones to you. If the recruiters would stand up as I call you out, we can give you each a brief patter of welcoming applause.' Pactman pulled a card out of his pocket. 'So– and this is alphabetical, I can assure you, no favouritism at Hunt Associates– we have: CCC, the Cairo Cramming Centre; EEE, Exam

Excellence, Eritrea; GSSMS, The Good Shepherd School of Mogadishu, Somalia– and I've been assured that the administration do all they can to shield their staff of committed Christians from any negative popular, political and press attention; PDDADU, the Paragon Dream Academy of Donetsk, Ukraine-- who promise me that the civil war is well and truly over there; and, last but not least, SHI, Swineforth Hospital International, which I'm proud to say will be the first ever international school in Kebapistan.'

Randolph rose for his personal trickle of applause and gave a casual wave. He noticed an attractive middle-aged woman sitting on a bar stool waving back, however, which he thought a tad odd. 'Okay then folks, there are some strategically located dishes of nibbles and we have waiters circulating with a couple of trays of wine courtesy of Hunt Associates. Kindly bear in mind, however, that thereafter the drinks are on you, but don't indulge too much-- we want to see everyone, candidates and recruiters alike, bright-eyed and bushy-tailed at 9 am sharp tomorrow morning! Any further questions, I'm going to be here for the next 30 minutes or, if you don't catch me, simply go and see one of the lovely girls at the Hunt Associates welcome desk. So, without further ado, *The Hunt Is On! Tally-Ho!*'

A few people who knew the ropes shouted *'Tally-Ho!'* in response. Randolph joined in with the *'Ho!'* bit and someone blew a kazoo in imitation of a hunting horn, at which everyone laughed. Suddenly the room was in flux with most of the recruiters heading like a pack of hounds toward the bar. Randolph followed suit, trying to be one of the pack. He couldn't quite make out the fox who had waved at him from the bar stool as she now had a group of recruiters around her, tongues hanging out, queuing up to buy her a drink, it seemed. He could see she was wearing a tautly tailored skirt suit in rust orange, whereas many of the other candidates clearly lacked adequate knowledge of how to present themselves.

A lumpy looking elderly fellow introduced himself to Randolph as Brian Eider-Drake. He had a heavy Birmingham accent and an oddly nasal voice, as if there were a clothes peg on the end of his nose. Randolph raised an eyebrow at his attire, a saggy Christmas novelty pullover the front of which was machine knitted so as to represent a mallard. There were not so much bags under his eyes as suitcases. Randolph found it hard to look upon him but, as he was one of the only science candidates at the fair, engage in him he must.

'I was in the British state system for 40 years, Walmley Ash Comprehensive mainly. I did actually retire last year but the wife finds I'm getting in the way of the vacuum cleaner so she's suggested I come to this do and sign up for an adventure,' Brian intoned ponderously.

'Well, let's get you booked in for an interview,' Randolph jollied him along, masking his horror of the quivering downy white tuft atop his pate, 'What say you to first thing after the sign up tomorrow at 9:45?' Brian promptly agreed and Randolph inwardly congratulated himself for bagging the old duck before anyone else could get at him. He was saved from having nought else to say to the man by the waving woman from the bar stool sauntering toward them.

'So, the fox has broken away from the hounds!' Randolph quipped. She had dyed black hair in a straight Cleopatra cut, large twinkling green eyes and a wide, full-lipped mouth thick with red gloss and a slight yet enticing gap between her two front teeth. As soon she saw him, she let out a rich, fruity laugh.

'Why, Tristram, don't you recognise me?' she boomed.

There was something familiar about her but he couldn't quite put his finger on it. 'Gosh, yes, we've met before haven't we, but I can't think where! Rosy, isn't? Definitely a flower name-- Daisy? No? Pansy or Posy or something?'

'No, none of them. I can vouchsafe that I was thoroughly deflowered before I started my O-Levels!' she belted out.

This was clearly a tad much for Brian who excused himself, mumbling something about getting in forty winks in order to be fresh as daisy in the morning. 'It's Gemma, Gemma Bridle," she shouted as if he were hard of hearing, 'Or Gemmy as my friends call me, and as you called me too, in a certain hot spring in Reykjavik!'

The crotch almost fell out of Randolph's pants. 'Good God, I'm sorry, I didn't recognise you. You've changed your hair. It was blonde and cut at an angle then. It must be four or five years since we, umm, met?'

'Speaking of blonde hair, where has all yours come from?' she crowed, 'Is it a toupee?!' She lunged forward to grasp it but he evaded her snatching hand, causing her to lose her balance on her high heels and fall towards him.

His old stage instincts kicked in and he caught her by the waist, as if they were doing the tango. She let out a shrieking laugh as several other recruiters turned and gawped at them.

'I had a hair transplant,' Randolph whispered close to her ear as he righted her.

'A hair transplant!' Gemmy sputtered. Eventually, after she'd composed herself, she asked him what he was doing there and the other recruiters gradually moved on. After five minutes or so of her incredulous responses to his explanation of his unanticipated and meteoric career surge, she told him she had indeed seen the posting for the English with drama teacher, and was even considering putting in an application and working in Kebapistan where, she reported, licking her glossy lips, there was a tribe which supposedly had 'the best hung men in the galaxy'.

'Shh! I don't think we should talk about that quite so loudly just now, Gemmy,' he was hoping she wasn't suddenly going to blurt something out alluding to his own nether regions.

'Look it up,' she challenged him, 'they're called the Dalibor. An old friend from uni went out there for a glamping holiday. You stay in a beautifully embroidered sheepskin tent, gnaw on skewered barbecued squirrel-type animals and have a lot of 'traditional' sauna massages. I hit the Big 5-0 this past winter, Tristram, and I tell you, I'm game for a *nude* awakening before it's a goodbye to all that.'

'Well, all that aside, I'm, umm, familiar with your credentials and would love to welcome you to the Swineforth family.' He recalled now that she was English *and* Drama, likely the only one at the fair.

'Hm... 'Family' substituted for 'School!'' Never trust a school that portrays itself as a family. It always ends up being entirely the opposite.'

'Oh, it's nothing, Gemmy, just a spot of marketing talk.'

'Plain speaking, Tristram, tell it like it is. It's a damn school— four walls and a lot of exam prep. Worst years of your life, made more bearable-- for pupils and colleagues-- solely by the handful of teachers like me who somehow manage to maintain a good sense of fun.'

'Yes, I suppose you're right in a way but tell me, Gemmy, how come someone of your talents is at this fair? Bit of a last minute gig for you, isn't it?'

'It gradually dawned on me how banally analogous the virile Egyptians were... there was the jolly good fornication followed by the what can we get out of the affluent foreigner interlude which is when they were given their marching orders. Someone like me shouldn't be asked to pay for sex. So, after nearly a year of that, I left the country and now here I am, looking for the next bodice ripper.'

Randolph noticed the room was thinning out now and suggested Gemmy accompany him to his room to watch the slick video Zara had sent him of the school, possibly to sign the contract on the spot. He felt he had this one in the bag but, to his surprise, she told him she'd drop by and have a look later as she'd first promised to discuss a post in Thailand with a recruiter who was sitting waiting for her at the bar. As she swaggered back towards him, Randolph nodded in the direction of his strapping, snappy suited rival, before heading back to his room, recalling that short affair of four years ago.

It had all started when a mischievous pupil doctored the back of his clipboard so that ISDIC (for International Schools Drama Immersion Conference) became I♥DIC. Randolph had strolled all around the conference, quite unaware of it for a couple of days until, in a lift full of people, there was Gemmy before him, grinning.

'And I would have had you down as a straight man,' she winked.

'What? I *am* a straight man!' Randolph gasped, 'What gave you the idea I wasn't?'

'Well, for one thing, the way you're so fervently denying it and, secondly, because of what's written on the back of your clipboard,' Everyone in the lift laughed when he turned the clipboard around and it dawned on him what they'd been giggling at for the past two days every time he'd walked into a room.

'Oh, gosh, which dastardly tyke's gone and done that?!' and then Randolph decided to guffaw with the rest of them, thus demonstrating his light-hearted side.

It was amazing how a bit of tomfoolery like this could break the ice and get people to lower their guard and have a laugh together. After the incident in the lift, he'd walk into breakfast and inevitably someone would shout out something like, 'Hey, Tristram, will you be having some *sausage* this morning?' And sure enough, the following evening Gemmy had asked him to come out with her little group of the most attractive drama teachers at the conference. They'd gone on a pub crawl but they had become separated from the others and found themselves at a hot spring. Perhaps she'd engineered it that way, he didn't know, but without a moment's hesitation, she'd tossed off all her clothes and plunged in, beckoning him to do the same, quite without concern for his bald pate that caused him such agonies of self-consciousness. And what a glorious feeling it had been, to be in that warm pool with her.

After the hot spring incident, she'd turned up at his door each night for the remainder of the conference. Then they had all gone home and that was that, no email, no mobile number, nothing. He presumed she had someone else and these conferences were her means of her letting off a bit of steam, which she'd certainly done in the hot spring. As he sat in his hotel room's token chair untying his oxblood brogues recalling this, there came a knock at the door. He opened it to find Gemmy framed there, as if his reminiscence had conjured her up. Between the fingers of each hand were three miniatures.

'Just stole them off a housekeeper's trolley,' she confessed as she stepped in. She unscrewed the caps from three Baileys and poured them out into one of his tea cups. Then she slipped off her shoes and sat on the bed, leaning back against the headboard with his two pillows behind her. Randolph sat coyly at the desk and made ready the film on his laptop, coming out with the odd jargonistic phrase in the hope of impressing her with his newfound managerial prowess, 'Of course, once we're up and running, we will assess the dynamics of the curriculum for our 21st Century learners and, it goes without saying, we will utilize group-based presentations to evoke cognitive disequilibrium.'

'Ha! Who the hell are you? Robot Randolph from the Planet Pedagogos?' Gemmy scoffed, 'Yes, it bloody well should go without saying; it's bad enough to *read* that crap!'

'Sorry, you're right, me babbling on again with all this highbrow educator talk,' Randolph apologised and Gemmy took a long slow sip of her Bailey's.

The video had loaded and he flumboyantly clicked on the play icon only to reveal a blank screen. 'Whoops, wherever have you gone?' he burbled. He fiddled again, thinking better of filling the air with eduspeak. She sized him up meticulously. Then, whilst the video was running, Gemmy watched with what appeared to be interest and, from what Randolph could deduce, she seemed to be impressed. The opening shot showed the imposing marble entrance to the school site, panning across at the intensely watered lawns dotted with palms. Then, the camera tracked up a grand set of granite steps to the reception area, they were lead into the headmaster's office which was all done out in teak. 'This is where muggins will be ensconced now that he's made the grade,' Randolph bantered. Then there was a shot of the Olympic size swimming pool and, behind that, the sample teacher's apartment, all terracotta tiled floors, sumptuous bedding and expensive appliances. The image faded and the words 'The Swineforth Hospital International Family, Kebapistan (SHIFK) brand new and waiting for you...'

'So, what do you think?' Randolph was on the edge of his seat.

'Looks dandy, Randy, dear boy,' her lip curled lasciviously, 'but you'll have entice me with your package if you want to me to come.'

Seeing how things stood, he duly obliged there and then, first setting out the tax free salary on the bed where she reclined, next reviewing the excellent professional development provision on the room's lone chair and finally laying bare the generous insurance and flight allowance on the desk. Yes, the package was thoroughly perused that night, within an inch of its life, in fact.

Waking up the next morning, Randolph felt

somewhat frayed so took a long hot bath into which Gemmy slipped shortly after him. 'You're not still contemplating Thailand after all that are you, Gemmy?' he queried, 'You do realize that contracts there tend to have a greater appeal for men of our age than women?'

'I have to at least put in an appearance, Tristy. I can't leave them all in the lurch,' she really was a stunning lady for one past her 50th birthday. Admittedly, her breasts had ripened and were beginning to fall from the tree, but he found himself rather relishing her, which surprised him as he generally had fixed ideas about how women he became involved with should look. On the other hand, it now dawned upon him that she might well expect this level of managerial attention to continue in Kebapistan, which could put a major damper on his prospects with Zara Zoran.

'I have to say, Gemmy, last night you challenged my beliefs about the libido of the older lady,' Randolph quipped. 'Are you on some medication to help that along?'

'Oh you mean the DTI pill?'

Randolph was confused.

'Delay The Inevitable and no, I'm not on medication but will be on double the dose when that doleful day arrives or I will have nothing to live for.'

'Surely, being an English teacher, you live for literature too? Who are your favourite authors?'

'I suppose you'd want me to say Jilly Cooper and all her cheeky horsey novels... *Stirrups, Stallions, Jodhpurs, Tack* and the really dirty one, *Manure*, but no, I'm more of an old classics girl myself.'

With that, Gemmy retired to her room to dress, while he donned his headmaster's garb, topped off by the gold-rimmed half-moon spectacles. He put on his Kebapi flag tie, pinned on his matching lapel badge, clipped his fountain pen into his breast pocket, slung his ID around his neck, tucked his welcome folder under his arm and made his way downstairs with a skip in his step in the wake of last night's diversions.

5

The conference room had been set up with tables around its periphery and large notices hanging behind each featuring the school's name and a list of vacant positions. Randolph noted with a sinking heart that many recruiters were, like him, in search of a teacher for almost every subject, although he, at least, had the excuse that his was a new school. At all but one of the others, the staff were walking out en masse, rats deserting sinking ships, which didn't put Swineforth Hospital International in the best company. He was relieved that Nigel Dare wasn't there to make one of his wry comments. He noticed Gemmy going from head to head, maintaining the mask of a smile as she listened to their similar spiels. Brian Eider-Drake was circulating around the room too, still in his mallard jumper, which was more rumpled now, as if he'd slept in it. He gave Randolph a little wave and came over to explain that Swineforth Hospital International remained his top choice and he looked forward to his interview after the sign up.

'You see, Mr Randolph,' Brian droned, 'I have a bit of an ulterior motive in wanting to come out to Kebapistan in that the Natural History Museum in Diskebapisbad houses the world's largest collection of early waterfowl fossils.'

Randolph feigned interest and smiled, perhaps a little too politely. But what else could he do? Brian was the only Chemistry and Biology teacher in the room.

'Something you need to understand, Mr Randolph,

straight from the first hopscotch box, is that most of my adult life has been defined by a quest to untie the Gordian knot that is the taxonomy of the Anatidae, which is to say, the avian genus more commonly known as geese and ducks.'

'Are you sure all this sort of stuff is in the museum, Brian?' Randolph interjected, 'When I was in Diskebapisbad last month, it seemed more of an arid climate, not really a suitable habitat for ducks.'

'That maybe so today, Sir,' Brian retorted, 'But millions of years ago, in the Paleogene period, the area where Kebapistan now lies was a vast wetland in which our modern waterfowl friends took the first teetering steps in their evolution from their dinosaur ancestors. As far as I can fathom from the rather sketchy website of the Kebapistan Natural History Archive and Museum or the KNHAM as it's fondly referred to, the ancestral fossils of the following are currently locked within its vaults... the Eurasian wigeon (*Anas Penelope*), the common merganser (*Mergus Merganserous*), the smew (*Mergellus Albellus*)—'

'Oh, gosh, that many! Who'd have thought it?' Brian's nasal voice had a soporific quality and Randolph felt he must jolt himself out of the enveloping monotony and get back to the task in hand, even if it meant recruiting Brian.

'Lichen is another of my great interests.'

'Lichen? The scaly stuff on rocks and tree trunks?'

'Oho, not only scaly, Mr Randolph, sometimes leafy or hairy! Yes, I was Secretary of the British Lichen Appreciation Society (more commonly referred to as the BLAS) in my younger days. We certainly had some fun on our lichen rambles! I am something of an amateur lichenologist, you know.'

'Lichen...' Gemmy suddenly appeared in front of Randolph, 'Well, that's about as exciting as the leaders of the realm of international education lining the walls here. Of course, they would have all made awful teachers, which is usually why they were slipped into 'management', out of a necessity to remove them tidily from the classroom and lock them up in an office out of harm's way, or out of the way of doing further harm. Present company excepted, of course, Tristram; I'm sure you were a wonderful teacher, when you chose to be. Ah, no matter on which continent, I've watched it happen time and again with bemused chagrin; while I have been consigned to remain perpetually at the coalface, with precisely zero prospect of a meaningful raise in gratitude of being a top notch teacher. Figurehead headmasters, how well I know them. They have the required genitalia and stature for prize-givings or prospectuses and, given that they're made of wood, they'll never say or do anything beyond the quotidian that might ruffle parental or proprietary feathers. Safe and sound marionettes with pull cords on their backs. Tug the ring and out comes the right fittingly hollow phrase. Funny to see you, Tristram having a crack at it now with your new hair. Hopefully, you'll be a bit different.'

And then she was gone, leaving him speechless and Brian nodding off. He didn't know what to make of it. Did it mean she wouldn't be coming to Diskebapisbad after all?

'Of course, an old uncle of mine urged me to pursue an interest in budgerigars,' Brian began.

'Budgerigars?' Randolph echoed, distracted from staring after Gemmy.

'Yes. You might have heard of him as he was Britain's leading expert in his field, William Watmough, Fellow of the Royal Zoological Society (FRZS).'

'Can't say I have, Brian.'

'You'd probably know him as W. Watmough though, which he used as his pen name to preserve his privacy, being such a celebrity on the caged bird fancying scene in the Midlands right the way through the middle decades of the previous century. Authored the definitive works *The Cult of the Budgerigar* and *Practical Inbreeding.* The budgerigar is the lapdog of the bird world, however. I am preferring a bird that roams free among the marshes and waterways so, although Uncle William's works impressed me, I stuck to wild waterfowl.'

'How fascinating! You know, we absolutely must delve further into it but –'

'Not just now though, if you don't mind, Sir. This sign-up thing has worn me out. I think I'll wander over to the cafe for a cappuccino,' Brian sighed and, rising, waddled off.

Terry Pactman had been right– there were *a few* more candidates this morning but, by the looks of desperation, thinly masked with forced grins on the recruiters' faces, it wasn't going to be enough to fill their quotas, and their candidate searches were going to spill over into their summer holidays. Like them, Randolph found himself assuming his most amiable face as a means to ensnare the somewhat bewildered looking people milling around the room. A young man, short and slight but with a tense wiriness, a sallow complexion and a skull cap of crow black hair suddenly pulled up at his table.

He placed his palms wide apart on its surface so that his close-shaven angular face was only a foot away from Randolph's and barked: 'Kebapistan. In the same part of world as Afghanistan, isn't it?'

'Yes, I do believe it is,' Randolph cooed in his most soothing voice, 'But I can assure you it's an entirely different sort of country-- stable, peaceful, free of ethnic conflict and religious fanaticism.'

'I could've been in Afghanistan right now,' the young man continued, 'If the British Army were still an outfit worthy of the name, instead of some namby-pamby global peacekeeping taskforce.'

The fellow was clearly a head case. Desperate though the recruiting situation at the fair might be,

Randolph resolved to politely brush him off. 'And what subjects do you teach, um...?'

'Gall. Mark Gall,' the lad growled, 'Maths and Physics.'

Maths and physics teachers, the gold dust of educational recruitment, as even the greenest of school heads such as Randolph well knew, 'In that case, Mark,' he flip-flopped on the spot, 'I'd be delighted to meet with you later. Kebapistan is very much an up-and-coming country and Swineforth Hospital, my school in the West Country, is helping to mould this sister institution.'

'But what's in it for me?' Mark Gall scoffed, 'It's all very well trying to impress me with meaningless talk about moulding foreign schools by giving them figurative siblings, but what do I get out of it?'

'Well, you'd a receive salary in line with what you'd get in the UK but totally tax free, a luxury apartment gratis, top-notch health insurance and annual flight to and from home– pretty nice package if you ask me,' Randolph boasted, smiling at how Gemmy would've reacted to the innuendo.

'What are you smiling at?' Gall snapped.

'I was just recalling reading your impressive CV,' Randolph assured him, 'You went into officer training in the army after uni but later 'resigned'. Why was that, if I may make so bold as to ask?'

'Because the British army have gone lily-livered,' Gall sneered, 'I was too forceful for their delicate sensibilities, or as they claimed, overly eager to dispense with ineffectual negotiation and move straight into the real work of fighting. One day I hope to join a legit army that's more about action and less about talk.'

'Well, I imagine that makes you a formidable presence in the classroom,' Randolph hypothesized.

'Look mate, I've come down all the way from Rothley in Leicestershire and I don't have the time to make idle chit-chat. If *I decide* to come to your school, I'll inform you– no interview necessary!' and with that, he stalked off, although Randolph observed, without stopping at any of the other schools' tables.

By email, Randolph had secured an appointment with someone who went by the unfortunate name of Gabby Scroggins. She hadn't been able to attend the sign-up session due to being delayed on her way back from a two year stint teaching art in some far flung provincial city in China. She'd suggested they meet over lunch, to which Randolph had flamboyantly offered to treat her as a ploy to get her on board.

He was sitting in the rather smart hotel restaurant, next to a fountain featuring chubby little frolicking cupids. He'd written a brief description of himself so she'd know him instantly– slim, strong features, full head of fair hair, exquisitely tailored suit.

'Mr Randolph?' a voice with a lilting Welsh accent enquired.

He glanced up to see a comely elfin face looking down at him, framed by a jolly pixie-like hairstyle in a rich chestnut brown. 'Ah, yes, Gabby?' he stood up quickly, upsetting his glass of red wine so that, for a moment, he was in a quandary, hovering between wanting to mop up what he'd just spilled and staring in wonderment at the positively spherical form that was now squashing its way around the table toward the chair opposite him. 'Right, I'll– erm – just sort this out,' and he dabbed at the spilt wine abstractly with his fingertips, forgetting to use a napkin.

'What a nightmare journey,' she dropped down into the unfortunate chair and fanned herself with the menu, '38 hours, including a 6 hour delay in Beijing. They only gave us two meal tickets as compensation.'

'Oh, no!' Randolph sympathized, 'Well, they have some very nice salads here if you want something light after all that.'

'Not a chance, Mr Randolph, I'm ordering the full Monty! I haven't eaten any *proper* British food for two years so with you having so generously offered to pay,

I'm pulling out all the stops,' she started to leaf through the menu, smacking her lips frequently as she went on, before waving over a waiter. 'I'd like your triple cheeseburger– less salad, more cheese please– with extra relish and a double order of curly fries, onion rings, deep fried cheese balls and an extra-large coke with ice and lemon. Can you leave the menu, please, because I'd like to peruse the desserts while I'm eating?'

Randolph ordered one of the salads he'd mentioned, feeling somewhat dismayed to be in the company of a shape of person he normally made a point of cold-shouldering. Now he'd have to sit there, watch her eat and lick her overstuffed boots as she was one of only two art teachers at the fair. She hadn't taught Design Technology before but, as it often went with art, Randolph felt confident in giving her that too. With people like Gabby and Brian on the books, what would the staff photographs look like? He supposed he and Gemmy could be positioned seated at the front with Gabby behind, so her body could obscured. Luckily, her face was fairly pleasant so her mugshot on the website would be favourable enough.

'You're very quiet, Mr Randolph,' she piped up, interrupting his fattist revelry, 'Feel free to distract me from my gnawing hunger with a few questions, if you like.'

He presented a cheery smile which he hoped disguised his horror, 'So, tell me, why are you leaving your present job in China?'

'Ooh, it's not easy for a Westerner to get to know people out where I am, Mr Randolph. Hardly anyone can speak English,' her features became pained, a deep furrow in her brow, 'I must admit that tubs of ice-cream and rolls of cookie dough became my only friends. Having said that, one of my pupils did end up making a sculpture of a hippopotamus out of all my empty tubs, which he dedicated to me at his final exhibition, so it wasn't all for nothing.'

'So, you put on a bit of weight out there, did you?' Randolph commiserated.

'Well, yes, a little, though I can't exactly say I was slender before I went over. You know, I often had no idea what I was eating. I'd wander alone through their culinary street markets with all manner of things sold from wagons. I'd just point at stuff and they'd pop it on a little paper tray for me with some chopsticks. I suppose I'm what you might call a gastronomical risk taker– but it's often backfired– quite literally! I've been in China so long, Mr Randolph, I've forgotten what it's like to have a solid stool.'

Randolph shuddered within but felt he had to grasp the cow by the horns as she was the only one of the two art teachers attending the fair. 'And do you feel, Gabby, with what is, to all intents and purposes, a weight issue, you'd be up to managing a group of eager children in a lively art class?'

'I decided to teach art for a reason, Mr Randolph...it's the only subject in the curriculum that allows the teacher to totally step back and allow pupils to express themselves as individuals, thus permitting the possibility of hardly ever needing to leave one's seat.'

Randolph begged to differ-- inwardly-- the 'pupil empowerment projects' he had cunningly set up for his drama pupils had meant that he could even be on a train heading to the opening night of something in the West End while Friday afternoon classes were underway. Admittedly Swainson had ultimately disagreed with his methodology, but he'd benignly shunted him over to Swineforth, where, in his new role, he'd actually been able to get away with doing even less.

'I've even dallied in my own art practice when I've had the energy during class and I can say it has inspired my pupils as they were given the opportunity to watch an experienced artist at work.' Whereupon, she produced a pocket portfolio of snapshots of her art, which exclusively featured paintings and drawings of desserts. 'As you can see, I'm irresistibly drawn to sweets as my subject matter. Do you notice the sensuous impasto effect I create, reimagining the icing by laying the paint on thickly with a palette knife, or sometimes even piping the paint out, whipped cream style?'

Her colossal meal was now set before her upon a wooden platter, as was Randolph's minimalist Caesar salad before him. She asked him to take a few photographs of her almost unhinging her jaw to accommodate the height of her triple burger. 'Nom, nom, mouthgasm,' she blissfully gurgled, her mouth filled with meat juices. Then, putting one of her curly fries under her nose like a ridiculous moustache, she posed for another photo. Randolph was made most uncomfortable by her antics, but was determined not to show it. She told him all about various food sites on the web and revealed that she even had her own food blog, 'Ooh, you should see me on that, Mr Randolph, *Gabby Gobbles* it's called-- 'Eating Everything Under The Sun' is the subtitle. Nothing's escaped my gullet, from monkfish eyeballs to pregnant witchetty grubs, from fermented shark fin to creamed tripe. I'm up for trying everything and I've garnered a bit of reputation for it on social media with over a thousand followers on that blog of mine.'

By the time he had finished his slimming salad, she had concluded her grease fest with a gratified belch, which she announced was customary in China, though she admitted she'd have to adjust now she was back in Britain. She began scrutinizing the dessert menu, her eyes popping out. She selected the raspberry pavlova, which choice she justified calorie-wise as it was, so she contended, 'mostly fruit'. It was described on the menu as 'a sharing dessert for 2-3 people'. 'Ha! Not for all the daffodils on St. David's Day would I share that!' and she didn't, downing the entire confection in roughly 15 minutes, while Randolph tried to focus on telling her about the package.

He'd brought out his lap-top and was setting up the short film about the school when she broke wind so long and loudly that everyone near them in the restaurant turned in their direction, 'How many times have I asked you not to do that in public?!' she exclaimed.

'That wasn't me!' Randolph squawked, reddening while she giggled at him, her chins wobbling, a noisome miasma enveloping them, like gasses risen from the Neogene swamp Brian had mentioned.

Later Randolph saw Brian who signed his contract, allowing him to fulfill his biology and chemistry quota.

Following that, he wandered around, having little chats with his counterparts from other schools with the devious intention of putting off any candidates in the vicinity... 'How's it going, Simon...Must be a tough sell, Liberia?' or 'Did you fill all your vacancies, Trevor? Always fancied Honduras myself but the murder rate put me off,' and so on and so forth. He went up to his room to meet Gemmy at 9pm but was still alone, twiddling his thumbs, half-an-hour later. He didn't know which room she was in so he couldn't go and find her. He was hoping that during their rendezvous that night, she'd sign her contract. Was he selling his body for his job? Maybe so but fair enough.

Sitting on the bed watching the television, he kept nodding off during the incessant commercial breaks so he stepped out of his clothes and slipped under the sheets naked, as was his want. He had an uneasy dream... He was at the airport in Diskebapisbad waiting to collect the new teachers but every time a plane landed, no teacher disembarked. The first day of school arrived and bus load after bus load of children was turning up but he had to teach them all as there was no one else. He stood at the board and watched them pile into his classroom, filling up every chair, then sitting on tables, then the floor, then appearing at windows after scaling the building like vampires. He woke up suddenly in a cold sweat and walked into the bathroom to relieve himself, the door slamming shut behind him. He couldn't see where the toilet was and then realised he wasn't standing on tiles but on a thick carpet.

Looking to the left and right of him, he saw he was in the corridor, naked and locked out of his room. 'Damnation!' was all he could mutter. His first reaction was to tap the place where his pockets would have been if he'd been wearing clothes. He then tried to force the door but with no luck. He looked down the left hand corridor, down which he'd seen Gemmy disappear after she'd spent the night with him. Calling her name in a stage whisper, he tiptoed along, without actually needing to as it really was a thick carpet. He heard a group of people approaching in a merry humour and squirmed to one side facing the wall. By good fortune, he had paused at a broom cupboard and, when he leant against the door, it swung open.

He ducked inside and froze until the group had passed, then found the light switch. He was in a tiny room containing several mops, a zinc bucket, a vacuum cleaner, dirty rags on hooks and– lo and behold– a lemon yellow polyester maid's apron! He put it on, for it was that or a dirty rag or a bucket to hide his manhood. It then struck him like a thunderbolt why he was in this predicament in the first place-- he had needed the toilet urgently; the zinc mop bucket before him would have to do. The sound of his deluge as it was released was like hail on a tin roof, so he leaned in to reduce the drop distance which dulled the pitter-patter somewhat. After a shake, he listened for a moment, then peered out and made his way along the corridor, back to the wall, continuing to call Gemmy's name in the stage whisper.

He arrived at the end of the corridor and was there faced with two options, either to linger flasher-like in the hall, or go down to reception in the lift before him and request help from whomsoever was on night duty. As he pondered this dilemma, the lift doors slid open and out stepped Gemmy, keenly followed by the

Thailand headmaster. There was no time nor place to hide himself.

'Tristram? Good grief, what *are* you doing?' she laughed.

Randolph was standing with his hands behind his back, mimicking the demeanor of someone admiring a garden, 'Oh, nothing, just a stunt me and a few of the other chaps set up.'

'Have you actually got nothing on under that apron?' she peered around to the back of him.

'What the heck do you look like?' the Thailand headmaster tutted, shaking his head in disbelief, his accent and diluted swearing revealing to Randolph that he was of a heartily prim American type common among heads on the international circuit.

'Tristram, I'd like to ask you a serious question,' Gemmy had an intense look on her face, to which he decided to respond to with nonchalance.

'Fire away,' and he leaned one buttock casually upon on occasional table, only it had a glass top and a fold of skin caught between it and the wooden surface beneath, causing him to wince slightly as he lifted himself off and leaned phlegmatically against the wall instead.

'Do you have anything on tonight?' she asked.

'Ha, ha, I don't think he does!' the Thailand headmaster quipped.

'Oh dear, Freudian slip,' she smiled, 'I mean planned, do you have anything planned?'

'No, nothing much, I think the fellows have disbanded now but I just felt like a late night stroll.'

She turned to the Thailand headmaster, 'Brad, thank you so much for dinner but I did promise Tristram the last dance so I'm afraid I'll be spending the night with him.'

'What, you'd actually sleep with him, loitering in a hotel corridor dressed like that?!' Brad scoffed.

'Certainly with him dressed like that! What lady can resist a fine figure of a man in backless, polyester chiffon attire? But sleep will only follow much later, once he's made me a few turnovers in his pretty apron,' at which she put her arm through Randolph's and ushered him to her room, with Brad watching aghast as Randolph's bare bottom disappeared along the corridor.

6

Two weeks before the day of departure, Randolph went to stay with his parents in their semi in Twickenham. They were a quirky old pair whom he rather missed if he didn't see them for over a month. On the other hand, they had quite a few idiosyncrasies that niggled him after a fairly short time in their company. For example, his father, Giles, was always going through the kitchen cupboards discarding any 'bulky packaging', whilst muttering about its being 'a bloody waste', which meant you could never find anything quickly; you always had to peer through the unlabeled plastic wrap to identify the contents. And then there was his mother, Jocelyn, whose main topic of conversation these days was friends and acquaintances who had died in what she saw as relative youth... 'Her husband had just turned 80,' she would tell him, 'and was in the bloom of health, slim, athletic, but he got into his car after a bowls match and promptly had a stroke at the very moment he turned the key in the ignition.'

Randolph usually stayed with them every summer for the whole six weeks of the holiday, but he'd been tied up with the sale of his flat in the West Country. He reckoned he wouldn't need it any longer now he was going to follow the international headmaster trail. The sale had necessitated sorting through his possessions, many of which were fragile. He'd spent hours packing everything in swathes of bubble wrap ready for conveying to his parents' house for storage over an indefinite period. He'd kept every costume he'd ever worn on the stage, the majority of which were from the school plays he'd directed whenever he'd cast himself, feeling an actor with more maturity was called for in one of the larger roles. There were also a couple of costumes from his stints with the Lincoln Theatre Royal, his favourite being the outfit for the role of the golden fly from Offenbach's Orpheus operetta. He was pleased to see he could still fit into the leotard and tights, but the spandex was corroding and the wings were a little on the tatty side now, despite his always having kept them in a box. From time to time, alone in his flat, he attired himself in this particular costume and relived the seduction of Eurydice, singing along with the CD, playing both parts himself, whilst his bedroom's fourth wall of full length mirrors also allowed him to be the audience. He also had in his possession the costume worn by the actress who had played Eurydice which he had rather sneakily made off with immediately after the last night. Naughty of him, he acknowledged, but he could barely control his urge to collect theatrical outfits. Eurydice's costume, a low-cut air-blue gown of the most exquisite shimmering gossamer, delighted both the eye and the fingertips. It was such a fragile fabric but he had still donned it from time to time when he wanted to act out Eurydice along with some subtle touches of fresh, girlish makeup and one of his long blonde wigs.

When the removal van arrived in Twickenham, Randolph issued terse reminders to the men to handle the boxes with care. Everything was placed in Randolph's bedroom where he'd had fitted wardrobes built the week before in order to store his elaborate outfits appropriately. He barely came out of his room for the next two days while he unpacked and put away. This made his mother, Jocelyn, a little unsettled. She would listen out for his footsteps from the dining room below and, every so often, pop into his room with a sandwich or a bowl of crisps.

Giles was at a loose end that summer and fidgety, peering into Randolph's room now and again, asking how he was getting on. He was a tall man, agile for one approaching 80 and with a thick mop of floppy grey hair which, to Randolph's sorrow, he hadn't inherited. Randolph's hair line was descended, alack, from the Vainglories, his mother's side, generations of bald men with photographic evidence to prove it stretching back over a hundred years. Giles made his money as an inventor. These inventions would keep them ticking over financially for a few years but, when the products went out of fashion or were surpassed by a superior model, then the money gradually would dry up and he'd have to invent something new.

The last invention, patented nine years ago had been a curious aid to long-distance lorry drivers and was no longer in use in a meaningful manner. The 'His-Pis', as it was called, consisted of a miniature electric pump, to the inflow end of which was mounted a metre long section of reinforced surgical tubing terminating in a smallish rounded latex funnel, while on the outflow end of the pump was another meter of surgical tubing ending in a plastic spigot. The gadget's purpose was to enable the full bladders of busy lorry drivers to be conveniently and tidily emptied in transit through an open window.

The seed of invention had sewn itself on a walking holiday in Spain ten years ago. Giles had been deeply perturbed by the number of plastic drinks bottles filled with urine he kept coming across by the roadside. He had then learned that the poor lorry drivers had such punishing schedules that even a short toilet stop would jeopardise their time sheet, so they always had to make sure they had an empty plastic bottle in their cabins for long stretches of driving. Giles puzzled long and hard over their predicament. Not only was it shockingly unsightly litter that would take several decades to biodegrade, it was also frightfully inconvenient for the lorry driver if, say, he needed to pass up to a litre of urine but only had a half litre bottle. The spillage would no doubt make the fellows uncomfortable for the rest of the day. Over the next twelve months, he nurtured his creation, building the model himself and testing it in the car with Jocelyn taking R&D notes on a clipboard. They tested it in all driving conditions, hairpin bends, steep gradients, ice and gravel. Giles had to drink like a fish to provide enough raw material to feed through the contraption.

Only when the design was perfect did Giles have it patented and sold to a company who had it made in China and packaged in Britain, giving him a healthy return. The His-Pis sold like hot cakes to its target audience, namely haulage companies. It was a neat, efficient way of avoiding mess in the cabin and helped drivers focus on the journey, instead of being distracted by the time-consuming activity of finding empty plastic bottles, along with having to aim through the constricting bottle neck. One company had even written to Giles to ask if he could invent a similar device for solid waste as an additional time-saving device. Two years after the His-Pis went on sale, Giles was the proud recipient of the 'Trucking Invention of the Year Award' by the European Haulage Society, where he and Jocelyn were the guests of honour at a function held in a hotel in Calais.

In the last couple of years, however, serious issues had arisen due to consumer tomfoolery and some of the tabloids had taken an interest. Certain rumbustious lorry drivers had taken to using the His-Pis to target hitchhikers, traffic policemen and the like. Soon there was a highly remunerative spike in sales with bored office workers, pupils on freshers week, delinquent comprehensive school boys and so on all buying the device. When Tory MP, Jacob Tree-Frog, had fallen victim he'd become incensed and spearheaded a successful campaign to have the His-Pis banned throughout the EU. Giles had been proud of the positive impact on the environment his invention had had, along with the improvement to the quality of life of thousands of lorry drivers. He felt that all of his hard work had now being washed away, so to speak, by a handful of troublemakers. Meanwhile, across Asia, Africa and the Americas, unlicensed knock-offs were being flogged for two-a-penny. The His-Pis had had its day.

Randolph could sense his father lingering at the door as he sorted out the burgundy plumes on a Charles the Second hat, 'Please come in, dad, tell me what you've been working on.'

Giles ambled in and plonked himself down on the bed with a sigh, his head propped up by the green velvet padded headboard, 'Well, I'd better get something finalized soon. You know how your mother loves to spend, as you saw at the V&A on Tuesday. It's not *exit* via the gift shop, it's *enter* via with her. What the hell does she need a William Morris Strawberry Thief umbrella for? We have dozens of umbrellas in the cupboard under the stairs. Along with that rather morbid William Blake 'Ghost of a Flea' paperweight. No one uses paperweights these days! I don't like to say anything as spending is one of her few interests, always has been.'

It had worried Randolph that they were getting low on the shillings as they'd always been there for him to fall back on, which was generally a couple of times a year. He remembered how this time last year his Viola Dolce Fiat 500 had given up the ghost outside Welwyn Garden City and he'd had to push it off a busy road onto what looked like a playing field. His father footed the bill for the recovery truck, only the operation wasn't a success. By the time the mechanic got there, as he called Randolph to tell him, his little bubble car was surrounded by tinkers who'd had no option but to build a scheduled pop up fun fair with the Fiat 500 in the middle of it. Teenagers had promptly broken into

Randolph's car and were eating their McDonald's on the back seat and by the time the fun fair folded, the Fiat was a virtual write-off.

'What's- his-name, the writer... Tom Sharpe couldn't have written the stuff that befalls you, my boy!' his father laughed, ever one to make light of Randolph's misfortunes.

'So, any new inventive ideas?' Randolph asked as casually as he could, despite latent panic.

'Say what?' his father was rather hard of hearing these days.

'Any ideas about the next invention?'

'Well, there is one weasel in the pipeline,' he put his finger in his ear and wiggled it, as if trying to dislodge the mustelid from there, 'but it's a computer programme, so not my strongest suit.'

'Oh really?'

'Yes, it's satellite navigation with a twist, in that it includes an historical narrative. Excellent for tourism. Saves bothering with all those guidebooks. You get a running commentary on the landscape of the past as you drive along, you see.'

'Hmm, wouldn't that be distracting?'

'Directing? Yes, it directs you too.'

'No, I said *distracting*, wouldn't it be distracting for the driver if they were told to look at this and that at the side of the road?'

'I don't think so but your mother and I will have to test it for ourselves. We have Major Meredith Silliphant on board to do the vocals. Remember him? Used to a trick with the kiddies where he'd make an old pre-decimal penny stick to their foreheads. You always hated that. Great voice though. He's just published his book, *This Vile Porridge,* a history of the British underclass, an ideal companion piece to *This Sceptred Isle*, so he tells me.'

'Good God, who'd publish something with a title like that?' Randolph contemplated.

'It's self-published,' Giles clarified. 'He was your scout leader for a few months, wasn't he, when old what's-his-name cried off with a hernia? We'll be giving it a dummy run when we come out to visit you in Kebapistan in October.'

'Ah, great,' Randolph nodded slowly, trying to make sense of the emergent invention. 'Your inventions always seem a little way out at first but you've done pretty well out of them all so I'll not poo-poo it all with my reservations.'

'Knows all about Kebapistan does the Major,' Giles continued, 'Went over there on a bus tour in the early '90s on a tour called *Battlegrounds of The Great Game* after the fall of the Iron Curtain. Took a load of photos and invited people over to his house for a very long slide show, which he periodically digs out if a new couple decide to retire to his neck of the woods. The chap certainly knows his stuff though, I'll give him that.'

'Sounds like a useful fellow for you with this latest project.'

'Well he is,' Giles affirmed, 'The script was all basically ready from this slideshow he created.'

His mother entered with a tray of tea cups and chocolate biscuits, almost bumping into her son and upending the thing– ever the metaphorical bull in the china shop, or cow rather. Her spatial awareness and sense of physical boundaries had always been lacking so jostling was one of her less endearing features, hence the fittingness of her being named Jocelyn. "Thought you might need a little energy boost to keep you going," she sat heavily on the bed next to his father, sloshing the tea into the saucers, then picked up a biscuit, dunked it and popped the soggy thing into her mouth before it collapsed. Randolph sighed and frowned at her when he saw she'd drawn on her lipstick a tad lopsided again. She knew exactly what he meant and, looking sheepish, picked up a napkin and dabbed at the edges of her mouth. At least, nowadays, she was keeping up with dying her roots black, thanks to his fortnightly reminders. Her once-luxuriant mane was straggly now and wisping down her back. 'So, all packed up and ready for the next chapter?' she chirped. There was chocolate on her teeth.

7

And so it was that, a few days later, Randolph departed for Kebapistan. It was mid-August and Heathrow was heaving with family holidays thwarted due to the usual delays. No reason was given, not so much as a leaf on the runway. The air was ripe with cursing and threats to whining or wailing children. Some of the older ones had already mastered mimicry of their frightful parents to excellent effect. Randolph passed a girl not yet into double digits, dolled up in a halter top, sunglasses and platform clogs drawling out, 'I ca-an't bloody believe this!' to which a woman nearby, whom the girl was clearly trying to impersonate, scolded her with 'Pipe down and eat yer burger, London.' London? The hoi polloi must have grown weary of using Paris as a first name and were now working their way through the other capital cities, Randolph pondered. Before long, there'd be names like Pretoria, Beirut and Moscow spat out by disillusioned mothers. Randolph sat for a while and noticed a boy of 11 or so trying to focus on the homicidal game on his tablet whilst his fractious preschool age siblings wriggled around him. He was able to ignore them no longer and spat out 'Right, you lot better sit down and shut up now or I'll crack you one!' to which they responded with siren-like wails. What a glorious country to be leaving behind, Randolph thought.

Fortunately, Randolph's flight was on time so he'd be putting all this behind him very soon. He'd be flying to Munich, where he would board a Kebap-Air flight to Diskebapisbad. He strolled over to the departures queue which was almost spilling out of the doors. Despite it being Britain's summer rainy season, the majority of travellers going through security were dressed in flip flops and shorts. When he arrived in his seersucker suit, specially imported from Haspel in New Orleans, he caused a few heads to turn. His Aquascutum trench-coat was draped over his shoulders, cape-like and his brogues freshly ox-blooded. His hand luggage consisted of an Aspinal leather 'shadow messenger' bag, a present from his parents, which he had his suspicions, due to the incorrect packaging, might be 'unused secondhand'.

He often wondered, when standing amidst the public, as he did now, whether anyone from the West Country might be present, who'd recognise him from what he liked to refer to as The Golden Age of his teaching career, when, for want of a better actor, he had awarded himself main parts in several school plays. His tragicomic Malvolio was said to have made several audience members weep-- whether with tears or laughter, he did not know-- and, after playing the rake Harry Horner, well, the suggestive fan mail from certain parents-- a handful of mothers, as well as one father-- had made him blush. Then there were the numerous times he guest-starred at the Lincoln Theatre Royal, his crowning glory having been the Golden Fly cameo. As he stood there, moving ahead a foot or two every few minutes toward security, he scanned the hundreds of faces around him for a flicker of recognition, and felt certain that there was an occasional lingering look, as if they were trying to place him.

Zara had booked him into business class and he tried to make it appear that was how he always travelled, masking his delight at the cordon bleu meal that was laid before him and nonchalant about the numerous offers of expensive beverages, even refusing at one of the five junctures when drinks were offered. He'd have to get accustomed to living high off the hog now he had transitioned into the top pay bracket in his career. He knew what these international school heads were raking in, and though it had to be said, Swineforth Hospital International was not a huge hike from his former salary, he saw it as a stepping stone to the top packages. Of course, if he were to bag Zara Zoran, he'd be looking forward to possessing, in the not-too-distant future, an oriental manse with a garage of vintage cars, including a DB5. His parents had always teased him about money burning a hole in his pocket, hence their having had to put up the funds for the hair transplant, amongst other things. Now, he would finally show them that he could stand on his own two feet in style.

In Munich, Randolph ambled over to his connecting flight, a small plane that flew but twice a week between Munich and Diskebapisbad. The seats in business class were taken up almost entirely by German business men and Randolph struck up a conversation with a man called Egon sitting next to him, whom Randolph had asked what line of work he was in.

'We Germans are all here on this plane for one reason, Tristram: Flocken, Knete, Kroten, Lappen, Moos, Pinke-pinke or, in my case, literally, Fleisch.'

'Flesh?'

'They are all nice German slang words for money, but yes, my firm deals in hormones, which we are selling to the Kebapi farming industry as part of an initiative set up by their government think tank.'

'Oh, so you're in the meat business?'

'Exactly, and what meat, Tristram! Meat like you never see in Europe because our fussy governments won't let us use the latest cutting-edge technology in hormone research! We are, therefore, in partnership with Kebapistan's government to produce—' Egon lowered his voice, 'super-beasts!'

'But, I've read that too many hormones may very negatively affect whomsoever partakes of the augmented flesh...5 Year Old Boy Grows Breasts, and similar attention-grabbing tabloid headlines.'

'No, research has disproven this about the new, artificially synthesized hormones my company is using, Tristram. And in a dry, developing country like Kebapistan, they need boosts like these to have enough to feed their people efficiently. Though, in truth, the best cuts of this *super beef* is only affordable to the elite so now they have too much so that *super meat* is being exported for the wealthy in the neighboring Stans and even back to Europe on this very plane. Extremely lucrative for the Kebapi government...and for me!'

'But didn't you say the hormones aren't legal in Europe?'

'Ah, yes, Tristram, but there is a – what do you call it? A hole in the loop?'

'A loophole?'

'That too. The hormones are not being *administered* in Europe and we have crossed the beasts with wild bison so that the meat is not classed as beef but as game. It is no problem to bring it into Europe like that. In fact, you are about to have some on this plane– this flight showcases our fleisch.'

And, indeed, at that moment, the stewardesses were placing huge oval plates precariously on the little tray tables. The meal was extraordinary– a steak the dimensions of which Randolph had never come across before without an ounce of fat on it and, as a token offering at the side, a little pile of wilted yellow cabbage. Last time he flew to Kebapistan from Munich, in economy class with his pupils, he'd been given only a small bowl of greasy stew. Now, in business class, as Egon had told him, he was receiving preferential treatment with this mammoth steak.

'You see,' Egon grinned, deftly wielding his knife and fork, 'that is beautiful meat.'

Randolph nodded politely and sliced off a little morsel to try. Unfortunately it was rather on the rare side for him with the blood seeping out, but Egon and the other Germans seemed to have no problem with that so he did his best to enjoy it. It tasted like steak but the texture was different, tightly compacted, more like venison somehow. He was but half way through when he had to lay down his cutlery as he was both full and feeling queasy. Egon had finished his steak already and rebuked him.

'Really, I can't eat another mouthful, delicious though it is,' Randolph apologised, 'and hopefully I shan't be growing a third testicle tonight.'

'Why not? Three is better than one!' Egon proclaimed.

In arrivals, a woman was holding up a card with Randolph's name on it. He gathered this was Golmar, whom he had previously been informed in an introductory email from her, was to be his PA. She was about 30, wore practical, flat shoes and a simple shift dress, topped off by brown shoulder-length hair in no particular style, a picture of plainness. After introducing themselves, they walked out to her vintage Lada sedan and set off for the school.

There appeared to have been an increase in billboard erection beside the long, straight road from the airport to the capital and Randolph was surprised to see most of them adorned with a fellow who looked a lot like a much younger version of Anomaly Zoran.

'I'm sure that's Zara's old man,' he pointed out, 'President of Zoran Oil.'

'Yes, it is, Mr Randolph,' Golmar nodded, 'There's the election in January and the usual landslide victory is expected.'

'What? He's standing for president?' Randolph exclaimed, thrilled to be right in the epicentre of the country's ruling class.

'He *already is* the President, has been for the last 40 odd years.'

'Really?! Not just the president of Zoran Oil and Minerals?'

'No, not just that.'

Randolph shook his head in awe at the billboards, whilst Golmar stared fixedly ahead, her eyes on the road.

'So he's *President* Zoran?!' Randolph was deeply impressed.

'Yes, President for Life, Dearest Leader, the Great Basha, Comrade Zoran-- the Poor Man's Friend, and numerous other titles in the press, which he also owns.'

'He owns the press too? What a remarkable man!' Randolph was bowled over.

They passed one of those groups of people whose job it was to sweep, making quite lethargic progress, the grey dust creeping back to the road a mere 100 metres behind them, the guard on the moped hovering next to them. *Like painting the Forth Bridge,* Randolph thought. In the spaces between the billboards, he caught sight of something he hadn't noticed on his previous drive to and from the airport – on the horizon were vast stockyards. These must be the homes of Egon's quick-grow cattle, the providers of the super-steak he'd just eaten on the plane.

'Huge beasts, aren't they?' Golmar had looked over to see what he was peering at, 'Genetically engineered to feed a nation.'

Here and there were little half-built buildings that had been all but been reclaimed by the desert, dunes forming right up the sides of them.

'In the past,' Golmar explained, 'people tried to live along this road, they wished to start small businesses to benefit from the airport traffic, but the conditions proved....too inhospitable so now almost everyone lives in the three cities of Kebapistan; our government prefers it that way. They turn a blind eye to the nomadic Dalibor people who can tolerate the most inhospitable conditions. They're renowned for their –'

'Ah, yes, I've heard about that!' Randolph jumped in, stopping her in her tracks.

'Their exquisitely embroidered tents,' Golmar continued.

They were suddenly turning onto a road to the left, which perturbed Randolph somewhat as he was expecting to go to the city, not to be heading into an area of dreary desert. 'Erm, are we supposed to be going *this* way?'

'Yes, Mr Randolph, this is the site of the new school– don't worry, it is heavily irrigated so it has the appearance of an oasis.'

Randolph could see it in the distance, high white walls angled inwards slightly like an ancient Egyptian pylon. Some buildings were still covered in scaffolding and people were working on them, teetering at great heights without any kind of safety harnesses as they clad the muddy-looking concrete structures with slabs of white marble hoisted up to them on rickety pulleys. Security guards armed with submachine guns got to their feet as they drove up to the gates. Golmar stopped so they could check her citizen ID and Randolph's passport, after which then looked inside the boot and under the car before giving them permission to drive through. The ostentatious pillars of the main building rose before them.

They parked to the side and Randolph made his way up the steps feeling like the Pharaoh Ahkenaten with a handmaid of Nefertiti following after him when he first went to inspect the new capital of Amarna in the desert. So be it if it wasn't in the city. The complex was on its way to being a palace of epic proportions. Golmar showed him through the flamboyant polished black granite reception area, where there was a life-sized standing portrait of Anomaly Zoran in a heavy gilt frame. He was sideways on, his left arm resting on a balcony, beyond which a crowd thousands strong was blurred in the background. Golmar showed Randolph into the grand office that was to be his. He immediately took up his position in the large leather swivel chair behind the showpiece desk and sighed, leaning back, swiveling, speechless for a while.

'This is marvellous, Golmar, just marvellous!'

'You wear it well, Mr Randolph.'

'And there's Mr Zoran again!' Randolph nodded irreverently toward another framed portrait of the president, just his head and torso this time, with a smattering of medals on his lapel, looking a lot younger than his 70 years.

'Yes, his picture is in every classroom, office, business and home.'

'But not in the toilets?' Randolph jibed, at which poor Golmar looked dumbstruck so, to change the subject, he asked her to take a few photos of him sitting there, for his parents and his theatre friends in Lincoln. When his parents came out there at half term, perhaps Mr Zoran would have the three of them round to dinner in the presidential palace, he mused, but his mother might embarrass him. Whenever they went into Harrods food hall, she had a tendency to gasp at the prices, rather than maintaining a blasé demeanor as everybody else did, whether they were ridiculously rich or merely pretending to be. He'd need to give her a pep talk before they went, should the invitation be proffered.

After the photographs, Golmar showed his apartment in the teachers' block, the self-same swanky bachelor pad that featured in the film. He wasn't quite sure how that would go down, living cheek by jowl with the teachers. It could also prove awkward with Gemmy, he thought, if she wanted to pay him one of her nocturnal visits, which would no doubt undermine him in front of the rest of the staff, if they found out.

'This is lovely, just lovely, but would there be any chance of my having an apartment in the city, rather than living among my staff? Usually the headmaster is set apart from the rest, you know.'

'Oh? Is that so? Then I shall ask about it, but for now you will have to stay here. At present, no foreigners are permitted to reside in Diskebapisbad, other than at government approved guest houses.'

'Of course, no rush whatsoever, but ultimately I'd prefer to be in the capital, or perhaps even on the presidential estate near Zara and her father.'

'Alright, Mr Randolph, leave it with me, I will see what I can do.

The doorbell rang and Golmar walked over to let in two men in lab coats and hairnets. Apparently, these were the caterers who would be delivering lunch to the teachers before the term started as there wasn't yet an up-and-running kitchen. Randolph noticed that each of them had an enamel button pin with an image of Anomaly Zoran on their left lapel. 'Because of the election,' Golmar explained, 'and on the left to demonstrate where their heart lies. I have one too, but I didn't wear it just to pick you up from the airport.' The pair subserviently placed a large plastic box on the table and departed. Golmar started unpacking it and scooped the hot food out onto the dishes. A heady bouquet of beef permeated the air, redolent of the odour in the airplane cabin at lunchtime, much to Randolph's dismay.

'This is jiz-biz,' Golmar declared, indicating the two dishes of beef stew replete with vertebrae, 'national dish of Kebapistan. Of course, jiz-biz consists of the offcuts and offal of the superbeasts. The prime cuts go to the Kebapi elite, naturally.'

Randolph wondered briefly whether 'jiz-biz' might be a suitable name for the erectile dysfunction gadget his father had been toying with for the last few years, even if the bowl of stuff in front of him was more like what might have come out of the solid waste extractor that he'd declined to invent. He sat down gingerly as Golmar poured out two glasses of concentrated, unnaturally vivid orange juice from a carton. To give his palate a little rest from all this richness, he also drew a glass of water from the cooler, the tap water being non-potable.

'No vegetables, I suppose?' Randolph asked.

Golmar reached over and retrieved two apples tightly wrapped in Clingfilm from the bottom of the plastic box. Randolph nodded in resignation.

As they ate, he went over his plans for the next few days, prior to the teachers' arrival. It was down to him to organise a two day staff induction. This would be followed by an informal picnic at the end of the week in which pupils, parents and staff would mingle. Golmar made notes as he spoke. "I've dug up a few drama games I used to do, which will serve as ice-breakers, along with a scavenger hunt that I hope will familiarize the teachers with their environment, so they'll know their way around before the pupils arrive. Other than that, they'll be unpacking and resting after their journey so I don't want to overwhelm them. For the picnic, I'd like you to print out a set of polo shirts in the main school colours, the Swineforth beige and sage, so the staff are easily identifiable in the crowd– let's say with the Swineforth logo on the front pocket.

'Anything on the back?' Golmar asked.

'Hmm, Swineforth Hospital International Team would be a tad lengthy, I think. Just the initials will do, in the Swineforth trim – chocolate brown.'

'Would that be dark or milk chocolate, Sir?'

'Milk, definitely milk.'

Golmar then excused herself and offered him the opportunity to rest in his apartment and unpack his things. She added that she would need his passport to take over to the Interior Ministry that evening in order to notify them officially of his arrival in Kebapistan in a long stay capacity in order to begin to process his visa. She promised to return to his apartment first thing in the morning and politely instructed him under no circumstances to attempt to leave the school compound in the meantime.

But he didn't see her in the morning. He waited until 10.30 and then, dressed in smart casuals, he strolled over to his office to see if she'd meant to meet him there, but it was all locked up. He walked back in the vague direction of his apartment but now there was a little tension in his step, as he turned his head right and left, seeking any sign of another living soul. He became disoriented and ended up at the far end of the campus among all the incomplete buildings, where a few men were at work on the scaffold right at the top.

Around the windows of the unfinished buildings, dead starlings had been strung up by their feet and monstrously large blue bottles buzzed around them, the likes of which he'd never seen before. He looked more closely but one collided with his cheek and he recoiled. He presumed this practice of hanging up the dead birds was some primitive custom to dissuade them from nesting there. He walked on, eventually found his way back and, feeling ravenous, was happy to discover some meagre provisions on a shelf in the cavernous interior of his brand new Bosch refrigerator: a box of breakfast cereal which translated tantalizingly as 'Mouthfuls of Wheat', a carton of UHT milk, some sliced white bread, something in a tub that he took for margarine, six very large eggs and a pack of little triangular spreadable cheeses. He put together some scrambled egg and spreadable cheese on toast and, as he ate this, opened the 'Swineforth Hospital International Welcome Pack' that had been produced for the international staff. Inside this, a few papers had been stapled together with the title *A Foreigner's Guide to Basic Kebapi*. With the intention of learning a few key phrases so he could get by to some degree, Randolph perused this. He was surprised to see, on the first two pages, *When dealing with the police and the military* and that the first thing one should say, rather like 'Hail Caesar,' should be 'Long live President Zoran'. *Fair enough*, thought Randolph, *When in Rome...etcetera*. He hoped he'd never have cause to interact with the police or military anyhow so he turned the page. The following page, *At the hospital,* had some useful key phrases such as 'Is my friend alive or dead?' *One hopes that one won't come in handy,* Randolph raised an eyebrow. The ordering food page was very brief, barely extending beyond jiz-biz with bread or without bread.

Slightly ruffled by the bleak nature of the phrases, he moved over to the lounge area and tried to find an English channel on the television. Scrolling through a slew of marching bands, he eventually came to a repeat of an Open University programme from the early 1980s judging by the presenter's garb... a brown shirt with a woven tie of mossy hues to which a microphone was clipped. The presenter had flyaway facial hair which held Randolph horribly transfixed. He introduced himself as Norman Coat and began twiddling the knobs of an archaic frequency measuring device with wide-eyed wonder through his magnifying spectacles. Over a rather bored-sounding narrative droned in Kebapi, Randolph could made out odd phrase from the enthusiastic English scientist... 'the total spectrum', 'now to increase the current' and 'the notch'. Giving up on that one after a time, he moved on and a few channels later, Randolph came across the children's programme *Bagpuss* with the same nonchalant narration in Kebapi. Randolph scrolled on until Roger Moore in a turquoise shirt and loosely tied orange cravat in an episode of *The Persuaders* piqued his interest. He watched it to the closing credits and was transported blissfully from his current predicament for a time. Following this, he resumed his scrolling and, on channel 44, he came across Zara's actress sister, and presumed she must be a permanent fixture of television in Kebapistan. He quickly recognised the drama playing out before him, despite its not being in English: It was *Hedda Gabler* so that, whereas before, she had been in Boudiccan garb on horseback, now she was a refined but histrionic lady in a red satin dress ensconced in a drawing room, drinking liqueurs from cut glass.

Eilert Lovborg entered and there was much berating, along with a dozen or so expressive close-ups that reminded him of the exercises they used to do on his drama course to tone up their facial muscles. Hedda then made a dramatic sweeping exit, revealing a fine figure even under all those Victorian ruffles, but the slamming of the door made the whole set shudder and a picture fell from the wall. Randolph stifled a laugh. He must make a point of taking this sister of Zara's aside-- hopefully by that time he'd have a residence in the city-- in order to take her through what her people could do to create a sturdier construction, impressing her thereby with his intricate knowledge of kinetic forces in relation to theatrical sets, over a glass or two of fine cognac.

At the end of the play, there was still no sign of Golmar so he set about ironing his clothes and hanging them in the wardrobe. When he was nearing the end of this task, the doorbell rang. *Finally!* he thought, but it was the caterers again in their hairnets bringing in the plastic box.

'Excuse me, do you know where Golmar is?' he asked but they shrugged apologetically, not understanding him, wherewith they picked up yesterday's box and off they went.

With dread, he lifted the lid of the new box. Jiz-biz again but this time with the addition of a small packet of wafer-style biscuits with a picture of a hazelnut on the front. He ate this first, then turned to the jiz-biz but managed only four spoonfuls before nervously peeking inside his shirt and then down his trousers to make sure there were no changes starting to bubble up. After four more spoonfuls, he packed the remainder away and left it by the door. For the rest of the day, he peered out of his windows at the moon base landscape, and started to wonder whether he'd made a terrible mistake in landing there. When night drew in, he heard distant and agonized bellows which he presumed were coming from the penned-up wunder beasts. He fancied they may be lamenting their dead friends whose remains sat in a plastic box by his door.

Randolph was awakened the next morning by Golmar at the door, earnestly apologetic for not turning up the day before. She had had problems, she explained, getting the visa stamp and the authorities had actually gone and confiscated his passport. This perturbed Randolph, making him feel like a captive and he gazed dismally out the huge window into the desolate landscape. Golmar explained how she had spent the whole day in the government office remonstrating with them. 'It is very complicated because foreigners are not normally allowed to live here, except in the official tourist hotels. For you and the other teachers, they must create a new kind of visa. This is only possible because it is Ms Zoran's wish. I will try to get your passport back when I take in theirs on Friday.'

On a lighter note, she told him the faculty polo shirts for the picnic were already done and bagged up in her office. She had located a few vegetables for him at considerable expense to herself and promised him that she would instruct the caterers that they must provide him vegetable dishes because he wasn't accustomed to eating like a Kebapi. Although anxious about the whereabouts of his passport, Randolph was delighted to see her and, for the rest of the morning, they went about together, writing clues for the teachers' treasure hunt.

8

On the day the teachers were arriving, Golmar drove out to the airport in her ageing Lada, whilst Randolph sat in his office putting the finishing touches to his letter to parents. The top half of the letter was taken up by one of the photographs Golmar had taken when he'd first arrived, with him posing at his desk. These had turned out rather well and he'd seen that a lot of headmasters included such pictures in their letters, more often than not, with fountain pen in hand in the act of writing, cementing the specious image they wished to portray of being men of letters. He had not thought to put paper under the fountain pen but no one was likely to scrutinize the photograph that closely.

He had also completed the school's policy statements and philosophy. This was easy enough to do as there were hundreds of such documents cluttering the web; he just had to find them and tweak them here and there so it wasn't blatant plagiarism. The only such documents the original Swineforth Hospital had were ones that had been knocking around since the 1980s, although Hastings Culpepper was planning to update these. Perhaps, Randolph mused, he could use the material he had just uploaded for the sister school.

He found he was a little nervous about seeing Gemmy. After Reykjavik, he'd never heard another thing from her, and the same had happened after their fling in London. He felt this gave him the all-clear to see how the land lay with Zara. Still, in one hour he would see her again and that didn't stop him spraying on a dash of Kilian 'Straight to Heaven' luxury cologne, and going over to the mirror in the little toilet that adjoined his office to style his hair one more time.

At 6pm the teachers would be gathering in Randolph's flat for drinks, followed by a three course meal, properly catered, with no jiz-biz, and waiters, so Golmar had informed him. The waiters had been in there all afternoon so it promised to be a decently run event. Randolph strolled over just before his guests were due to start arriving and found the scene that met his eyes quite awe-inspiring. Six life-size boars' heads carved from butter were stationed around the room on plinths and the table centrepiece was a boar-rampant in Phrygian cap fashioned from a block of ice. A problem with this symbolic reinterpretation of Swineforth Hospital's heraldic emblem was the slight deviation in that each of the butter boars had an apple in its mouth. Then there were sculptures made from watermelon on the sideboards – a swan, an elephant and...was that one Elvis Presley? 'Anomaly Zoran,' Golmar explained when she saw him staring at it. She herself had gone through a transformation... her hair styled into an up do, a sleek black cocktail dress, eye-shadow, rouge and lipstick. Randolph raised an eyebrow in astonishment.

Gemmy and Gabby were first to arrive, the door opened for them by one of the waiters. They were arm in arm, cackling like a pair of lewd witches.

'We met on the plane, didn't we, Gobbles?' Gemmy tittered, and then walked over to Randolph and entwined him in an overly-lengthy embrace, her fingernails digging into his back.

'Well, I wish I'd known he was bonking the female applicants. Then we both could've had a go in London,' Gabby belted out a raucous Welsh valleys laugh.

Happily, Golmar appeared unfamiliar with Gabby's vernacular diction and looked puzzled. Randolph extricated himself, took a few steps into the middle of the room and chuckled, 'Ha, ha, Gemmy and I go way back. Now, haven't the waiters done a marvellous job? Have you seen the butter boars' heads? By the way, that's not Elvis over there; it's President Zoran, tastefully rendered in watermelon.'

Golmar cleared her throat pointedly and Randolph looked around to see the waiters, all wearing the little Zoran election badge in their lapels, had frozen with their trays of champagne and turned to him with expressions on their faces that blended astonishment and anxiety. The awkward moment was fortuitously averted by the doorbell. Brian Eider-Drake had arrived and made a surprisingly animated entry. Randolph was pleased to see he'd spruced himself up a little with a haircut and a colourful Hawaiian shirt. Perhaps he'd thought he was coming out to a holiday destination.

Following him were the two local hires, the humanities and Kebapi language teacher, Pyro Envany, and the sports and citizenship teacher, Volta Kovet, both in early middle age. Envany was a small man with intense green eyes that were hard to look into for more than a few seconds. His wavy hair grew upwards in reddish flames. He was wearing what was probably his best suit, but it was threadbare at the cuffs and worn shiny at the elbows. Former Olympic bronze medalist in pole-vault, Ms Kovet, clearly descended from the Amazons, was one of those gym teachers who couldn't keep still. When she took Randolph's hand, it was like shaking hands with a sea anemone and Randolph didn't know what to make of it, at first thinking she might be making a play for him. Observing her slyly for a time, however, he saw her fingers were constantly on the move, even when she was just standing alone. As Pyro shook hands with his new colleagues, he presented each of them with an election badge, which Randolph noticed Volta was wearing too. After thanking him for the gift, Gemmy said she probably wouldn't wear it as she didn't wear badges as a rule.

'I think it would be better for you if you did, so that

you may fit in better,' Pyro advised her.

'I pride myself on never fitting in,' she replied, placing the badge on the coffee table, at which he turned away from her sharply.

Golmar pointed out to Randolph that the boars' heads were starting to melt and that she would go see where Mark Gall had got to while he made a start on his welcome speech. Randolph tinkled his champagne flute as if he were addressing a room full of people and not the small gaggle of teachers before him. 'So, here we all are, ready to embark on one of the most challenging episodes in our career. We are not simply slotting into a long-established school. We are *starting* a school and what an honour it will be to mould it in our likeness!'

At this point, Mark Gall sloped in like some sullen teenager and leant on a wall, carelessly placing the sole of his Adidas trainer against it, whilst surveying the room with a face like thunder. Golmar, who had walked in behind him, was shaking her head and raising her eyes heavenward. 'My brief from above,' Randolph continued, 'is that we *Anglicize* our pupils, create a little bit of Britain out here in the desert, sharing with them our traditions and our steadfast British mores. So, before we sit down this fine meal together, the first of many we will share, no doubt, I'd like you to raise a glass with me to toast not only the new school year, but a new beginning. To Swineforth Hospital International!' They chorused the phrase back to him, then took their seats at the long table, Randolph at the head. With a flourish, the waiters placed a gigantic steak before each of them.

Gabby started laughing, 'Another one of these, Gemmy!'

'Oh, no!' Gemmy stood up dramatically, 'Why must the people in this country eat like lions?'

'I'm sorry, ladies, we do have some vegetable dishes,' Golmar waved her hand and the waiters brought them to the table in silver serving dishes.

'That's a relief!' Gemmy handed her steak back to a waiter and piled vegetables on a clean plate. They were overdone and clumped together but she ate them anyway, making a few grimaces at Gabby.

Brian dined with lethargy but, on the opposite side of the table, Mark Gall cut at his steak like some feral animal, droplets of blood from it gathering in the corners of his mouth. Volta and Pyro ate meticulously, with barely restrained hunger.

'In Kebapistan,' began Pyro, looking over at Gemmy with displeasure, 'we are brought up by our beloved president to savour all food that is given to us, not to take it for granted.'

'We are raised to be himble, sumple peoples,' Volta continued in the same kidney, 'who are graceful for everythings we are given by our dear motherland.'

'And we have no wanting for any extras, we have enough and are contented with it!' Pyro concluded.

'Isn't that lovely, everyone?' Randolph beamed, 'What a charming and modest nation you Kebapis are!'

'Ha!' Mark Gall snarled, 'I don't think so! I couldn't help but note the manner in which that one was staring at my trainers when I walked in just now?'

'Me?' Volta gasped, she spread her broad hand upon her chest, her long fingers fluttering, 'Well, of course, as I am the sports teacher, I take an interest in trainers, naturally.'

'All I can say, madam, is you have a wandering eye, rather like a magpie I once shot with a pellet rifle at Rothley Park Golf Course,' Gall muttered.

'Good God, why on earth did you shoot a magpie, you horrid thing?' Gemmy scoffed.

'Because it was eyeing up my trainers!' Gall spat, and no one dared to make any further enquiries.

'Well, let me tell you about the programme for the next two days!' Randolph trilled, deploying his chipperest tone to move them on from the magpie incident, 'Tomorrow we start at 9 sharp with ice-breaker games!'

'Ooo, goody gum drops!' Gall piped up.

'Then onto the scavenger hunt after lunch, which is a dual-purpose activity designed as jolly good fun in addition to helping to familiarize your good selves with our palatial campus.'

'Is there a prize for whomsoever wins?' Brian Eider-Drake enquired, his eyelids drooping as he languorously said 'whomsoever'.

'Prizes, Prizes, all must have prizes,' Gemmy laughed, 'And I shall personally present our maths teaching colleague with an elegant thimble, lest he prick his finger upon his sharp tongue.'

Gabby had already devoured her whole steak and a waiter was hovering to serve her a second when she declared, 'I'm one of these people who'll eat absolutely anything. When I visited Shenzen, I nipped in for a meal at the famous Fangji Cat Meatball Restaurant. I was the first European to go in there to eat in years and some of the regulars challenged me to a cat meatball eating contest. No one thought I'd win and everyone in the place was laying bets. The match went on for over an hour and people were cramming in off the street outside until there was, well, not enough room to swing a cat, even a dead cat. Eventually, my last remaining opponent slumped over onto his piled up empty plates in a faint. When I was declared the victor, the crowd went mad and twenty or so of them hoisted me into the air, cheering me in Cantonese. I'd consumed 144 cat meatballs, which is considered a highly auspicious number in China, being 12 times 12. Someone made a video of the event and it went viral, getting over 20 million views on YouKu, which is like Chinese YouTube. But when I got back to the city in the northwest where my school was, everything went pear shaped. You see, they don't like eating cats up there. People pointed at me in the street and whispered about me behind their little hands. Oh, it was terrible for weeks.

'Well, there's the fickle finger of fame for you, Gobbles!' Gemmy quipped.

The second course was served and Randolph was bemused to see it was soup.

'It may appear strange but in Kebapistan we have the soup in the middle of the meal to cleanse the palate after the meat,' Golmar explained.

It was a golden brown molluscan broth with dozens of tiny snails floating in it.

'Do we, um, eat the shells?' Randolph stirred his spoon around in the broth with trepidation.

'Yes, they are quite soft,' Volta demonstrated by taking a spoonful into her mouth with a light crunching sound.

'Marvellous,' said Brian Eider-Drake, 'This is the closest I've ever been to actually being a duck. Did you know, Miss Bridle, that Kebapistan once played host to the ancestors of the majority of Old World ducks known to ornithologists today?'

'No, actually, I didn't know that, Brian, but I think I'll just play it safe and dip some bread in, not being blessed with a bill or webbed feet.'

'Where could all these snails come from in such a dry country?' Randolph asked the table at large.

'We have snail farms,' Pyro explained, 'They are harvested each month from snail corrals under polythene. Excellent source of protein. I intend to take my classes to one I know well near the school.'

'Isn't that brilliant, everyone?' Randolph beamed, his forehead glossy with the steam of the soup. He noticed the boar rampant centrepiece was also covered in a sheen of dampness as it started to melt away. 'The world is your classroom! I'd like you all to take a leaf out of Pyro's book and find subject-relevant venues to take your pupils and inspire them *beyond* the four walls!'

'So, Golmar, where might an English and drama teacher take her precious charges?' Gemmy asked.

'There is the Kebapistan Unified National Theatre

(KUNT), but it is in Kebapi language,' Golmar replied.

'Ah, yes, and the principal actress is a *huge* talent, she's the president's daughter, don't you know? I am acquainted with the family personally,' Randolph trumpeted.

'So, what is there for mathematics?' Gall asked. Golmar had no ideas, which made him tut, 'Then we shall go out into the desert and count the grains of sand until the vultures tear the flesh from our bones.'

'Lovely... You know, Tristram, I've just remembered where I've seen this flat before,' Gemmy suddenly announced, 'In that film you showed me in your room at the fittingly named Undershaft Hotel.'

'Ay, you've got a point there, Gemmy, ours aren't like this one at all!' Gabby exclaimed, white flecks of snail shell flying from her mouth.

This pushed Gall over the edge and he flung his soup spoon onto the table, 'I agreed to come to this school in part on the strength of the accommodation, which I see now was *falsely* portrayed in the publicity material. I would have turned tail and headed straight back to the airport if Golmar here hadn't already sped off with our passports. How is it you get the posh bedding, Randolph, while I have scratchy, starchy rubbish that's worse than what you get in barracks for basic infantry training? Moreover, my mattress is lumpy and the flaming Soviet refrigerator gave me an electric shock earlier.'

'So what other factors influenced you to come out to Kebapistan, Mark?' Brian inquired civilly.

'Guns,' Gall snapped back, 'All Kebapi men are trained in use of arms in mandatory military service, and are obliged to keep up that training until they reach pensionable age at 74. Diskebapisbad is full of government controlled firing ranges, all stocked with classic Soviet weaponry. First chance I've got to get off this bloody campus, that's where you'll find me with a nice, warm Makarov 9mm in hand.'

A dessert was now placed before them, to Randolph's relief, as this indicated the meal was nearing its conclusion. 'Desert Snow', as it was called, was a bowl of smooth white, tasteless pap akin to an old fashioned paste you might find on the tables for a school craft project. Brian took a spoonful and declared 'Heavens above! The porridge here is remarkable!' Golmar told them white bread was the main ingredient...and white bread was the overriding flavour.

After a few spoonfuls and a good amount of lip smacking, Gabby gave her opinion, 'I'm a bit of culinary expert, and I think a generous sprinkling of cinnamon would give this dish some form of identity.'

'Snails, then a dessert of bread, I really am in the realm of the duck,' Brian effused, shoveling it in.

'Careful or you might start honking, Brian,' Gemmy sighed.

'Quack,' was his ironic riposte.

'I beg your pardon?' she smirked.

'Geese *honk* but ducks *quack*,' he explained.

Following coffee, Brian nodded off on the tablecloth, which prompted the teachers, one by one, to make their excuses. Gall had already left after one spoonful of the dessert, which he'd described as what sounded like 'effing pole milk'. The waiters half-carried Brian to his apartment on their way out once they'd cleared away the dishes. Gemmy was last to leave and Randolph braced himself, preparing to tell her that they couldn't really pick up where they'd left off with him living among the staff, which reminded him that he must prompt Golmar again to try and find a smart city residence for him.

'Well, here we are!' she yawned, looking out across the empty desert into the heavy darkness, not a flicker of a light. 'Quite, quite alone.'

'Yes, profound, isn't it?'

'As you are probably aware, Tristram, I am a woman with certain needs, minimum daily requirements, in fact, to be scrupulously honest, twice or thrice daily requirements.'

'Ah, yes, of course, Gemmy but—'

'However, after that heinous snail soup, I feel fairly certain my nausea would be much worse if I do any jiggling around.'

'Oh, yes, I mean no, one mustn't jiggle after snail soup.'

'So I'm going to have to take my leave of you.'

'Oh, right-oh, see you in the morning, Gemmy,' Randolph breathed a sigh of relief, 'Hope you'll be fresh as a daisy for the ice breaker games.'

She retired, looking green about the gills.

9

Randolph was ready and waiting for them in the unfinished gymnasium the following morning, decked out in his black fitted top, black leggings and black ballet pumps. He found himself pleased with being back in his garb from the old days as a drama teacher. It still fit perfectly, he felt, enhancing his sleekness. As each teacher entered, he'd beckon them over to join him in stretching exercises. He'd asked them to wear loose, comfortable clothing. Brian was in some worse-for-wear jogging bottoms and Gabby in an orange t-shirt and pink knee-length leggings, which showcased the only part of her body that was verging on slim, her shins. Volta arrived in nylon running shorts and an A-shirt bearing the Olympic logo, her long, pale, cable-like arms and legs extending from them like mooring rope. Gemmy wandered in a red crocheted dress with lingerie of a matching hue. Mark Gall was wearing the same stiff jeans, black roll-neck and trainers he'd had on the night before. He refused Randolph's suggestion to remove his trainers, casting a wary look over at Volta who rolled her eyes.

Volta and Randolph rivaled each other in flexibility, whereas Brian and Gabby did their best, restricted by their respective infirmities. Gabby's mind wasn't on the stretching, however, as she kept harping on about how the sliced bread and eggs left in her fridge were just plain boring as a breakfast. Gemmy sat to one side, legs wide apart and elbows to the sprung floor, complaining to Golmar that she had woken up with two different sized pupils. Golmar said it was probably caused by the

Kebapi champagne, which, being carbonated cheap white wine with grain alcohol added, was known to affect some people thus. Mark Gall point-blank refused to take part, sitting at a distance on a plastic chair, arms and legs crossed.

Pyro appeared toward the end of the stretching session, rather flustered, wearing the same suit he'd worn the evening before. He took off his jacket and draped it carefully over the back of a chair revealing large circles of sweat on the underarms of his shirt. 'I am so sorry, there was a roadblock coming out of the city: the president is on the move. Of course, it would be easier if Volta and I were given the opportunity of having flats on the campus but being Kebapis, we are not awarded the same privileges as you foreigners.'

Randolph commiserated then asked them all to gather around him for The Human Knot. 'Come on, squish in everyone, that's it, don't be afraid of body contact. They're not known as ice-breakers for nothing, you know. Thanks for soldiering on and joining us, Gemmy, your eyes are starting to look a bit more symmetrical now. Could you step in a teeny bit closer, Brian? Mark, will you be taking part in this one?'

Gall suddenly stood bolt upright from his chair and marched, ramrod straight, right into the middle of the little group, carelessly stepping on bare feet with his trainers and nearly knocking Gabby off balance. He was opposite Volta, his slate-grey eyes glaring up at her.

'Now, what we're all going to do now is close our eyes, reach our arms into the air then grab the first two hands you chance upon. Don't let go whatever you do! Now open your eyes. What we need to do is undo this knot... duck under other people's arms or crawl through their legs as we untangle ourselves. You're relying on each other to problem solve here so do talk to each other.'

And so they began to unravel themselves, twisting here and there, going over and under each other's arms.

Apart from Volta and Gemmy accusing Gall of digging his nails into their hands, Randolph was thrilled to see how much fun they were all having. They ended up in a circle, apart from Brian who was in the centre holding his own two hands before him, not having realised until half way through the unknotting process that he had somehow grabbed hold of his own two hands at the beginning.

The next exercise was one of Randolph's favourites and never failed to thrill children of all ages, Blind Man's Buff. Gall surprised everyone by volunteering to wear the blindfold.

'Now Mark, you have to guess the identity of first three people you come across without touching them,' Randolph tied the blindfold, 'How many fingers?'

'How would I know, I cannot see?' he drawled sarcastically.

'Good, then everyone stand in a space in the room.' Randolph turned him about in the customary way to disorient him but stopped and jumped away as the fellow was wielding his arms like a pair of jack-knives and almost jabbed him in the stomach.

After steadying himself for a moment, Gall prowled, sniffing about him. He rounded on Brian first, putting his ear to his face, listening to him breathing, then sighed, disappointed, 'The torpid, rasping breathing of the decrepit Mr Eiderdown.'

'It's Drake, Eider-Drake,' Brian whispered.

'If we were the seven dwarfs,' Gall continued, 'would you be Sleepy or Dopey? Tricky one that. Of course, Gemma with all her subtleties would be Bashful.'

'Well, that must make you Grumpy,' Gemmy snipped, giving away her location.

Gall made a beeline toward her but she dodged him and instead he stopped at Volta, paused awhile, head cocked, then suddenly hissed 'Let me tell you this, javelin woman, these trainers will not leave my feet while you are in the vicinity of them.'

'Nonsense!' she sneered, 'Your feets are tiny; your trainer is too small for my big toe, they are nothing to me!'

He moved on, arriving at Gemmy who faced him full on, with an exaggeratedly revolted expression at his blindfolded face. He took in a long lung-full of her, 'Ah, essence of salaciousness, Mistress Minx. Didn't get your five-a-day yesterday, did you? And I'm not referring to the soggy vegetables at dinner, Ms Gemmy Bridle. How long will you be able *bridle* yourself in out here on our drab, dry desert campus? I hope you thought to bring along some nice, hefty latex supplements to keep yourself going.'

'How many fingers do you see, Gall?' Gemmy asked dryly, brandishing her middle one in front of the blindfold.

Randolph stepped in to put an end to the round by untying the blindfold. As soon as it came off, Gall snarled and made a lunging motion toward Gemmy's neck, but she stood her ground.

'Did it ever occur to you, Gall, that math rhymes with wrath?' she scolded, 'Appropriate that you deal in cold, dead numbers without feelings.'

'And feelings are *all* you deal in,' he returned, 'Feeling this and feeling that whilst being felt all the while.'

Gemmy walked away from him, calling over her shoulder, 'Partially true and I'm entirely unashamed of it. But never in million years with you, not if you were the last man left in the world.'

Trying to create a chipper mood, Randolph let out a bogus laugh, 'Right, everyone, that's enough of the ice-breakers. Time for the scavenger hunt now!' his voice was somehow similar to that of a compere at a children's party. 'Now team up with someone you don't yet know so well and Golmar will pass out the first clue... Remember, there is a prize for whichever pair completes the hunt first!'

Volta chose Brian who was already yawning after the morning's endeavors, and Pyro ambled over to Gemmy who gave him a forced smile. Gabby tottered over to Gull, 'I'll go with Mark then– don't worry, I'll cheer you up, little chap,' she teased and gave him a light poke in the ribs. He rounded on her, brandishing a clenched fist but she giggled, as if he were playing some sort of game.

Then they were gone. Randolph went off to get changed back into a suit. It would give him that edge over his staff. He was not comfortable with the way his warm-ups had turned out and felt he needed a sharp suit to rein in Gall, who was obviously a fiendish handful. He was looking forward to next week when classes began and he'd see little of them. He supposed he'd mainly be spending his time having tea with prospective parents after they'd been shown around the school by Golmar. Getting their children signed up would be a breeze, given that his was the sole English medium school in the country. Perhaps some of the spare buildings could eventually be used as dormitories so pupils from across the length and breadth of Kebapistan, or indeed the entire Central Asian region, could be enrolled. And he, Tristram Randolph, would be on convivial terms with all their families: Heads of state, senior ministers, captains of industry.

Little did the teachers know that Randolph had made *himself* the prize at the end of the scavenger hunt. After he'd changed into his smart suit, he positioned himself behind his desk to wait for the winning pair to claim him. The prize was to be an evening with him at the Irish pub.

After twenty minutes or so, Randolph turned behind him to look out the window to see who was going to get to him first. It looked as if Volta had gone entirely wrong as she was walking toward the car park and where in heaven's name was Brian? Meanwhile, Gemmy seemed to be advancing, in spite of having an animated disagreement with Pyro about which way to go. There was no sign whatsoever of Gabby and Mark.

'They will all know the campus of by heart, after this, Mr Randolph,' Golmar congratulated him.

Gemmy appeared at the office door with a look of triumph on her face, Pyro behind her, exasperated. She slunk into the office and sat on Randolph's desk reading out the final clue, '*A leading man in the theatre and now in a school, this ultimate clue will lead you to his domain so woody and cool!* It was sufficiently self-congratulatory that I knew it had to be you. Pyro here, whose English is a bit rusty, was determined to debate the issue with me, insisting that he was as fluent as I am, which was tiresome.'

'Well, Pyro, old chap, you may not be as fluent in English as our English teacher but you both get to go out to the Irish pub with Moi, just as soon as we foreigners get permission to leave the campus.'

Next to turn up was Volta, only without Brian, 'He wanted to go for a line down,' she explained.

'I'm afraid we beat you to the prize,' Gemmy gloated, 'Pyro and I got here first and get to go with the Head to Ye Olde Irish pub.'

'This of no interest to me. I live with my parents on the same parvenue as the tourist pub. I can go there whenever I wish but I do not wish.'

'Because she cannot afford it,' Pyro chimed in, 'One bottle of Guinness costs a whole morning's wages for us.'

'You still live with your parents?' Gemmy marvelled.

'Of course,' Volta replied, 'That is normal here in Diskebapisbad because the cost of apartments now is similar to in London, which is certainly not fordable on our local teachers' salary.'

They went into the reception area outside the Head's office, where the caterer had delivered meat paste and pumpkin sandwiches for lunch, 'Ah lovely, what we had for lunch and dinner yesterday only ground up!' Gemmy muttered.

'Again, you are voicing the dissatisfaction,' Pyro scolded her, 'Here in Kebapistan, people receive prison or the sweeping duty for constantly finding faults like this.'

'Ha, imprisoned for being sad about dining on meat paste! What kind of country have you brought us to, Tristram?!' Gemmy fumed, while Randolph's broad smile failed to mask his own reservations.

They watched Mark Gall amble in, pick up a sandwich and devour it noisily in three bites.

'Where's Gabby?' Gemmy demanded.

'No idea, the whale couldn't keep up with me,' he answered, his mouth full of a second sandwich.

'I'll go and look for her,' Golmar called back, already heading for the vast, tinted glass front doors.

'Well, enjoy your meat paste!' Gemmy scolded as she ran to catch up with Golmar. Randolph scuttled after her, thinking that's what a conscientious headmaster should do.

The trio walked across the campus, from the pristine completed facades to the half-finished area to the rear with its cement mixers, scaffolds and stone cutters throwing clouds of dust into the air. They walked on planks across muddy puddles, tiptoed around a newly laid cement path, and scuffed up clouds of cement dust, calling Gabby's name. Eventually they heard her muffled cry. It took some time to locate her but eventually they did, wedged tightly into a concrete pipe.

'Good God, Gabby, what *are* you doing in there?' Randolph exclaimed, praying he wouldn't have to get his fine suit dirty extracting this blockage.

'Mark told me the clue was through the pipe and I had better get it if I knew what was good for me. When I got stuck, he told me now I'd have to stop eating for a week until the pupils arrived. He said he wasn't going to tell anyone where I was as my punishment for being a fat sow.'

'Oh poor Gobbles, how dreadful!' Gemmy shook her head, 'Let's see if we can tug you out.'

Gemmy and Golmar each took an ankle and pulled. Randolph thought it best to stay at the front end and shout managerial encouragement. They pulled and pulled, but it was no good. Soon enough, terrible howls from Gabby made the builders down tools and come over to investigate.

'However are we going to get her out, Golmar?' Gemmy whispered.

'I think I will have to get them to crack open the pipe,' Golmar worried, 'They won't want to do it, believe me. If there is a further delay in the building completion and Ms Zoran hears of it, she will probably blame me.'

'No, it is not the only way,' one of the builders took Gemmy aback with his surprisingly proficient command of English. He untied the cloth around his face which he'd been using as rudimentary protection against the dust, 'We can squirt oil into any small cavities, and wriggle her out gently.'

Nodding sagely, Randolph observed that Gemmy looked as keen on the idea as she did on the builder with his dark, south Asiatic eyes and complexion, his strong brow and jawline, his finely shaped nose and mouth. She watched intently, possibly even jealously, as he deftly oiled her lucky friend, spreading the lubricant with a dirty old rag, apologising all the while. For his part, Randolph was glad to let the workmen get their hands dirty and look on with leaderly concern. Gemmy, however, wanted to be involved so she sat astride the pipe, leaning forward to get a better look at the goings on. The handsome builder and two of his colleagues then attached ropes to Gabby's ankles, which they protected with rags and began attempting to ease her out, with Gemmy shouting words of encouragement. After twenty minutes of twisting, and more lubricant applied as gaps in Gabby's rolls presented themselves, she finally started to slide.

'I can see your knees now, Gobbles, that's it, keep going! Oh God, it's a breech birth, but we can do it! Don't forget to breath,' panted Gemmy from the pipe, 'Yes! I can see your bum! Now squeeze, squeeze...and you're out!'

Gabby lay upon the concrete, streaked with oil, heaving and wailing. Randolph found it all grotesque.

'Thank goodness she's breathing!' Gemmy cried, having jumped down to her friend and cradled her in her arms, 'It's alright, it's alright.'

Looking away, Randolph noticed that the handsome builder appeared much moved by the tender scene.

'Your friend will be fine very soon,' he said, 'My people have a saying in the desert– the earth will spit back what is wrongly thrust into it.'

'Your people? Who would they be?' Gemmy asked through her tears, but it was clear from the coquettish tone in her voice already she had guessed the answer.

'The Dalibor, the first people in this land, and its true guardians, famous for our—'

'Oh, I know!' Gemmy gushed, 'I've heard all about you!'

'Richly embroidered tents.'

'Oh?'

'Yes, Gemmy, I heard that too. Maybe the rumours you picked up were exaggerated,' Randolph jested but she barely registered his presence, so taken was she now by the Dalibor builder.

'If you like, I can collect you one Friday and take you on my motorcycle to our village. It is only about 20 kilometers from here,' the man said.

Gemmy grinned perhaps a little too eagerly, her eyes shining, 'Oh, I'd like that very, very much. I came to work in this country in order to learn more of your tribes'...ways.'

'Come and find me here, working on the construction. I will be waiting for you when you need a friend.'

With his fingertips, he wiped the tears from her face, patted Gabby on the shoulder, gave Randolph a salute then returned to his labours, the weighty tool belt rhythmically tapping the dusty seat of his trousers as he strode away.

'Is that one of the fellas you told me about, Gemmy?' Gabby asked after a time.

'It is, Gobbles, it is,' Gemmy sighed as she heaved her friend to her feet, 'Tristram, Gabby needs a warm bubble bath and some sweet tea. I trust you'll explain to Mr Gall what a rotten trick that was?'

Randolph assured them he'd speak to Gall directly, even though he dreaded the thought of being in the same room as the man.

At Randolph's request, Golmar had arranged a minibus for the following morning to take the faculty out on a jaunt around a few local landmarks. Their first stop was the snail farm Pyro had mentioned, which Gemmy claimed smelt like old bandages. At the end of the tour, they were offered free tastes of snail paste and extract of snail on Eucharist-like crackers. Randolph politely declined to sample these local specialities and even Gabby admitted to finding them repellent. Next up was the ruin of an old fortress from the days when the region was known as the Sultanate of Mish Lope. There was little left of it now but it was said that the ghost of the Sultan visited regularly to inspect the remains and that he could be seen on moonlit nights in summer reposing in what was left of his sunken garden, where the fountain was still fairly intact.

The third and final destination was a bizarre natural feature out in the desert some 20 kilometers from the school. It was a deep pit, some thirty meters in diameter, roughly circular, smouldering with fiery seams in burning black rock and reeking of hot tar. The seven faculty members stood near the brim peering in, an arm's length between each of them, but with Gall being given a double wide berth...presumably, thought Randolph, for fear that he might suddenly shove one of them over the edge.

'The name of this place is translated as Hell's Mouth,' Golmar began, 'Kebapi legend has it that it was here sin was spat into the world and it is here where it will be swallowed up again someday.' Six of them took an involuntary step back at this, while Gall went one closer. 'For there is a saying in our country that what is spat out from hell, will one day be thrown back by the forces of good,' she added.

'I am hoping, Ms Golmar," drawled Pyro, "That this is not the veiled comment on our government.'

'You may interpret it as you wish, Mr Envany...Old sayings may have many meanings,' she replied.

'You forget to mention, Comrade Golmar, that in past times, this was how the Sultans disposed of their arch-enemas, who were flung, screaming, into this pit, whereas our Dear Leader is merciful and places even worst enemas of our state in his citizen rehabilitation camps,' Volta soothed the others.

'Well, that's a relief, I think,' laughed Randolph, 'I'd choose a nice camp over the fiery pit any day!'

'Yes indeed, Mr Randolph,' Brian nodded in agreement, 'I'd say a camp is more likely to have some semblance of a bed at the very least.'

'I wonder, could you fry an egg on one of those rocks toward the side?' Gabby mused after a pause.

'And I wonder if there'd be enough heat to cook a very large lady to the core on a spit laid across the thing, or would she remain raw in the middle, in spite of having been carefully gutted?' Gall growled, glaring at her, 'You could eat yourself, that might be fun for you, and leave the raw bits for jackals.'

'Oh, just ignore him, Gabby, he's not worth tuppence,' Gemmy huffed, linking arms with Gabby, at which they turned back to the minibus, the others following in dribs and drabs.

10

Randolph's big day arrived – the informal welcome barbecue and picnic out on the newly laid artificial school playing field. There was an ample turn-out of a couple of hundred people, families of the children starting this year, and those of others interested in joining the next, once more year groups were open. The cuisine had a British theme and the serving tables were laden with beef burgers and sausage rolls. Strawberries had been especially flown in for the event and waiters were serving them in little plastic finger bowls with cream. Randolph caught a glimpse of Zara Zoran, walking about like royalty in a leopard print dress with her bodyguards in tow. He hadn't been able to get near her though, with all the guests stopping him to ask questions. The faculty t-shirts were clearly doing the trick, making the teachers clearly identifiable as he saw little groups around them-- another stroke of brilliance attributable to his good self. But then he noticed Mark Gall, standing alone, seemingly eating sausage rolls in his usual black turtleneck. After a moment though he realized that the madman was biting them one after another and putting them back, whereupon Randolph resolved that it was a blessing in disguise that he'd refused to play ball with today's faculty dress code.

It was time for him to climb the podium for his welcome speech. Golmar was up there with the list of new pupils whom he would welcome to the stage, one by one. He smoothed down his hair, took out his speech and tapped the microphone. Everyone politely took a seat but just as he drew in a hefty breath to begin his delivery, there was a terrible clashing of symbols and a drum roll and everyone jumped up again, Randolph thought it was some special Kebapi welcome heralding his arrival and he duly waved his arms, gesturing to them all to be seated again, but at that moment cacophonous march music blared from the speakers and everybody began to sing, standing ramrod straight, their arms glued to their sides. From their glazed, deadly serious countenances, Randolph assumed they'd been suddenly bewitched. He turned to Golmar for clarification but she was doing the same, except that she seemed to be lip-synching, as opposed to actually singing. The torturous sound went on for some two minutes, ending in a static scratch; then everyone relaxed and returned to their chairs as if nothing had happened.

'Thank you, everyone, for that spirited and unusual welcome– I am very honoured,' Randolph announced into the microphone, his voice reverberating, bouncing off the buildings and across the desert. He beamed at the crowd and Golmar handed him the programme which informed him that they'd just sung the national anthem honouring Anomaly Zoran and all he had done for Kebapistan. 'And, I'm sure that, if President Zoran could have been with us today,' he quickly corrected himself, 'he would have been delighted with each and every one of you.'

Randolph turned to drink some water while he unfolded his speech. 'It is my honour this afternoon to welcome you to the Swineforth Hospital International Family,' a patter of applause. 'I am Tristram Randolph, Headmaster, and I am absolutely thrilled to be leading this new school on its first steps toward greatness. Acorns grow into fine oak trees, as the saying goes'...more patter. 'I shall be leading my staff of six accomplished teachers in laying the foundations of what promises to be an outstanding educational institution, modeled upon our 800 year old sister school, Swineforth Hospital in Somerset, England. I and my four fellow British teachers have had such a warm welcome in Kebapistan, one that has made us feel very much at home and, with these firm friendships now in place, we shall go forth together, in the spirit of Sir Hubert Swineforth, who himself ventured to eastern lands during the Fourth Crusade, founding the original Swineforth Hospital to perpetuate the learning he had acquired there...' Suddenly, he just couldn't resist slipping in a favourite phrase from the educational jargon generator, which he'd never found the opportunity to use at the Undershaft, 'Together, we will morph open-ended liaisons with a laser-like focus! So, without further ado, I'd like to individually welcome our 35 pupils-- our inaugural group!' Golmar handed him the list of new pupils. 'Hmm, in reverse alphabetical order, at the top of the list is Felicity Zoran...'

Golmar whispered something in his ear as a beautiful girl with bouncing blonde curls mounted the podium. 'Ms Zoran ordered that her children must be first; that is why it is *reverse* alphabetical order.'

Randolph shook her dainty hand, and he arched an eyebrow: the idea of entering into a relationship with Zara was suddenly a little less appealing now he saw there were children in the equation. Felicity promptly sat in the most prominent central position of the chairs which were arranged in a crescent, and elegantly placed one leg behind the other like the Queen of England.

'And next on the list is Gerald Zoran!' Felicity's younger brother now sprung onto the stage, with a manic, wicked look in his eyes. When Randolph held out his hand, the boy made a rude sign, thumb to nose. Randolph laughed along with everyone else. He had to; this was the President's grandson.

When Randolph looked at the next name on the list, he could not, for the life of him, fathom how to pronounce it. He gave a long whistle and noticed the audience suddenly became animated, writhing in their seats. 'Could you say this one for me please, Golmar? If I try, it will probably come out like Rhubarb Rhubarh Rhubarb!' Golmar pronounced the name. He shook the hand of the studious looking boy who had appeared on the stage and looked down at the next name with so many unusual letters in peculiar arrangements. He shook his head and whistled again, and the audience again became visibly uneasy.

'Mr Randolph,' Golmar whispered, 'In Kebapi culture, to whistle is a bad omen, implying that someone is too lazy to work hard, which is against our country's ethos.'

'Oh, good lord, how interesting, right-oh, won't do that again then. Sorry, everyone, I haven't quite got the hang of the Kebapi language— thank goodness for good old Felicity and Gerald. Of course, their mother, President's Zoran's daughter, whom I am fortunate to be able to call my friend, is such a great Anglophile, which provided the inspiration behind our all being gathered here today. You should see her in tweed!' No one followed this inane banter and Randolph's chuckles at his attempted humour echoed hollowly around the field. He therefore decided on the spot to add a bit of fun to the proceedings, 'Right then, one thing I have learned about Kebapi names is that they all have meanings, so now our ever-prepared school secretary, Ms Golmar, will translate all the other names *into English*, saying each of them loud and clear into the microphone. Maybe we can even stick to these Anglicizations once school starts to make it easier for their British teachers to remember names!'

In Golmar's eyes there was a look of trepidation. 'If you like, Mr Randolph,' she said behind her hand, 'but please be aware that our Kebapi names may not translate so well into English. What is one word to us is, more often than not, a whole phrase in English.'

'Just do your best, Golmar,' Randolph grinned,

'What's your name translated, incidentally?'

'Well, it's a bit embarrassing, Sir.'

'No, I don't believe you. Come on, spill the beans.'

'Very well, if I must, it's Dimples.'

'Well, Ms Dimples,' Randolph declared in to microphone, let's have the first name.'

'Don't call me that please!' Golmar hissed through clenched teeth barely moving her lips, a blush spreading over her cheeks and neck.

'Ah, okay, right you are, Ms Golmar, who's up next then?'

'Moon Rock Cactus,' Golmar spoke in a monotone into the microphone. An obviously embarrassed fourteen year old girl walked up to Randolph and shook her hand. 'Birth in Spring Rain,' and another came forward, a boy blushing to his roots. 'Steel Boy' was next, a tiny wisp of a lad with a shocked expression. The names continued in the same vein with confused bursts of applause... Molar Cusp of the Setting Sun, Love Betwixt Two Perfect Beings Engenders Greatness... and so on. Some of the pupils did not immediately recognize their translated names and took some time to come up but Randolph kept on smiling. He could tell that his impromptu plan was backfiring as the phrases no longer sounded like names at all, but he certainly wasn't going to admit he'd made a mistake up there in front of everyone. That wouldn't be what a Headmaster did at all.

When all 35 pupils were on stage, Randolph decided to take a leaf out of Pettistone's book and invited everyone to join him in the Swineforth rugger song, 'It's very simple. It goes like this. Now repeat each phrase after me: 'To the east...To the west...To the south...To the north...Nobble their de-fence...Scramble their off-ence...Let the swine go forth!'" Following these instructions, a smallish minority of audience members did the rallying cry back to him. This wasn't good enough for Randolph so he split the audience into two sides and tried to set up a little competition based on which side was loudest, adding 'Now when you do 'West', I want everyone to wave to the west to my dear old mum and dad in Twickenham, England.'

Sadly, Randolph's crowd-riling skills were lost on his audience, most of whom had never been out of Kebapistan and were unfamiliar with rugby songs. The response to his call only got quieter each time until it dwindled to almost nothing. He decided he'd best move on. 'And now I'd like to introduce you to our fabulous faculty, whom many of you have already been mingling with, thanks to the special polo shirts I had commissioned for this event. Swineforth Hospital International Team, please come up and join me at the podium.' All of them, apart from Gall, whom Randolph hadn't seen since he'd spied him with the sausage rolls, trotted up the steps and were introduced by name and subject taught.

'Love what you did with the polo shirts, Tristram,' Gemmy tittered, squeezing his hand as she walked toward the steps that led off the podium.

'Jolly good fun, aren't they?'

'Yes, especially backside!' she called over her shoulder.

And as they retreated down the steps Randolph saw, to his horror, the huge error he'd made in having the initials of Swineforth Hospital International Team emblazoned in chocolate brown on the back of the shirts. He stood there gaping in silence for a while, only coming round when Golmar tapped him on the shoulder.

'So,' he returned to the microphone, eager to beat a hasty retreat at the earliest opportunity, 'Thank you to Ms Golmar for designing those lovely faculty polo shirts....aaand, erm, nothing else.'

A few people put their hands together and Golmar, befuddled, gave a little bow.

'Thank you all so, so much for joining us and enjoy the rest of the picnic,' he burbled before hastening away.

Just as he was about to duck into his office, where he intended to lock himself in until everyone had left, two men, whom he recalled as Zara's main bodyguards, intercepted him.

'Ms Zoran like see you her office,' one of them said robotically.

'Oh, very well. Her office? Where's that then, chaps?' Randolph replied, open-mouthed, at which the other one placed him in an iron grip just above the right elbow and guided him next door.

Randolph had no idea she had taken up residence in the room next to his office. He'd noticed the door but thought that behind it there was only an empty room. The bodyguard knocked and the word 'Enter' resounded from within. Randolph opened the door to an office slicker even than his own, if that were possible. There was an ornate marble fireplace with a realistic flame gas fire and a tiger skin hearth rug splayed before it as if worshipping the flame. Three rigid, tightly buttoned Chesterfield sofas were positioned around the tiger and, on a tartan carpet, was an ebony desk behind which, upon a throne-like high-backed chair, was seated Zara herself.

'Tristram! Hello! Come in!'

He breathed a sigh of relief at her jovial tone and shook off his tense expression. 'Zara! Hello! So good to see you!'

'How's it all going?' she walked around her desk and invited him to sit with her on the Chesterfields.

'Well, apart from that little boo-boo with the whistling—'

'Ha! How were you to know? An outdated, superstitious belief!'

'And then the muddling up with trying to say the pupils' names—'

'To be expected. You're new here. I'm not sure it will be any easier for you with the literal translations, but try it if you think it will help them with their English.'

'And then the error of judgment with the design of the team's polo shirts—'

'Yes, now that was a bit silly but I think you successfully passed the blame over to your PA. It is part of what she is there for and she will understand. What I wanted to talk to you about is the teachers. Gemmy, her name suits her. What a little gem! A perfect mature English rose with such a lovely clear speaking voice! But Tristram, I *cannot understand* Gabby. She told me she is from The Mumbles and all I can hear is mumbles whenever she opens her mouth!'

'Well, The Mumbles is in Wales. She's Welsh.'

'But we don't want our pupils getting a Welsh accent. An English accent is what you must foster here, and we have assured parents their children will develop this. They see it as one of the main things they are paying for. Then there is Brian who tells me he is a Brummy. Where is this Brummy?'

'Brummy? Oh, it's slang for Birmingham.'

'Again, this is not a real English accent—'

'Well, it is actually. Birmingham is in the English Midlands.'

'Hmm, I am now thinking we did not fully express our expectations because we had to hire you in such a rush so we are *partly* at fault. Never mind, we will make the best of it, but get rid of them at the end of the year and hire new people who talk like Gemmy and like you.'

'Right-ho.'

'Good, I am so glad we have an understanding. From acorn to oak tree. I like that.'

'Great that you have an office next to mine!'

'So that we will be able to work together closely on developing the school. And now, you've met my children, Felicity and Gerald?'

'Yes, they seem absolutely charming.'

'They are, of course, in years 7 and 9, which is why we are starting with these two years. The school has been founded around their needs. Father doesn't want

107

them sent out of the country for their English style secondary education. It is too much of a security risk. Instead, we have brought English schooling to them. We will be adding years 8 and 10 next year. It was father's suggestion, clever as ever, yes? Another reason I wanted to move my office here was to, let us say, keep an eye on them. Gerald can be a little brazen. We had the Olympic size swimming pool built with him in mind. A vigorous swim gets rid of his excess energy and helps him to concentrate better in lessons. He will be here every morning before school starts with his coach. He has enormous potential, you know. Could become an Olympic athlete. Anyway, I will be visiting my children's classes from time to time to check the teachers are doing sterling work. I think you call it 'walkthroughs', rather like an informal co-director, let us say.'

A knock at the door heralded the entrance of a sallow, portly fellow with a box of papers. 'Leave them there, Max.' With a resigned look, he placed the box on a side table and had a good, long gander at Randolph before departing. 'You remember my ex-husband, Max? He will be the office boy. You and the teachers can pass him all your photocopying. He can also put letters in envelopes and such like. Don't let him address any envelopes though because his handwriting is not very neat. Now, let us have some tea with your PA and you can tell me all about your plans for the first week.' She pressed a buzzer on her desk and within two minutes Golmar entered with a tray of tea things. It was strange, thought Randolph, that Golmar had neglected to tell him that Zara would be in the office next door.

The first item Randolph wanted to cover were the accommodation arrangements, which he said were less than ideal with the leader living among the staff, from the point of view of his being a separate entity entirely from the run of the mill teachers.

'Yes, Golmar has mentioned this to me, Tristram,

but it has to stay as it is for the time being,' Zara asserted, 'We will look at changing it next summer.'

Randolph nodded and smiled, feigning amiable acceptance.

That evening, Gabby went over to Randolph's apartment, with Gemmy accompanying her, to complain about the dinner that had just been brought to them, which was left over sandwiches from the picnic. 'It's bloody awful, Mr Randolph, how am I going to survive? I need proper meals. I'm starting to become lethargic,' she whinged.

Randolph invited them in and sat with Gabby to make a list of the kind of meals she'd like to have, using his gold plated fountain pen and the HA! Hunt Associates pad he'd received from the fair. He promised he would discuss the matter with Ms Zoran but he imagined nothing would be accomplished. Still, at least he was going through the motions, like a good headmaster should. As they sat there, Gemmy stared preoccupied out into the desert night, probably dreaming about that Dalibor builder, Randolph surmised, carrying her off to his 'richly embroidered tent' on his motorbike, her arms low round his waist and her inner thighs pressed to his hips as they rode along the excitingly bumpy desert track.

'What the hell's that?' Gemmy asked.

'What? Meatloaf?' Gabby replied.

'No, that, there!' she pointed outside. They came over to the window and looked at something that Randolph initially thought was a mirage. Nearby there was a building entirely decorated in Chinese paper lanterns with what sounded like the steady beat of formulaic East Asian pop music jangling out.

'A Chinese restaurant?' Gabby offered, 'Shall we go and investigate?'

Within two minutes, the three of them were walking across the campus and toward the glowing apparition, with Gabby veritably wheeling along making it difficult for Randolph and Gemmy to keep up. The building was a ruin, but one that had been repaired with colour: tarpaulin covered over by bright polyester fabric had been strung up to serve as a temporary big-top-like roof. The windows were sealed over with waxed paper parasols painted like Chinese fans and red paper lanterns swayed in the desert breezes. A carefully hand-painted sign hung above the empty doorway, Michael Oh's Cosmopolitan Emporium. They stepped inside to see several high metal shelf units laden with goods ranging from the quotidian to the ridiculous, from cornflakes to dried shiitake mushrooms, from pop tarts to salted spiced crispy crickets. A man in early middle age with dyed blonde hair, tubby yet nimble, was up a ladder hanging accordion bunting that was unfolding to reveal the 12 animals of the Chinese zodiac.

'Well, hello, I've been waiting for you. I am Michael Oh and this is my fantastic emporium!' he said in a strange accent, something between East Asian and South African.

'Are we dreaming?' Gemmy asked.

'Yes, we all are,' said Michael, coming down to their level and shaking their hands, 'I take it, you're from the new school? I've set up shop here to serve as your convenience store and cafe. When I learned about the school starting up from my dear friend and English conversation partner, Golmar, I knew instantly that I could never let an opportunity like this pass me by, not only to make good money, but also to make good friends. Now, may I get you a welcome dish of cha-gio, ergo Vietnamese spring rolls?'

'Yes! We'll have that to start with!' Gabby gushed.

'Piyotr darling, will you set a table for these two lovely ladies and their rather dashing friend?' he called over to a petite man behind the counter with his hair styled in exactly the same way as Michael Oh, dyed blonde with a Tintin style flick at the front, who was basically a slightly younger, scaled down version of Michael.

'Welcome, welcome,' Piyotr crooned, dashing out with a tablecloth, cutlery and a yellow candle.

They were invited to sit in the middle of the shop at a pale blue plastic picnic table, hastily covered with a vinyl tablecloth in a cartoon panda print, with a little tea light candle between them. Randolph found it all somewhat makeshift but went along with it as the food smelled good. They were served the spring rolls, followed by the Vietnamese salad known as nom, bowls of pho or Vietnamese noodle soup, then bun cha, which were crispy grilled snippets of spiced fatty pork, and for dessert, ban ranh, alias crispy fried balls of glutinous rice, filled with sweet red bean paste and covered in sesame seeds. Gabby got Randolph take pictures of her eating everything for her blog, while Gemmy waxed lyrical to Michael and Piyotr over discovering their gustatory oasis amidst the culinary wasteland of Diskebapisbad.

Michael related to them that he was a 'baffling beigeian' relic of the vanished Communist world, the son of two engineers, a Mozambican father and a North Vietnamese mother, who had each been chosen to undertake their doctoral degrees in the Soviet Union, and had subsequently been selected to stay on and work in a top secret Soviet biological warfare programme, which had been based in part in the small city of Breshnevisbad, long since re-christened Zoranisbad. Michael had met Piyotr in a 'citizen reconditioning camp', whither they'd both been sent after being deemed unfit for compulsory military service due to 'unmanly tendencies'.

The reconditioning hadn't been successful and they'd been together since, living as flat mates in an apartment inherited from Piyotr's parents who'd been high Communist party apparatchiks, originally dispatched from Russia, doing one thing or another on

Diskebapisbad's limited hospitality scene, including working at the Irish pub for a couple of years. They were always on the lookout for a business opportunity, however, and when Michael had heard about the new school out on the desert road, they had driven out there and claimed the ruin. 'We knew if we put out our lanterns we would, sooner or later, attract some beautiful butterflies of the night. Now you can bring your friends too and we can find more friends who'll take us as we are.'

'Well, I'm sorry to have to say this, Michael,' Randolph admitted, 'but there are only two other international faculty at present.'

'And one of those,' Gemmy sniffed, 'is someone I promise you don't wish to meet.'

'We're not worried about that; we'll grow alongside the school,' Michael smiled, ever the optimist. We always get by, whatever we do, don't we, Piyotr?'

The diminutive man agreed and took away their dishes as Gabby went around the shelves filling a basket with all manner of snack foods. As she did so, Randolph and Gemmy watched Michael go outside with a tray of plastic beakers filled with bottled water. They saw him approach some of the sweeping people and hold out the tray to them. Some of them took the water, downed it quickly and furtively, then carried on sweeping.

'They take it like they're not supposed to,' Gemmy said when he came back inside.

'You're right, they're not supposed to. And I'm not supposed to give it to them either. But that doesn't stop us. Piyotr and I know what it's like to be in their shoes. We worry they're dehydrated and we are able to be quite certain they go hungry. Of course, they're being punished for 'serious wrongdoings'.'

'What sorts of wrongdoing?' Gemmy asked, but Michael only gave a sad smile, put his finger to his lips and went over to help Gabby with her purchases.

11

The school uniform of Swineforth Hospital International had been based on the uniform at its English counterpart, only jazzed up a little with the addition of satsuma orange tights for the girls which, Randolph had to admit, looked rather fetching under the Swineforth beige and sage tartan kilts. The boys' uniform, was along the same lines, with the Swineforth tartan slacks and satsuma socks. Both girls and boys wore the chestnut brogues and the white shirt with the ruffle at the neck. The blazer, also in the Swineforth tartan, had been stylishly tapered to appeal to the Kebapistan elite and Randolph had managed to procure a larger one for himself, free of charge, when the uniform shop was accidentally left unlocked for a brief period. He'd make good use of it, he thought, when he went on hiring trips and so forth.

Randolph had read that a headmaster needed to make sure he had a high profile during the day about the school, if he wanted to get on in his new career. One of the things he did to achieve this was to stand at the gate and welcome the pupils as they got off the buses and walked into school. 'Hello, and how are you today, my friend?' He had decided that this was to be his main form of address as he wasn't good with names. Once he'd seen in the last bus load of pupils, he'd make his way to the central quadrangle where the children would all line up and sing the national anthem in that funny way with their arms stuck to their sides like little toy soldiers. The rather tinny-sounding music came out of loud speakers up on one of the balconies from a system operated by Max who, once he'd turned it on, would come out and stand on the balcony with his chin up like Mussolini. They would all fix their eyes on a Kebapi flag with President Zoran's face printed in the centre. Randolph had tried to memorise the anthem but it was quite the tongue-twister so he mimed as well as he could. Zara had told him that *all* the teachers were supposed to be out there singing, but only the local hires generally made it. Randolph thought he'd let this slide as it redounded well on him being the sole foreign faculty member who attended the patriotic pomp.

For the first few weeks of school, Randolph sought incessantly to cement the image of himself as hands-on leader. He would stroll about the campus aristocratically, his hands behind his back, with Golmar bringing up the rear, taking photographs of him in various scenarios. These photographs were now on the school website along with being framed on the walls of the foyer. There was one of Randolph kicking a ball around with a few lads in the central quadrangle, another of him awarding a certificate for excellent homework at the front of the English class. He had passed the classroom as Gemmy was about to award it herself and had nipped in and substituted himself.

The piece-de-resistance, however, was carefully engineered by Randolph to appear on the front of the prospectus, and was currently the cover image for the school's website. It included what appeared to be a range of nationalities even though everyone in the school was 100% Kebapi. Felicity Zoran with her blonde locks would pass for a Nordic beauty, a couple of young lads whose mother was from the Dalibor tribe, and had just so happened to marry the son of a Kebapi millionaire whom she met whilst he was earmarking sections of the desert for landfill, would pass for Asian, and a redheaded girl with distant Russian ancestry was, in Randolph's eyes anyway, the Irish representative.

He was sure this photograph would stand him in good stead when he moved on to a more lucrative position in a European country in a couple of years' time. He quite fancied Brussels or The Hague.

No photographs, however, could possibly be taken in the dreaded canteen as what was served up in there rivaled in crudeness the very worst offerings in British state primary schools. It was all very well wanting to imitate meals in British schools but Randolph was mystified as to why they'd chosen the plastic segmented tray-plate with a dollop of mince in one segment and a dollop of pink blancmange in another– basically two forms of diarrhea, dog and robot. He had mentioned his reservations to Zara who told him the model would have to remain this year but they could look into alternatives for next year. Felicity and Gerald, meanwhile, took their own gourmet lunch separately with their mother in her office.

Randolph would have liked to have said the first month of the school year passed without incident, leaving him with little to do beyond his photo-ops but, sadly, this was not the case. Every day there was at least one parent lurking outside his office wanting to see him, and all too often the same parents came back day after day, anxious and bored mothers mainly, who would drivel on and on, taking up an hour of his precious time-- and Golmar would be there too since most of them required a translator. If one, just one, of these mothers had been attractive, divorced and fluent in English, the cloud might've had a silver lining but, alas, none of them ticked all three boxes. Worse still, they were, every one of them, pushy, entitled members of Kebapistan's politico-economic elite, with neither jobs nor interests, their all-consuming focus being their mediocre children. Randolph's plea of 'If you wouldn't mind giving us all a little bit more time, just to settle in,' didn't seem to be having much effect.

Brian came under the heaviest fire for his

'confusing accent', which one addled parent had described as 'Bummy'. This was but one complaint among others in a letter to Randolph signed by 10 mothers who were clearly doing this in search of some purpose in life as well as to cause trouble. In addition to his accent, they criticised Brian's project on wetland fowl, which none of the parents could locate on the prescribed British syllabus, and which they quite rightly deduced to be 'time-wasting'. They claimed they had read the syllabus 'from cover to cover' and had found no mention of wetland fowl. Randolph marvelled at their threshold for tedium, he had barely skimmed through any syllabus, including ones he had delivered in the past.

Then there was Pyro in his 'ragged suit' with its foisty smell, repeatedly asking the pupils whom he taught first thing in the morning to bring in class breakfasts. Of course, the parents all felt they must excel in this as he, after all, would be giving their children a handful of their grades, so the man was breakfasting with all manner of treats beyond his budget each morning. The litany of complaints carried on with Mark Gall, who frightened the pupils with his fury when they got an equation wrong, Gabby with her sluggish apathy and Volta with the remarkable rate at which pupils' valuables were going missing from their lockers in the changing rooms. Even Gemmy came under a bit of fire for getting the pupils to do embarrassing things in the drama class such as having girls and boys work together in pairs.

'In Britain, we encourage girls and boys to work together,' Randolph explained.

'Not when it's having them carry a tennis ball between their necks across the room,' a parent explained, 'not when she is naming the game 'beast with two backs'. We have looked this idiom up.'

'Oh, that's just Miss Bridle breaking the ice between the pupils,' Randolph responded, brushing this off, 'I did similar things myself when I was a drama teacher.'

To which the perplexed parent replied, 'I did not know they were doing things with ice. This also must stop immediately. It's dangerous.'

Zara appeared in Randolph's office one afternoon dressed in a black velvet tuxedo style trouser suit with a satin blouse with a pink pussy bow collar. He hadn't seen her for a week or so and had presumed she'd been away, but no, she'd been there all along. 'Tristram, how is everything going?' she enquired.

'Oh, hiiii Zara, it's all going brilliantly, did you see my little photo exhibition in the foyer?'

'Yes, it looks like you're getting on well with the pupils. But my question is, how are the pupils getting on with their teachers?'

'A few kinks to iron out in the cuffs and collars but, you know, getting better all the time.'

'That is not what I have been hearing. You must remember that we are one big family here at Swineforth International. Many parents here are the children of my father's close associates whom I grew up with. We feel that there are issues to be sorted out, wouldn't you agree?'

'Oh?' was all Randolph could say, feeling himself pinned and wriggling beneath a magnifying glass.

'I think the time has come, Tristram, to do the rounds. Felicity's artistic talents aren't being stretched and Gerald was at the brim of tears last night because he could not do his maths homework.'

Randolph sighed. He supposed he'd have to act on the complaints now that Zara was in the know. He had hoped they'd have petered out by now. He dropped in on Gemmy first, since she was the teacher receiving the smallest number of gripes. He asked her to tone down the drama games as the prudish parents couldn't deal with them.

'But the pupils *love* them, Tristram! I'm not

changing a thing. I am simply guiding these eager girls and boys in their first tentative steps towards intimate relationships, almost like an informal sex therapist.'

Randolph didn't really know what to say to this so he traipsed off to pay a visit to Gabby. She was behind her desk writing her *Gabby Gobbles* blog when he came into her unruly year 7 art class.

'Working on the blog?' Randolph nodded toward a picture of her on the screen with what looked like a beard of rice noodles hanging from her mouth and Piyotr and Michael either side giving the thumbs up.

'Yes, it's become really therapeutic to lose myself in this with the general lack of food on offer around here,' she whined, not looking up at him, while she added a bit more to her blog entry, 'Plus I have over two thousand followers now so I have to give something back to my fans.'

'How are they doing?' Randolph nodded as casually as he could toward the neglected class.

'They're discovering their independent artistic creativity,' her eyes remained fixed on the screen.

Randolph surveyed the room. Some pupils were colouring in photocopies of Disney characters, while others were merely chatting or playing games on their phones, 'Seems they don't need much help on this one?' he observed.

'No, this is one of the filler activities I use where they don't need me at all– helps them to refine hand-eye coordination and come to their own conclusions.'

Randolph had to admit, he knew nothing about art, yet even to him, the pupils didn't appear adequately engaged colouring in Dumbo and Bambi. But then again, what could he really do about it, anyhow?

'Do you know what I keep dreaming of, Mr Randolph?' she stopped typing and looked up at him beseechingly, 'A crombone.'

'Whatever is that, Gabby, or shouldn't you mention it in front of your class?'

'It's a delicacy from the Valleys, a tubular crumpet in the shape of a trombone, served hot and dripping with melted butter.'

She invited him to view a video of herself buttering and devouring a crombone, close up in slow motion. As she watched, her eyes centimetres from the screen, her mouth open and her hand disappearing under the desk.

'Well, I'd better leave you to it,' Randolph concluded and wandered off back to his office, attempting to erase from his memory what he'd just witnessed.

The next morning, Randolph popped along to Pyro's classroom. He was teaching Kebapi history with the government's prescribed slant on world events, which contrived to place Kebapistan in a central position on the world stage, with a reconfigured world map above the board to support this. The debris of extravagant breakfast foods was spread over his desk and he held forth at the board with propagandistic passion, the pupils making notes all the while. When he saw Randolph enter, he grinned cunningly and switched to English for the boss's benefit. 'In 1885, the British, eager to claim our wealth of minerals for their own, sent over an army numbering some 3 million men. We defeated them in a matter of weeks, in the same way we did the Romans...by luring them into the desert, where their poor survival intelligence caused them to perish gradually without a single shot being fired.'

Randolph listened with interest as he had never heard about this singular episode in his country's history, though he could've sworn that the British army hadn't swelled to 3 million men until the First World War was well underway, and that through the 1880s the entire British Empire had been secured using only around 125,000 troops. On the other hand, his mother had told him that his great, great grandfather, Sir Gannet Vainglory, had been involved in some sort of short-lived campaign in Kebapistan at about this time, but it had involved no more than a handful of men, and was largely to do with delivering a gift to the Sultan of Mish Lope. The gesture had backfired, however, with Sir Gannet ending up in jail as the gift was somehow not to the recipient's liking. Following the lesson, Randolph asked Pyro about the breakfast tradition he had started.

'It is a fair trade, Mr Randolph-- the British teachers have their breakfast food provided by the school yet I receive nothing! I am coming early in the morning from the city, where there are more and more roadblocks with the election on the way. I have no time to make the breakfast before I leave. You have to remember, the children eat, too. They like it– it is, I think you say, a communal breaking of bread.'

'More like waffles, apple strudel and chocolate chip cookies, it seems. I didn't even know you could get this sort of stuff in Kebapistan.'

'These rich people have foreign cooks brought in at tremendous expense– why shouldn't I get a piece of the cake?'

'Literally,' Randolph swept up a chocolate chip cookie for himself and the gesture provoked Pyro to regard him with narrowed eyes. 'Do you think they may feel compelled to bring it all in so they will gain good grades in the subjects given the most weight by the Ministry of Education?'

'What nonsense is this? If they don't bring anything in, they simply cannot join in with eating, it is nothing to do with grades!'

Randolph, content with what he'd heard in that the breakfasts had nothing to do with grades, now had a denial to report back to parents and continued breezily on his way to the state-of-the-art science lab.

No class was in progress and at first he didn't see Brian because his head was on his desk behind heaps of papers and a huge balsa wood model of a what appeared to be a coot. When he did finally spot Brian, stock still and papery pale, he froze with horror. *Good Lord, I hope the old duck hasn't died on me,* was the first thought that leapt into his head.

Max emerged from the lab storeroom carrying what looked like a test paper and hesitated, surprised, when he saw Randolph. A wily look came over him and he placed the paper in his hand behind his back, obscuring it from Randolph, and whispering, 'It is okay, he is not dead, only sleeping,' as he passed him at the door. Randolph looked after him, wondering exactly what it was he'd taken.

Brian raised his head and peered about puzzled with his small, round brown eyes. 'Ah, Mr Randolph you appear to have caught me in a moment of deep meditation. I was contemplating the profound mysteries of science, particularly as they relate to the taxonomy of waterfowl. I was, so to speak, communing with my daimonion.'

'Your daimonion?'

'Yes, daimonion, my familiar spirit, a shadowy being which guides my hand in times of uncertainty.'

Randolph didn't like the turn the conversation had taken but thought it best to play along, 'And does it, by any chance, have a name, this familiar spirit of yours?'

'It most certainly does, Mr Randolph; it is called Pervetus.'

Randolph blanched, 'Brian, I fear that an elderly man who claims to have his hands guided by a spirit named Pervetus, and who has unfettered access to young people, is a far from reassuring thought to me as your immediate supervisor.'

'Oh dear, Mr Randolph, you need have no fear! My affections are entirely engaged by ducks, geese and the occasional swan. Pervetus refers to pervasiveness, rather than perversion. Anyhow, Pervetus is only his familiar name. His surname is Presbyornis. Have you never heard of Presbyornis Pervetus...or in English 'The Pervasive Old Man Bird'?'

'Sorry, Brian, but I'm forced to admit I haven't.'

'Why it's the most likely common ancestor of modern waterfowl and a creature of true wonder! Imagine, if you will, the body of a duck but on the scale of an emu, surmounted by the neck and head of a goose far larger than that of any alive today, balanced on the graceful, stilt-like legs of a crane or a flamingo. There you have the image of my daimonion. They haven't walked the Earth since the Ypresian Age of the Eocene epoch, which ended nearly 48 million years ago. There is said to be a fossil of another species of the genus, the only one of its kind in the world, in the National Museum of Natural History in the city centre, which I have been persistently enlisting Golmar's assistance to arrange for me to see.'

'That sounds consumingly captivating Brian, but some of the parents have asked when you'll complete your waterfowl project and move onto the syllabus?'

'All in good time, Mr Randolph, we're nearing the end of the first part of the waterfowl study and, although the material could easily take up the whole six years of secondary education, you may rest assured that I am mindful of other topics we must touch upon.'

'Good, well if you'd start touching on those ASAP, so I will not have to have dissatisfied parents hanging around my office taking up my time, I'd be most grateful,' and with that Randolph gave him a short, curt smile and marched out, though his smug sarcasm was plainly lost on Brian. He was already getting quite weary of having to spoon-feed these teachers, who should've known what they're doing by this stage in their careers.

He walked past the mathematics room– dead silence, everyone with their heads bowed down writing, textbooks open in front of them and Gall sitting at the front in a pair of enormous black padded headphones, staring fixedly at a spot on the wall at the back of the room. What Randolph didn't know was that he was listening to the loudest, angriest kind of Heavy Metal.

He did this often whilst teaching a class as he found the pupils so infuriating. Gall either ignored Randolph's little wave at the door or didn't notice it. *Now that to me seems like a mathematics class that's running very smoothly*, thought Randolph who could see no evidence of Gall being angry toward the pupils at that moment.

Gall had been aggressive toward him, however, on the couple of occasions he'd dropped by to cajole him into covering Gabby's art class, when she'd been struck down with food poisoning, a frequent complaint given her adventurous eating habits. Gall had point-blank refused to do the cover so Randolph had taken to sending Golmar on his cover-seeking missions. She'd had no luck with Gall either so now, when no other teacher was available, she ended up sitting at the front of the art class instead. Although Gall made it perfectly clear that he hated everyone on staff, he had struck up a strange friendship with Max. Randolph had spotted them together a few times smoking cigarettes in the alleyway at the side of his office. He had looked and listened in on the sly one time. The topic of conversation had been the many ways to kill a man with your bare hands, with Max demonstrating and Mark Gall attempting to copy his actions, with an awestruck look on his face.

Randolph now moved on to his last stop of the morning, Volta Kovet who was dismissing her PE class as he walked in.

'Don't forget to take your personal belongings as you leave!' she bawled after them.

'Ah, that erroneous phrase!' Randolph entered, smiling and shaking his head sanctimoniously.

'What is wrong with it? I learned it from an expansive online English conversation class, the Cheltenham System.'

'Your belongings is sufficient. Adding the word personal is surplus to requirements, even though everyone seems to be saying it nowadays.'

'Well, if everyone is saying it, then I will too!' she brayed at him, raising herself up to her full two metres, her cable-like neck muscles tensing, 'Besides, how do you daring to kryptonite my English when you are not speaking *one word* of Kebapi?'

'Ah, yes, you certainly have a point there Volta,' Randolph faltered.

'Why have you come here for anyway? Can't you see I was about to take the shower? Or maybe that is why you come?'

Randolph felt slightly uncomfortable about broaching the issue at this point as she towered over him drumming her fingers on the wall, her pungent post-athletic body odour filling the air, like mown grass fermenting in the sun, 'No, not at all, Volta, it's just a little thing, you see the pupils are claiming a few bits and bobs have gone missing-- an iPhone or two, couple of watches of Russian make, Shorokoff and Denissov, whatever those are, a Bulgari necklace-'

'And why do you come to me about this? Do you think I am some thief? You heard me just now tolling them to take their *personal* belongings. If they leave things lying around, how can I help if a cleaner takes them, or more like they take from each other?'

'Well, I suppose in some cases it may, Volta, but I understand it was things from the changing room lockers and that you issued all the combinations.'

'What roughage! How am I doing that?'

'You don't have them all on your computer, then?'

'What are you employing?!' she was furious now and Randolph took a step back as she leaned down and her face lurched toward him.

'Absolutely nothing! Those silly parents! How could they think such a thing?' he snivelled, before scuttling off, nearly losing his footing over a bin brimming with plastic cups.

After his thoroughly thorough walk through, Randolph was convinced no one could accuse him any longer of failing to investigate complaints. He sighed as he made his way across the marble floored central quadrangle, feeling slightly overawed by the huge responsibility he'd agreed to take on in becoming a headmaster at a startup school. There were few people, he thought, who were up to this sort of task so it was a great stroke of good fortune for Zara that she'd chanced upon one who was. Still, it was a burden that was tough to shoulder alone so he was relieved to pass by Gemmy who, seeing he was looking a tad the worse for wear, linked her arm through his and, walking along with him, invited him out to dinner at Michael Oh's Cosmopolitan Emporium with Gabby, Brian and herself.

Walking over there together, Brian told them that he didn't actually mind the fleshy fare he was presented by the school catering service, which Randolph had observed he ate as if in a trance, sometimes missing his mouth. He'd agreed to join them as he always agreed to everything, nodding and nodding, as if attempting to converse amicably in a language he couldn't fully comprehend. Randolph strongly suspected that Gemmy and Gabby weren't actually interested in spending time with dozy Brian, but had invited him along primarily to get more business for Michael and Piyotr, whom they had taken to referring to as 'Diskebapisbad's most fabulous entrepreneurs'.

'Wait Brian, it's just over here,' Gemmy pointed when he started ambling off in the wrong direction, 'You'd probably wander off into the desert without stopping, wouldn't you, if someone wasn't there to guide you?'

'Quite possibly,' he smiled vaguely, 'And who knows, I might find a fascinating waterfowl fossil while I was at it.'

'You're going to love Michael and Piyotr's cooking, Brian,' Gabby took him by the arm to speed things along.

'Michael and Piyotr? Who might they be?' he

enquired, even though they had already told him.

'The proprietors of the most excellent emporium at which we're shortly to dine in rare style for this barbarous land, Brian,' Gemmy reminded him.

He stood still and thought for a while, 'Are they, uh, living together as man and wife then?'

'Husband and husband I think you'd describe it as, Brian old chap,' Randolph explained.

'Ah, Barbara told me I'd be coming across all sorts when I went abroad. I hope they won't try anything on. In the duck world, you know, it's all too often drake on drake when there are no ducks to be had. Sometimes even the unfortunate coot or grebe may unwittingly get caught up in the shenanigans.'

Gemmy rolled her eyes, 'Fear not, Brian, they won't be asking you to nest together, although an omelet may be on the cards.'

'Which I hope is not a euphemism for the mating act,' whimpered Brian with a worried look in his eyes.

'Besides Brian, you're of somewhat advanced years for them and they're both spoken for,' Gabby added.

'And another thing, Brian,' Gemmy said, looking him over seriously, 'You may have turned 65 but you've really let yourself go. I'm not surprised Barbara sent you packing. Look at Tristram here, for example, he's not sooo much younger than you but he spends a great deal of time on his presentation. You don't have to be like him, of course, but you need to make the best of the basics and the M & P partnership will help you learn to do that.'

'Ooh, like a makeover?' Brian burbled, brightening a little.

'Not exactly, more 'make slightly less awful',' Gemmy elucidated, 'May I enquire of my old gentleman, why, oh, why he doesn't keep his fingernails better trimmed? And they're looking rather dirty too, I fear. I bet your toenails are a sight to behold. Do they clack when you walk barefoot on the bathroom floor?'

'Yes, I think perhaps they're starting to,' Brian grinned impishly, 'Barbara had been doing them for me these last few years and I seem to have neglected them somewhat since coming out here.'

They arrived at the Emporium, where Michael and Piyotr made much of Brian on this, his first time there, taking his jacket, tucking a napkin in his collar, slipping a colourful cushion onto the chair just before seating him upon it. All of this Brian regarded with some trepidation, although he went through the motions of being polite, looking about at his new surroundings with all the anxiety of one who doesn't like to set foot outside their house.

'What can I get for you, Brian?' Michael asked, 'A choice of the finest Vietnamese cuisine to be found between the 50th and 80th parallels of longitude, or the all new, all day full cooked English breakfast?'

'Ooh, the latter please, thank you,' Brian quacked, reddening.

'And how do you like your eggs?' asked Piyotr.

'Look, I don't have eggs, I'm not a duck, I'm a drake, and I'm in my twilight years, so I'd prefer you didn't make enquiries of that nature,' Brian warned, suddenly riled.

'Steady on, old fellow!' Randolph jibed, slightly horrified.

'Oh, don't mind him, he's a bit of a befuddled old fowl, just bring him the breakfast with no variety of eggs whatsoever,' Gemmy explained and Piyotr darted off to get it all ready.

Thankfully, the remainder of the meal proceeded without further incident. Following it, Randolph returned to his apartment, had a long shower, put on his fleur-de-lys bathrobe and, thus in repose, gave his parents a video call to review their plans for the half-term holiday.

'Hello Tristram!' his mother said. Her lipstick had missed the mark again and Randolph dispensed with a salutation in order to tell her off.

'Don't berate her too much, old boy,' his father chipped in, 'she's putting off buying her new glasses til our finances rejuvenate, aren't you, Jocelyn, old stick?'

'Oh, good lord, do you have enough for the air fares to here for half term?' Randolph asked, hoping he wouldn't have to reach into his own pocket.

'Don't worry yourself, Tristram, we have our tickets,' Jocelyn smiled sweetly, 'I'm so looking forward to seeing you again, my darling.'

'She's been missing you, you know,' Giles winked, 'and we are really hopeful about the Major Silliphant Navigator which finally has a name– the Silligator– we've been testing it around Twickenham and it's ready for its trial run in Kebapistan!'

'The Silligator?' Randolph was skeptical about the choice of name.

'We've been practising with Major Silliphant and hopefully haven't missed out a single gory detail of the history of Kebapistan,' Giles beamed, 'Your mother's started packing, she's so excited.'

'Well, don't forget your rubber turkey hat,' Randolph quipped.

'Do we need to bring a turkey hat?' Jocelyn looked confused.

'What, do they have Christmas early over there?' Giles wondered aloud.

'No, just joking,' Randolph replied, but the conversation continued with them befuddled, Giles asking her what he was saying and Jocelyn repeating something about the turkey hat that he couldn't quite hear. 'Look, you two, I'm still here! Just forget about that. I'll collect you at the airport so you don't need to worry about a thing.'

'Is there anything else we need to bring you?' Jocelyn asked, 'Can you get Marmite out there?'

'Mother, you know I detest the stuff.'

'What about Y-fronts?'

'Marmite and Y-fronts, those essentials in life, along with the rubber turkey hat!' Randolph quipped but his razor-sharp wit only muddled them further

'If there's anything else you need, anything at all you need, you let me know,' Jocelyn pleaded.

It had become too exasperating to talk to them. He suspected they'd had wine with their lunch and were not entirely compos mentis, so he signed off. Opening up his email he saw to his dismay that Roger Swainson had written to him reminding him of his imminent visit with his accomplice and Randolph's nemesis, Nigel Dare.

12

'I've just seen High Trousers Man lurking outside my classroom!' Gemmy burst into Randolph's office laughing. He'd mentioned the sobriquet to her privately in passing, the day after he'd informed the teachers in an email that 'representatives from the sister school will be making a flying visit to see what they can learn from our exemplary work'.

'Yes, High Trousers Man does tend to *lurk,* doesn't he?' Randolph smirked.

They had already met up with Randolph outlining the shape their 'inspection' was to take. The word had jolted him; it hadn't been called this at the board meeting. Dare would be carrying out his own impromptu walk-through, with Randolph in tow, recording– literally, on Dare's antediluvian Dictaphone-- 'examples observed of both desirable and less desirable educational practice', whilst Swainson would be meeting with Zara and then Golmar about Randolph's own performance, in addition to going through all the new unit planners and policy documents to get a picture of how things were panning out, hopefully in preparation for an official accreditation visit the following school year.

Nigel Dare, dressed in officious black, skulked down the corridors making commando hand gestures to Randolph who could only guess at what he meant. He was muttering observations into the Dictaphone for which, Randolph had been astounded to find, he still had a supply of long discontinued miniature cassette tapes, 'Approaching room 27 now. Mathematics stationed here. Repeat, mathematics. Preparing to record lesson sample now.'

Randolph followed after him, bemused by his spy moves and military parlance. 'Is it really necessary that you act like this, Nigel?'

'Shh, approaching point of interest now,' and he waved Randolph down, as if suggesting he take cover, which was fair enough as this was, after all, Mark Gall's room.

'No, no, no, no,' Gall's flinty voice cut a fissure into the air, 'You've done it wrong, again, Moon Rock Cactus! Practice the formula from the textbook. I do not want to see crap like this!'

Randolph saw Nigel Dare flinch at the usage of the c-word but then he smiled slyly, probably at the damage it would do to Randolph's position. He followed Dare's suit in peering around the corner to see most of the class standing in a straight line down the middle aisle, waiting to show Gall their work. Dare took a sneaky photograph of it with his antique Rollei 35 camera on which the film had to be advanced and the shutter cocked by thumbing a ratcheted lever at the top, an action which Dare obviously relished. Randolph supposed the photo must be High Trouser's Man's way of recording Gall's method of having nothing to mark of an evening, in addition to facilitating his public humiliation of those who had no natural inclination toward mathematics.

'Actually Moon Sock, I just want to ask you something– how are you so bloody thick? You even got the warm-up questions wrong. Your parents named you well. You're dumb as a rock and your mind's on the moon.'

The girl shrank into herself, 'I just don't like numbers, sir, they're spiky and I blank out when I look at them. Sometimes I feel sick.'

'You blank out because there's a blank where your brain should be,' and he picked up a giant wooden compass and directed the sharp point millimetres from her forehead, 'I could pop your head like a balloon and we'd see the little void within. Now remove yourself from my immediate line of vision and return to your chair at the rear of the class.'

Gall was dissatisfied with the next pupil's work too and he took his yardstick and sliced it down on the table with an exclamation of 'Why are you all so bloody simple minded?' They stood there in line, terrified, as if awaiting the guillotine. Some teared up, others stoically raised their chins.

'I think I've got enough evidence on tape here,' Dare whispered, 'Moving upstairs to Scroggins in the art studio.'

Dare crept up to the art studio door on tiptoe, Randolph rolling his eyes behind him. There was no class going on but they heard a gurgling sound from within a storeroom. More sign language commands from Dare seemed to be suggesting that Randolph get on the other side of the storeroom door and crouch. Randolph duly did this. Dare inched forward and pressed his ear and his Dictaphone to the door. The sound of a rhythmic, pulsating motor reverberated followed by a woman's moans. Randolph's eyebrows knitted, surely she wasn't in there engaged in unschoolworthy activities with herself? They listened again... 'Infuse that vibrant jet! Oh, oh, oh. Adulterate with cream. That's it, whirl it in. Yes, do it! Do it now! And, yes, saturate in blood red globules that burst, burst all over!'

Randolph could see that Dare was in two minds as to what he should do. He had Gabby's bizarre discourse on his Dictaphone, which would probably be enough to hammer another nail into the lid of Randolph's coffin. But, if he should burst in and take a photograph of her in the act, then he would have a very juicy piece of bonus evidence indeed. He signalled to Randolph that he was going act on the latter notion, placed his hand gently on the handle, his other hand holding his old-fashioned pocket camera poised. Under his breath, he counted to three then flung open the door and took a photograph with flash. The site that greeted them wasn't exactly what either of them had imagined. An immensely corpulent woman lay on a pile of rags on the floor, shielding her face. The source of the whirring engine had come from her laptop upon which appeared to be a montage film demonstrating the erotic art of paint mixing.

'What? What's happening?!' she lowed, rolling over, blinded by the flash.

'I could ask you the same thing,' Dare boomed.

'I...I don't know what you mean. I have a free lesson. I can do what I like in my free time,' she struggled to a sitting position in an attempt to regain some dignity.

'What were all those noises I was hearing outside the door? What were you doing during school hours?' Dare probed.

'It's only a harmless little interest of mine. I...I watch paint mixing films. I love them, they calm me down. I'm finding it a stressful experience being here. There's not enough diversity of meals and that's a serious problem for me. I've told Mr Randolph about it before but nothing has ever changed, has it?'

'Well, Gabby, you know I've tried my best with the powers that be to get the menus improved,' Randolph reminded her.

'I know but now we're buying most of our food from the shop down the road because we got sick of having the Kebapi beef all the time. It's been a bad move coming here as most of my wages are going on meals from Michael Oh's Emporium– that's the name of the local shop.' She teared up.

Randolph could see Dare regretting his abrupt entry, although he would still almost certainly be using the recording and the photographic as evidence against Randolph's leadership. Dare squatted down on the pile of rags, intrigued to find out more about the paint mixing fixation. 'So, you're feeling very stressed being here and these films have a calming effect you say?'

'Yes, they do. And I also watch films of cutting into soap and ones featuring slime, how to mix it and the like. I've been making slime with my year 7s. They love it, but we've been at it for a few weeks because they struggle to get the consistency right. The parents are up-in-arms with all the ingredients they have to go out and buy, but it absorbs the children and that's what Art is all about, isn't it, Sir? Look, I've stored some samples of their more successful slimes on these shelves. I come in here, shut the door and play with it sometimes. It helps me unwind.'

And she proceeded to show Dare her range of slimes in labelled jars, from a bright blue slime filled with microbeads that cracked when you squeezed it, to a gold sequin star slime with, to a slime that resembled real mucus to a rust-coloured magnetic slime. They sat there and, for want of a better word, did slime-play together.

'You sit outside and close the door, Randolph, while I chat with Gabby here for a while longer,' Dare said, repeatedly squeezing a lump of blue microbead slime, 'She may wish to divulge something about your leadership but feel impeded by your presence.'

Randolph did as he was told and stood outside the classroom, waiting at the door like a boy who'd been naughty. The next class arrived and Randolph greeted each of them with his customary, 'Hello, my friend!' hanging around ever longer, looking over messages on his phone from yet more parents with various petty quibbles. So engrossed was he in answering the quibbles that it slipped his mind that Gabby was still in the storeroom with Dare. The year 7 class quietly took their seats and waited. The conversation must have sounded highly curious to the pupils but it washed over Randolph as he thumbed his upbeat responses to the parents.

'Turn the light off, you see how it glows in the dark?' came Gabby's voice from behind the store room door. 'And it feels so good when you press your fingers into it, Mr Dare, lovely isn't it?'

'Oh, yes, it's got a most interesting consistency– a bit squeaky at first but it when you work it, it goes all slippery,' Dare replied.

'It's edible, you know, but I wouldn't eat it because the kids have had their paws all over it.'

'Edible? Really? Miss Scroggins, I have to say, I don't think I've had this much pleasure in years.'

Absorbed as he was in his phone, Randolph didn't immediately notice a certain mischievous look playing at the corners of the eyes of Gerald Zoran who bounded to the front of the class and began performing matching lewd gestures each time the voices emerged from behind the door. The class regarded this strange choreography with nervous disbelief. After all, this was the President's grandson.

The conversation continued for the next four minutes, during which time Year 7 became sufficiently bored or embarrassed that, one by one, they took out the ingredients they'd brought from home and started making their latest batches of slime with new recipes they'd found on the internet.

Nigel Dare finally emerged from the closet squinting, followed by a bleary-eyed Gabby Scroggins.

'Oh, whoops-a-daisy, looks like our session ran over a bit, Mr Dare.'

'It seems it did, Ms Scroggins, the time just flew by! Thank you so much for showing me what you've been working on. I'd better let you get on with your class now,' and he loped out of the studio and, followed by Randolph, headed for the room assigned to Humanities and Kebapi.

'Now in vicinity of number 52, classroom of Mr Envany, local hire,' he smartly told the Dictaphone. More commando hand signals to Randolph before halted at the door and cocked his head to one side like a puzzled dog. Randolph could see that Dare was not able to make any initial judgments as everyone was speaking in Kebapi. But it did all sound rather informal, not as if there were any teacher leading the class, but rather as if ten or more people were chattering at the same time. Dare pivoted forward on the balls of his feet to peep around the corner and Randolph followed suit. Envany had his legs up on his desk reading a magazine, whilst three boys with screwdrivers appeared to be disputing the best way to repair a coffee machine. The rest of the class were either absorbed in their mobile phones or talking together. Dare decided to enter, the better to comprehend what was going on. Randolph hung back at the door.

'Yes?' Envany asked, barely glancing up from his reading matter.

'Yes, hello, I'm Nigel Dare from Swineforth Hospital in England, the authentic one. What is your lesson about today, if you don't mind me asking?'

'It is not *about* anything until we get the coffee machine fixed. How can I conduct a lesson without caffeine? The international teachers have coffee-making facilities supplied with their apartments but since I am not given an apartment because I am local hire with a lower salary, I must provide my own coffee-makings, so now we wait until machine is repaired.'

'Right, thank you. I won't take up any more of your valuable time,' Dare quipped, unable to mask his disapproval. He swept out of the room and, without a word to Randolph, continued on to his last visit of the morning before lunch, 'I will now investigate science, I repeat, science, with Mr B. Eider-Drake, room 65,' he enunciated into his Dictaphone as he stalked down the corridor, keeping close to the wall.

Brian was conducting an experiment. Year 9 pupils were gathered around a table sitting on stools. A Bunsen burner was sending out a blue flame and every pupil was holding a forceps, in each of which was clasped a feather.

'I have to say, girls and boys, that I do find the smell of singeing feathers quite soporific.' Brian was fading, his head drooping over, his sunken eyes two disappearing points. "Is it your turn, my dear?"

'Ye-es, Mr Eider-Drake,' a beautiful girl with blonde locks chanted; it was Felicity Zoran.

'Very well, put your feather into the flame and we will record the moment of combustion— it's the filoplume of a goosander, I believe.'

'Yes it is, Mr Eider-Drake.'

Brian went into a sort of hypnosis at the sight of the smoking feather, his head rolling forward, his mouth falling open, his tongue lolling and a goose-like honking hum now emerging from his slack mouth.

Felicity's lovely face was rapidly transformed into an ugly leer as a wicked idea seemed to bubble up into her imagination. She moved her feather, now with a little flame at its tip, to Brian's downy tuft of hair while the rest of the class watched, mesmerized. It crackled and caught within seconds. Hands were slapped over mouths suppressing giggles, but no one did a thing as a single flame gained momentum atop Brian's head. Nigel Dare burst into action, dashing into the room with a long-legged canter and grabbing the fire extinguisher. He directed it at Brian's head, pulled out the pin and squeezed the lever. The pupils looked on, amazed. Unfortunately, Dare could not see how to halt the spewing foam and Brian was swiftly turned into a kind of baked Alaska. Randolph came over to try to advise him, while Dare fiddled with the valve at the top, which only served to eject the foam at a faster rate. The pupils became excited and began jumping about the room, wrestling each other to the floor into piles of foam.

Randolph's cries of 'Felicity, please!' and 'My friends, get back into your seats!' fell on deaf ears as the repressed fourteen year olds enjoyed their impromptu foam party. When the extinguisher was finally spent, Nigel Dare cursed the state of his trousers while the pupils continued to frisk about.

The foamy mound that was Brian shuddered slightly and a pair of eyes opened, like two chips of coal in a snowman's face. 'What was the combustion period of the feather?' he asked no one in particular.

Swainson bumped into Randolph and Dare in the reception area. Dare was making his way back to the apartment block in order that he might change his trousers before lunch. 'How was everything, Nigel?' he asked his loping assistant.

'As predicted back in England, not good, Roger, not good at all,' was all Dare could muster, at which Swainson looked to Randolph with a hint of a frown.

Following lunch, the pupils and faculty gathered at the school's entrance as Zara Zoran had sent out an urgent mail announcing that she had something special to unveil. She'd commissioned a carved stone coat of arms to match that of old Swineforth Hospital, featuring the seven wild boars upon the heraldic shield, which was to be hoisted up and mounted onto the marble facade above the great glass doors.

'It gives me great pleasure to share with you, during our first visit from Messrs. Swainson and Dare, this special symbol which links us even more closely with our dear sister school in England,' Zara effused.

Everyone clapped on cue and the two elder statesmen of English education, standing beside Randolph, smiled and waved, waved and smiled. Zara removed the velvet cloth to reveal a rather nicely executed, much enlarged copy in ruddy sandstone of the Swineforth family coat of arms, only there was something not quite right about it that Randolph couldn't quite put his finger on.

'Oh dear, oh dear,' Randolph heard Dare say to Swainson, 'She's got the boars going the wrong way! They're supposed to be running *toward* the boar rampant in the centre but this lot are running *away*!'

'Ah, yes, so they are!' Swainson exclaimed, 'Someone put a lot of work into that-- shame they didn't notice. Still, probably best not to mention it just now, Ms Zoran seems so pleased.'

"And there was a good way off from them an herd of many swine. So the devils besought him saying, 'If thou cast us out, suffer us to go away into that herd of swine,'" Dare intoned to Swainson in his best pulpit voice, 'And the big one in the middle in the fool's Phrygian cap is our friend Randolph.'

'Why thank you, Nigel, but I don't need the cap now I've got my hair back,' Randolph countered.

'So, what are we seeing before us on the shield, Nigel?' Swainson asked, 'The swine before or after the devils have possessed them?'

'I'd say if it's anything like what I've observed thus far today, the swine are running amok, with the devils already firmly in place,' Dare sighed.

'Crikey, they're all running away from me! Leaving me in the lurch!' Randolph squeaked, recollecting the dream he'd had of himself all alone at the whiteboard with hordes of children before him.

'Fleeing the sinking ship perhaps?' Dare contemplated, 'Come along, Randolph, let us venture forth to the gym and see what delights await us there.'

Arriving at the door to Volta's office, Dare suddenly froze, ears pricked. There were some peculiar sounds reminiscent of toilet straining, which seemed to put him in two minds about whether or not to quench his natural curiosity. He told Randolph that they'd better take a quick peek to put his mind at rest so, in unison, they craned their necks around the door frame. Volta Kovet stood trying on a heap of clothes over her gym clothes, albeit without success as all the articles were too small.

Nigel Dare stepped forward and cleared his throat, 'Sorry to bother you, Miss, but is everything alright?'

'As you can see, it is not,' she panted, sweating and red-faced, 'It is both a gift and a curse to be so powerfully framed! The one who can be the bronze-medal-winning Olympic athlete, cannot so easily wear the dainty garments: The pupils have brought in these donations for the earthquake victims in Afghanistan but nothing fits me!'

'Should you be trying on the donations?' Dare challenged her, whilst Randolph boldly held the rear guard just outside the door.

'Why not? I will only take what fits me. The rest will go to the Afghans.'

'Er, don't you think, Ms Kovet, that they are perhaps needier than you?'

'All I think about, old mister English man, is that the Afghans do not notice if a few items are not in their donation– they are happy to have anything!'

Dare appeared to Randolph to have decided that trying to reason with this teacher would be a fruitless venture so he marched them off to make the final call of the day upon Gemmy. As soon as they entered the corridor, they could hear reading poetry from her room, the door to which was always open...

'The gemmy bridle glitter'd free,
Like to some branch of stars we see
Hung in the golden Galaxy.
The bridle bells rang merrily
As he rode down from Camelot:
And from his blazon'd baldric slung
A mighty silver bugle hung,
And as he rode his armour rung,
Beside remote Shalott.'

Dare edged forward to spy on the source of the Victorian verses, but she spotted him immediately and skipped over, pulling him into the classroom.

'You mustn't miss this, o' plenipotentiary from the far off sister school! It's suppressed sexuality in Tennyson today!'

She seated Dare at the front of the class, where he writhed a little and squeezed out a false smile. Randolph stood at the back of the class, enjoying his bugbear's discomfort.

'Now class, which words and phrases in this stanza of the poem might well be 'double entendres', implying to the reader that the Lady of Shalott is rather attracted to Lancelot? You talk about that in pairs for five minutes while Inspector Dare gives me the once over.'

'Well, I'm not exactly an inspector, more of a monitor.'

'Ooh, a monitor, that's a kind of big lizard, isn't it?'

'Yes, but I'm not that.'

'Well, what a shame. Alright, Mr Monitor, fire away, what would you like to know?'

'Er, just a brief outline on how you're doing really.'

'I was doing pretty awfully until I started seeing my Dalibor fellow– talk about 'a mighty silver bugle hung'!-- yes, class, that's a clue – I could blow that instrument all day! Of course, before coming here, I had a second coming with Tristram at the Hunt Associates fair-- I told him in London exactly why I wanted to work in Kebapistan, didn't I, Tris?... to explore the 'customs' of Dalibor, renowned far and wide for their – keeping to the theme of the lesson – blazon'd baldrics slung. Now I spend every weekend round at his camp over in that general direction across the desert. I'd like to go every night, but he claims he has to conserve his energy.'

Randolph wondered whether the pupils really had picked up on the implicit content of the poem, or if most of them were merely pretending to work but were actually listening to what Gemmy was saying to Dare. Several of the girls appeared to be giving their partners knowing looks, especially Felicity Zoran, who looked to be having a sneaky laugh at Dare as he sat there, mortified, in front of the class.

'Thank you, Miss Bridle, I'll let you get on with your lesson now,' he warbled, beating a hasty retreat for the door with Randolph trailing after him down the corridor.

The next morning, Randolph was surprised to find himself invited into Zara's office for an 'emergency meeting', a locution that somewhat alarmed him. They were ready for him when he tapped on the door, Swainson and Dare seated together on one Chesterfield and Zara on another. They had already gone over the agenda, whereas it would be sprung upon him out of the blue so that he'd have no choice but to respond with unprepared answers to their well-prepared questions. He sat on the empty Chesterfield with the glass eyes of the tiger rug fixed upon him. Zara's, Swainson's and especially Dare's eyes were similarly directed toward him, matched by polite smiles. He knew he was in for it, but he didn't yet know what *it* was.

'Morning, Randolph, thanks for joining us,' Swainson reeled off, 'It's been a most enlightening experience coming here and we've dug down and thought about what makes the place tick and what makes it flounder. Let's start with the positives, Nigel.'

'Well, it's going to be a great campus when the building work is completed and I've seen a few examples of good teaching practice so there are some solid foundations to build on. Gabby Scroggins is a great gal who has tapped into her pupils' slime craze and is really giving them what art lessons should be – good honest fun. They're able to unwind in the art class and have a break from the important subjects. And there's Gemma Bridle who is, perhaps, a little on the earthy side but is admirably ambitious in covering some pretty mature topics with her classes.'

'Unfortunately she is far too much on the earthy side, Mr Dare,' Zara said with a pinched, prudish expression, 'Her cleaner informs me she is constantly moving the portrait of my father into her bedroom when the designated place for all presidential portraits in the home is in the living room. It is a law which has been passed these last twenty years and she is flaunting it! Whenever the cleaner returns the portrait to its rightful place, Gemma is moving it back to her bedroom again. We have left her notes in English explaining the custom but she is ignoring them!'

'Perhaps she is missing having a man in her bedroom,' Swainson jested.

'That is precisely what I was thinking, Mr Swainson, and it is unacceptable!' Zara snapped outraged, 'What is she doing in her bedroom in full view of my father? Is she disporting herself in the presence of his portrait while being unclothed!'

'Like I said,' Dare reiterated, 'she's rather on the earthy side.'

'I thought Gemma was quite promising when I first met her, with her nice appearance and accent, but I now doubt she was a sensible hire, Tristram,' Zara complained, making a pursed, pained expression.

Randolph gazed at her blankly, surprised with himself at how badly he had misjudged her during their initial meetings. She really was a dreadful prude whose heart always had and always would belong to Daddy.

'Well, let's not be too hasty, writing her off over moving a portrait,' Swainson reassured her.

Randolph waited for Dare to reel off some more examples of good practice but he did not. He laid his notes aside and waited for Swainson to move on to the next topic.

'Nigel has, however, seen several examples of less desirable teaching practice, snapshots, I know, allowing for time constraints, but these can give a fairly vivid impression when collated.'

'Let's tackle Brian to begin with,' Dare picked up a new paper, which appeared to have much more writing on it. 'Brian fell asleep in the lesson we observed together and then the lab was set on fire.'

'I'd also like to draw your attention to a test Brian will be giving to year 9 next week,' Zara added. She clicked her fingers and from the corner of her office, Max emerged and handed her several sheets of paper. 'We have already had parents complaining about Brian, and I'm aware that Tristram has broached this issue with him. Yet the man persists in teaching only about wetland and wildfowl. He is positively monomaniacal. I am now unsure whether anyone you hired is up to scratch, Tristram. Ducks are not even on the syllabus! Look, this entire test is about ducks and, what's more, one quarter of it is three pages of photographs in which the pupils must pair the duck with its characteristic penis.'

'Well, I hope you haven't shown Felicity that test to ensure that she'll be getting top marks,' Randolph observed. He'd suddenly put two and two together as to why Max had been walking out of the science lab with some papers the other week, and wondered whether the man went prowling around the other classrooms scavenging for master copies each time one of his children had a test. With Max revealing this penchant for cheating, Randolph wondered whether he dared to be dishonest at his evening chess matches with Anomaly Zoran, an act which would surely warrant a sentence of banishment, or worse.

'That is by the by, Tristram,' Zara sniffed, brushing off his comment as Swainson and Dare perused the duck penis section of the test with grave faces. 'Then there is the issue of Mark Gall, of whom my little Gerald is terrified. The fellow appears to have no care that he is speaking so strictly to the grandson of the President. When I sent Golmar to warn him that there might be serious consequences for this, he laughed in her face. I won't have her treated like that, even if she is only a PA.'

'Quite right,' Swainson agreed with her, 'All staff

should be treated with respect whatever their social standing.'

'In addition to the international hires, there are some issues with the local hires,' Dare resumed, turning a dour bulging eye upon Zara, 'Your sports teacher was in the act of stealing charitable donations when I was on my rounds and I understand that many of the pupils' belongings have been reported missing in the vicinity of the gymnasium. Then there is your humanities teacher who is so eaten up by what the international teachers are getting and what he is not, that it is disrupting his teaching. When I visited his classroom, he seemed to be on strike until the pupils figured out how to mend his percolator for him.'

'I may have hired them, Mr Dare, but it is Mr Randolph's job to support them,' Zara was on the defensive. "Volta Kovet is an Olympic bronze medal athlete and needs nurturing as she is new to teaching, while Pyro Envany just wants a few simple home comforts and he will do anything for you.'

'Which is exactly why I've been encouraging him with his programme of potluck breakfasts in class!' Randolph chimed in mendaciously.

'You need to remember, Ms Zoran,' Dare warned, 'that the Swineforth name is currently *on loan* for one year, pending review, and that its renewal will be dependent upon positive reports from Mr Swainson and myself.'

'There's also the issue of the food, Ms Zoran. Two of the international teachers have mentioned that they're finding it very difficult— it's simply too meaty for the British palate, what with the steak and the stew,' Swainson said, 'It's a sound enough meal once in a while, but they're getting it every day, which strikes me as overkill.'

'More like roadkill,' Dare muttered under his breath for Swainson's ears only.

'Jiz-biz is our national dish and many Kebapis

would give their eye teeth for a serving,' Zara replied haughtily, 'When in Rome...as your wise English saying goes. I do not eat these dishes myself, for health reasons, but if they are good enough for the people of Kebapistan, they should suffice for these teachers who are guests in our country.'

'Actually, I heard from Gabby and Gemma that they're eating every evening at a little place next to the school, so possibly you could strike a catering deal there as they seem to prefer it,' Dare suggested.

'Where do they mean? What little place?' Zara sneered, 'We have given no permission for a business to be situated next to the school— Max, please go and investigate immediately.'

Max made his exit instantaneously with the blank eyes of a shark gliding toward the scent of blood.

To conclude the meeting, a five part action plan was introduced, mainly involving extra work for Randolph, which left him somewhat miffed, although he judged straightaway that he could palm off much of it on Golmar. Nevertheless, he was now going to have to formally observe all six teachers on a weekly basis, when it had been tedious enough to do it on that one occasion. He was to ensure that their conduct toward pupils was professional and that their content of their lessons was germane-- as if that were actually something under his control! He was also to properly check over all their lesson planning on a half-termly basis; there was no way around it. Zara would continue with her walk-throughs, but now they would be more regular and rigorous, and not just about checking up on her children.

A few perks were to be introduced for the local hires to help them feel less hard done by. The caterers would be instructed to provide a different meal for each day of the week, which must amount to more creativity than minor variations on jiz-biz and steak. The teachers' apartments would be fitted with appliances and furniture to match Randolph's by the end of the term. Lastly, Swainson and Dare would return just before the Christmas holiday, to determine whether adequate progress had been made-- and the all-important Swineforth imprimatur renewed.

Zara excused herself and a moment later Swainson stood up and put on his suit jacket, as if to draw the meeting to its close but then suddenly paused, 'Ah yes, Randolph, I nearly forgot to say 'Best of Luck' from Diana Von.'

'Diana Von...Diana Von...' Randolph stood there processing. He'd once been highly complimented on his hors d'oeuvre waitering skills during his acting days in London by the famous fashion designer Diane von Furstenburg but she was hardly likely to remember that and how would Swainson know such a person anyway.

'Frau von Ravensbruck...your former colleague, now first Headmistress of Blindefellows,' Swainson brought him out of his revery, 'You had quite the crush on that beautiful niece of hers when you were a young chap, didn't you?'

'Well, Roger it was more the other way round but thank you for conveying her good wishes. They really do mean a lot to me. I often thought Frau von Ravensbruck the most attractive and accomplished older woman I've known, and that if I were an older woman myself that's how I'd like to be.'

'I hadn't known that was something you, ah, gave much thought to, Tristram.'

'You know, in a purely hypothetical sort of way that one might.'

'Naturally...naturally. Anyway, she specifically said she knew better than any of us could ever imagine just how hard the road you're going here could turn out to be. But not to worry, Nigel and I will be behind you all the way,' and with this uncomforting reassurance, Swainson pumped his hand once vigorously and left him to his own thoughts.

13

With the half-term holiday coming up in a couple of days and still no passports returned eight weeks after having been submitted for the mysterious working visa process, all five international staff members would be remaining in Kebapistan. Gemmy claimed not to mind in the least as she'd be disappearing into the interior with her Dalibor friend for the whole week to 'blow off the cobwebs', as she said. Gabby, however, minded greatly as her blog and her palate had gone stale on the same old fare, even though Michael and Piyotr had done their best to discover or invent new dishes to sate her indefatigable appetite. She'd been hoping to do a whistle stop culinary tour of central Asia, with one day in each capital city, but instead was having to settle for Kebapistan's other two cities, where she'd have to see whether she could ferret out anything different to eat.

Mark Gall was putting on his usual show of fury but Randolph knew the truth; the man was thrilled about being taken on a 'gun tasting tour' of the shooting ranges of Diskepisbad by his newfound mentor, Max. Brian too had found half-term happiness locally. With a little help from Golmar, whose uncle was Director of the National Natural History Museum, he had been offered an invitation to peruse the very fossil collection that had lured him to Kebapistan. Golmar had also facilitated Randolph's own holiday arrangements by securing him a self-drive hire car, a service not normally available to tourists, who were required to hire only state-approved chauffeured vehicles. He and his parents could now drive about testing the Silligator. Other than that, they'd be having a relaxing time. Goodness knows, he needed it!

On the morning of the day his parents were due to arrive, Golmar had arranged for the hire car to be delivered and the keys brought to him in his apartment. For the amount the car was costing him, Randolph was expecting something spectacular. Golmar had assured him, it would be 'a reliable car', which sounded like it would be something dull, but when a tall, dark and slickly dressed man in a black suit and dark wrap-around sunglasses came to his door, he was suddenly hopeful.

'Golmar tells me she's rented something reliable,' Randolph prattled as they walked down to the car park.

'Yes, reliable is what she has book for you,' he said, handing Randolph the keys.

There were two cars in view and Randolph made a beeline for the black Range Rover.

'No, not that one,' the car rental man called to him.

Randolph was confused. 'So, it's the other car?'

'Yes, other one is special self-drive hire for foreigners,' said the slick man. He was pointing at an orange Robin Reliant. It had been polished until it was glossy, which only served to make it stand out like a lifebuoy. Randolph's mouth fell open. What was Golmar thinking? Was this some practical joke at his expense?

'Seriously? I wouldn't be seen dead in that contraption. It looks like a giant wedge of Red Leicester.'

'But is classic British car,' the man frowned, 'We have none other at this time.'

'For the money I'm paying, I was expecting something a little more...up to date.'

'I am sorry, Mr Randolt, is only self-drive car available-- arrange by special government permission just for you. Is newly renovate with A/C, radio-cassette player and mini-bar.'

'I don't care if it has a chandelier and bandstand, it's a bloody *Robin Reliant* and I'm not having it!' He pulled out his phone, jabbed his finger on Golmar's number and waited, but there was no answer. Was she anticipating his reaction and ignoring him? He'd thought at first that she'd be the Miss Moneypenny type, loyal and admiring, but all this smacked of snickering, sneering even. There was nothing he could do now. His parents were landing in half-an-hour. He snatched the keys off the slick man and opened the creaky fibreglass door to a lurid fake leopard fur interior, the same hue of orange as the exterior. 'All we need now is a furry dice hanging from the mirror as the piece de resistance, in orange of course!' he jested sardonically but it was lost on the rental man. Glowering, Randolph squeezed into the driver's seat, turned the key in the ignition, listened a moment to the thrilling rattle of the 750 c.c. engine and trundled off to the airport.

He had never driven anything so antiquated. His foot was all the way down on the accelerator yet he could do 70 miles per hour at best. Unless he eased the clutch in and out with the greatest care, the thing juddered whenever he changed gear, as if it were suffering from the automotive equivalent of advanced Parkinsonism. What on earth would he tell his parents? He was supposed to be coming out here for promotion, a salary hike, a stepping stone to an illustrious career, yet here he was in a car fit for doing a newspaper delivery round thirty-five years ago. Then he had a cracking idea– one that he had to admit to himself reflected his old improvisational brilliance onstage-- he'd tell them he'd got it on purpose as, he now remembered, that a Robin Reliant had been their very first car when they were just married. There were even photographs of him in the back seat as a baby in a carry cot.

He stood in the deserted arrivals area. There was a glassed-in corridor that arriving passengers had to walk down to get to the doors letting them into Kebapistan. It was manned by two soldiers in dress uniforms bedecked with golden braiding, wearing shining chromed helmets and standing to attention with rifles the muzzles of which were surmounted by gleaming bayonets. Why there should be such strict security for anyone entering this hell hole of country, where no one with any choice in the matter would wish to remain was utterly beyond Randolph. He now had his eyes fixed on the corridor as he'd seen a plane land just as he was parking. An officious little man who looked like a retired bank manager was the first to appear, dressed in a bottle green pinstripe suit with a knee-length tweed overcoat and matching pork pie hat at a jaunty angle. He was carrying what looked like a viola case.

Behind the little man were Randolph's parents who caught sight of him immediately and began waving excitedly. There was something odd about his father though. It looked as if he were wearing a turban on his head. Why, oh why, would he do that? Did he think he was coming to a country that required religious head coverings for men? And as Giles drew closer, it appeared to be a fleshy-coloured, bumpy sort of thing. Randolph moved up to the glass for a better look. No, it couldn't be! What had he done? He was wearing a rubber turkey like the centrepiece of the Christmas feast up there on top of his head. Randolph banged on the reinforced glass to get their attention but no sound penetrated and they weren't looking at him now, but were fiddling with the zip on one of their pieces of hand luggage, which his mother seemed to have got her sleeve stuck in. Randolph started shaking his head exaggeratedly and indicating with his arms to take the turkey hat off. When they noticed his animated movement, they thought he was waving back enthusiastically and returned this with their own exuberant greeting.

It felt to Randolph as if the next part of the proceedings melted into slow motion. He stood there, hopelessly, as if he were a spectator of some calamity occurring underwater but he couldn't swim so that standing idly by was all he could do. A member of the armed forces dashed at his father, although it was just the arm and leg motions of dashing, decelerated to a few feet per hour, and rugby tackled him to the ground. His mother stood agape in a frozen scream, her uneven lipstick making her mouth look all the more distorted. Then she was down on the ground too and Randolph didn't know if she'd fainted or died of a heart attack. A flurry of military activity involving flourished handguns and truncheons massed about his parents and his mother was suddenly being carried away on a stretcher, while his father was dragged off in handcuffs, his nose bleeding profusely. The turkey hat had been confiscated and dropped into a plastic bag with Ziploc seal, the military personnel regarding it as if it were a very hazardous item indeed.

Randolph rushed to a woman at an information desk and cried out, 'Where are they taking my parents?' But she didn't understand him and carried on gawping at the drama like everyone else.

'Probably to jail for a very long time,' the little man in the bottle green suit who had come out before them appeared at his elbow. 'Edwin Sneed, bank manager, retired,' Sneed held out his hand for Randolph to shake, which he did in a daze.

'Oh, my God, my God, what can I do? How could he have been so stupid! I expressly told him *not* to do that!'

'Your wires must have become crossed,' Sneed said, matter of fact, 'Come with me and we'll see if we can talk some sense into the police commissioner to nip this in the bud. You can follow me in your car if you have one, or if you don't, you can be driven with me.'

Randolph thought it would be best if he didn't bring up the rear in his Red Leicester clown-mobile so, denying he had a car, he followed Sneed outside and to a vintage burgundy Bentley with little flags on the front bearing the dragon emblem he had seen on the gates of the presidential palace. He would come back to collect the cheese wedge another time. The chauffeur closed the door after them and Sneed instructed him to head for the central police station.

'You may be wondering what line of business I am in, Mr.. er?'

'Randolph.'

'The president is a very dear friend of mine, Mr Randolph; I am bringing him a rare barometer.'

'Oh, yes, I know him too! We took scones together. I saw his barometer collection. Most impressive.'

'Suffice to say, it is a shared interest that binds us.'

At the police station, Sneed and Randolph were immediately ushered through several long corridors into a small, windowless interview room with what looked like years of bodily fluids smudged over the walls. Sneed advised Randolph to let him do the talking. The Commissioner of Diskebapisbad's Central Security Police, a chunky fellow with a thick moustache and a great deal of hair on the backs of his hands, listened to Sneed with reverence.

'You see, commissioner,' Sneed summed up in English, 'What has happened was through no fault of Mr Randolph senior. I saw it with my own eyes. Someone *put* the turkey hat on his head. I cannot say who but, in the confusion of collecting the hand luggage, I saw a hand, just a hand mind you, as my line of vision was obscured, and that hand deposited the turkey hat on Mr Randolph senior's head. I am certain that if you dust the turkey for fingerprints, you will be sure to find your man. Mr Randolph senior is, shall we say, in possession of a somewhat befuddled mind, as is his wife. It was obvious that, in their excitement at their reunion with their son, they were not even aware of the offending headgear. I think it would best if we were to sweep this matter under the rug. We already have a chap in jail for life for 'donning the turkey' as President

Zoran is wont to say. It is enough that he has been made an example of. It has attracted a good deal of criticism from other nations and we don't want to cause a diplomatic incident by incarcerating a British pensioner, especially on the eve of the presidential election.'

The commissioner nodded slowly and looked over to Randolph who responded with sad eyes set in a face tinged with grave regret. 'I am inclined, as always, Mr Sneed, to agree with everything you say. We will prepare the Randolphs for immediate release. Thank you for coming in to assist the Central Security Police today and my regards to President Zoran,' wherewith he sloped out of the room.

'Mr Sneed, I don't know how to thank you,' Randolph gasped.

'No need...No need. Best to let these little incidents pale into insignificance before they get blown out of all proportion, as the other turkey hat incident did...If only I'd been on hand to diffuse that bomb, too. You see, with the election coming up, critics of the government will use these incidents to slight the president, not that what they have to say makes the slightest difference, but it can still be so irritating.'

Giles and Jocelyn Randolph entered the room, Jocelyn being pushed in a wheelchair by her husband who had cotton wool plugging each nostril.   'Good God, mother, are you alright?' Randolph exclaimed, jumping up.

'I don't know what happened. I think I blacked out. Where am I?' she looked about wildly, 'Did anything untoward happen to me whilst I was in custody?'

Edwin Sneed arose, assured her decorously that it had not, shook hands with her husband, then drove them to the school in the Bentley, listening with gracious interest to Giles's explanation of the Silligator. Sneed seemed quite the computer wiz and offered Giles some tips. Just before he left them at the main entrance, Randolph turned to him and told him he hoped President Zoran would like his new barometer. Sneed looked confused for a moment, as if he knew nothing whatsoever about any barometers, and then suddenly nodded, adding an 'Ah, yes, I'm sure he will.'

After warm baths and a few gin and tonics, his parents seemed to be recovered from their ordeal. Jocelyn chatted excitedly about a children's book she'd penned following Tristram's departure and had already sent out to literary agents, though she had not heard anything back yet. Randolph tried to share her enthusiasm but felt the title, *The Canine Jamboree,* was more than a tad dated. He asked whether the word 'jamboree' was even used in Britain these days, after which they moved on to discussing plans for the holiday. There was now far more to the trip than merely trialling the Silligator. Jocelyn had decided, in addition, to retrace the ill-fated steps of her great-grandfather, Sir Gannet Vainglory, on his diplomatic mission to Kebapistan or, as it was then known, the Sultanate of Mish Lope. It had ended with his languishing in jail, following the presentation of some gift that had affronted the sultan. His companion, Viscount Barnaby Glibly, the last peer to inherit the title, was imprisoned too. The pair had, Jocelyn continued, been pawns in The Great Game, the British Empire's long race with Imperial Russia to win over the statelets of Central Asia as economic partners and political vassals. Vainglory and Glibly had been dispatched to Mish Lope to ensure that the precious metals and minerals beginning to be mined there on a modern scale were traded exclusively with Britain.

'Hang on a mo,' Randolph exclaimed, 'If my great-great grandfather was a Sir, doesn't that make me one? Am I actually Sir Tristram Vainglory Randolph, perhaps one day to be Sir Tristram Vainglory Randolph, KBE?'

'Oh, I say, that does sound rather good!' Giles nodded.

'I'm afraid he was only a life peer, my darling, it died with him,' his mother lamented.

'Bloody hell!' Randolph was crestfallen.

'The other one, Viscount Glibly, *was* a hereditary peer, but as there were no known offspring, that title became extinct. The story ends here in Kebapistan...no one heard anything more from Sir Gannet after one last letter shortly after he was jailed. He and Glibly were presumed dead five years later, based on this letter from the Diskebapisbad Dungeon, which appears to have possessed something akin to the infamous Bug Pit of Bokhara.'

'And what in God's name was that?' Randolph blanched.

'It was a foul form of torture, a deep hole only accessible by means of a rope, into which the Emir of Bokhara threw the worst prisoners, and into which his prison guards rained down on the poor fellows below all manner of vile creatures-- scorpions, giant cockroaches, centipedes. After Sir Gannett and Viscount Glibly's ill-fated mission, the borders of Mish Lope were sealed. No one could get in or out of the country and nothing more was heard of them. Of course, this left my grandfather quite shattered. Can you imagine, Tristram, being a boy of ten and told you'd never see your beloved father again. It's a chapter of our family's history which is shrouded in mystery. Was he really dead when presumed to be so and what actually was this gift that so offended the sultan?'

'Well, I'm sure we can do some digging around, but only with my PA's help because I wouldn't know where to begin,' he muttered vaguely, retreating into his bedroom, focused upon giving Golmar an earful as to her choice of rental car, 'I'll ring her up now.'

Golmar was apologetic, confirming that she'd asked for a British car and that she had no idea what a Robin Reliant actually was. She sought to redeem her misdemeanor by eagerly agreeing to come around with them to various city offices in their bid to uncover the family history mystery, even though it was her holiday.

When Giles and Jocelyn saw the Robin Reliant the next morning and Randolph told them his little tale of its being a special request for sentimental reasons, their initial dismay turned to delight and, for the next 20 minutes, they insisted upon detailing the memories surrounding the photos of him in it half a century earlier. In spite of there being no carry cot to hand, Randolph did agree to pose with his mother's handkerchief on his head tied up to resemble a baby's bonnet. He even did a bit of thumb sucking with a silly face. They collected Golmar from in front of the Irish pub and she directed them to their first port of call, the very building where Vainglory and Glibly had been held, which was still a prison to this day. She was carrying an enormous brass-latched briefcase and looked more business-like than usual in a sharply cut black suit and patent leather shoes.

With Jocelyn's manila envelope of old papers tucked under his arm as they walked toward the forbidding main gate, Randolph felt a little nervous about entering the prison of a country near the top of the Amnesty human rights violations list, but did his best to show some enthusiasm for the quest. 'How are we actually going to get inside?' he asked Golmar.

'Getting in is all too easy, Mr Randolph, it is getting out that can be tricky.'

'Really? Are you sure we should be doing this?' he asked, beginning to panic.

'Don't worry, I have my papers with me to show that you and I work for the Zoran family. That's usually a pass into-- and out of-- everything.'

'Usually?' Randolph repeated anxiously. He was not a risk taker, as a rule.

The entrance to Diskebapisbad Prison looked like that of some ornate oriental castle, turrets, arrow slots and what not. There was even a modern take on a

spiked steel portcullis, which slowly slid upwards on an electrically operated chain, granting them access once Golmar had shown her classified identity card to the digital camera eye mounted at eye level on the stone portal. They emerged into a central courtyard where they were asked by a loudspeaker to wait. Perhaps it had once been a spacious place of execution but now it was full extra cells because the old fortress was nowhere near big enough for the demands of the Zoran regime.
Before them rose a tower block of rusty shipping containers that had been crudely converted into prison cells. Golmar explained that each cell held twelve prisoners and contained two features-- a dozen camping mats, one per every two prisoners, so that sleeping had to be done in shifts; and two buckets, one for faeces and urine, and the other for 'fresh', if it could be called that, water. There was absolutely no privacy, with the guards able to see into every container through large, glassless, steel grated windows, as if the prisoners were chickens in a battery farm.

Quite suddenly, Golmar approached the cells on ground level, clicked open the latches on the briefcases and started passing bread rolls with both hands to the grasping hands reaching out through the bars. Randolph stared in astonishment as she darted up to the next level via the external steel staircase and continued to place rolls into outstretched hands. Randolph's heart pounded as he thought of the trouble he and his parents might get into being associated with her. A guard soon spotted her and ordered her down.
He didn't seem too ruffled and she spoke with him calmly but authoritatively.

'I told him that I was sure the President would like to see healthier prisoners,' she said, rejoining Randolph.

'Would he?' asked Randolph, surprised.

'No,' was all she replied in a flat tone and with a completely neutral expression which terrified him.

A corpulent middle-aged man in a mustard-coloured

suit came over to them, introduced himself and shook their hands. 'Hello, I am the, how do you say, Were-don, of Diskebapisbad Prison, In fact, my family have franchise of all prisons in Kebapistan. You, Mr Randolph, may know two of my brothers. They are prominent Kebapi judges. Their childrens attend your new Swineforth school.'

'Ah, a family business. So your brothers help you fill the cells, eh?' Giles quipped.

'Exactly,' the warden chuckled, 'We don't have one mat empty for long here! And the families from each convict must contribute to the upkeep of their brother, father, son or whatever, which helps our government to make endings meet.'

'And what happens if the families can't contribute?' Giles continued. Randolph didn't like this line of socialist questioning.

'We receive basic rate from state per prisoner but that is our management fee,' the warden explained, still reasonably cordial, to Randolph's relief, 'What families pay covers prisoners' foods and guards' wages.'

'Shape of things to come in the UK, I'd say,' Giles gibed.

'Yes, it is the excellent system and one that government and business profits from alikes. My brother-in-law in the States has obtained our first contract for running prison there on slightly modified version of model here. We have eagerness to expand into UK, which has become ideal new market for us under your current government. If you happen to have contacts in that field, you may consider to become an investor; you would be finding yourself well rewarded if were ultimately awarded contract?'

'Oh, no, not my line of work at all– I'm an inventor.'

'Really? Then perhaps you can invent somethings to keep these filthy dogs quiet at night? When one start up they all join in and our guards cannot sleep at night.'

'Ah, we have something that might do the trick in

the UK,' Randolph chipped in, 'a bark-activated electric shock collar for the excessively barky dog.'

'Now that *is* good idea and one I will investigator further, thank you!' whereupon the warden drew a line under the chit-chat to move on to brass tacks, 'Now what can we to do for you today?'

He listened with interest to Jocelyn's explanation of why they had come.

'Ah, yes, I know all about this!' he boasted, 'The cell from the two English diplomats– come, I will show you.' They followed him into the older part of the prison made of the same pitted black volcanic rock as the entrance. 'We are keeping certain prisoners in this wing in isolationism due to nature of their crimes and danger they are posting to others.'

They passed a cell in which a man dressed in nothing but some torn up briefs was scratching with snaggled toe nails on the floor as if looking for something. Randolph paused for a moment, transfixed by the strangeness of his movements, which made him think of Edgar feigning madness as Poor Tom in *King Lear*, a role he'd always fancied playing-- though in a loincloth of deerskin, rather than shredded and discoloured tighty-whities which was what the man's underwear appeared to have been, in bygone days. The man caught sight of Randolph and let out a terrible noise that could only be likened to the gobble-volley of a turkey cock.

'Come away from there, sir, she is one of maximum security prisoners and has to been kept in strict isolationism,' the warden warned.

Randolph rapidly rejoined Golmar and his parents and, looking shaken, asked, 'What did he do?'

'She was offensive in her choice of hat wear,' the warden replied before moving them all on.

'Is that that poor turkey hat man whom you were telling us about, Tristram? The one that Amnesty is campaigning for?' Giles asked.

'It is indeed,' the warden affirmed, 'But I can't imagines they want him back now, eh!'

'Don't say anything else,' Randolph hissed at Gilon, 'It could have been you in that cell if they hadn't been so lenient thanks to the good offices of Mr Sneed.'

'No need to worry about cell we are going to entering now. No prisoners are holding there nowadays. We use it for interviewing primates in privates. It is little isolated from rest of prison so that are having necessary privacy.'

They climbed a winding staircase until they reached a little room at the top of the tower. Jocelyn walked in and took a deep breath, as if trying to catch a scent of her ancestor. There was a sturdy steel desk in the corner with steel chairs to one side, a single narrow window with a sliver of light and what looked like a large ironing board with leather straps suspended from the ceiling and leaning against a wall. Randolph wondered whether interview was too mild a word for whatever went on in there.

'Terribly pokey little place to spend a few years of your life!' Jocelyn seemed to be a bit choked up, on the verge of tears. 'I promised myself I wouldn't cry, but here I am, welling over.'

'We thought it'd be much worse though, didn't we mum?' Randolph tried to ebb the flow of Jocelyn's tears, which he found rather embarrassing, 'We thought there would be some dreadful bug pit.'

'Oh, yes, the British were in the bug spit for a month or so, but the sultan kindly gave them the token of protection in the form of a yak-hair fly-whisk. Then came instructions to move them here,' the warden informed them, 'We still have the bug spit, but is covered with the metal grid and has not to been of use since 1980. We are more up to date in our methods in these days thanks to our enlightenment president.'

'Well, that's something of a relief,' Jocelyn sighed, 'I've had some horrible images in my head of my great grandfather dying in that terrible way and it gave his son, my grandfather, nightmares all his life. I only wish he could have been here with me to find out that the horror was relatively short-lived.'

'And when they were in this particular cell, where did they go to the toilet? Where did they sleep and wash? And what did they get to eat?' Giles asked earnestly.

'I am afraid that treatment of prisoners here in that time was less humaned than is today,' the warden told Giles, who looked sceptical, 'There would have been a pile of straw with perhaps an old blanket, a bucket in the corner for the toilet and a minimal amount of food.'

'So, rather similar to what we saw out there, really?' Giles suddenly piped up, at which Randolph shot him a stern glance. In so doing, he noticed that Golmar was once again wearing her fixed, blank expression, that somehow suggested a struggle, barely won, to contain murderous fury.

'A little more primitive I think you'd find,' the warden purred, giving Randolph a mean smile.

'Ha, ha!' came Randolph's nervous laugh as he recollected Golmar's warning that it could be complicated to get out of these places, 'I'm sure you do sterling work here and who are we to judge with the state of British prisons today?'

'Exactly!' the warden bellowed.

And at that moment it popped into Randolph's mind to ask the warden if Golmar could take a photo of him strapped to the ironing board contraption. It'd be a giggle for his Lincoln friends to see him exotically trussed up in that way. The warden allowed this and Golmar reluctantly did the deed which she clearly found distasteful.

'Do you have any information on when my great grandfather and his friend died?' Jocelyn sniffed.

The warden invited them downstairs to his office, where he showed them the prison log books that were kept on the tall shelves behind his desk.

'The more recent ones from Soviet period on lower shelves are bounded in cloth with black Cyrillic lettersing,' the warden explained, 'while the leather-bounded books on higher shelves with Arabic script in gold are from time of Sultanate. While I may easily help you with Soviet ones, I am fearing volumes from Sultanate are beyond me.'

'Not a problem, Sir, I can read them,' Golmar volunteered in the same flat tone she'd used in the yard.

'Aha, your young guide is proper scholar,' the warden remarked, 'No wonder that she has find employment close toward our steamed Presidential family.'

Golmar completely ignored this compliment and asked, 'Do you know in what year your great grandfather was imprisoned here, Mrs Randolph?'

'I believe it was in the late 1880s,' Jocelyn ventured with uncertainty.

Golmar turned to the warden and, rather than asking, informed him, 'I will stand on your desk chair now in order to reach the required ledgers.' She pointedly did not take her shoes off and elevated herself from the seat to the arms of the chair in her quest. When, after some scanning of spines and looking quickly into dusty tomes, she found what she was looking for, the warden extended a hand to help her down. Randolph felt pleased with himself when he was able to pick up on her tart, 'No, thank you!' in Kebapi. Having jumped back onto the floor, she then not so much requested as ordered the warden, 'I shall sit at your desk in order to locate the relevant entries, alright?'

'Bit of steel in there, I'd say,' Giles quipped to his son, raising his brow and widening his eyes.

'Please, do sitting down,' the warden urged the Randolphs, indicating a Turkish style divan and pair of low antique chairs, whilst Golmar leafed slowly and intently through the antique ledger, running her forefinger slowly along the lines of writing just above the yellowed paper.

They sat, the warden and Randolph opposite one another in the chairs and his parents on the divan.

'Do you think she'll find anything?' Jocelyn enquired worriedly. A suspenseful silence then descended for some minutes, punctuated only by the occasional deep breath and turning of pages from Golmar, who suddenly declared, "Man onro joftam'-- that's Sultanate Persian, Mrs Randolph, for 'Eureka'-- I have found it.'

'I'm almost too scared to look,' Jocelyn put her hand over her eyes dramatically, but then, decisively, put on her glasses and went over to Golmar.

'Here's their *release* date, which I didn't expect to see because I thought they would, most likely, have died in custody,' Golmar declared.

'Yes, so everyone back in England thought that for the last hundred and thirty years,' Jocelyn replied, cleaning her glasses with the front tail of her blouse, as if this might clear up the whole mystery.

'And look here, Mrs Randolph, converting from the Islamic to the Christian year, it's evident that their release date was only a year or so after they were imprisoned.'

'I wonder what possibly could have happened to them after that, Miss Golmar?'

'I, for ones, cannot say,' the warden called over, 'We only have record of them while they were here.'

'I know where to find out and just the person to tell you,' Golmar announced, closing the prison ledger and rising smartly, 'If, warden, you would escort us back to the main gate so that we may continue our investigation elsewhere, I would be grateful.'

'Of course, dear ladies,' the warden answered, 'I hope you will being so kind as to communique your impression of how helpful I have be today to your illustrious employers.'

'You may be certain I will do that, Warden,' she assured him dryly in another snippet of Kebapi that Randolph was chuffed to be able to slowly decipher. Back in the prison yard, Golmar reopened her briefcase, almost ostentatiously, and placed her remaining bread rolls into various prisoners' hands.

Randolph veritably held his breath until they were outside on the street, where he protested in a stage whisper as he walked with her a few paces ahead of his parents, 'Golmar, may I ask you not to engage in politically provocative behaviour whilst I am in your company!'

'Oh, come now, Mr Randolph, how can giving bread to the needy ever be dangerous?' she responded, giving him a solicitous pat on the shoulder and adding, 'I like your parents very much. You should try to be more like them.'

14

Their next port of call was the National Historic Archive, which apparently contained all surviving state documents from before the Soviet annexation, as well as numerous objects of historic import. Golmar said she could direct them there with her eyes closed because it was her favorite place in Diskebapisbad. She promptly amazed the Randolph family by being as good as her word. She removed the Persian silk scarf she'd been wearing on her neck and tied it around her head instead, asking only to be told whenever the Robin Reliant was approaching a crossing. Giles, immersed as he had been in his Silligator project for the past several months, was especially impressed, informing her that she was 'a wonder', at which her cheeks coloured below the scarf. It turned out the she knew the way so well as the Archive was attached to the National Natural History Museum, of which her uncle, the renowned Kebapi polymath, Dr Kalamuz Preyn, was curator.

The complex was the former palace and harem of the Sultan of Mish Lope, a fantastical pile decorated in colourful geometric tiles of mythical animals and exotic flowers. There was a whimsical fountain to the front elevation featuring a circle of bronze geese spurting water from their beaks. The overall effect, Randolph reflected, was somehow like a hybrid of Brighton Pavilion and the Kremlin. They followed Golmar through a courtyard of curlicue arches toward the former Sultanate library, where they found her uncle at the very top of a rolling ladder, not holding on at all as he leafed through a leather clad tome plucked from a high shelf with no anxiety whatsoever about teetering in high places. Like uncle, like niece, Randolph mused, recollecting Golmar's balancing act on the warden's chair half an hour earlier. Dr Preyn was a small round man with sparrow-thin legs supporting a rotund torso and sandalled feet which appeared too large in relation to his diminutive stature. At the bottom of the ladder stood Brian, of all people, chattering away to the learned doctor above him with a degree of animation exponentially greater than anything Randolph had ever seen, or even thought possible, from him before.

'Hello there, Brian!' Randolph called over jovially, 'How's your half-term going?'

'Oh, hello Mr Randolph, I'm having a marvellous time! Dr Preyn and I have already started planning some weekend fossiling fossicks into the desert, to culminate in an expedition over the Christmas holiday during which we hope to finally unearth the fossil of the long-lost Lophogallus in what was once the inner delta of the ancient Oxus up in the north of the country, which will allow him, with a little help from myself, to complete his monumental work, *Fossil Hunters of Kebapistan.*'

'So, I guess you won't be home going for Christmas?' Randolph asked.

'Certainly not! I've never had so much fun!' Brian beamed, 'I've asked Barbara if she'd like to join me here but she prefers not to leave England during the holiday season, which is for the best, perhaps.'

'Mr Eider-Drake will be an asset worthy of his name on this expedition!' Dr Preyn heartily avouched, 'The particular fossil I am seeking shall shake this country, shake it, I say, to the core! We have already found fossilized footprints and fragments of fossilized eggs of Lophogallus but an entire skeleton will tip things over the edge! Brian is a first class assistant and soon we will begin in earnest, venturing out into the desert every weekend! I only wish I could take him sooner but he feels he has a mission with the children at Swineforth School to imbue them with his love of waterfowl. What a noble enterprise!'

'Uncle,' Golmar called up the ladder, 'You mentioned to me that you have some information about the notorious gift to the sultan, you know, the one that provoked his locking up the two British diplomats? This lady is the descendant of one of them, Sir Gannet Vainglory.'

Dr Preyn pottered down the ladder, chortling to himself, 'It certainly put those two fellows into a serious pickle. They were fortunate to get out of it alive. I doubt they'd have been so lucky today. Follow me.'

They left Brian in the library, soaking up an essay on the nesting habits of the Harlequin Duck. Dr Preyn led them through rooms of dust-covered glass cases of taxidermized wildlife, many of which were not so well stuffed, with glass eyes askew and straw escaping through seams. Then they proceeded through a network of corridors which opened out into what had been the sultan's reception rooms, behind which were his private chambers, a large room for his wives and children with wooden filigree screens on the windows looking out onto a courtyard and finally a study just for the sultan.

'Of course, that was the golden age of the Sultanate of Mish Lope, as this region was then called. It is all long gone now, just my humble and simple desk in the middle of the room supplanting the palatial bed, but I ponder, from time to time, on what might have taken place on that as I sit evading my scholarly work,' Dr Preyn smiled with a faraway, glassy look in his eyes, not unlike that, Randolph thought, of the taxidermized animals they'd just passed. He shook himself out of his reverie and led them to a door, 'In the corner here, you see, this little room? It was the water closet, the very first flushing WC in Kebapistan and, lo and behold, what do you see next to the toilet?'

Randolph and his parents looked into the room. There was an old-fashioned toilet with blue tiles around the bowl and a worn, wooden seat, squarer and more ungainly than the toilet seats of today, with a cistern above and a long metal pull chain with a crazed porcelain handle dangling. But, as they peered around the corner, a staggering sight met their eyes...

'To answer your question before you ask it, no, it isn't solid gold,' Dr Preyn pronounced, 'If it had been, the Soviets would have made off with it long ago, and if not them, then that rogue Zoran and his spoilt daughters. Rather, it is something that was far more unusual at that time-- engraved electroplate. Already an everyday technology in Britain, which was then the most industrially advanced nation in the world, out here on the far reaches of the old Silk Road, it was nothing less than miraculous.'

Randolph, who had thoroughly absorbed the national habit of demonstrating awe for Kebapistan's president in public, was preoccupied by Dr Preyn's political candour. Not so though, his parents. Giles gave a low whistle, while Jocelyn murmured, 'So, they brought the sultan *a gold plated bidet*! But why would he take offense at that?'

And it was then that Dr Preyn told them the story of the golden bidet... 'Your great-grandfather, who was working for the British foreign office, had heard that the sultan had recently received Kebapistan's first flushing toilet from Tsar Alexander III of Russian so he thought to outdo the Russian by bringing the sultan the perfect companion piece-- a bidet. But not just any bidet, mind you, the government commissioned one plated in gold inscribed with meditative verses in the original Persian from 'The Rubaiyat of Umar Khayyam', which was just then all the rage among Britain's literati thanks to the inspired translation by Sir Edward Fitzgerald. Then too, there was the quandary of transporting the cumbersome yet delicate bidet from its final maritime destination at

Trebizond, over the mountains of Georgia and Armenia, across the southern reaches of the Caspian sea, and through the wastes of Turkmenistan. It was in solving this that your great-grandfather and his dear friend, Viscount Glibly, came up with an idea as remarkable as the golden bidet itself. They would bring it by hot air balloon, thereby presenting the sultan and his court with yet another triumph of British engineering.

'The balloon appeared in the sky above the palace one afternoon, emblazoned with the image of the fiery phoenix of Mish Lope, to the delight of all the sultan's wives and children. It hovered there a while and then made its graceful descent, landing in the dead centre of the courtyard through which you, yourselves just walked. The sultan, of course, had been expecting them and knew they had something to present to him before their trade negotiations began. His servants helped the two distinguished Englishmen out of the basket and a group of strong men carried the gift to his very feet, where, with crowbars, they loosed it from its wooden crate. Its gleam brought a smile to the sultan's face. His wives and children reached out to touch it but he warned them off, reminding them it was a gift first and foremost to him. He then thanked Queen Victoria's two emissaries heartily and had them shown to their luxurious quarters in this very museum. They would feast together that night and tomorrow begin their negotiations. At the feast, the sultan thanked them again for the gift and told them he was having it installed that very night and it would be his honour to show it to them the next morning.

'So, the next day came and, after breakfast, the sultan led the two fellows outside. All of his wives and children and the courtiers were arrayed, sitting on silk cushions in the formal garden and the sultan unveiled the golden bidet which he had had set up right in the centre, no less. He pushed the lever, it spouted, he inclined his head and drank. Looking up, smiling at his two astonished guests, he bowed down and drank again. The Englishmen were at first confused. Then they turned to each other and let forth hearty laughter. Finally, they shared their source of humour with the confused sultan and his whole court was in stitches. The whole court, that is, apart from him. He had been humiliated and had Vainglory and Glibly dragged off to the dreaded Diskebapisbad Dungeon. For the remainder of the sultan's lifetime, no one in Mish Lope was allowed to utter a word about the incident on pain of death!'

'Crikey!' was all Randolph could say.

'Oh dear, what a truly terrible tale of cultural misunderstanding!' Jocelyn whimpered, tearing up.

'But we've just heard that they got out of the prison and went into house arrest,' Giles ejaculated, 'How did that come about?'

'A good question and we can only guess the answer,' Dr Preyn replied, 'Perhaps he had the bidet installed in its rightful place, where you have just witnessed it standing still, and thinking in hindsight that it was quite a useful and charming little contraption, reconsidered his punishment. That, anyhow, is my theory, such as it is. Alas, such pardons are unheard of under Kebapistan's present sultan. Should you land in jail for giving offense to the almighty Zoran, you will never get out, even if you went in for a trivial reason like not being animated enough in clapping after a presidential speech at a football match.

'The point is, however, that Vainglory and Glibly were, I suspect, forbidden to return to their homeland for fear that they would spread the tale of the sultan who drank from the bidet. And one certainly cannot say that they led difficult lives here. Glibly ultimately married one of the Sultan's daughters and fathered a veritable tribe of offspring, while Vainglory went native on, I think you say, the other side of the fence, taking up with a handsome Tajik falconer from the Sultan's retinue, though he did father a single daughter with his official wife for form's sake. I believe she was married off to Glibly's eldest son to sustain the Britishness of the two family lines. I can check it easily enough. They were persons of importance so it is all recorded in the court annals of the Sultanate.'

'Well, not such a dreadful tyrant after all!' Randolph chirped but Jocelyn was shell-shocked by the disclosure. Golmar, sensitive to the older lady's distress, suggested they return to the beautiful old library to drink Turkish style tea with Dr Preyn and Brian. Whilst they did so, Jocelyn kept repeating mournfully, 'You'd think he might've managed to send word he was alive and well just once.' To this, Brian offered a brief disquisition on the primitive condition of telegraph and postal services in Central Asia during the late 19th century, while Dr Preyn suggested, with his obviously habitual frankness, that the sultan would not have looked kindly upon any attempt at correspondence with England, and that maybe a man who had experienced the sort of 'conversion' undergone by Sir Gannett Vainglory might find it wiser not to divulge the details of his new life to family and friends in late Victorian England.

15

The following afternoon, Golmar appeared at the door to Randolph's apartment in a state of high excitement. She urgently wished to speak with Mrs Randolph, to whom she brought news that Jocelyn's third cousin was almost certainly alive and well in the provincial capital of Jizbizisbad! She had checked the microfiche records of the Soviet censuses, from the first, of 1930, shortly after Stalin's annexation of Kebapistan to the Soviet Union, to the last, of 1990, just before independence, and during those 60 years, three successive generations of Barnaby Gliblys had resided in that grim industrial city of lead and mercury mines. The last two censuses, carried out in 2000 and 2010, under the Zoran regime, tended toward the ropey, but there was still a head of household by the deeply un-Kebapi name of Barnaby Glibly, at that time aged 45, living there. Randolph did not share his mother's hoots of joy at this news. The present day Barnaby Glibly would, he supposed, nothing like his noble English ancestor. Living, as they did, in that toxic industrial backwater, not only did he and his family seem destined to be on the uncouth side, they would also, most likely, be hard up and looking for a handout, something his parents could scarcely afford these days.

In the face of his mother's near-hysterical insistence, Randolph soon ceased his protestations and it was determined that rather than test the Silligator around the outskirts of Diskebapisbad, they would do so on the day long drive to Jibizisbad. This did not seem likely to prove much of challenge for the device since Kebapistan's only three major cities were connected by a badly drawn triangle of dual carriageways. Since both foreigners and wealthy Kebapis journeyed there rarely, and then only briefly on business, there was scant provision for overnight accommodation in the city. Golmar booked them into an Soviet-era state boarding house for one night, reassuring them that it was the best of the few options available. She also warned them they should get out of the city as soon as possible because the air was not safe and the locals, poor and unaccustomed to tourists as they were, would stare at them in the streets and possibly beg for coins.

Giles set up the Silligator on the dashboard ready for its trial run and they put their overnight bags in the back. Giles tinkered about for another 5 minutes then gave the thumbs up and they rolled away, Golmar waving them off with a wry smile on her face. A minute or two later, as the Randolphs left the school campus, the voice of the Silligator emerged loud and clear from the speaker, 'Take the next left and drive in a straight line following signs to Jizbizisbad for 300 miles.'

'Ah, not too complicated then,' Randolph drawled.

'Yes, now we can sit back and enjoy the ride with a commentary on the history of Kebapistan,' Giles enthused.

'Fingers crossed!' Jocelyn piped up.

Randolph did the left turn and the voice of Major Sillifant launched into a monologue, 'Over on the right you will see the Leng Mishi Oasis, which the British and Russian fought over in the wake of the natives' retaliation. In the centre of the oasis, you may be able to catch a glimpse of the stone lean-to used by the British commanding officer, Scudamore Scudamore Stanthorpe as a latrine.'

'Gosh, pretty meticulous attention to detail there,' Randolph nodded, impressed.

'Shh, there's more!' Giles held up his hand.

'Beyond the shelter,' continued Major Sillifant in a voice that seemed to bristle through a military moustache, 'Evidence of the battle has been discovered mainly from the Russians with their outdated weaponry left over from the Crimean War. Make a left turn now!'

'What?' Randolph was confused, 'I thought I was driving in a straight line for 300 miles!'

'Now, I say!' came the metallic command, which Randolph obeyed. 'You may park here and venture to the rear of the lean-to where you are free to mooch about and discover bits and bobs in the sand. Recommended stopover time is 30 minutes.'

Randolph pulled over. In front of them was a scrubby looking excuse for an oasis with no evidence of any latrine. Randolph didn't quite think they could spend 30 minutes there so he turned the car around and got back onto the main road.

'Make a U-turn NOW!' the Silligator commanded.

'What? Why?' Randolph was dumbfounded.

'You failed to spend the prescribed 30 minutes at the oasis where you might have been making interesting military historical discoveries in the sand,' the Silligator replied.

Randolph was spooked, 'Good lord, did he just answer me?!'

'No, no,' Giles shrugged it off, 'just clever programming.'

They continued in an uncomfortable silence for ten miles before the Major spoke again. The sound of a sharp intake of breath on the Silligator warned them he was about to announce something and they all looked at the speaker on the dashboard. 'If you look to your right now, you will see the sight of a famous skirmish between the Sultan's army and British forces. The Mish Lopians, armed with clubs and scimitars, were confounded by the indomitable fighting skills and spirit, not to mention the modern firearms, of our soldiers. The skirmish was over within 20 minutes and many prisoners were taken.'

They all looked to the right at a scrubby patch of desert with no distinguishing features whatsoever. Randolph feigned interest and Jocelyn began to doze off.

'Straight ahead of you,' the Major began five minutes later, 'was where the British held the native prisoners within a fenced compound, which conveniently served as a buffer against the Russian forces. The British possession of the oasis was, from that day, regarded as a fait accompli by the Russians.'

Randolph nodded again, hoping now there would be a long stretch of silence as there really was nothing, absolutely nothing to be seen anywhere in the grey desert which spread, featureless, in every direction.

'Incidentally,' the Major added, 'this desert road was built with British funds to facilitate movement of troops. Of course, many Mish Lopian tribespeople had to be enslaved in order to accomplish this.'

'Bit of a naughty detail about our colonial past there,' Randolph quipped to his father.

'You may think this an unsavoury aspect of our colonial past,' the Silligator went on, at which Randolph swerved slightly, 'but it was the way of the world then and we have to learn to live with it.'

Detail after detail dogged their journey. Randolph didn't have the heart to tell Giles that it was information he, and most people, could live without, and that, in fact, he found it a chore to listen to.

'You will be at your destination, Jizbizisbad in 20 minutes,' the Major's voice finally announced after six dusty hours on the road and Jocelyn woke up, taking a while to recall where she was. 'Allow me to tell you a thing or two about this interesting city. The Mish Lopians have been mining for cinnabar in this area for centuries. Traces of cinnabar have been found embellishing graves from nearly two thousand years ago, the dead even being mummified using the red stuff. The famous Red Lady of Jizbizisbad can be found in her sarcophagus in the archaeological museum in Diskebapisbad.'

'Nowadays, Jizbizisbad may appear an utter backwater, but it was the setting for an important skirmish which decided the direction of The Great Game in this nook of the world. A mob attacked the small British occupying garrison in the central midan and Sir Scudamore was forced to admit that his forces were unable to subdue the bellicose natives. Forthwith, he struck a deal with the sultan: His troops would ensure the longevity of the sultan's rule by assisting him in quashing his warlord rivals. Thereafter, Sir Scudamore's soldiers were pretty much granted a free reign and, drumming up support from bands of local ruffians, set upon the Russians who fled with their tails between their legs. The Sultan was temperamental, however, and frequently acted on a whim if he took offence. You may find the people of today's Jizbizisbad somewhat backward, but present them with toothpaste and other toiletries and they'll be your friends for life! Enjoy your stay in Jizbizisbad.'

Randolph looked over at his father nervously who showed him a carrier bag filled with toiletries between his feet in the Reliant's passenger seat and winked. *But do we want them to be our friends for life?* Randolph pondered. The bedraggled city came into view, a contaminated haze hovered above it veined in crimson, as if an angry rain cloud lingered and dilated there but never released its load.

The Silligator directed them in a confused, roundabout manner toward the boarding house. The streets had an unfinished look about them: the pavements, where present, were of uneven slabs of cracked concrete, rickety mid-rises of chipped brick in uneven courses, where one floor seemed tacked upon another rose up, either with hardly any space at all between them, or else interspersed with empty lots full of shanties built up from waste materials. Children dressed in rags and covered in red dust huddled in doorways and a bent old man trailed along collecting pieces of scrap wire and metal in an improvised cart mounted on old bicycle wheels. The only shop they passed seemed to sell nothing but canned food, which could be seen piled in pyramidal stacks through its dusty window. The Silligator announced their arrival at the guest house which looked, as Golmar had reassured them, a little more habitable than the rest of the town.

It was an old three storey wooden house down a little unpaved alley. Just inside the door behind a counter of laths sat a woman whom Randolph thought would be perfect for playing the troll in production of *The Three Billy Goats Gruff.* He approached her, his parents looking on from the rear, and said in a spirited tone, 'Good afternoon. Randolph, party of three. We have a reservation.'

The troll woman scowled and said something in rapid fire Kebapi, to which he replied, 'Pardon?' in response to which she clarified her meaning, switching to English by assertively grunting, 'NO!'

'Ah yes, right, I see,' Randolph ventured. He took out his mobile phone and rang Golmar. Fortunately, she answered. He informed her of his present predicament and she asked him to hand the troll woman his phone. Repellent though he found the prospect, he complied. The troll pressed the phone to her lank, grey hair and he heard Golmar's voice buzz in her ear. After a time, she snorted out a single sentence in Kebapi. Golmar's voice buzzed again briefly, whereupon the troll handed him his phone back. It felt oddly greasy, smelt like mutton and an ear hair appeared to have bonded itself to the receiver. He took care to hold it slightly away from his face.

'Just give her a thousand Zoran note; that should solve the problem,' Golmar informed him, 'I'm sorry, Mr

Randolph, that's simply how it is in our country, outside of the little enclaves where people have been familiarised with the government's special expectations for dealing with foreign visitors.'

She rang off and in putting his phone back in his pocket Randolph took out his wallet. Opening it below the level of the check-in counter, he removed the required bill, equivalent to roughly five Pounds Sterling, palmed it and casually laid his hand on the counter's dirty white Formica top. In response, the troll, to his mild horror, patted his hand solicitously. Having allowed him to remove his hand, she slid her own much beefier one from the countertop. She then turned heavily to the key rack behind her, removed one of the keys hanging there-- all of which were attached to vintage star-shaped, red enamelled brass fobs, embossed with the hammer and sickle on the front and engraved with a room number on the back-- and handed Randolph one, grunting again and pointing to the staircase opposite.

They deposited their hand luggage in the grim little room, in which there was a sagging double bed made up for his parents and a tiny single bed for himself along the foot of the double. Jocelyn was keen to get a move on with meeting her long lost relations and Randolph preferred to give other bleak surroundings a try rather than remain in these. Leaving the room, the key stuck in the lock and he waved his parents onward to wait from him in the cheese mobile while he attempted to free it. As he did so, he heard weighty treads and wheezing ascending the stairs and wondered whether his parents might've managed to rouse the troll to his aid with the lock. But instead he looked down the corridor to find Gabby approaching him.

'Bloody hell...I mean, good gracious me, who'd ever have expected to find someone posh like you here, Mr Randolph!'

'I'm here with my parents,' Randolph sputtered, 'On

a sort of quest connected to a branch of our family history. My great-great grandfather was a rather significant player in British Imperial politics in these parts a hundred and thirty odd years ago.'

'That figures, I suppose. I'm here to write about the origins of jiz-biz for my blog. I can take you to the place that does the best one in the city but they're all much of a muchness, truth be told. They also serve a sort of crude lentil paste with a bland roast marrow but I wouldn't recommend it. It's had a fairly dire effect on me, if you take my meaning. Still, we could meet there for supper this evening, if you fancy?'

Randolph definitely did not 'fancy'. On the other hand, he was finding his mother's current crusade more than a little irksome and it struck him that if were to accept her invitation, the burden of keeping them contented would be lifted from his shoulders for the evening...so he did.

She held out a paper. 'Here's the address and they drew a map for me on the back so I could find them again... Are you having some trouble with your key there, Mr Randolph? Maybe I could help.'

'I doubt it,' he said sharply, taking the paper, 'But you're welcome to give it a go, if you insist.'

He stepped out of the way and let Gabby try the lock. The key came away almost instantly. 'There you are, Sir. Art teachers, you know...well developed fine motor skills and all.' He told her they'd meet up with her at 7pm, after calling on his erstwhile distant relatives and hurried downstairs.

Meanwhile, at the side of the car, Giles was surrounded by a gaggle of children, handing out little tubes of toothpaste to them. A couple of them seemed a bit confused by it and were sucking it straight from the tube as if it were some sort of penny sweet. Shooing away the child crowd, he hustled his father into the passenger seat and took his place at the wheel. He turned the key in the ignition and the Silligator, plugged into the cigarette lighter, crackled to life. When he began to tick off his father for encouraging beggary, the Silligator appeared to reprimand him in turn 'The child beggars of Jizbizisbad are the progeny of parents who labour from dawn until dusk in the cinnabar and galena mines. It is for this reason that they hang about the streets in packs. Adults who work in the mines are not long enough lived to become grandparents, while parents cannot afford the nominal sum for after school childcare... So, treat them with decency, for pity's sake.'

16

They arrived at the address Golmar had given them and ascended four floors on a rough staircase of crumbling concrete running round the outside of the building. Randolph just wanted this over and done with and to get out of this hellish conurbation at first light tomorrow morning. A piece of heavy duty blue plastic sheeting was strung across a door frame with 'ГЛИБЛЫ' daubed roughly on it in red paint.

'It says No Entry', Randolph blurted out, 'Best move off, I suppose.'

'It does not!' Giles exclaimed, 'It says GLIBLY in capitals.'

'Dad, please, you're talking nonsense.'

'I am not, Tristram! I was in the Royal Signals for my national service. It was the height of the Cold War and we had to know the Morse code for all the Russian letters so we could take them down for the intelligence chaps. This reads: G-dot-dot-dash/L-dot-dash-dot-dot/I-dot-dot/B-dash-dot-dot-'

'Alright, fine, that's quite enough!' Randolph muttered, 'I'll see if anybody's in.'

'There is a baby crying on the other side of that plastic sheet, Tristram,' Jocelyn stated sternly, 'Obviously, there is someone in!'

Since there was nowhere to knock, Randolph lifted the blue plastic slightly and, peering in, calling out a greeting. The dwelling was basic, to say the least, with a concrete floor and crates improvised into furniture. A baby sat ensconced in a larger crate, while a care worn woman was seated on another smaller upturned one trying to stop a pair of small children, a girl and a boy barely a year apart in age, from fighting tooth and nail. Blood had been drawn but the woman clearly no longer had it in her to mollify them. She stood up, flustered and confused as, simultaneously, Jocelyn, pushed her way in past her son.

'Erm, mother, I think this may be a bad idea,' Randolph mumbled, following her, 'I'm not really sure this is an entirely fitting environment for old age pensioners such as yourself and dad.' Jocelyn, however, didn't hear him, so transfixed was she by this poignant tableaux of her distant relations.

'Me Vain-glory, Ing-land. You Glib-ly,' Jocelyn enunciated Tarzan-style, pointing first at herself, then at the woman and her children. The woman smiled, revealing an appalling lack of dentistry, and offered them crates to sit on. Giles promptly handed her toothpaste, which she accepted graciously.

'Where Bar-na-by?' Jocelyn continued. She put her hand above her brow and looked about as if scanning the horizon to indicate searching, 'Bar-na-by, where, oh where?'

'We've obviously come to the wrong place, Mum,' Randolph pattered out with false sympathy, 'I think it's best we take our leave now and stop intruding upon this poor woman.' He stood up. One of the children who had been fighting when Randolph had first looked in, the boy, approached him tentatively, smiling sweetly, but then punched him in the privates and scuttled away laughing ghoulishly. Randolph sank down onto a crate gasping.

Jocelyn took no notice of it and tried once more, 'Baar-neey?...Baar-neey?'

Given the short form of the name, the woman suddenly understood. She began to wail, 'Vaaar-neey! Vaaar-neey!' This set the baby in the crate off screaming. The woman went over and picked it up, then shuffled across the room and from the sill of the window, which was tacked over with a sheet of thick clear plastic rather than being glazed. There she retrieved what appeared to be a pocket-sized gold plated diptych photo-frame, which she brought over and placed Jocelyn's hands before collapsing and throwing her arms around the old woman's knees like a suppliant.

Randolph rolled his eyes. *This is where the wallet comes out,* he sighed inwardly. He hoped his mother would get it over and done with quickly, give the hag a wad of notes and let them go on to their delightful jiz-biz supper with Fatty Scroggins. But, alas, it was not to be.

'Var-ney mur-da ast!' the woman wept and, when the little girl joined in, her brother gave her a shove.

'Dear God!' Jocelyn gasped, 'Our poor cousin, the father of these children, has been murdered, Tristram!'

Fortuitously, Randolph had acquired just enough Kebapi to clear this up, 'No, no, as it happens in Kebapi 'murda' doesn't mean 'murdered', only 'dead'. So, it's all okay. He hasn't been murdered; he's just dead.'

But as quickly as everything appeared to have been cleared up, Randolph was thrown into confusion again. The woman now began jabbing her chilblained forefinger at the photo frame, whilst smiling rapturously and calling out, 'Ammo Vaar-neey zinda ast!'

'Oh, hang on a mo', mum. 'Zinda' means 'alive'. Now she's saying he's alive. Perhaps she's trying to tell us that he had some terrible accident and...and was in hospital in a coma or something but he's recovering now. Or maybe she was seeking to gain our sympathy in order to get more charity out of us but has now decided honesty is a better policy. I really couldn't say.'

As if she sensed his changing tone, the little girl stopped sobbing and crossed to Randolph's crate, leaning in toward him. Then, brushing the tears from her eyes with her forearm, she blew her little nose into her hand and laid it affectionately upon his cheek. He recoiled, removing his handkerchief from his front blazer pocket, wiping his face and pushing her gently away from his person. Randolph felt deeply unnerved by these impish creatures with their dirty faces. Could it truly be that they came from the same gene pool?

'Oh, Tristram, you don't understand because you cannot see these two photographs,' Jocelyn gushed ecstatically, 'What she is telling me is that her husband has died but that she has a grown up son who is alive and also called Barney! We can bring him back to England with us and sort out his title! Once he masters English, he shall have a seat in the house of lords! Talk about from rags to riches!'

'The Viscount is dead!' Giles brayed, 'Long live the Viscount!'

Randolph did not like this one bit. Why should this chap be entitled to a hereditary peerage, when he, with all his expensive private education and refined manners, would remain a mere commoner? Furthermore, it was going to be a drain on his parents' flagging resources to elevate the lad thus and he had a bad feeling he was going to be expected to chip in, too. 'Mum,' he said sweetly, 'surely it's better that the boy remains here to support his widowed mother and three young siblings?'

'I think the least we can do, Tris,' Giles ventured, 'is to send Mrs Glibly some money each month until such time as we can sort out a way of bringing over the whole family. With you living in the capital, you can drive over here each month to check up on them personally.'

Randolph was horrified at the plan that was hatching. 'But Dad, I'm only renting the Robin Reliant,' he extemporized, 'A car isn't included in my package and it'd be a terribly long haul on a public bus.'

'Nonsense, you can't leave our near relatives living here in this hell-hole!' Jocelyn exclaimed, 'As soon as Miss Golmar can arrange it, Mrs Glibly and the younger children can relocate to the capital and live in that enormous school flat of yours with you. You've got four bedrooms and two full bathrooms, for goodness sake.'

'Now, now, mother, you cannot be rude about other people's homelands like that,' Randolph scolded her, scrabbling for a way to strangle this emergent stratagem in the cradle, so to speak, 'Moreover, Kebapistan is a very strictly run nation with a strong sense of social hierarchy. I hardly think that Ms Zoran, who is an absolute stickler for rules and traditions, is likely to allow the Headmaster of her elite private school to bring his raggle-taggle distant relations to live in his on-campus luxury flat with him.'

'Shame on you, Tristram Vainglory Randolph!' Jocelyn tutted, shaking her head, 'You are revealing the selfish character of a cosseted only child.'

'Well, if I am, I wonder whose fault that might be?' Randolph scolded, 'Look, this is hardly the time to discuss these matters. I ran into one of my staff at the guest house and I promised we'd meet her for dinner at 7. That's in half an hour. We need to go. We can talk about these grand plans of yours in the cold light of day tomorrow morning.'

'But we haven't had a chance to meet the young Viscount yet!' Giles protested.

'He isn't a Viscount *yet,*' Randolph snapped, rising, 'And is unlikely ever to be, in my opinion, for whatever that's worth. But, as I have said, we can discuss that later. Now it is time for us to depart.'

'Well, maybe he could join us at dinner?' Giles suggested, 'I mean, you must know where we're meeting your colleague. You could give Mrs G. the address and Barney could meet us there.'

'Mrs G.! Barney!' Randolph remonstrated, 'Shall I get the names of Little Snotnose and her brother, Punch-Crotch here for you so you can send them postcards when you get back to London?'

'How dare you speak to your father like that...and in

front of family members, too!' Jocelyn quavered.

'God help me,' Randolph sighed, resting his forehead Hamlet-like between thumb and forefinger for a moment. He took the paper Gabby had given him and handed it to the Widow Glibly, who raised it to her eyes bewildered, leading him to wonder whether she was literate.

Next, he pulled his phone from his pocket, opened Google Translate typed in some simple instructions and the translation into Kebapi popped onto the screen. He held it out for her to read, but she did the bewildered look again, cementing his suspicion that she was illiterate so he had the Google Translate robot speak it. She responded with amazement, then threw her free arm around him, enveloping him a cloud of sour milk and stale sweat. He stepped away from her and walked decisively to the blue plastic sheet, holding it aside with one hand and making a sweeping exit gesture to his parents with the other. Jocelyn wrung 'Mrs G's' hands in hers, Giles patted Punch-Crotch and Snotnose on their grubby little heads, pulled a funny face for the baby and then, thank Christ, they were out of there.

They met the young cuckoo himself approximately an hour later. Randolph was sitting with his parents and Gabby at the back of what was supposed to be the best jiz-biz cafe in the hometown of jiz-biz. There were long rough sawn tables with benches either side and an area behind a counter where the stuff was constantly simmering in vast vats. They brought it over to you in what looked like stainless steel doggy bowls, and plonked down a plate of white bread in the middle of the table, like a cannibal feast with internal organs and wads of cotton wool to soak up the gravy. It wasn't a place where the locals came in to chat over their meal but more akin to a human filling station: they paid, ate as quickly as they could with their heads close to the bowl, and left, probably to dash back to the mercury processing plant or to pop back down the mine shaft for a ten hour shift.

Barnaby Glibly the Sixth had obviously done the best he could to scrub up before meeting his distant relatives. He was petite with half-open eyes and a mushroom cut of ginger hair that certainly made him stand out from the rest of his countrymen. He wore a bow tie, an ironed but slightly soiled white shirt, tight polyester trousers with frayed hems, imitation Adidas trainers (spelled Addass on the sides) and a little black satin waistcoat that he'd long grown out of. The overall effect reminded Randolph of one the bewigged and costumed P.G. Tips chimps from the television advertisements of his boyhood for Britain's favorite tea. When he saw them all sitting there, the lad smiled and possibly reddened slightly, it was hard to tell with his cinnabar-stained skin. Upon catching sight of him, Jocelyn stood up and flung her arms around him like a long lost son. Randolph rolled his eyes.

'It's like one of those long lost family reunions on that *Who do you Think you Are?* on the telly!' Gabby exclaimed, a bit choked up.

'Indeed, who *does* he think he is?' Randolph sniped aside to her, 'I was hoping he wouldn't have the nerve to show up.'

Barnaby sat down at their table, where they were all furnished with their doggy bowls of jiz-biz by a surly waiter who dropped a heaped plate of thick cut wedges of white bread onto the centre of the table causing the tower of bread thereon to collapse. He didn't try to repair the damage.

'Thank you for inviting me. This is the nicest cafe in town,' Barnaby Glibly smiled, trying hard with his accent as he dipped his bread in the gravy with a shaky hand, plainly famished.

'Where *did* you learn such good English, Barnaby?' Jocelyn patted his arm.

'My father wanted me to speak English, so we conversed for an hour every day until he died down the mine last year. We knew we had an ancestor from England and we were very proud of it.'

'And not just any old ancestor, Barnaby,' Jocelyn assured him, 'Viscount Barnaby Glibly, no less. We intend to reinstate that peerage and within a year or two, get you into the House of Lords!'

Randolph shook his head in disbelief, 'Why are you telling the boy all this before you've made proper enquiries? What a travesty.'

'What is the meaning of Viscount?' Barnaby asked.

'Well, it's a bit like a king but not quite as royal,' Jocelyn winked.

'It's nothing at all like a king, mother. Don't get the lad's hopes up,' Randolph was becoming more and more infuriated by this charade.

Gabby summoned one of the friendlier waiters to take photos of them all eating the jiz-biz for her blog. 'Oh, this'll make a great story with little Lord Fauntleroy here!' she cooed. Randolph fixed his teeth into a smile as the camera flashed. Waiters were always at Gabby's beck and call, fluttering about her, like bees around a honey pot, asking her if she wanted this side dish or that extra serving, and she usually did, she couldn't resist, so they ended up serving her with a larger bill at the end.

Jocelyn then excitedly told Barnaby about the plan she was hatching for his lordly future... 'You'll come back with us in the car tomorrow-'

'Tomorrow, Mother?' Randolph was shocked. 'How will we all fit in the car? I've agreed to give Gabby a lift back.'

'Oh, we can squidge together in the back, we're family after all!' she chirped. 'Then you'll stay with us at Tristram's place-'

'Will he?!' Randolph wasn't at all pleased with the way his life was now having to fit around this distant relation.

'And in two weeks, when we go back to England,

you will come with us!' she announced, 'I'm sure Ms Golmar, Tristram's secretary will know a way of sorting you out with a passport, if she pulls a few strings, plus I'm going to ask her to gather all the birth and marriage certificates and other documentation so we can prove indisputably that you are the heir to rightful heir of your family's baronetcy.'

'Ahem, she is supposed to be *my* PA doing work for *me!*' Randolph griped, tapping his spoon on the table twice.

'And you don't need to worry about providing for your mother and your brothers and sisters. We will take care of all that,' Giles assured him.

'Good God! Why, oh, why are you telling him this?' Randolph raised his voice, unable to hold in his temper any longer. 'You are making all these promises with the idea this Silligator thing is going to succeed and see you through for another ten years! I have to say, I have grave reservations about that contraption!'

'I've always had faith in my inventions,' Giles was downcast, 'And you have always had faith in them too...in the past.'

'Alright, alright, I'm sorry, Dad. All I'm saying is, don't count your chickens and so on. Get your money coming in before you start making promises to desperate people in shanty towns!'

'But they're family, Tristram!' Jocelyn sounded on the verge of weeping.

'That really is stretching it, mother! They're cousins about 20 times removed! I'm probably more closely related to Winston Churchill than I am to him!'

'But Tristram,' Giles began, 'With your new career as a headmaster, it will hardly put you out of pocket to support this enterprise wholeheartedly.'

Randolph was gobsmacked. 'Support it? Support it? Have you even asked me once whether I *want* to channel my hard-earned shekels in this direction?!'

Gabby had been observing the discussion with

interest and now put in her two penn'orth, 'He's quite right, Mr and Mrs Randolph. If my parents asked me to support a far-flung relative I'd say no, too, I'd much rather channel my finances into fine dining.'

'Well, that's your loss, Gabby, even if you aren't capable of seeing it yourself. And the same goes for our son who I now see would prefer to put his money into fancy outfits and sports cars, instead of the things that really matter, such as making a difference to world poverty,' Jocelyn scoffed.

'Ha! I say Ha! to that!' Randolph stood up, 'And, I'll have you know, Gabby, that this comes from a woman who has never done a day's work in her life, and has made a habit of buying all manner of frippery from every shop she puts her nose into, while my poor father here has struggled to make ends meet!'

'Oh, come now, Tristram, I mainly buy essentials,' Jocelyn insisted.

'Cast your mind back, mother dear, to the booty you amassed on our last visit to the V & A, along with buying a bag for life every time you go to a supermarket. You'd have to live 500 years to use up your stash of bags for life!' And with that, he stalked out of the cafe, his jiz-biz barely touched.

The main event the following morning at the state rest house was the blocked toilet, courtesy of Gabby who had birthed an entity the size and shape of one of the lesser dinosaurs, and had the nerve to come knocking at Randolph's door, requesting advice, possibly assistance, in dislodging it. In the light of this, Randolph, with no advice to give, opted to relieve himself in the garden once he'd packed up the Robin Reliant ready to put Jizbizisbad far behind, determined never to lay eyes upon the miserable hole again. Now, of course, they were bringing their own little piece of it along with them, and lo, there was the future viscount now, at the front gate in the same absurd clothes he'd worn last night and holding two plastic carrier bags, no doubt containing all his goods and chattels. He caught sight of Randolph as he was zipping up his fly and gave him a friendly wave. Randolph did not wave back.

Wedged into the backseat were his parents, Barnaby Glibly between them, and in the passenger seat sat Gabby who was now making the light bodied three-wheeler keel. Giles insisted on turning on the Silligator despite Randolph's insisting he knew the way. Major Sillifant therefore told them *again* about the same landmarks he'd pointed out on the way there. Whenever he spoke, Gabby awoke for a few seconds and feigned a modicum of interest. Randolph kept his window open as Gabby broke wind from both ends as she slumbered, mumbling apologies in her sleep as she did so. In the back, Jocelyn and Giles chatted and laughed with Barney, getting on like a house on fire.

Randolph's pride was smarting. It was as if another son had replaced him while he, Tristram, was just there to be chauffeur and provide financial assistance. He brooded upon his current predicament as he drove the enclosed fibreglass bathtub down the desolate desert track...an obese woman snoring next to him whilst his parents bonded with their new and improved son behind. They were welcome to take the boy back to England with them and play about with their outrageous idea of his becoming a viscount– good luck to them– but they'd receive no assistance from him, financial or otherwise. He had no need for them anyhow, now he'd been promoted to top dog. His fury at the embracing of this new child in his parents' affections was suddenly replaced by a devil-may-care nonchalance. *Good riddance to them*, he thought, *about time I struck out alone.*

'Now, to your right are the remains of an ancient amphitheatre,' the Silligator piped up. 'If you turn down the track in 100 metres and drive for five miles, you will get a better look at it. The track is a tad stony though, so hold onto your hats!'

This was the first historical feature that hadn't been of a military nature so Randolph was somewhat interested. Smiling cruelly, he relished how jounced around they'd be in the back if he drove carelessly so he took the turning sharply. His plan worked a treat. His parents paused in their prattling and bounced about, clearly in great discomfort with their heads occasionally bumping on the roof, but too nervous to complain to him when he was in this foul state of mind.

Gabby awoke, displeased by the sudden change in motion, 'Mr Randolph, why are we suddenly off road? I don't have a sports bra on at the moment, you know.'

Randolph recoiled at the image this conjured up, but pressed on until the Silligator informed him he had arrived at his destination. He pulled the handbrake up sharply, stepped out and stomped off, looking for the amphitheatre. The others peered out as if too afraid to put a foot on the ground in the emptiness. He walked around for some time and it came as no surprise that there was nothing more than a hint of a flat area suggestive of a circle, hardly any change from the desert around him. He strolled into the centre of this flattened area and closed his eyes for a few moments, recalling his glory days as an actor, all eyes upon him, delivering some great comic speech, but was soon distracted by the billowing flames of oil fields on the horizon. *There was no rich theatrical tradition here*, he scoffed. The only tradition was the art of survival in this barren landscape, duly depicted on the richly embroidered tents of the aboriginal Dalibor people. He walked back to the little orange car, where the Silligator was finishing off a pompous spiel on the origins of tragedy... 'Strophê, Antistrophê, Epode.' Sighing loudly, Randolph turned the car around and they trundled back down the track.

After 20 miles or so, the Silligator imparted another gem of knowledge... 'Bear left to see the remains of the defences the British set up prior to suppressing the insurgencies from Jizbizisbad during the fifth wave of

Russian-backed uprisings,' the Silligator revealed.

Another futile snippet of colonial history, thought Randolph. He glanced to the left and, low and behold, there where there were no remains whatsoever. All that was there was more of the same grey and miserable Kebapi sand. 'What a surprise...how refreshing...no remains whatsoever, as per usual,' he muttered to himself.

'If you bear left and look *very* closely you will, I assure you, see the stumps of the defences, just stumps, mind you,' the Silligator affirmed.

'No, nothing, not a damn thing, not a crumb of concrete, a void, a vacuum, and you, Major Sillifant, are about as interesting as this mind bogglingly dull desert road– a straight line to nothing.'

'Make a U-turn now!' the Silligator commanded.

'No, I bloody well won't make a U-turn, Major Silligator, I do not wish to look for your stumps,' Randolph shouted into the speaker and his parents in the back seat fell silent.

'I can assure you, there are the remains of that noble stockade,' the Silligator reiterated.

'Sorry to disappoint you, Major, but there is NOTHING! It's all bloody gone– like you and your whole outdated, moustached, imperial lot– gone with the wind! Incidentally, I thought you'd died years ago after you went off to live in that thatched cottage in Nether Backwater.'

'It was Clacton-on-Sea, Tristram,' Jocelyn corrected but it was no good.

'What was written on the sign as you drove into that diabolical void? *Nether Backwater, stay a while amid its ancient charms...* Stay awhile amid its ancient population, more like it. And, by the way, you were a rotten scout leader too! I've never been so bored in my life—'

'Giles, control your bloody son. I will not be spoken to in that manner!' came the Major's voice, flustered and possibly tearful. Randolph looked over his shoulder at his father and stopped the car abruptly. The voice came again... 'I've done this for you as a token of goodwill, Giles, and I do not deserve this treatment.'

'Are you actually telling me you're there *now*, doing this *live*? You aren't a recording?" Randolph shouted into the Silligator but there was no answer, just a static crackle.

'I think you've upset him, Tristram,' Giles said quietly.

Randolph leaned back and let out a hollow, vicious cackle. 'You were right when you said your computer skills weren't up to much! Oh, lordy lord! This was supposed to be your meal ticket for the next ten years?'

'This is only a trial run, we still have a few kinks to iron out,' Giles pleaded, 'We just wanted to see if it'd be something worth developing.'

'Well, I hope you can see now that it damned well isn't!' Randolph turned on his father with fury, 'It's boring, it's irrelevant, it's not even bloody real! So, you'd better get on with inventing something new because I am not funding *that*!' and he jerked his thumb in the direction of Barnaby who looked petrified and close to tears.

The rest of the journey passed in silence. Randolph fixed his eyes upon the road, his foot jammed all the way down on the accelerator, speeding the overburdened cheese wedge along at 50 mph.

17

Randolph claimed he had work to do in his office to avoid spending the last days of his holiday with his parents and their new 'pet' project. Come Monday morning, he was in his usual position, at the school entrance, greeting the pupils, shaking hands with them before going off to wash his hands, figuratively as much as literally, during the patriotic anthem singing in the quadrangle. He was hoping to spend the rest of the day in his office streaming some classic BBC radio drama but Golmar poked her head around the door and disturbed him the moment he sat down at his desk. She apprised him that Gemmy had had been rushed to hospital from a Dalibor village in the back of a pick-up truck over the weekend. Her condition was stable now but she had been seriously injured. He asked what the problem was but Golmar said that the doctor dealing with her case had been evasive about it. She also reported that Brian was absent, stuck out in the desert with her uncle, Dr Preyn, whence they had called in by satellite phone to report that they were awaiting assistance to repair a Land Rover gasket failure on the way back from a fossilling expedition recce. Randolph instructed her to set up the cover or do it herself, if she didn't wish to grovel to the remaining four teachers.

As the end of the school day, Randolph dropped into Brian's lab to see if he had made it back yet. He was more inclined to loiter around the campus as he continued to be appalled by his parents and their Viscount project.

Gabby was sitting at one of the benches and not only was Brian present, but also looking outright lively for a change, chatting away as he prepared coffee with the aid of a lab stand, a Bunsen burner and a Pyrex flask.

'Ah, Brian, good to see you back! How was the desert?' Randolph breezed.

'Very exciting, Mr Randolph. Dr Preyn and I believe we may well have evidence of Lophogallus having originating here in Kebapistan within our reach. We've found fossilized egg, or rather I found it, as Dr Preyn was busy meeting with the Dalibor excavation team when the momentous discovery occurred.'

'Exciting times!' Randolph cheerily exaggerated. Then, turning to Gabby, he asked about Gemmy.

'Well, I don't suppose she'd mind too much if I told you, Mr Randolph,' Gabby confided, 'I suppose you must be familiar by now with the reputation of the Dalibor tribe.'

'Oh yes!' piped up Brian, 'They are world renowned for their fossil hunting skills. No fossiling expedition in Kebapistan would get very far without them and they're frequently taken on as scouts for digs in other parts of the world, too.'

'To the rest of us, Brian, Dalibor men are famous for soft body parts going rock hard in quite another sense than that of fossilization,' Gabby pointed out.

'But what's that to do with our Gemma?' Brian was befuddled.

'Just as you, Brian, are on a mission to find rare waterfowl fossils, Gemma's guiding interest in life is seeking out another sort of rarity, one which rhymes with duck; only this time she took it too far and did herself a serious injury.'

'Dear, oh, dear!' Randolph exclaimed.

'Her trouble sprang from wanting to have her cake and eat it, you could say. Do you happen to have any cake, or biscuits perhaps, to go with the coffee, Brian?'

'I don't remember what I've got in the cupboards, Gabby, but you're welcome to have a look while I sort out the coffee.'

Whilst Brian shuffled about filling the kettle and washing out two mugs, and Randolph started texting Gemmy to ascertain when she might be up to returning, Gabby's ever edacious eye was caught by a large and colorful cake tin bearing a flying duck motif stowed on an upper shelf. Idly prying off the lid, she discovered, nested in thick wads of cotton wool, what appeared to be some sort of rock sugar candy curlicues like delicate crazy straws in pastel shades of pink, blue, green, and less appetizingly, grey or brown.

'So, she wanted to have her cake and eat it, did she?' Brian called over, 'Sounds more up your street, Gabby.'

'I wasn't speaking literally, Brian. What I mean is that Gemmy was, at the time her accident occurred, trying to have it both ways...straight up both streets, if you catch my drift. What with Gemmy being a petite sort of lass and the tribesmen being gifted in the way I alluded to earlier, when matters, shall we say, reached their crescendo, it all went suddenly awry, transmogrifying, to use Gemmy's own words, from incomparable orgasmic pleasure into unendurably excruciating pain. She's had to have emergency surgery, you know.'

The mention of indescribable pleasure seemed to lead Gabby inevitably down the primrose path of gastronomic dalliance and, as Brian continued preparing the coffee, Randolph watched her take up one of the curlicues, a pink one, between thumb and forefinger and raise it to meet the tip of her probing tongue, which evidently liked what it found.

'Should you be licking that?' Randolph asked her.

But she didn't appear to hear him and snapped off a third of the sweetmeat with her incisors, masticated for an instant and paused to savour. She mulled the thing over in her mouth, drawing conclusions about it aloud. 'Mmm, the sensation is quite incomparable, one moment saline, the next sweet,,,and yet also strangely sour, with more than a hint of bitterness. I can also detect undertones of cinnamon and vanilla. It's like something Willie Wonka would've come up with.'

'It doesn't really look edible to me,' Randolph suggested but she appeared to be experiencing some shuddering sensation, as if her stomach were veritably lurching up into her thorax to seize upon the remainder of the tidbit. With a glance at Brian, whose back was still turned, she stuffed the rest of it into her mouth, barely able to suppress a loud, sensual groan as she crushed the sublime whorl between palate and tongue.

As Randolph watched her swallow the rare morsel, Brian turned to her and raising tufty, white brows, remarked, 'If only our Gemma had been a bird, all would've been well.'

'Mmmow's that then, Brian?' Gabby asked, the question mingling with the swallow. She returned to her stool to drink the coffee sitting opposite Brian and Randolph.

'Female birds have only a single orifice down there, not two like mammals. It's called a cloaca. Same with the reptiles. Dinosaurs too in their day. An enduring and successful evolutionary attribute.'

'What do the male birds have to say about that?' Gabby jested, and Randolph cringed as she licked the taste of her purloined snack from her lips.

'I shouldn't think most of them mind much,' Brian mused, dribbling creamer into their coffees, '97% of all male birds lack external genitalia. But of the 3% of bird species that do possess a phallus, geese, ducks and swans account for 97%. The 97:3 phenomenon is one of the great mysteries of avian evolution, and is among the prime reasons for my lifelong fascination with the Anatidae.'

'Why Brian, you naughty old bugger!' the rotund art

teacher chuckled, her serial chins wobbling.

'Oh, there's more to it than that, young lady. To understand though, you'll need to have a goosey gander at this.' He walked over to the table with the duck tin and placed it before her with a confidential air. 'Take a look at what's inside and have a guess what it might be! But be sure to handle with care: contents fragile.'

Gabby opened the tin, felt with false trepidation among the cotton wool, removed another of the crispy crazy straws, a bluish one this time, and feigned surprise. 'Is it something off a coral reef or some sort of fungus out of a tropical rainforest?'

'Au contraire, Gabby, what you now have in your hand is the ingeniously preserved male sex organ of the mandarin duck.'

'Oh, crikey, Gabby! Perhaps you've really had one of those mouthgasms you like to mention!' Randolph smirked.

'Blimey, how do you preserve them, and more curiously, why?' Gabby was transfixed by the avian curios.

'First the why, Gabby-- in our own species, we are fond of talking figuratively about 'the battle of the sexes' but among ducks that battle is a literal one. You see, most sorts of ducks mate for life, or at least for the season, yet most species also produce significantly more drakes than ducks. That obviously leaves a considerable proportion of drakes out in the cold, if you take my meaning. Consequently, drakes have evolved an elaborate range of penile morphologies, combined with a penchant for explosion eversion of that organ and a capacity for spontaneous ejaculation, which allows those without partners to employ a kind of hit and run reproductive strategy. Meanwhile, for their part, your female duck is aiming to lay eggs and raise chicks solely from the sperm of her carefully chosen mate, which has led the little ladies to evolve cloacae of contrasting complexity, in some cases even with a facility for changing cloacal shape in circumstances of duress, these being the unwanted advances of unfamiliar drakes.'

'My, my Brian, you truly do know your stuff,' she marvelled, 'Nevertheless, I find I'm still in the dark as to the wherefore of your severing and preserving the masculine organs of all those drakes, much less your method of keeping them intact in more or less permanent storage amidst wads of cotton wool inside a big old cake tin.'

'As you can well imagine, Gabby, the opportunities for studying the panoply of phallic forms among waterfowl in the wild, or in captivity for that matter, are infrequent and short lived. A few years ago, I hit upon the notion of flash freezing, wrought permanent and portable by means of good old fashioned candying, ergo crystallization utilising a scientifically tested range of sugars and salts.'

'So, in effect, Brian, this unique taxonomic collection of yours is also a premium example of 'delicatessen', as they say?'

'Oh, I wouldn't quite go that far, Gabby. In order to insure against bacterial, fungal or insect attack, they're positively shot through with disodium arsenate.'

'That's the stuff they put on Pringles to make them addictive, isn't it?'

'I should think not, Gabby, it's salts of arsenic, a thoroughly deadly, if somewhat slow-acting, poison.'

'Oh heck, Gabby, that is a bit of a drag for you!' Randolph exclaimed, not knowing what else to say.

Gabby winced and clutched at her neck, as if she could sense the beginnings of a slow and painful death creeping up her throat. Tears blurred her eyes and she cried, 'But I've eaten one of them, Brian!'

'What?' Brian was astounded, 'That object was important to the world of science– you've basically eaten evidence of evolution!'

Seeing that Brian wasn't going to be taking the action required to save her life, Gabby went into hysterics, begging Randolph to drive her to hospital. It was tiresome but what option did he have as her manager? She descended the stairs and hurried across the quadrangle into the car park, Randolph strolling after her. They drove off in the Robin Reliant, which took some time to accelerate up to road speed with Gabby in it. Randolph was nervous that she might at any moment vomit on the acrylic leopard fur upholstery and he'd have to pay extra for cleaning. Sadly, the trip didn't go to plan with the Reliant, not living up to its name, spluttering to a halt mid-way. Gabby was beside herself and said she fancied she felt a nauseous headache welling up in her skull. There were no other cars about and neither of them had phone reception. Randolph sat there for a moment, resigning himself to the only course of action as there would be no walking her the last three miles to the hospital. He would push the Robin in neutral with her in it holding the steering wheel. She repeatedly shrieked at him to go faster but how could he go with her inside, he wanted to say, instead biting his lip and putting his shoulder to the orange grindstone. Fortunately, as the car was flimsy fibreglass and the road flat, he did the job in under two hours.

At the hospital, Randolph, having consulted with Emergency reception, deposited Gabby, now jammed into a wheelchair, in the stomach pumping depot, where burly men were attired in wellington boots and rubber aprons. Then he went up to see Gemmy with one question at the forefront of his mind-- how long would she be off school? Getting cover out of the local hires or Mark Gall was like trying to get blood out of a stone. Brian, on the other hand, would always agree but he tended to forget or, if he did turn up, would nod off at the front of the class, which invariably ended up with one or both of Zara's children making mischief. Randolph did not intend to become the fallback cover teacher. Headmasters simply didn't do that sort of thing.

Gemmy was in a private room off a ward, lying on her back, her bottom propped up slightly with a foam support. She looked pale and wan, but registered his arrival with half-closed eyes.

'So, Gemmy, how's tricks?' Randolph greeted her sympathetically.

'No tricks until the New Year at the earliest, I'm afraid,' her speech was slurred. Randolph sat down on the side of her bed.

'I'm so sorry that this has befallen you, old girl.'

'Yes, two holes are better than one, as I can now avouch,' she sighed as her head lolled back in a morphine stupor, 'Seems une ménage à trois was a bad idea with the Dalibors.'

When she drifted off again, Randolph stood up, leaned over and gently tapped her shoulder until she looked up at him drowsily. 'But when can you come back to work? You can't leave me in the lurch, Gemmy!'

'More restorative surgery tomorrow then six weeks bed rest,' she murmured, her eyes slowly closing. They would be the last words he ever heard from her.

Randolph left the room and cursed under his breath in the stairwell. At the reception desk, he asked whether Gabby was alive and, if so, when she was likely to be back on her feet again? It was touch and go, they told him. Had it been any longer, the doctor quipped, she'd have had her chips. She's had those a few too many times, Randolph told him but he didn't get the joke. She'd be in hospital under observation for the next few days, then she'd need bed rest for a month.

'Damn and blast!' Randolph's cry met with deaf ears. With the Reliant in its defunct state at the side of the entrance, he had asked reception to call him a taxi, not a simple matter in Diskebapisbad. As he waited, he reflected upon how these two silly women had each fallen prey to their singular appetites in life, leaving him high and dry.

18

For the rest of the week, Randolph had instructed that Golmar set up Pyro and Volta with Gabby and Gemmy's lessons, which thoroughly infuriated them. When they bothered to turn up, they made no attempt to give any sort of lesson, not that they could've done much both being less than proficient in English and having neither interest nor ability in art. That weekend, Zara, who had been out of the country, learned via her children, and to her extreme annoyance, that the two foreign female teachers were both in hospital. She sent Randolph a curt email, instructing him that he'd now be required to do Gemmy's job. She also informed him that she'd found a cost-effective local hire to stand in for Gabby. A struggling young graduate of the Zoran National Academy of Arts, who lived in a Diskebapisbad garret, would be starting on Monday.

Randolph had never taught English before and had absolutely no desire to do so now. He found a couple of textbooks in Gemmy's room and had Golmar photocopy sets of pages from them. He most certainly didn't intend to give any written work that would require him sitting down doing marking, so he chose only spelling, grammar and comprehension exercises with fill in the blank or multiple choice answers. He saved time by letting the pupils mark each other's work in class while he read out the answers and, punctuated by plenty of his genial banter, they appeared to take to it rather well.

Drama was, of course, his specialty, but he found

that he couldn't be bothered with it any longer. He hadn't taught the subject for 10 years and had forgotten how tiring it could be with all the freedom of movement and expression it involved. He thought back to the old standbys, his pupil empowerment projects, which placed all the responsibility squarely on the shoulders of the pupils. He tried one out in class but these Kebapi children weren't up to it, accustomed as they were to being spoon-fed bite-sized tasks that never called upon their own initiative. He looked online for drama projects for primary school pupils, which seemed to suit their capabilities and stopped them rushing about the room, giggling and whacking each other. At the end of his first week of being the English and drama teacher, Zara summoned him to her office.

'It seems the parents feel short-changed by the loss of Gemma,' she exhibited a disappointed face, 'And that they much preferred her approach to yours.'

'Well, I'm sorry to hear that, Zara but, I am now doing two jobs, one of which is entirely new to me. The parents must understand that.'

'Oh, they do, they do, Tristram, but they don't like change and they'd become used to Gemmy, radically inappropriate though she often was. What you need to do is find some way of restoring school spirit, some special event planned by you. It should take place by the end of next week-- a drama production perhaps as that's your area of expertise.'

'It takes weeks of rehearsal to put on a decent pupil drama production, Zara!'

'Well, having witnessed your work at the drama festival last Spring, I am confident you will manage it. As I said, it's a question of restoring school spirit.'

School spirit? Randolph had never taken to the term. Hastings Culpepper had banded it around a few times on his arrival at Swineforth. The staffroom veterans had duly scoffed at it, asking him whether he was referring to the ghost of a long dead physics master who was said to roam the corridors after having run into trouble changing an incandescent bulb with the light switch on. Culpepper had quickly seen it wasn't going work at a school like Swineforth and had shut up about it.

'The other thing I have decided,' she continued, 'Is to fly Gemma and Gabby back to Britain this weekend. I am sure you will agree that they will better off in the care of the NHS.'

'But, Zara, their respective misfortunes only happened a week ago,' Randolph reminded her, 'I understood they needed bed rest and shouldn't be moved, particularly Gemma with her rather fragile...repairs.'

'Not to worry, Tristram. Provision will be made for Gemmy to be strapped into-- is it called 'a gurney'?-- on the flight to Munich. The second flight to London is under two hours. I am sure she will be fine. I have already had Golmar tell the doctors to make them ready for the journey.' She cocked her head and smiled, 'And all their belongings in their apartments have been nicely packed up and sent ahead of them to the airport. Rest assured, they will be paid until the end of the month: we look after our staff like family.'

The end of the month was in three days. The extent of her generosity concerned Randolph and he wondered how far it would extend should some misfortune ever happen to befall him.

'At the end of the day,' she continued, 'No one, not even you, Tristram, is indispensable.' Randolph inwardly disagreed, but decided not to dispute the point because the only thing he really wanted to know was when the replacements would be arriving.

'Oh, no, no, we cannot bring in replacements and have yet more change! You will do Gemma's job until the end of the school year and the art graduate will continue in Gabby's post. I have already had wonderful reports from my daughter about her. She has much more energy than Gabby had and is so grateful to be given employment such as this. I see now that fluency in English is not necessary in our Art teacher.'

At that moment, it properly dawned on Randolph that his current predicament rendered him well and truly worse off than he had been at his previous job where he'd had no teaching to do for the past 10 years. He now had 20 lessons per week, in addition to having to see disgruntled parents daily and write the chirpy weekly newsletter.

'Also, Tristram, Max tells me Brian has started missing his lessons on Mondays because he is out on field trips with Dr Kalamuz Preyn. Max asked him what he was up to and he told him he'd been out in the desert searching for the fossil of Lopho Phallus! Do you understand what this means for my family?'

'A fossilized phallus? Would that be helpful to your father...or to yourself?' Randolph replied deadpan.

'Quite the contrary, Dr Preyn's is seeking to prove to the world that *the turkey's* dinosaur ancestor, the Lopho, originated *here* in Kebapistan! Can you believe the cheek of the man? He only holds his position as curator of the Museum of Natural History thanks to our generosity. Yet, if this research comes to fruition, it could undermine the very fabric of our society, along with gravely insulting my father. Apparently, he has been searching for 20 years but has managed to keep it under his hat all that time.'

'I would think, Zara, that he's not going to find it if he's been looking for it for 20 years,' Randolph assured her over what struck him as an exceptionally petty fear, 'It's a big desert out there, you know.'

'Yes, you are probably right, Tristram. It is sure to come to nothing now it has been brought to our attention. I should not be burdening you with political concerns when you have so much work to do. You must start thinking about this school spirit event that will make us a family again. I'm looking forward to seeing it.

Let us say, provisionally, Friday next week at 6pm in the performance hall.'

Randolph returned to his apartment. Unfortunately, his parents had decided to extend their stay while they waited for Golmar to obtain the last few documents to prove Barnaby Glibly's entitlement to the vacant viscountcy and, in the meantime, to an entry visa that was being facilitated, God only knew why or how, by Edwin Sneed.

'Well, everything's gone well and truly tits up now!' Randolph said as he walked in and threw himself on the sofa, disturbing his parents' and their foster prodigal son over a game of Scrabble.

'Shush, Tristram, you'll teach Barney the wrong kind of language for a Viscount,' his mother mock-scolded him.

'What are tits?' Barnaby asked politely.

'It's just a silly phrase meaning things have gone wrong,' Giles explained.

'Well, I cannot make a word out of my letters so I think my tits are up?' Barnaby offered.

'No, no dear, a viscount doesn't say that, it's a bit naughty,' Jocelyn shot a look at Randolph from the corner of her eye to show him the trouble he was causing.

Randolph went out in a huff and walked to the Robin Reliant, which the hire company had returned to him with its clutch fixed and with a complimentary extension to his hire period as compensation. The summer weather had been replaced by a chill wind as the nights drew in. He would drive into the city to take refuge in the Irish pub, which had become his regular off-duty haunt since his parents had brought back Barnaby Glibly.

Randolph walked into the Irish bar and ordered the usual from 'Paddy' the Kebapi bartender. Paddy's English was decent enough and Randolph had been pouring out his sorrows to him on his visits. At the other end of the bar was a group of Kebapi creative types. A woman in her late thirties, he estimated, wearing a silver fur-- could it actually be sable?-- mini dress revealing magnificently supple thighs descending into knee-high suede boots. She wore her long and luscious blonde hair on top of her head, casually held in place with a Chinese-style comb. The two men she was with were tall, handsome and aquiline in fashionably distressed denim. They looked like they were annotating scripts, reading sections, talking about it and making notes. Randolph tried to catch her eye so he could give her a nod, but she was engrossed in her annotations so he rabbited on to Paddy instead.

'You know who's that?' Paddy whispered 20 minutes later, nodding over to the woman at whom Randolph had been casting frequent glances. 'Zina Zoran, the president's daughter.'

'Seriously?' Randolph's jaw dropped.

'Those are her body guards with her; they also do small parts in her plays and television shows.'

He'd had a few too many tots of watered down, probably counterfeit Irish whiskey and, before he knew what he was doing, had sauntered over to her table. 'So sorry to bother you but I'd just like to say—' he began but the two artistic-looking bodyguards got to their feet and blocked him, 'that you were brilliant, just brilliant in *Hedda Gabler!*' he called over their sinewy shoulders.

She said something that brought them to heel and they relaxed. He edged between them, taking the seat opposite her, his tongue on the verge of lolling out of his mouth as he took in her wide baby blue eyes, her fuchsia pink lipstick, her round, soft honey-coloured cheeks, her ample bosom...

'Thank you so much,' she smiled, 'Did you see it at the National Theatre or on the television?'

'Oh, on the television but I would have much, much preferred to have seen you perform in the flesh!'

He introduced himself as the headmaster of

Swineforth Hospital International and all of a sudden her interest was piqued. Caressing the crimson upholstery of the seat next to her, she invited him to sit closer, and sent the bodyguards to the opposite end of the bar. Zina Zoran, seemed to think it was 'very funny' that he had to work with her older sister on her 'little project', which was really just an excuse for providing an English school for her 'brats' because their grandfather thought it too much of a risk for them to be sent to boarding school in Britain.

'She's quite the bossy-boots, don't you think?' she winked, leaning toward him, possibly suggestively, so he hypothesized.

'Oh, yes! She's always summoning me into her office for a spank!'

'Really?!'

'No, not really...she saves that for Max.'

'Max! What a specimen!'

'I know!'

'Where did they dig him up?'

And thus they babbled on. Randolph hadn't had this much fun in months. Not only was she a match for his razor-sharp wit, she was also one of the most alluring women he'd ever seen...and he'd thought Zara was at the top of her game!

'Did you know she once did try to murder my Yorkshire terrier when we were children?' she pouted.

'You must be joking, why?'

'Other than her being totally—', Zina tapped her temple meaningfully, 'I suspect it was because I got the English dog for Christmas and she got the Dachshund.'

They laughed heartily. She poured him a glass from a bottle of expensive looking Georgian wine and he took a sip, crooned 'Mm, deliciously fruity with an accent of...honeysuckle.' He licked his lips. 'Well, I have to say, her playing at schools has gone totally pear-shaped. The teachers dropping like flies and she wants me to come up with some 'grand event' by next Friday night that will restore everyone's faith in the project! Ha, what a shambles! One week to put together a show!'

'Ah, but I am having a little idea that is going to help you,' she squeezed his knee, 'what if I bring my theatre troupe in and give a performance of our award-winning show *The History of Kebapistan?*'

'Mm, I wouldn't mind seeing you on the horse again in *that* tunic,' he cosied up to her and she met him halfway.

'But you must keep it a secret, don't tell anyone, especially not Zara. We'll surprise her with it,' she whispered in his ear sending a chill down his spine. 'Here is my personal card with my private number. We can start planning tomorrow. It will only take a couple of days to get things ready. I do it all the time. The show, I mean. I will be ready for you next week.'

'Zina, this is so generous of you,' and he took her hand and kissed it flamboyantly.

'I like you, I like you very much and I want to help you,' she breathed, stroking his hair. 'Let us have a dinner date after the performance to celebrate.'

As she left, she kissed him on both cheeks. Randolph was beside himself. Paddy the bartender looked over in astonishment and raised his thumbs once she and the bodyguards had turned their backs. Randolph ambled back to his bar stool and grinned with self-satisfaction.

'Good work, man,' Paddy went so far with his job as to try to speak English in as Irish a manner as he could muster given his limited exposure, 'You've got her eatin' out of your hand!' Paddy patted him on the back, 'Not only beautiful but rich beyond measure!'

'And about bloody time, after all her sister has put me through!' he consoled himself.

19

That weekend, Randolph became civil toward his parents again. When they were discussing their adoptive aristocrat, he listened cordially, albeit with a far-off look on his face. They showed him all the documents Golmar had assembled in preparation for their unveiling of Barnaby as the successor to the viscountcy and Randolph nodded and smiled encouragingly. 'Perhaps he's fallen in love again?' Jocelyn suggested to Giles, only half aside. Upon their departure at midday on Sunday, Randolph drove them to the airport, hugged his parents and shook hands with Barnaby, wishing him all the best. On Monday morning, Randolph had a skip in his step as he went out to greet the pupils as they arrived for school. He noticed Felicity laughing with another elegant looking sort of girl, beamed at their jolly mood and asked them, convivially, what they were laughing about.

'Oh, we shouldn't really say, Mr Randolph,' Felicity battered her lashes in exaggerated bashfulness.

'Surely you can tell me, Felicity! I like a good joke of a Monday morning.'

'Well, it's about Mr Gall,' she began, 'When he gets really angry there's this thread of spittle that forms vertically between his lips and we all watch it when he starts ranting. It's actually amazingly rubbery, wavering in and out like the thread of a cobweb. We've even timed how long it takes to snap. 7 minutes is the record at the moment!'

Randolph knew he shouldn't but he joined in with

their laughter and walked into school with them. What a shame Golmar hadn't been there to snap a piccy of them sharing a joke.

During the week that followed the indifferent look Randolph had previously exhibited in the classroom was replaced by the foolish smile and doe eyes of the infatuated man. By Tuesday afternoon, he'd become Felicity's favourite teacher and a number of pupils were eagerly following suit.

He certainly had something to look forward to! On Wednesday evening he'd be dropping in on Zina at the National Theatre, whilst she supervised the preparation and packing of costumes, props and technical equipment for the school's command performance of *The History of Kebapistan* at the end of the week. Together they would plot how everything, even the horse, could be smuggled into the performance hall to keep it a surprise. Randolph had sent out invitations to pupils and their families, phrasing it as a 'Surprise Gala' with refreshments. Zara had probed him about it, but all he told her was that it would be something very special indeed. Part and parcel of the plan was that it had to be kept under wraps so as not to spoil it, though he was sure it would 'restore faith in Swineforth International and bring everyone together in a grand celebration of school spirit.'

The following day, Randolph just happened to notice something that abruptly brought him out of his newfound euphoria. It was a tiny video camera and microphone embedded in a plastic aspidistra that had sat in the corner of his office since his arrival.

'Golmar, what is this?' he asked, annoyed.

He dropped it in her palm and she closed her hand over the device so that it could pick up nothing. 'She listens to your meetings. It is normal business practice in Kebapistan.'

'Well, that's just great, isn't it? So, I'm being spied upon!'

'No, purely monitored, at the moment.'

'Ha! That makes it so much better then!'

'I wouldn't mention it, if I were you. She will only have Max hide it somewhere else and it's to your advantage that she doesn't know you know it's there.' She walked him back into his office and replaced the bug precisely where it had been.

He felt sure the lovely Zina would never do anything so underhand. How different sisters could be!

On Wednesday evening, he spruced himself in preparation for his visit to the theatre. He donned what he deemed his most thespian outfit, which still erred on the side of headmasterly respectability: black blazer with black Levis, tan boot brogues and a white oxford shirt, made slightly risqué with a number of buttons open up top. He drove the Reliant over to the national theatre, a colossal concrete cube of brutalist architecture with a giant's doorway in the centre and a tremendous lintel supported by soaring iron girders. Randolph minced in and was swallowed whole.

Zina may have been from the richest family in the country but she wasn't afraid of mucking in, he thought as he entered the vast auditorium. He smiled as he watched her buzz about on the stage with her subordinates, carrying armfuls of costumes. After twenty minutes of this, she caught sight of Randolph.

'I'm so sorry, Tristram, I didn't see you come in. You should have told me you were here!'

'Oh, it's alright, I was just sitting here admiring the view.'

She led him to her office, arm in arm. She just so happened to be in black jeans too so they made quite the matching couple, what with their both being blondes. Her hair was loose this evening and her tousled tresses spread out over her black mohair jumper.

'Someone told me that the three-wheeled clown car was parked at the front, did you see it?' she asked him.

Randolph raised his eyebrows in wonder and

sputtered 'You call it that too?'

'Well, yes, because that's what it was, a car for the clowns to jump out of at my 10th birthday party. My father had it imported specially. He asked his assistant to find the silliest car she could. The clowns were dressed in orange to match.'

'I believe you're referring to the Robin Reliant, the car hire company fobbed off on me, I'm afraid.'

'Oh no, really? I think it's one of Zara's many crumby little businesses and she's making some money out of cast offs rusting in daddy's garage! she thinks she's such a serious business woman and she's hiring out the clown car! Wonderful!'

Randolph firmly resolved at that point, now that he'd been relieved of his parents, he would tell Golmar to call the slick car hire man to arrange to relieve him of the ridiculous vehicle. He'd be happy to see the back of it. Taxis would suffice in future.

They arrived at her office, a fun room done out in 1960s decor with white shag pile rugs, a kidney-shaped coffee table and egg-shaped armchairs that you could have a lot of fun swivelling round on. What a difference from Zara's Balmoral décor! They were served coffee and a plate of elaborately decorated cupcakes. Zina took a cupcake that was dotted with toasted miniature marshmallows set in pink icing. She opened her full mouth wide to bite into it, her blue eyes doubling in size, and purred through crumbs, 'Mmm, cream filled!'

They giggled together as they planned how her tech team would smuggle in all the costumes and props after midnight of the day of the performance and store it all in some of the empty classrooms on the top floor. Randolph had come across some newly built garages where the horse could be stabled. A groom would stay in there with it and keep it calm and quiet. What a ruse it would be and what a spectacle would be created–everyone was sure to be amazed.

'By the way,' Zina began, 'We are currently

rehearsing a British-style pantomime. Although we do not do Christmas here in Kebapistan, it will be performed over the festive season. Do you know anything about this distinctive British art form?'

'Oh, yes, of course, we're all very familiar with that 'art form' in Britain. Which one are you doing?'

'*Peter Pan*, with me as the protagonist. I have the legs for it—'

'You certainly do, Zina. But what about, you know, above the waist? Aren't you a touch generous for Master Pan?'

'Oh Tristram, you rogue! No one will mind. The Kebapi males in the audience will lap it up, their wives will all be jealous and the children just won't understand.'

'You're sooo right, now I think about it, darling.'

'And I do love being strapped into the flying harness. It squeezes me in just the right place which adds a little frisson of excitement to my flights...But you know we've had an awful setback recently. One of our actors took a bit of bad turn and is having to go into treatment for some time. I was wondering whether you might, especially for me, be willing to take his part.'

Randolph's heart missed a beat. 'Which...part is that?'

'It's the Dame.'

The Dame! Randolph's eyes widened. This was a part for a supremely talented comedy actor-- one who had mastered its Commedia Dell'arte origins and would know how to apply those techniques in front of a demanding audience consisting largely of children. He clasped his hands to his chest and gushed, 'Are you actually telling me, dear Zina, that I shall finally have the chance to play *the dame?*'

She nodded.

'I never thought this day would come!'

'So you'll do it?'

'Oh God, YES...a thousand times over! Thank you!

Thank you! Thank you!'

And she furnished him with the script there and then. Because of the day job, he'd only be able to attend evening and weekend rehearsals but with his background as an actor, he assured Zina, his hand on her lithe arm, he would manage perfectly. His life in Kebapistan had suddenly taken on a new meaning. His meeting with Zara and the headship had been merely an overture. This...this was where his fate had been leading him all along. He was to tread the boards again, a stunningly beautiful woman at his side illuminating the way. That night, he read the script of *Peter Pan* from cover to cover dissolving, over and over, in helpless laughter at the incomparable opportunity he had be given.

20

The evening of the 'Surprise Gala' was upon them and Randolph stood at the foot of the stage in the school performance hall looking out into the dimness, where he could out around 300 audience members-- ergo every pupil in the school along with their friends and family members-- all waiting for the stage to be illuminated and the mystery show to begin. Zara and her shadowy familiar, Max, were as much in the dark as everyone else in the auditorium. Randolph had caught Max in his office glancing through some papers, no doubt trying to find out what was going on at Zara's behest. Aware now of the surveillance in his office, Randolph had only spoken to Zina about the play from his phone, whilst walking about the building site at the back of the school, for fear his apartment was likewise bugged.

Zara sat on the front row next to Felicity and Gerald and between some of the wealthiest parents. A reasonable quantity of refreshments had been provided but whether it would be enough to sustain everybody through the 20 minute intermission in the four-hour extravaganza, Randolph had his doubts. The caterers had turned up their normally flagging creativity in response to his request for 'something a bit different' and had produced a prodigious batch of minced jiz-biz vol-a-vent with sprigs of parsley on top. Pyro Envany and Volta Covet were there, he suspected for the free snacks, which they'd begun pecking at as soon as the auditorium doors opened. Mark Gall was sitting next to Max, no doubt engrossed in some winsome topic of conversation such as garroting techniques. Brian sat at the end of the front row, finding it difficult to keep his head up.

The huge crash of a gong, concurrent with the lights suddenly up full on the stage revealed a tableau of the first people of Kebapistan eking out a living...skinning a hide, spearing an imaginary animal, gathering a berry or two. The recorded narration in Kebapi resounded in the oversized sound system, spoken by Zina's sensuously expressive voice. Randolph peered out into the auditorium expecting to see riveted faces but no...Zara's face wore a look of pained horror, her shoulders hunched as if taking a blow. Adults and children alike were sneaking out their phones to check the time and play a spot of Angry Birds, Candy Crush or Temple Run. Randolph was confused, but then Golmar was suddenly at his side to explain what was happening.

'Not one of your better decisions, Mr Randolph,' she whispered, 'They've all sat through this half a dozen times-- required viewing for prominent citizens.'

'But why does Zara look so done in?'

'Because she hates her sister and had forbidden her to come anywhere near the school. Swineforth is her pet project and, on pain of death, no one was to allow Zina to set foot in its campus. President Zoran himself is rumoured to have warned her off antagonising Zara in connection to it. I suppose you didn't know and that Zina put you up to this? You've been used as a prawn in a nasty feud, I'm afraid.'

Randolph looked out into the audience again. There were some empty seats already and many more people were looking around as if searching for an opportunity to sneak out. When Zina came on stage astride the horse in her metallic costume, a wonder to behold, Zara's reaction was to stand up haughtily and march out. Zina paused to watch her, a sly little smile on her face. Zara's departure seemed to be the cue for those who had been sitting next to her to follow with similar haughty gestures as they walked off. Felicity remained for a few moments, stifling laughter, then waltzed out after her mother dragging her brother by his arm.

'Will I lose my job for this?' Randolph asked Golmar, clutching his bowed head in both hands.

'As you were entirely ignorant of the feud, I should think you'll be alright. But confide in me in future, Mr Randolph, I am on your side,' she looked so sincere he was inclined to believe her.

The spectacle wore on and, at half time, the remaining audience members fell upon the jiz-biz vol-a-vent like flies upon daintily presented dung in pastry shells. Randolph mingled with parents and pupils and everyone who'd remained seemed to be enjoying the show, or rather pretending to.

'Mr Randolph, sir,' Brian appeared looking like a haunted soothsayer, his hair at sixes and sevens, 'I'm a little troubled by something I've just seen.'

'Not the show, I hope!' Randolph chuckled, wondering what had alarmed the old man.

'I have to admit, Mr Randolph, I did nip out half an hour into the proceedings with a sudden inclination to eat some spring rolls. I went over to Michael Oh's Emporium only to find it...gone!'

'Gone? Perhaps they moved to other premises?'

'No, gone as in razed to the ground, Chinese lanterns amongst the rubble and these too,' Brian held up a pair of Michael's black-rimmed spectacles.

'I'm not sure what to make of all this, Brian, but I'll ask around tomorrow,' Randolph proposed to jolly him along, 'In the meantime, why don't you try one of the jiz-biz vol-a-vent? Ooh, looks like they've all been eaten. Now there's a desperate audience for you, eh?'

The gong rang out to indicate the end of the intermission. Randolph assumed Zara's vacant seat on the front row, grinning and nodding to the other members of the thinned out audience. Whenever Zina entered in her different guises, she gazed into his eyes alone, as if she were acting only to him and they were the only people in the room. Randolph was beyond excited about their date after the show. To hell with Zara and her silly school project if she didn't appreciate his efforts here tonight to drum up the school spirit. The beautiful Zina could potentially offer him a permanent role in the acting company of the National Theatre. That would be something to write home about to his old theatre friends in Lincoln and they didn't need to know *where* this National Theatre was. He wondered whether he'd ultimately be invited to move into her villa and, at some later date, perhaps even be asked to dip his toe into fatherhood.

At the end of the show, the audience got to their feet for the mandatory standing ovation. Randolph stepped onstage with a bouquet of red gladiolas and bowed as he presented them to Zina. She made a deep curtsy to him, allowing him a glimpse of her divine décolletage. She was so captivating, his head swam and he went weak at the knees. Having recovered himself, he stood by the exit doors as the audience departed, shaking parents' hands effusively. When the last parent had left, Zina suddenly appeared flanked by her bodyguards, a vision of delight...fresh-faced and out of her stage make-up, a silken loose toga-like dress flowing, held together by a golden plaited cord that hung at her side, a beaver stole thrown over her shoulders against the chill of autumnal night.

'Now for the post-performance engagement I promised you,' she took his arm and they walked along... but they seemed to be heading in the direction of his office.

'Wherever are you leading me, Zina?' he simpered.

'You'll see...it's an intimate treat.'

They then walked past his office and one of the bodyguards flung open the door of Zara's office instead. Randolph recoiled slightly as this was a forbidden zone but she coaxed him in by his necktie. He was stunned to see that a candlelit dinner had been set up in the middle of the room, with a chef in a 'toque blanche' apron preparing food that didn't smell like gravy for a change. His shock turned to hilarity and he promptly burst out laughing at the naughtiness of it all. She embraced him, laughing with him and caressing his hair, then they sat down and were soon holding hands across the table.

Six courses of heaven were prepared by Zina's personal French chef and served to them by his waiter-assistant from the stainless steel preparation trolley. Each plate contained an intricate morsel, no more than a couple of bites, but what a sublime experience his taste buds were having! He felt he deserved it after putting up with Kebapi fare for so long. The waiter, who was also French, asked Randolph to try the wines. A recording of Mozart opera classics, just loud enough to allow their conversation to be private, was playing from Zara's laptop on the desk. Oh how cross she'd be if she'd known someone had touched that!

'I know all her passwords just like I know how to push all her buttons!' Zina snorted.

They laughed over Max's inability to discover what they'd planned and sniggered about Zara's walking out in a 'jealous huff', at that particular moment in the show, Zina said, 'because she knows I have a far better body'. Then they guffawed, imagining Zara's face if she could see them now, using her office for their fine dining. At the end of the meal, over coffee and liqueurs, Zina sent her staff away, locking the door after them and turning up the opera compilation. Sitting with her, talking and laughing, occasionally joining in with bits of arias, Randolph felt this was the most theatrically romantic experience he'd ever had. He was smitten to the core and reflected that had never been so happy in his life, except perhaps for his unforgettable turn as Offenbach's Golden Fly.

She led him over to one of the Chesterfields where

they became passionately entangled to the *Queen of the Night*. Randolph found her a little tentative and felt he had to take the lead in cherishing the angel before him. She leaned over and fiddled about with the dial on the fire but the flames suddenly leapt to half a metre and turned from gentle gold to luminous blues and greens.

'I didn't know it could do that,' Randolph said, sitting up abruptly, 'You need to be careful, Zina, it looks like it might be dangerous. Watch your dress doesn't catch fire, you'll go up like a Roman Candle.'

She didn't answer him but, with a brazen gesture, stood up and pulled on the golden cord around her dress. The whole thing slid to the ground, unveiling intricate crimson undergarments comprising straps, lace and Velcro. Randolph was taken aback. Then, with a ju-jitsu-like sleight of hand, she rolled him off the Chesterfield and onto the tiger skin rug as the finale of *Don Giovanni* struck up. It was as if contact with the tiger skin infused her with a kind of wildness. She tore open his shirt, buttons popping, and began biting at his face. He tried to keep up with her but felt too flabbergasted to match her fiery desire. She was atop him now, sinking her nails into his chest and running her fingers through his hair far too vigorously for his liking.

'Steady on, old girl,' was all he could utter.

She didn't seem to hear him and the flames reflected off her perspiring pearlescent skin, as if she were at one with it. She looked frightening, possessed, demonic. He tried to squirm away from the fire, the heat of which was making him gasp, but he was held in place by her thighs, which he'd formerly admired for their shapeliness, but now feared for their strength. Her hands were gripping his locks as she gratified herself on his Versace Medusa Head belt buckle, gnashing her teeth and growling, her eyes vacant. Then, quite abruptly, it was over. She shuddered, sighed and smiled up at the ceiling. She blissfully stretched her arms into the air but then, falling from her fingers, were blonde strands of *his* hair. She looked confused. Randolph's hands automatically flew to his head and he shrieked as he felt patches of skin. He flipped her off him and leapt to his feet, standing in frozen horror, clutching his scalp. There was a stunned silence of about five seconds and then she could hold it in no longer...it was one of the funniest things she had ever seen in her life and she laughed with cold-blooded callousness. Then there came a pounding at the door.

'Do you know how much that cost my parents?' Randolph shouted above her laughter but it only made her roar louder, 'And do you have any idea of the pain I endured to have hair transplants?'

Zara burst into the room and took in the scene-- her sister in her bizarre undergarments, laughing hysterically on the tiger skin and Randolph standing stock still looking like a plucked chicken. Behind her stood Max, a slight sneer of contempt disturbing his usual blank composure.

'How dare you set foot in this school and use my office as your sex pad!' she sneered at her sister who now found their predicament even funnier. 'Tristram, I will deal with you on Monday. Right now I need to throttle someone. Max, take him out, shut the door behind you and wait there.'

Outside the office, Zina's bodyguards and kitchen staff stood unfazed, as if they'd seen and heard it all before. Randolph put his hands atop his head, attempting to cover his bald patches, and slunk off, as composed as he could manage.

He spent most of the weekend developing a comb over technique in front of his bathroom mirror to hide the bald patches he now had to contend with. Would they ever grow back? His brief fantasy of Zina had been smashed to smithereens. She was absurd, deranged even-- certainly not the sweet girl he had taken her for. She had wounded his name and torn out his hair. He resolved to have nothing more to do with her. On Sunday afternoon, however, there came a knock at the door. He peeped through the spyhole and saw, in fish-eye, one of Zina's bodyguards standing there holding a heart-shaped, pink cardboard box tied up with a lavender bow. Randolph opened the door and took the box from the denim-clad Adonis who handed it over without a word and went on his way.

Inside the box were a dozen cupcakes of similar decoration to the ones she'd shared with him on his visit to her dressing room. There was a handwritten note on lavender scented stationery amongst them...*Tristram, please let us be friends, I don't know what came over me, I behaved like a wild animal! It must the effect you have upon women. I am so looking forward to seeing you at the Panto rehearsals next week. Don't let me down, darling... such fun we will have!* He couldn't quite believe it. He made himself some tea and helped himself to a couple of the cupcakes, re-reading the Dame's hilarious lines and almost forgetting about his hair. Zina had sorely abused him...but he was an actor and his craft must come first. He would put personal slights aside for...the show must go on.

21

As decreed, Randolph was summoned into Zara's office the next morning between two of his English classes. He knew he was meant to appear chastened before her but his frame of mind was actually one of indifference. He had a brilliant acting job before him. That was his focus now. Fortuitously, it involved a wig but what of other possible roles to follow? How might bald patches affect his prospects? Hopefully, his concerns would prove premature. His transplant had come with a three year guarantee. He'd return home over Christmas and get some restoration work. Naturally, he'd refrain from telling them that he'd been attacked by a wild cat. He'd have to ask Golmar *again* when his passport would be ready– they'd had it more than three months now!

'I see you as a victim, Tristram, hoodwinked into this by my sister who, beneath her superficial vapidity, has a scheming nature and is subject to bouts of manic hysteria,' Zara told him after inviting him to sit down, 'I presume you had no idea of the feud between us?'

Randolph responded in the negative, shaking his head slowly and putting on his best downcast look.

'I'm sure you can see how frivolous she is. Her name, after all, means 'charm', or rather 'trinket', in Kebapi, which just about sums her up...alluring at first but scratch through the plated surface and you will find a cheap piece of trash. My name, on the other hand, means 'queen' which, as father likes to point out, indicates my demeanor perfectly, a point well worth your taking note of.' She paused and looked at him intently, 'It is common knowledge that father *created* the National Theatre expressly *for* Zina to keep her out of mischief. It usually absorbs her and had, for some time, been keeping her on the straight and narrow-- until *you* came along, but you have merely been the catalyst. Of course, everyone in our social circle knows she is totally crazy. She once tried to strangle my Yorkshire terrier.'

'But I thought—' Randolph began but there was a knock on the door.

Golmar entered. 'Mr McNadger and Miss Mealy are here, Ms Zoran.'

Zara asked her to show them in and there they were-- all smiles, shaking hands with Randolph who hadn't the faintest idea who they were or why they were there.

'Nobby,' McNadger said in an Australian drawl, 'You must be Tristram. Pleased to meet you, mate. Heard a lot about you from Zara.'

'Really?' Randolph asked, 'Because I haven't heard anything about you. I've always wanted to meet someone named 'Nobby' though. Such a curious nickname. What's it actually short for?'

'Well, in my case, mate, it's not short for anything. My real name's Neil, so twice as many syllables there. How about yourself? What's Tristram meaning?'

'It's a bit of a contradiction. In Celtic it means 'one who makes a big noise' but in Latin, of course, it means 'one who is full of sorrows.''

'Well, I'm glad to tell you,' Nobby gave him a hearty slap on the back, 'Your sorrows are coming to an end, mate, 'cos it looks like you're on the road to Knowledge City.'

Randolph had known in theory that brawny, bluff Australians who repeatedly addressed one as 'mate' were out there but he had somehow managed never to meet one. How odd to come across one for the first time in Diskebapisbad of all places. 'And where, or what, is

'Knowledge City', if I may be so bold, Nobby?' he enquired.

Here Miss Mealy stepped in. She was a papery thin American with a smiling skull face and a dyed fuzz of black hair that looked like a child's drawing of a thundercloud tentatively balanced on the back of her head. She appeared to be attempting power dressing with chunky plastic jewelry and a pillar box red polyester trouser suit but to Randolph she was, by virtue of these appurtenances, a washout.

'Well may you ask, Tristram!' she crowed. 'And please call me Kay, okay? Knowledge City is both a 'where' and a 'what'. On the one hand it's the fastest growing private university in the Middle East, recently ranked in the Top 1,000 Universities Under 50 Years Old Worldwide.'

This immediately revealed to Randolph that it must be somewhere in the bottom 100, or else she'd have described it as being among the top 7, 8 or 900. He also wondered whether there were, in fact, more than 1,000 universities worldwide under 50 years old.

'On the other hand,' Kay Mealy continued 'It's the largest chain of for-profit schools across the Mid-Eastern/Central Asian/North African region... But let's not have me tell you the incredible story of the rise and rise of Knowledge City, Tristram. I've got our company video on my hard-drive so you can see it for yourself. As soon as Ms Zoran saw it, she got us right out here.'

The video revealed the tale of Knowledge City which began during the impoverished youth of its founder, Dr Abu-Walid Abd-El-Fadl, whom Randolph thought from the black and white photos of him in his early years bore a remarkable resemblance to Walt Disney. As a scholarship pupil at the American University of Beirut in the early 1960s, Abu-Walid, his Doctorate as yet a twinkle in his eye, had begun to tutor his wealthier, less studious classmates to keep his well-oiled head above water. His results were good. His reputation grew. Upon graduation, he invested his tutorial savings into starting up a crammer school for the Lebanese high school final exams and civil service entrance tests.

At first, all had gone well-- but to young Abd-El-Fadl's shock and dismay-- not all his staff shared his talent or his motivation. Their cramming sessions were lacklustre and so too were their pupils' results. What to do? What to do? Abu-Walid Abd-El-Fadl racked his overstocked brain. And hark, it came to him-- what if...what if...he could pre-package not only content, as in a normal textbook, but also delivery so that teaching could become nothing more than 'reading a script', a fully prepared one, with all the direction already in place. Teachers would become interchangeable cogs in one great big school machine. True, charisma and excellence might be eliminated but, on the flip-side, so could incompetence and indolence, which were far more frequent.

Thus was born the encyclopedia-wide set of extra-thick ring-binders known as the Curricula of Comprehensive Knowledge System, nowadays more conveniently situated in the Microsoft and Google, Oracular or Ali-Babian clouds and implemented at 48 schools, directly owned or franchised, from Mongolia in the east to Morocco to the west. With the dawn of the 21st century came expansion into the United States with Divine Intervention Charter Schools in inner city districts crisscrossing the Rust and Bible belts. In the present decade 'the Knowledge' had even arrived in England, reviving failing state schools under the flagship Treadwater and Slogmore Academy brand names in London.

The video ended with swelling music that Randolph instantly recognized as the martial closing bars of the Kebapi national anthem, which must've been specially inserted for the occasion.

'You know, Tristram,' Kay Mealy oozed, 'It is just so

great to touch base with you after Zara reached out to us.'

Randolph writhed inwardly but managed to twist his mouth into a feeble smile. 'Sorry but I continue to have no idea why you're both here. I *think* you're saying something about our school going 'under the umbrella' of Knowledge City. All I can say to that is, do as you wish. I can only suggest that you don't adopt the name. It's a silly name for a school, even more so for a university.'

'No sillier than *Swine*forth, I'd say mate,' Nobby-nee-Neil put in sarcastically.

'In some ways, yes, but Knowledge City is more immediately absurd in its redundant obviousness, isn't it? It's like calling a hospital 'Medicine Towers'. It's your choice, Zara, though I do wonder how many days it will take for secondary school pupils to reduce your 'Curriculum of Coordinated Knowledge' to its acronymic form.'

The two Knowledge City representatives eyed him as if he were a volatile substance but Randolph no longer cared. He was ready, there and then, to wash his hands of the whole asinine business.

'Tristram, if I may—' Kay Mealy insisted, 'As I explained, Zara reached out to us and we have come over here to devote ourselves, 24/7, to finding a way forward. I think your aura of negativity isn't contributing to that team goal at present. You need to give us some leverage to help us to help you.'

'Do what you will, I shan't thwart you,' Randolph shrugged, 'I'm sorry but I find your corporate bombast so exasperating that all I want to 'reach out' for right now is a stiff gin and tonic.'

Zara then gave him the news that Swainson had written to her, very disappointed about the termination of Gemmy and Gabby's contracts. Nor was he too pleased about Randolph doubling as the English and Drama teacher. Swainson was even threatening to withdraw his support and the Swineforth name with it so Knowledge City had now been brought in preparation to take the reins, should things go awry with the Swineforth partnership. They were, furthermore, guaranteeing a level of pedagogical quality control which they claimed Randolph's leadership had wholly failed to deliver.

Kay Mealy, being an ex-Head of English, informed Randolph she would be 'shadowing' him for the rest of the week, observing his English lessons. He objected that he was an impromptu English teacher who'd been press-ganged into the classroom. In response, she pointed out pertly that under the Knowledge City system this sort of thing would pose no problem, would it? She offered to let him give the English C.O.C.K. a trial. She had it right there on her hard drive. He was sorely tempted as it would have made his life easier, converting his lessons into a dramatic cold reading at which, no doubt, he'd have excelled. His pride got the better of him though and he declined, insisting on sticking with his resources and methods...for this week anyway. 'You can lead a horse to water but you can't make it drink,' was her only comment. She thenceforth tracked his every move in the classroom upon several pages of forms on a clipboard. He suspected that she'd determined from the outset to give him the worst possible score.

At the end of the school day, Zara took over observing him. As he walked out the ornate school gate to wait for his taxi, she casually asked him, 'Going somewhere *nice* this evening?'

'Well, yes, actually, I'm starring in the National Theatre's Christmas panto!'

Zara's eyes widened, in admiration he thought for a moment until he realized it was rage. 'I would have thought you had learned your lesson. But since you have not, may I remind you it is stated in your contract that you may not do any work outside this school, paid or otherwise!'

'But I'll let down the show if I don't honour my commitment. A real actor just doesn't do that.'

'Let me tell you, Tristram, if you continue to take part in this panto, it will not be the first nail in your coffin but it may well prove the last.'

He dithered for a moment, then threw caution to the wind and got into the taxi that had stopped in front of him. The days might be dismal as he watched his headmaster career ebbing away but the rehearsals for the panto were tremendous. There was Zina in her green tunic and tights, a sight to behold. She'd had her wicked way with him, achieved what she'd wanted with Zara so there was fortunately no prospect of further shenanigans. The company was so welcoming and eager for his tips about British humor and making the most out of the gags. He felt truly appreciated.

The following morning Randolph was staggered to see Nobby McNadger sitting at *his* desk wearing headmasterly half-moon, gold-rimmed spectacles, with Kay Mealy bringing him papers out of *his* filing cabinet.

'G'day Tristram, mate,' McNadger gave him a wry smile, 'Just checking all your papers are in order.'

'Why?' Randolph enquired, 'Am I going to die?'

'Ha, ha!' brayed Kay Mealy. She laughed too much for Randolph's comfort, and when she wasn't laughing, the shadow of her mocking skeleton smile was etched into her drawn, translucent skin, even when she was saying something serious. Randolph resolved to call them inwardly the Big Mac and the Happy Meal from that moment forward as a humorous coping mechanism for his inevitable demise.

'You know, Tristram mate, that if Swineforth International were to become Knowledge City Diskebapisbad, you wouldn't need any of this. Vision statements, policy documents, schemes of work, assessment rubrics, your faculty handbook, your behaviour code, the whole kaboodle, it's all provided for you from corporate HQ in Dubai. Why reinvent the wheel? At plenty of KC schools, the head's the bursar because the only thing that needs human monitoring is expenditure. No need for principals because whatever a parent asks about something, or complains about something, it's all there in black and white already. And if something does come up that's not in the paperwork, then all a school has to do is ring up head office and they tell you what to do within 24 hours. Whether for the kids or the adults in charge of 'em, it's a no-brainer. And because nobody needs to sit round scratching their heads thinking all day, everyone can get on with what matters.'

'So, what is it that matters, Nobby?'

'Learning, Tristram.'

'Yes but, learning what?'

'Skills and facts, mate, facts and skills. The stuff needed to excel on exams and eventually land a well-paid job. What else are primary and secondary education for, tertiary maybe even more?'

Called upon to defend his realm for the first time, Randolph determined to rise to the occasion with grandeur he knew himself to be capable of in a serious role upon the stage. He drew a deep breath, raised his chin, looked out of the window into the middle distance and made ready to perorate:

'Well Nobby, I'm afraid I must beg to differ. I studied Theatre at university and there were no drama lessons at my school. My father read Philosophy at Oxford but went on to become a successful inventor, though the two are unrelated in any practical sense. What is more, I am a product, as both pupil and teacher, of British public, which is to say private, schools. In such schools, the Head hardly fulfils the mundane managerial and administrative functions to which you have alluded. He or she is instead primarily a symbol-'

'Oho, I see, very posh,' the Big Mac interrupted,

'And what do you symbolize in this place, Tristram? How to wear a designer belt?'

'In a sense, yes, Nobby,' Randolph continued unswayed, 'One's role, if I may draw the analogy, should be likened to that of a captain of a ship of the line in the heyday of sail. The mates and the middies run the vessel. Other than in times of crisis, the Captain is simply present, available for consultation. Kurt Hahn, the founder of Gordonstoun, which was attended by Princes Philip and Charles, was once asked what his function as a Head boiled down to, do you know what he answered?'

'I dunno, Tristram? I guess you'd enlighten me, being a mere Australian state school man myself.'

'It was, 'To walk about', which is to say, 'To be...to see...and to be seen seeing!''

'Well, 'Veni, Vidi, Vici' for him, mate, or should I say, Cap'n, and in your case, Tris, one who'd better get ready to go down with his ship.'

At this opportune moment, it happened that Brian wandered, lonely as a cloud, his hair upstanding upon his pate, into Randolph's office. 'Mr Randolph, sir, any word on what became of the Emporium?' Brian didn't even seem to notice it was the Big Mac and not Randolph sitting symbolically at the head's desk, probably because he had something of a look of Randolph with the gold-rimmed, half-moon glasses and all.

'I'm over here, Brian,' Randolph called from an armchair upholstered in vinyl in the corner where he was quickly looking up an activity for his next class, 'I can't think what Emporium you mean.'

'You know, the Asian cafe and shop Gemma and Gabby went to of an evening. Sold lovely noodle soups and suchlike and you could buy, prawn crackers and other crunchy novelty foods. I tagged along with them now and then. I asked you about it during the Kebapistan play...don't you remember, the little place that got knocked down. I found the fellow's glasses among the rubble. I still have them if you know where I can send them to,' and he held the glasses up, scratched, twisted and beyond repair.

'That was an unlisted business, Brian!' Zara walked briskly up to Randolph's former desk with further paperwork for the Big Mac's perusal. 'We don't allow these pop-up enterprises in Kebapistan so Max organized their eviction from the property and it was then demolished to prevent any further illegal activities taking place there. Besides, the proprietors were mentally disturbed and in need of treatment.'

'I had my doubts at first but I came round to liking them very much,' Brian opined cordially.

'Randolph, I'd like to see you in my office, please,' Zara said as she bustled out, presumably expecting him to follow her. It was the first time she'd ever addressed him by his surname alone and he, therefore, suspected the worse.

'I had nothing to do with this Emporium Brian was going about,' was the first thing Randolph said as he followed her into her office.

'Shut the door please and sit down,' she replied. He did as she asked and lowered himself into the chair in front of her desk to receive his next telling off. 'Messrs. Swainson and Dare have just written to me to cancel their visit during the first week of December due to false flags being raised by troublemaking western NGOs that my father's election on the last day of November will not be a 'free and fair' one. I strongly suggest that cancellation of the right to use the Swineforth name will follow at the end of the term, not that I care; there is nothing they can do about my continuing to use it as I long as I like. That is why I have my Swineforth replacement lined up. I expect that you will support me in this as it is I who pay your wages, not to mention ensuring your continued security and liberty, if you take my meaning.'

Randolph sighed. 'Very well, Zara, and what is your plan for me?'

'You will continue as headmaster slash English teacher until the end of the school year for the sake of continuity. However, the Knowledge City Recommended Pay Scale will be implemented immediately, which will result in a reduction of your salary. If you wish, you are free to reapply for your job, or another post here, in Spring as we prepare to complete the changeover to Knowledge City.'

Randolph smiled and nodded. He had absolutely no intention of grovelling for his silly job, but he wouldn't be showing her his hand. He would stay the year out on his slashed salary and then either go on to be head at a better school, or see if Zina offered him a permanent place in her acting company. 'And what of Brian?'

'Brian is not able to move on from the ducks so close to his heart so I won't be retaining him after this school year. He's also had some unexcused days off, I suspect for fossil hunting out in the northern mountains with that Preyn character. We will, however, retain the local hires who have been superb members of staff and haven't missed a day."

Hmm, thought Randolph, *if they're incomparably cheap you can forget about the theft and corruption.*

'And I am thinking what to do with Mark Gall,' she mused, 'He may be a little harsh with Gerald and seems totally indifferent to Felicity-- which is odd when she is such a beautiful and well-mannered young lady— but he has formed a firm friendship with Max, and that is of great value as Max is a very solitary person.'

How sweet, Randolph mused, *A psychopathic match made in heaven.*

The following Tuesday, Golmar brought Randolph news that Brian had, yet again, been detained in the northern mountains after what was supposed to be another weekend of fossil hunting with Dr Preyn. Golmar had been out there herself taking one of the two annual personal days she was entitled to.

'They will be back as soon as they can, Mr Randolph,' Golmar apologized on Brian's behalf, 'It's just they've found the Lophogallus fossil, which will turn the avian world on its head. It's a major scientific discovery which will also, as I have mentioned, prove very embarrassing for the president.'

'Why would that be again, Golmar? I find it difficult to keep track of these things.' Randolph puzzled.

'Let me show you the little recording I made of Brian on my phone at the site yesterday,' she said and pressed play...

'Have a gander at the auriculars on this one, Mr Randolph!' Brian was in a state of animation, chipping at a fossil at the rock face, 'Almost certainly the Lophogallus. We've been out here the last few weekends, but I've done most of the unearthing as Dr Preyn has to be in his tent with our Dalibor guides perusing maps and such like along with making the armory of our evidence shipshape as he tells me we have to be prepared for hostility in the wake of this find. Barbara, my wife told me I needed to break out of my boundaries and that's certainly what's happening for me now, Mr Randolph, thanks to you.' Brian pointed at part of the fossil which looked very abstract to Randolph, 'You see that across from the speculum, there is some faint evidence of a single feather and the faint outline of a tassel at the chest which is the proof that this is indeed the Lophogallus and that the turkey originated in these parts. Oh, if only fossils would show us the iridescence of those long vanished plumes that once astounded their avian neighbours!' There was then a long shot of Brian's face with a far off look as if he were imagining the ancient creature upon its primeval heath, the screeches of other avian dinosaurs filling the air.

Walking up the steps to his front door, Randolph heard the sound of a running bath coming from Gemmy's flat and the sound of a woman singing something military in Kebapi from Gabby's apartment. *Replacements?* Randolph speculated. He knocked on Gemmy's former door, then knocked again louder. The bath was suddenly turned off and angry footsteps stomped to the door. Answering the door in one of Gemmy's flimsy dressing gowns was none other than Pyro Envany!

'Pyro! What on earth are you doing in there?' Randolph exclaimed.

'And why shouldn't I be here?' Pyro barked, being his typical confrontational self, 'I heard it was your phoboxenic decision that we shouldn't be given accommodation from the start. Can you explain this?'

'What a load of tosh and you have no right to speak to me in that way!'

From Gabby's old apartment just along the corridor, Volta stuck her head around the door. 'It is not tush, Mr Randolph. That is what we were told and that is what we are believing.'

'Well, it's rubbish. What difference could it make to me whether you two lived on campus or in town? Anyway, Pyro, why the hell are you in woman's dressing gown, or shouldn't I ask?'

'I am simply using what was in here when I arrived.'

'So, they didn't do such a good job of sending on Gabby and Gemmy's things then?' Randolph mused more to himself.

'Those things are of no use to me,' Volta shouted over, 'The Gabby was wider than she was tall which means the clothes are not fitting me. However, I will be cutting them to pieces to use as handkerchiefs.'

Randolph enquired as to how they'd got the keys and they told him Golmar had eventually handed them over when they had been to see her a few times, 'suggesting' they should use the empty flats. They then had the cheek to give him a veiled threat, advising him to keep quiet about the arrangement or they would put even less effort into their classes. Finally they reminded him that he couldn't do anything to them now anyhow because he was 'washed off' and only a 'head figure' since Swinelorth International would soon be part of the Knowledge City. He rolled his eyes and sloped off to his apartment to get changed for rehearsal.

There was a strange atmosphere in downtown Diskebapisbad that night. Randolph, travelling by taxi as usual, was stopped at three roadblocks. Apparently, there was always an intense army presence in the week before the presidential election but this put Randolph in mind of a war zone-- armoured barriers, soldiers in flak jackets armed with assault rifles and festooned with ammunition and gas canisters, bazookas and mortars propped up and ready to fire. He still didn't have his passport to show them, but had a letter on National Theatre stationery and signed by Zina, which he carried folded in his wallet that seemed to appease them. Golmar had promised him that the officials handling his visa and holding his passport had promised them that it would be back in his hands next week, allowing him to take his flight home for Christmas the week after that.

It was to be an important rehearsal, the first full dress, but many members of the cast were late due to the roadblocks. Zina laughed it off, 'It is like this every five years when Daddy has his election...he is just being over-cautious in case the small minority of jealous people who dislike him try something reckless. There is no need at all to worry, Tristram. Unlike its neighbours, this country has been at peace since the fall of the Soviet Union because Daddy has been in power dedicating himself to ensuring that.'

'But will the show still go on in these times of tension?' Randolph asked her.

'Of course!' she scoffed, 'Except for a handful of nervous ninnies who have run off to Russia, the whole Kebapi elite is here. They are just staying at home, lying low. We have an assured full house.'

It was going to be a great show and Randolph, in his role as Mrs Smee, secretly felt sure he was sure to steal the limelight. His costume consisted of a bodice with a well stuffed chest in a brocade of turquoise and silver, which attached to a hoop skirt that gave him a stunning hourglass figure that was like a caricature of Zina's own. He had a wig of tightly curled royal blue hair topped off with a plum-coloured velvet ribbon, punishingly high pink platforms, and make up consisting of thick curling false eyelashes, turquoise eyeshadow and purple lipstick. Strangely enough, Zina couldn't leave him alone when he was in costume and kept fondling his false bust in the wings. They had joked with the cast that he'd been eating too much hormone-pumped superbeast steak.

The run-through went on into the wee hours and, as they left the National Theatre when it was over, the cast's laughter rang out in the cold, deserted streets. Randolph suggested they all go out for drink but one of Zina's denim-clad bodyguards told him everything was shut. There was a curfew in place and everyone had to be at home by 7pm, with the exception of Zina's cast whose names were on a special list. As no taxis were permitted to be out either, a fleet of armoured military jeeps were at the cast's disposal, lined up at the front of the theatre.

22

The following morning, Randolph went to his usual spot at the main entrance to greet the pupils as they came off the buses. He looked at his watch. They were running late today. Must be the roadblocks, he thought. Twenty minutes later, still standing about aimlessly, he looked at his watch again, wondering whether it might be some national day of which Golmar had neglected to apprise him. Then he heard footsteps running behind him and there was Golmar herself, carrying a cardboard box, her eyes wild, as if she were fleeing the building.

'What on earth is going on, Golmar? Is there a fire?'

'The revolution. It's started!' she panted, looking more excited than fearful.

'So, is there no school today?' Randolph asked confused.

She suddenly stopped in front of him, placed a hand on his shoulder and, looking straight into his eyes said, 'No school, Sir. Today is an undeclared holiday, one I have been waiting half my life for, and Kebapistan since before I was born.'

Then she continued on, rushing toward her old Lada. She flung open the door, threw the box into the passenger seat, got in and turned on the engine. But before she moved off, she rolled down her window, and leaning out while waving her raised fist, shouted joyously in his direction, 'Down with Zoran! Free Kebapistan!'

'Wait! Where's my passport?' he shouted back, but she was already far away.

Randolph looked over toward the city. He saw smoke rising and then heard gunshots. He noticed that a group of about 10 people who had been sweeping the road to his right suddenly stopped what they were doing and looked over toward the smoke. They appeared to collectively notice that there was no armed guard shadowing them on a scooter any longer and began talking in hushed voices. The next moment, they had all thrown down their brushes and were jogging off in different directions into the open desert in pairs, or singularly. Perhaps, he thought, that gives them more of a chance to escape...every man for himself and all that. But escape from what? What was coming? More gunshots, with mortar fire, seemingly closer now. He dashed for cover, heading for the back of the school site to see if he could find any Dalibor labourers for a lift to the airport on a motorbike, a quad bike, a donkey cart... anything. But it was deserted. They'd probably downed tools and gone off to join the revolution. He shot across the quadrangle, glancing up for any evidence of snipers, and saw that the giant Kebapi flag with the image of President Zoran had been ripped down and trampled in the dust. *Oh God, they're here!* he thought. He darted to the front of the school again to see if there was anyone at all he could stop who was heading to the airport. Driving toward him with the city behind them was an estate car loaded with people, followed by a van with a huge fold-up satellite dish on top. Randolph waved wildly. They noticed him and swerved off the main road into the car park in a cloud of dust.

The man in the passenger seat rolled down his window and, in a Newcastle accent, asked Randolph 'Are you the contact?'

'What? Er, no, what do you mean?' Randolph stuttered, 'I'm the headmaster of Swineforth Hospital International, the school behind me.'

Seven or eight people in flak jackets, armed with microphones and cameras disgorged themselves from the car and rushed to him. Randolph tried to take a step back but they engulfed him.

'Could you tell us your name?' the first reporter demanded, lunging at him, Randolph saw on his identity badge that he was from the BBC and even recognised his voice from Radio 4, which was permanently on in his parents' kitchen.

'Randolph's the name, Tris Randolph,' he smiled into the cameras, taking care to show his best side.

'Chris Gandalf?' one of them shouted out, 'Sorry, the eardrums have been a little pummeled by the mortar blasts.'

'Tristram Randolph,' he proclaimed again in best received pronunciation with an added rolling of Rs. 'Great Great Grandson of Sir Gannet Vainglory, British Ambassador to the Sultanate of Mish Lope, as this country was known in the age of Victoria. I came here to continue his great work-- where he held out the golden bidet of peace, I came to offer the boon of a public school education in the hope for-'

'Have you closed your school down?' a woman interrupted Randolph's oratory. He had seen her before on the telly. She was that hard-as-nails Northern Irish one who always covered the riskiest stories.

'Well, of course, we have to put safety first in any school environment, wherever we are in the world, thus instilling in foreign countries an example of British conduct in times of great danger.'

'And will you be staying in the school with us?'

'Of course I will stay. As the captain goes down on his ship, if necessary, so the headmaster with his- But, sorry, did you just say you were staying *here*?'

'That is alright with you, isn't it?' someone said, 'We were told there was a half-built school here with empty flats that we could use a base for reporting over the next few days.'

'Yes, it's alright with me but aren't you heading to the airport? I was hoping you'd be able to give me a lift.'

'Naw, we've just come from there yesterday, bro,' another chipped in. He pointed round to the others one by one. 'BBC, CNN, Reuters, UPI, Al Jazeera, freelance, freelance. You can count on us turning up at times like these to show the world democracy in the making.'

'You mean the rebellion won't be quelled?' Randolph asked.

'No, looks like Zoran's reign of terror is at an end and the rebels will win,' the Radio 4 man smiled.

'Reign of terror...?' Randolph echoed.

They piled back into the car, Randolph directing them toward the faculty housing block like an experienced car park attendant. Then he stood there smiling and waving them on their way. As soon as they were out of sight, he whipped out his mobile phone. No network. No wonder-- it was called Zorantel and had probably been shut down to thwart rebellion communication. He dashed into his office to try the phone on his desk. He had a few landline numbers on his contacts list, Zina for one, who'd be sure to help him, if only because Zara wouldn't. He couldn't get a dialling tone but it didn't stop him pleading 'Hello, hello, is anybody there? Please answer me! Please! It's Chris Gandalf– I mean Tristram Randolph. I'm...I'm still here, waiting, at the school I need to get out of here. Please help me!'

'You didn't run away with the rest of them!' a voice finally replied.

'No, I'm still here, can you help me get out?' Randolph blurted into the phone.

'I'm amazed you had the balls to stick around this long,' the voice came again, but it wasn't on the phone, it was behind him.

'What on earth?' Randolph spun around to see Mark Gall regarding him from the vinyl chair in the corner, attired in the uniform of the presidential guard...brown trousers tucked into knee socks, 'Are you supposed to be dressed like that Gall?'

'I've been recruited to fight in the president's security force,' he smiled smugly, 'Get a load of this weaponry!' He held open his jacket to reveal two guns strapped to his chest on crossed holsters and another strapped to each thigh. He took a grenade out of one of the jacket's several bulging pockets and started to repeatedly throw it a couple of inches in the air and catch it again. 'I'm looking forward to blowing the brains out of any reb that crosses my path. I plan to be the last man standing and I have a special confession just for you 'boss', when I have no one left to fight with, I'll *wound* myself.'

'You want to be careful that doesn't go off by accident, Mark,' Randolph said, starting to edge around his desk.

Gall nonchalantly drew out a pistol and pointed it at Randolph's head, gazing down the muzzle with dead eyes. 'I wouldn't go anywhere if I were you. We'd need to have a word, if you don't mind sitting down on that chair there.'

We?' Randolph murmured as he lowered himself into the chair.

Max entered, also in the full military attire, with an accordion file folder under his arm, 'I would like you to know, Mr Randolph, that there is an extensive file on you in the Ministry of Security.'

'What? Me? I don't know what you're talking about!' Randolph exclaimed.

'What do you know about the fuck?' Max snarled.

'Sorry, Max, I'm not following your English, do you mean, 'What the fuck do I know about.... something or other?''

'He means what he says,' Gall snapped, 'What do you know about the fuck or, as it appropriately translates into English, the F.U.C.K., the Freedom & Unity Committee of Kabapistan. The gutter press are having a field day with it.'

'I have absolutely no idea what you're talking

about—'

'Preyn,' Gall snarled, drawing out the vowels, 'Dr Ka-la-muz Pre-yn.'

Randolph recalled the name, 'You mean the little old man from the museum?'

'We are aware you have had a secret meeting with him,' Max was in his element, unveiling all the underlying aggression that he had barely been able to mask in his role of office boy.

'For Christ's sake, he told me and my parents a story about a golden bidet. It was hardly revolutionary plotting!' Randolph would have found the situation laughable if Mark Gall hadn't still been pointing a gun at him.

Max opened the file he'd been holding and spread surveillance photographs of Randolph out on the desk, including a couple of him looking shifty holding a manila envelope. Randolph stared at them for a while in disbelief until it dawned upon him that they were pictures of him from the day he'd visited the prison with Golmar and his parents. He remembered being terribly nervous about going in there but his facial expression made it look more like he was up to something dodgy, glancing over his shoulder in one, putting the manila envelope inside his jacket in another.

'This is the day you entered the prison under false pretences with this person of high priority interest,' and Max laid his heavy index finger on Golmar's face, covering it over as if to eradicate her.

'What? It wasn't false pretences...my parents were researching one of our ancestors! Which is also why we went to see Dr Preyn. Ask them!'

'How can I?' Max shrugged, 'They are in England and we cannot call them as the phone lines have been cut across the city and the country by your Dalibor friends.'

'They're not my friends! I don't know anything about the Dalibors except that they have—'

'A few weeks ago Golmar smuggled keys into the prison in your presence-'

'No, she did not! She distributed bread rolls! Oh God, were there keys inside?'

'Exactly. You are complicit.'

'No, no, I had no clue. It just dawned on me! Please!'

'This morning most of the convicts broke out using these keys in what the rebels have called 'Operation Pandemonium' and now I hear they have released the mammoth beefs who are running amok, interfering with our advance on the rebels surrounding Diskebapisbad in the desert. In Jizbizisbad and Zoranisbad there is widespread looting and hijacking thanks to the actions of your friends. Senior government officials connected with national security have been murdered.'

'Listen, Golmar isn't my friend,' Randolph pleaded, 'I only see her at work. It was Zara who appointed her as my PA.'

'Please, be careful what you say, Mr Randolph, as you are now implicating the president's daughter in this revolution. This is an offence that could lead to summary execution.'

'I'm not! I swear! I'm sure Zara had no idea about Golmar either!'

'Your PA is now on her way to join the intellectual leader of this revolution, Dr Kalamuz Preyn, who is out at his mountain base with his deputy Brian Eider-Drake, yet another colleague slash friend of yours.'

'Brian is hardly a revolutionary deputy!' Randolph almost laughed, 'He's out there collecting fossils! He was obviously being used as a red herring.'

'Lies, Mr Randolph. I know herring is a fish and it is not even imported into Kebapistan. What is your connection to the assassinated revolutionary cell leader from Jizbizisbad, Barnaby Glibly? For what purpose did you have your parents smuggle his teenage son out of the country?'

This was too much for Randolph. He felt hysteria

rising, 'I...I...I didn't. It was all mother's idea. Because...because he's a distant relation. They...think they can get...get him a viscountcy.'

'So, you are a related to a known revolutionary in the eastern provinces. And you plotted to come to Kebapistan in order to give succour to his family. You are being arrested for treason, Tristram Randolph. You are to be interrogated and I promise you, we will learn exactly what is this viscountcy.'

Randolph recalled the interview room at the prison where he'd had his photo taken for a giggle on the ironing board thing. He clung onto the armrests of his chair, pleading with them in tears. Then there was Zara, suddenly striding into the room wearing a military-chic jumpsuit, of the same brown hue as Mark and Max's only with exaggerated martial embellishments, sewn on stripes, golden frogging and the like, topped off with a fascinator modelled on the dragon-like creature he had noticed on her ring when they first met and on the gates of the presidential palace.

'Zara, please don't let them do this, please!' Randolph blubbered.

'I've been listening to this entire litany of treachery from my office and I am appalled, just appalled!' she hectored him, 'Worse still, I have learned from Pyro and Volta that you gave them permission to live on campus and told foreign correspondents that they were welcome to break into the faculty apartments and use these as their base in the full knowledge that they are supporting this rebellion.'

'That was Golmar, who told Pyro and Volta they could live here, not me!'

'Blaming Golmar again, eh! Like with the t-shirts *she* designed?'

'Alright, it was me that time but she gave the local hires the keys! And someone had already told the journalists they could set up camp here when I met them. Maybe it was McNadger and Mealy?'

'I think not, Tristram. I had them flown out of the country in the early hours. In any case, I have no time for this inane back and forth. Take him away.'

Gall stepped toward him and put the gun to the side of his head. Randolph winced with terror and he shut his eyes. A few moments later, he became aware that he had wet himself.

'Ha, look Max, he has pissed his fancy pants!' Gall sniggered.

Max guffawed. It was first time Randolph had ever heard him laugh.

'Move!' Gall marched him out into an army jeep waiting at the front of the school. Randolph could see that it was particularly gratifying for Gall to handcuff him the front seat. It must have been more gratifying to him still when Randolph slumped over in a dead faint as they roared off down the airport road to deliver him to jail.

23

When Randolph awoke, he was afraid to open his eyes. He was lying on what felt like a plank of wood and there was a stench of stale urine and body odour all around him. He heard a shuffling sound which abruptly ceased. Slowly, he built up the courage to open his eyes. Standing over him was a wild-eyed man with tangled hair and wasted cheeks. Randolph cried out and recoiled, putting out his hands to shield himself from the repugnant being. He couldn't believe what he was seeing, but - the horror, the horror - it was the shredded underpants turkey man and he was locked up in a cell with him.

'Did you wear a turkey hat too?' the man asked coyly in a Liverpudlian accent.

'No, I didn't do anything. I shouldn't be here,' Randolph whispered back aghast and edging toward a slop bucket in the corner.

'I shouldn't be here either. That's why I'm scratching a tunnel.' The man indicated a tiny depression in the floor and demonstrated his digging technique with his gnarled toenails. 'Sorry, I'm forgetting my manners, Tom Thomas, pleased to meet you.'

Randolph was momentarily stunned by the coincidence. How bizarre that this man who had made him think of Poor Tom when he'd first seen him, should be a real poor Tom. He had no wish to shake Tom's hand as he smelled appalling, but felt he should strive to maintain a civil relationship, given that the fellow was, as befit his name and appearance, mad. 'Tristram...How long have you, erm, been in here, Tom?'

'I'm not sure, Tristram. I was doing a tally on the wall over there but then, because each day was the same as every other, I found that often I couldn't remember whether I'd done it or not so I gave up.'

Randolph looked across at the hundreds of little lines scratched into the brick and shuddered. He turned to Tom sadly, 'Why on earth did you come to Kebapistan-- and in that turkey hat, of all things?'

Tom laughed and scratched his unkempt head. He sat down on the plank bed, a tad too close for comfort. Randolph sought to avert his eyes as Tom's shredded underpants scarcely shielded his modesty. 'You know how lads are on their stag do?' he began, 'My best mate suggested Kebapistan out of the blue as something completely different. I'd never heard of it, personally, but I was game for going somewhere off the beaten track. I was about to get married so why not do something outlandish while I still could? Anyhow, my best mate handed me the turkey hat as we got off the plane and said, 'Put it on, go on, we'll take some photos, it'll be a laugh.' Next thing I knew I was being wrestled to the ground and put on trial in a language I couldn't understand. I've found out since from the Amnesty fella they let in to see me that it was a set up. The guy who was my so-called best mate went back to Liverpool and married my fiancée a few months later!'

'Crikey, Tom, that's just awful!'

'I tell you, if I ever find myself back in Liverpool, I'll peck him and peck him and peck him!' Tom let out a volley of gobbling and, in his agitation, resumed with scratching his feet over the floor turkey-like.

'Peck him?'

'Yes, peck him and peck him within an inch of his life. He'll be but a worm beneath my talons.'

'But in the meantime, you're stuck scratching around here indefinitely.'

'Scratching? Yes, but don't take that too literally, Tristram. There's method in my madness. I'm hoping that by doing all the turkey stuff: scratching, gobbling, shivering my tail—' here Tom demonstrated the quiver of his lower half so that the shreds of his briefs began to oscillate—'that they'll put me in a mental hospital. I've heard they're better than this place. The beds are more comfortable and there's TV for an hour at night. But there is the drawback that they put the inmates out to work as road sweepers. Still, at least they get some sunshine and fresh air.'

A guard materialized with a tray of food, at which Tom sprang to his feet and resumed his turkey persona, gobbling vigorously and twitching his head left and right. The guard squatted and slid Randolph a dish of watery jiz-biz with a doorstep thick slice of bread turning to a paste on the top. Tom got a dish of seedy porridge on the floor with no spoon.

'How long will I be kept in here?' Randolph warbled to the guard as he stood up.

He shook his head, 'No English.'

'You have *some* English. You just said something in English,' Randolph was desperate, 'I must speak to the warden. He knows me. We had a pleasant chat over old ledgers in his office once. Please!'

But he had gone and Randolph sat down feeling wretched. He then watched Tom, amazed, as he deftly pecked at his porridge, tossing globules of the stuff into the air where it sailed in a graceful arc into his mouth.

In the days that followed, Tom was polite company, graciously turning around when Randolph had to relieve himself at or on the bucket and chatting amiably about this and that. Nevertheless, Randolph could not relax in the dreadful little cell with gunshots and mortar fire jerking him awake through the night. Sometimes when he woke up, Tom was perched on the end of his bed in the moonlight throwing a monstrous shadow on the wall, and Randolph thought he was in the middle of a nightmare in which he was in a production of *Birdy* but hadn't learned any of the lines. On the third day, the warden appeared at the door in the same linen suit but with a dandy silk handkerchief in the breast pocket. Randolph patted down his hair and tucked in his shirt in an attempt to look more presentable.

'We're ready for your interview now, Mr Randolph,' he said without smiling.

'What sort of interview?' Randolph backed away a little, 'Don't you remember me? I met you with my parents. I'm the great, great grandson of Sir Gannet Vainglory!'

'No, no, no, no interview!' Tom began running around the cell like a headless turkey.

Two guards lumbered in, took Randolph's arms and escorted him down the corridor and up the spiral stairs to the room at the top of the tower. Once inside, they strapped him to the ironing board contraption on which he'd posed but a few weeks ago for the jocular photo and now, with a crude pulley, he was being raised heavenward, parallel to the floor.

The warden addressed him: 'Mr Randolph, it is partly dues to some of your actions that we now have the state of emergency in Kebapistan. As you are the solely rebel leader to be captured so far, I am sure you can give us informations that will lead to the capture of your comrades,' the warden said calmly from the desk. Only his silhouette was visible in a shaft of light coming down from the high barred window.

'This is all a horrible mistake, I know nothing at all,' Randolph cried. His denial was not well received. The warden gave a hand signal and the guards began walking clockwise pushing the ends of the board until the cables above it were in a taut twist and the board became further elevated above their heads. The warden said a single word in Kebapi and the guards released him with a powerful shove anti-clockwise. The board spun wildly and in an instant Randolph was sickeningly dizzy. As the board came to rest jerking clockwise and anti-clockwise, the warden loomed over him and shouted in his face, 'You will be telling us the presence location of Golmar Preyn Niyaz!'

He eagerly related the circumstances of Golmar's departure in her old Lada, adding helpfully that she must have gone to join her uncle in the northern mountains. When he said that he had no idea where specifically, he was spun again, in the other direction this time. The warden asked him about her whereabouts yet again. He'd have been happy to suggest anything but he didn't have the faintest idea about names of places out in the northern mountains. He was spun a third time and his most recent bowl of jiz-biz lurched from his stomach in a projectile spew that drew a near perfect circle on the stone floor.

More questions came, of an increasingly bizarre nature...'What were the names of those members of the Dalibor tribe working on the construction site at the rear of Swinefilth school who were involved in the rebellion? Which degenerate actions did Michael Oh perform in front of his guests under the covers of his grocery store and what was his connection to the rebels? What were the revolutionary responsibilities of Mr Elderdrake, deputy of Kalamuz Preyn? Where was the evidence that Gabby Scroggins ate and of what kind was it?' All of it resulted in more spinning when he couldn't give the warden the answers he wanted. Already suffering from loose stools as a result of the prison food and terrible nerves, Randolph emptied his bowels in his suit trousers, begging them over and over to stop. Finally, when he was reduced to hysterical weeping so that he could no longer speak at all, the guards unchained him, tilted the board and let him drop to the floor.

They half carried, half dragged him back to his cell, tossed him onto the bed where he fell into a nightmare that he was one of the shaved-head sweepers, endlessly plodding the streets in blazing sun and freezing wind simultaneously. His parents passed by on a scooter and consoled him that it was alright; they had little Barney Glibly to take care of them now. When he came round, Tom was sitting by him dabbing water on his face and giving him sips of water from a metal cup. When Tom offered him blobs of seedy porridge from his fingers, he turned his head away.

He lay there thinking about the farce he'd lived through for the past few months. What a fool he'd been to deceive himself that becoming a head was his future. Zina had used him badly but only to get at Zara who had used him far worse. But, in being used, he'd come to see the truth.

The rehearsals for the panto had been the only work he'd done since starring in his final school show at Blindefellows that had brought him any satisfaction. He could deny it no longer. A life on the boards was his real vocation. He'd suppressed it while pursuing the more lucrative career in education, but he could do so no longer. Yet what was the good of his epiphany? It had come too late. After a few more torture sessions, they'd grow tired of their fun, accept that he knew nothing, take him out to some lonely courtyard, put a blindfold on him, shoot him through the head and bury him in a shallow grave. His apotheosis in the role of Mrs Smee at the National would never be realized. Some Kebapi ham actor would be thrust fumbling into the part and throw it away. Oh, the waste of it, the sorrow and the pity. Generous tears for himself flowed down his face and onto the plank and he realized he was sobbing convulsively. Such profound grief and no one to witness it but poor Tom, roosting by the bars of the cell, watching Randolph, still and silent, out of the corner of his maddened, mottled turkey's eye.

24

Randolph was awakened by a figure at the door of the cell. Although slightly obscured by the raking winter sunlight, he appeared to be dressed in a black suit and bowler hat and holding an umbrella and briefcase. He thought it might be a hallucination a la Magritte, only there wasn't an apple where the face was, just a concerned expression.

'Mr Randolph?...Tristram?' came a vibrato voice like a radio newsreader from the 1940s, 'Am I addressing Mr Tristram Randolph?'

Randolph sat up and squinted. 'Is it Mr Sneed, the barometer man?'

'Correct. Make yourself presentable, young fellow. You're coming with me.'

Tom rushed up to the bars and began gobbling frantically. 'Mr Thomas, I must ask you to step away from the door and under no circumstances to attempt to leave your cell with Mr Randolph. If you comply, you have my word that I shall return very shortly to deal with your situation. However, if you do not follow my directions now, I shall not be returning. Is that understood, Mr Thomas?'

Tom demonstrated his reluctant acquiescence by strutting away from the cell door, doing one of his bizarre underpants oscillations with each step.

Sneed then produced an enormous, strangely shaped key from his Chesterfield pocket which he used to let Randolph out. He relocked the cell door, gave Tom a small salute and told him, 'Not to worry, Mr Thomas. I am a man of my word.' He gave Randolph a gentle pat on the back and asked, 'Steady on your pins, I hope, Mr Randolph? I did put in a call to the warden to warn him not to be too hard on you.'

They then walked, without a word, down the corridor and into the main courtyard with the stacked shipping containers, now all empty, and out through the portcullis gate, which was up. Sneed opened the back door of the Bentley, spread a newspaper upon the seat and invited Randolph to sit upon it. Both the smell and the sight of his trousers, Randolph surmised, must have led him to take these measures. Sneed then walked round to the other side and got in. He spoke two words to the chauffeur which had become the most beloved in the Kebapi tongue to Randolph during the previous weeks 'Milli Teatri'...National Theatre. The city had been transformed since Randolph last saw it. As far as he could tell, it looked as if the revolutionaries had gained the upper hand. Buildings were smoking. There were burnt-out military and police trucks. The army checkpoints had been abandoned. Zoran's soldiers were no longer maintaining anything other than a fleeting presence. And the whole 'after-battle' look and feel of the streets was heightened by the dim December dusk.

'Has President Zoran stepped down?' Randolph asked in bewilderment.

'My friend, Anomaly Zoran, is not the 'stepping down' type. His government will only ever fall, as he likes to say, over his dead body. No, Tristram, it is merely that a state of stalemate has temporarily been reached in Diskebapisbad since most of the presidential forces have left the city for the northern mountain to fight the insurgency,' Sneed informed him, 'It should all be under control in the next fortnight or so. Tonight, however, the Diskebapisbad elite are quietly wending their way to the national theatre for a morale building exhibition.'

'But why bring me to witness it? I won't understand

a word.'

'Witness it, Tristram? You're an integral part of it! I am bringing you to play your part in the national panto.'

'I played it already. I was the head of a school. I had bad reviews. I got arrested and tortured.'

'You need to buck up and stop feeling sorry for yourself, young man. You've got a full house of several hundred children and adults to entertain.'

'And then straight back to jail...or will they let me go home for Christmas?'

'That depends upon you, doesn't it Tristram? Make my old friend Anomaly, his lovely daughters and his lively grandchildren laugh, despite his being surrounded by a sea of troubles, and you'll be on your way. But let them, yourself and, most importantly, the theatre down and, yes, I suppose it'll be straight back to jail.'

A brief silence passed between them during which Randolph struggled to maintain the sulky pretence that he wasn't utterly thrilled with the way things were turning out. Then he looked Sneed in the eye and said, 'Whether or not this revolution succeeds in bringing the house down, you can be sure, I will!'

'Spoken, Mr Randolph in the indomitable spirit of the great British stage actors: Kean, Tree, Irving, Olivier, and especially Sarah Bernhardt, in whose footsteps, you are, in a sense, following tonight.'

A checkpoint the size and shape of a fortress had been set up in front of the theatre but they were saluted and waved straight through. Fortunately the bunker-like building hadn't been damaged. The Bentley went round to the back where Randolph had seen Zina's crew loading up the costumes and equipment for the debacle at Swineforth International. Sneed, or Edwin as Randolph now ventured to call him, stayed in the car, explaining that he had pressing counter-revolutionary business to attend to in the intervening hours until the curtain went up. He told Randolph not to dally chatting with anyone but to head straight to Zina's office-cum-dressing room.

Zina must've known he was on the way because she was standing waiting for him, already in her Pan costume, albeit without the hat, her abundant locks still loose. She had likewise assumed a Peter posture, arms akimbo, weight on her right leg with the left out front on point. She looked taken aback for a moment when she saw him but composed herself and pointing at him playfully declared, 'Well, I hear that Mrs Hook and her former Mister have accused one of my lost boys of being very wicked and had him shut away.'

Randolph looked down, shuffled his feet and agreed, 'I'm afraid they have and they did, Peter. But I swear not a word of it is true.'

Zina pointed to an open door into the bathroom, where there was a high backed freestanding bath in the with a powerful looking standpipe tap coming out of the polished concrete floor immediately to one side of it. 'Off with those filthy school togs then. Time to get cleaned up, dressed up, made up and go out to battle.' She walked over to the bath and turned the taps. The water roared into the tub steaming. She untied a green suede string pouch she had looped to the broad belt slung loosely round her waist and tipping its contents into the tub trilled, 'Crushed Lush 'guardian of the forest' bubble bath elixir, brought personally by moi from Neverland.'

Randolph walked over to the tub and took off his shirt. He noticed her catching a whiff of him, her mouth curving down with revulsion. He pulled off his shoes with his feet. It dawned on him that owing to the 'peculiar' manner in which their intimacy, such as it was, had transpired, he had not previously been naked in front of her. She stood there staring at him as nonchalantly as before. He dropped his grimy trousers and stepped out of them but found his 50 Pound a pair Swisstouch briefs were pied brown and stuck to his skin by his dried excrement. He peeled them off, wincing when they took pubic hair with them. Zina turned away disgusted. He couldn't care less. All he wanted was to have a bath.

He woke to the sound of Zina purring, 'Treess-trahm, Treess-trahm, wakey, wakey.'

The bathwater had turned tepid and she was at her desk applying her makeup in a magnifying mirror, her hair now tucked atop her head inside her high Robin Hood hat. He looked about him. His costume and wig were on an abstract wooden manikin by the desk. His rancid clothes were gone from the floor, replaced by a large heart-shaped pink shag bath mat. A luxurious purple bath towel with the monogram 'ZZ' in pink at its corner lay folded on the standpipe. He stepped out of the bath unsteadily onto the mat and wrapped himself in the towel, feeling rather like some reeking dog that had been packed off to the grooming parlor.

Zina helped him on with his costume, wig and makeup, chatting with him the whole time, her agenda transparent from the outset

'Could I be a successful actress in England, do you think?'

Randolph smiled, 'Ah, Zina, it was hard even for me with my cornucopia of dramatic talents and skills to find regular work as an actor over there. Exceedingly stiff competition. That's what drove me to give it up and go into education. You might get the odd bit of work here and there but it's not what you know, it's – '

'--Who you know,' she jumped in, 'But if I were to have to move to London, I could afford to go to all the most exclusive parties and arrange to meet everyone I needed to know.'

He realized he was treading on thin ice and an image of Tom in his shredded pants in their jail cell flashed before his eyes. She was helping him on with his wig and he lay his left hand on her right, which was resting on his shoulder. 'It's terrible Zina but precisely because of your incredible looks, your accent--'

'I don't *have* an accent in English!'

'You do, darling; it's ever so slight and tantalizingly exotic but--'

'Do I have more of an accent than Zara?'

'Zara speaks in highly artificial received pronunciation, like someone doing a bad imitation of the Queen making her Christmas speech. Your voice and enunciation are infinitely more alluring...But to continue, I fear you'd be typecast. You'd be relegated to playing parts like the female sidekicks of Bond villains, famous ballet dancers in exile and all that sort of thing. It'd be a waste of your gifts.'

'Mmm, I see what you mean, dear Tristram,' she sighed, eyeing herself sidelong in a full length mirror.

'Something you could do, given your exceptional resources, would be to start your own, off-off West-End alternative theatre company to pursue your own vision. That's how Complicite, the finest theatre company in Britain started out when its founder members couldn't find work because they were not stock material. You should know that if you were to go that route, I would, for a moderate stipend and the honour of a place in your company, be right there by your side helping to navigate the way.'

She contemplated this a while. 'Hmm, I'll stay here unless the rebels win.'

'They might win?' Randolph writhed in his swivel chair, 'But not tonight, I trust!'

'No, not tonight but sooner or later perhaps. Daddy is pretending that it is all okay but there is fierce fighting around Jizbizisbad and the rebels have taken the northern highland city of Zoranisbad, which is a great sorrow to him as he grew up there, though obviously it was still Breshnevisbad back then.'

A moment later, the speaker on Zina's desk flashed pale pink and purple and its pacifying computer generated airport announcer voice said in English, 'Places for the performance, please. Places please.

Places.'

They walked backstage together and parted ways, she to her place and he to his. Randolph peered out into the auditorium from the wings. Every seat was taken and the atmosphere was electric with nervous tension. In the high upper circle, Randolph could make out the servants of the wealthy. He'd picked up enough from the pupils at Swineforth International to realize it would've been unimaginable for them to be allowed out to go out to the theatre during peacetime. When Anomaly Zoran took his place in the presidential box, accompanied by Zara, Felicity and Gerald, everyone stood up and applauded uproariously. Zina came onto the stage and a giant Kebapi flag with the image of President Zoran, like the one they used to use at the school, unfurled into the air above her.

How fitting, Randolph reflected, that a performance of *Peter Pan* should become a rallying cry for the regime. A panto-- what a perfect parable of this surreal Neverland and the histrionic antics of its ruling clan. Why hadn't that occurred to him before? He must've been too caught up in it all himself to realise. Being tossed into prison and tortured a bit had plucked the rose-coloured contact lenses from his eyes though. Zina was making a prefatory speech in Kebapi. God only knew what she was saying but it was certainly laden with earnest gesticulation and featured many a nod to Daddy. At the end of it, they were all on their feet again, applauding and stamping. This gave way to hands on hearts to sing the national anthem. Randolph wondered how his performance would go down after all this sincerity, chock full as it was of sophomoric innuendo, but he wasn't about to alter it now.

From the moment he set foot on stage as the dame, half-an-hour into the first half, he brought the house down with mid-revolution laughter that bordered on hysteria. His 'underwater' dance with the mermaids, a parodic tribute to synchronised swimming, showcased his fluid movement skills. Then there was his most raucous slapstick comedy moment when he pulled a rubber fish out of his bloomers and then sang a sea shanty with the pirates whilst engaging in chorus line calisthenics with swabbing mops. They ate it up too when he charged into the auditorium shrieking in operatic falsetto to escape Tick-Tock the crocodile. The children, in particular, were beside themselves with his escapades. In the past, during his years as a classroom teacher, he'd despised the loudness of the lower forms and thanked his lucky stars that he had nothing to do with primary pupils. Now, faced with a few hundred squealing, writhing kiddies, he was surprised to feel not a jot of repulsion. Rather, he found himself riding the crest of their wave of animation and felt positively ecstatic.

Everyone loved him, even that tyke, Gerald Zoran, whose eyes were now glossed over with admiration when 'Principal Randolph' did his curtsy in the curtain call to applause that matched Zina's. There was a certain longing in young Gerald's eyes and Randolph could see he too might reach a state of harmony attired in the fine chintz of the dame, if he ever were to admit it to himself. The cast returned to the stage in ensemble for a standing ovation, which Randolph perceived swelling to a crescendo when he stepped forward to take his encore bow. He had provided the star turn and he knew it. Zina was marvellous too though, in her way, with her gymnastic posturing in harness upon the high wire, but she erred toward the wooden in her speech. She'd made sure to steal the show in looks, however, intentionally selecting squatter, darker, frankly more Kebapi-looking, actresses for the parts of Tinkerbell, Wendy and Tiger Lily.

On returning to Zina's office to change, the exhilaration of his performance still coursing through him, Randolph found Sneed awaiting him and canvassed his opinion directly, 'Well Edwin, what say you?'

'Tristram, you have found your vocation in life. It is to play the dame!' Sneed exclaimed.

'So do I get out of jail free then, or am I to be flung back in, despite having passed 'GO' with aplomb.'

'You're free to go, Tristram and, not only that, it will be my pleasure to escort you to the airport.'

'But what about bidding Zina and all the rest of the cast farewell. I should think they'll be a splendid cast party. I don't want to miss that.'

'There is to be and you will. President's orders, I'm afraid. Best follow them before he changes his mind. He sends his congratulations, by the by, as do Miss Felicity, as well as young Gerald, who specially requested I convey that he liked you much better in a dress.'

'Yes, I could tell that from afar and it'll be in my current identity that I'll be travelling with you to the airport because clearly Zina has had someone dispose of my soiled clothes.'

'It would be my honour, Madam,' Sneed joked, chivalrously placing his Chesterfield, draped over his arm onto Randolph's bare shoulders, 'You can get changed at the airport. I've had your things packed up and your luggage sent ahead. Our side's still in full control of the airport road, which will, no doubt, please the Ruskies, in the event we lose control of the rest and Mr Putin needs to send in back-up.'

'Hmm, are you sure they got everything? They were a bit slap-dash when they packed up Gabby and Gemmy's stuff. There's a leather Aspinall Shadow Messenger bag amongst it, you know.'

'A shadow messenger bag, eh? Sounds more like something I ought to have. But yes, everything's there. I supervised the action myself after I dropped you off here.'

The two of them sat in silence in the back of the Bentley for a couple of minutes, Sneed gazing meditatively out his window, before Randolph worked up the courage to pop the big question. He felt his costume would render him sufficiently disarming that he'd get a frank answer, like Barry Humphries hosting talk shows as Dame Edna Everage. 'Edwin, my dear,' he ventured in falsetto, 'why do you do it?'

'Do what?' Sneed asked distractedly.

'Go so far out of your way to rescue idiots abroad like my father or myself, and plenty of others, I have little doubt...but also waste your obviously remarkable diplomatic talents serving Anomaly Zoran?'

Sneed turned and faced him, 'What makes you think that ultimately I do the things I do for Zoran, or you for that matter?'

'Then who do you do them for?' asked Randolph in confusion.

'For England, of course!'

'I knew it!' Randolph exclaimed, putting his hand to his shaven décolletage in imitation of a gesture he'd copied from Gemmy, 'You're MI6, aren't you?'

'If I were with MI6, Tristram, I wouldn't tell you, would I, unless I were about to kill you.'

Randolph's voice dropped an octave into the high end of his own register and he grabbed Sneed's hand, 'Oh God, you're not driving me out into the desert to shoot me, are you?!'

Sneed withdrew his hand and shook his head in dismay, 'No, because I don't work for MI6, do I?'

'But if you don't work for them, how did you learn to do what you do, to be as you are?'

'As I believe I mentioned when we first met, I was a bank manager.'

'But how does a bank manager learn—'

'I ran the back office at Baring's, bankers to Their Majesties...until it was brought down by a greedy, know-nothing, about whom I warned the toffs at the top but they wouldn't listen because I wasn't a public school man. I moved money all around the world for the wealthiest individuals in Britain and plenty of foreign

VIPs. Did you think I'd managed The Midland in Leighton Buzzard or some such thing?'

Randolph said nothing for several seconds...since this was exactly what he had thought. 'So that was how you came to know President Zoran? Not through your shared enthusiasm for barometers?'

'Exactly, though we do share an interest in barometers. That only came out later though.'

Randolph glanced out the window. Just at that moment, they were passing the Swineforth International campus. He waved it good riddance, in the style of the Queen, and strangely, with a touch of nostalgia. The notion of waving like the Queen brought him back to his train of thought. 'But how, Edwin, is what you do here in Kebapistan serving England?'

Sneed stared back at him with a strange intensity, 'Because, Tristram,' Sneed began with passionate intensity, 'The Great Game never ended. It was merely in abeyance for 70 years with Russia putting us in apparent checkmate with the offense known as the Soviet Empire. But it was not mate, merely check and, thanks partly to my discreet efforts, Great Britain is still at play on The Great Board of Central Asia.'

'Crikey!' Randolph murmured, adjusting his bodice, which had got into a twist, 'I had no idea.'

'I like to think that it is, in part, due to my quiet feeding of President Zoran's admirable Anglophilia that a goodly portion of Kebapistan's oil winds up in BP's refineries, rather than the lot going to the Russians. And that the lion's share of Kebapistan's metals have, for the past quarter century, landed in the mouths of the British lion and her cubs, Australia and Canada, which is to say our Commonwealth mining companies, instead of ending up in the hands of the Yanks, or more recently, the Chinese.'

They were approaching what Randolph surmised must be the first line of defence for the airport, a checkpoint of armored cars and heavy machine guns surrounded by sandbags. The Bentley slowed to a crawl. Sneed rolled down the window, letting in the frigid night air. Randolph shivered, more from nerves, but without cause for as soon as the officer in command saw Sneed's face, he stood to attention and saluted, allowing them through without a word.

'And then, Tristram, as you've seen just there, or at the central police station on our first meeting, there's the power. I daresay I'm the most powerful person in the country, outside of Anomaly Zoran's extended family, who run the important government departments and most of the biggest companies. From what I've heard about your run at Zara's school, you're not much of one for power over others.'

'You're a shrewd judge of character, Edwin. I do love to be admired and to impress, of course. But you're right, I've no interest at all in lording it over others, in giving orders or being obeyed and all that. Political ambition and potency in my family seems to have faded from our line since the days of my great, great grandfather.'

They slowed down and were waved through a second, more heavily fortified checkpoint, populated by many more soldiers. Again, Sneed lowered the window and they passed on without objection.

'Ah yes, Sir Gannet Vainglory and his friend Viscount Glibly,' Sneed mused, 'Like me, they made lives here, found influence in the court of the old Sultan, though they had a bad deal of trouble for a time. The connection between your past and my present was what motivated me to take an interest in the Glibly lad. Now wouldn't that be a coup for British-Kebapi relations, if it were to come off. It'd make all the tabloids and for a week or so Twitter, Facebook and the like, would be full of chatter about the quirky-looking ginger lad from the faraway nation with the funny name who'd come into a peerage.'

This speculation was not pleasing to Dame

Randolph who haughtily readjusted his hoop skirt and, arching his brows, muttered 'I suspect that on that count, your otherwise astute powers of political prediction are likely to be foxed, Edwin.'

Seeking to assuage Randolph's obviously fragile feelings on the matter Sneed added, 'Naturally, you too Tristram, as a descendent of Sir Gannet, hold a special interest for me through your ancestral connection to The Great Game.' They were approaching the entrance to the airport now and a third checkpoint with barbed wire, parked tanks and a couple of heavy artillery pieces. Sneed leaned over to extract something from his trouser pocket. It was a coin purse with a snap top. He shook its contents out into the palm of his free hand and a flurry of small golden coins dropped out. Sneed asked the chauffeur to stop and taking his overcoat, which Randolph had cast off, from between them, opened the door and stepped out of the car. Randolph watched as he chatted encouragingly with the officers of the Presidential guard who gathered round him. Into each of their gloved hands he pressed one of the small golden coins.

When they drove off again, Randolph inquired, 'Surely, you of all people, didn't have to bribe them?'

'No, no, nothing of the kind,' Sneed announced cheerily, 'Just shoring up their morale and polishing Britain's image in this time of crisis. Royal Mint, tenth of an ounce lunar year gold pieces. Year of the Dog currently, rather fitting given the present circumstances. They're only worth a couple of hundred Pounds each but that's an extra month's salary for these chaps.' Sneed put the dozen or so remaining coins back into the purse, snapped it shut and pressed it into Randolph's hand, 'Something to keep you on your feet for a month or so when you get back to Blighty. I suspect Zara won't be wiring you severance pay any time soon.'

Randolph plucked at his bodice and decorously

deposited the purse in his artificial cleavage, fluttering his false lashes and tittering, 'Ooh, you are too good to me, Sir!'

They pulled up at the small but extravagant terminal. Sneed's chauffeur got out and opened the door for Randolph. Randolph held out his hand, as if to be kissed but Sneed, turned it vertical and shook it firmly, saying 'Not a word about what I've done for you when you get back. I'm still a back office man and I like to keep a very low profile. I told your father the same on the phone in relation to the Glibly boy. He kept his word like a gentleman and I expect his son to do the same. Understood and agreed?'

'Understood and agreed, Mr Sneed,' Randolph repeated in his own baritone voice.

'Excellent,' Sneed said and, reaching into his overcoat pocket, pulled out Randolph's passport and handed it to him, 'Off you go then. No need for a ticket, you're virtually the only passenger and the crew, as well as passport control, have been notified you're coming. They know you're coming at the other end, too. No stop in Munich, straight to London. Less fuss that way. Finally, I'm sure that an actor such as yourself will be fully able to improvise a suitable tale to explain the circumstances of his departure from a closed country in the midst of a revolution.'

Randolph slipped his passport down the front of his bodice and stepped out of the Bentley. He had his wig box by its silken cord in his left hand and tucked his empty dress carrier under his left arm. With his free right, he shut the car door and stood waving frantically, now more like a queen than the Queen, as the burgundy chariot of the noble knight of The Great Game drove off into the wintry dark.

25

The airport looked abandoned other than that all the lights were on, putting Randolph in mind of a zombie apocalypse movie. The only people to be seen were young draftee soldiers in the sandy coloured uniform of the regular army standing-- or more frequently leaning, squatting or sitting-- on guard here and there. They gawked in wonder at him sailing by them in his sky-high blue wig and brocaded turquoise bodice. They must never have seen anyone cross-dressed before, definitely nobody so gorgeously cross-dressed anyway. To judge from Zara's nasty little comments about Michael and Piyotr, it was probably illegal. Approaching the border control gate, he saw that all the booths save one were empty. In the one that was occupied, the officer 'on duty' was fast asleep with his head on his desk. Randolph tapped gently on the thick Plexiglas. No response. He rapped smartly.

The policeman raised his head drowsily and stared at Randolph incredulous, probably thinking he was dreaming. Randolph plucked his passport from his bodice and presented it. When the fellow opened it to the photo page, he shook his head, as if seeking to dispel the pink elephant of some dreadful hangover. Randolph helpfully held his wig aloft and recognition dawned. Alas, following Zina's initial depredations and the stress of his week in prison, his hair was now nearly as thinned out as before his transplants so that he resembled his passport photo rather more closely than on his arrival five months earlier. A folded sheet of

Zina's lavender stationery bearing her autograph and an important looking seal dropped out of his passport. The immigration officer looked it over. 'Paper say you special permit go,' He proceeded to hold up the note and kiss the signature. Having popped it into his shirt pocket, he made a gesture in front of his chest of full breasts and nodding knowingly at Randolph said, 'Zina Zoran, number one beautifuls lady Kebapistan!' followed by an onomatopoeia that was plainly equivalent to 'Pfwaw!' in English.

All except one of the gates was closed. At the one that appeared to be open, a trio of burly male flight attendants in Kebap-Air uniform were sprawled out drowsing on the terminal seating by the boarding counter, in front of which were his half dozen pieces of Maxwell Scott luggage. They were from the previous year's collection, purchased at the Maxwell Scott outlet but Randolph had been fairly confident no one of his acquaintance would pick up on that. He walked over to his bags, unfolded and unzipped the suit carrier and pulled out his soft wool Fortnum and Mason blazer. A hand clamped down on his bare shoulder. It was one of the flight attendants, no doubt roused by the sound of the zip, who demanded, 'Passport!' He fished into his bodice once more, handed over his passport to the fellow and lifted his wig again. The man made a querulous face, let go of him and, handing back the passport, grunted, 'Okay'.

Randolph zipped and folded the suit carrier back up and opened the two holdalls. He'd had a damned hard time of it these past few months, days especially, so comfort would be his watchword for his return journey. He rummaged round in them until he found a comfy pair of plum-colored Oliver Spencer cords and a cozy Grayers & Harper flannel shirt, as well as a fresh pair of briefs and socks. Laying all this atop one of the holdalls, he opened his shoe carrier and extracted his Clarks chukka boots. He stood up with his clothes clutched in one arm, his wig box and dress carrier in the other and realized the three flight attendants were all staring at him. He rolled his eyes, sniffed haughtily and flounced off in the direction of the first toilet to catch his eye, which happened to be a ladies room.

He emerged a new man-- literally, all the more so with the purse of little gold coins, safely stowed in his left trouser pocket. At the gate he found the three stewards standing now. They looked decidedly better pleased with his appearance. The one who'd grabbed him by the shoulder now grunted 'Boarding time', at which he and his two colleagues stepped toward the gate. Randolph cleared his throat loudly and they turned round. He glared at them and indicated his luggage with a sweep of his hand. The lead steward gave a disgruntled snort but the three of them returned and picked up his bags. He trotted down the gangway after them and entered the empty plane.

'Lucky for me you're still flying,' he remarked, hoping to make peace with the snorting steward, who only snorted once again, 'Not fly for passengers. Fly for carry cargoes.' The stewards were heaving his bags up into the forward most overhead luggage bins.

'Cracking, what's the cargo then?'

'None your businesses!' the steward sneered, 'Order allow you fly first class. Sit. Sleep. No meal in flight.'

'That's a relief on this airline,' Randolph said drily, giving up on winning the fellow over. Shattered as he was, he dropped off to sleep again, just as he had in Zina's bath, almost as soon as they'd taken off.

'Good to be heading home,' Tom's cheery Liverpudlian voice said to him soothingly in his dream. Randolph was astonished to see him in white tie and tails but, above his collar, a brush-like turkey's beard stuck out and above that, knobbled, red and blue wattles hung pulsating. Over his beak-nose, on the side facing Randolph as they sat together, transported back to the plank bed in the cell, hung his turkey's snood twitching. He was horrified, but Tom had been so kind to him in there that his horror was mingled with a tragic pity.

Randolph began to weep and sniffled, 'Oh Tom, I thought you were going too far with the Turkey charade but I didn't say anything...and now look what's happened to you!'

'It's alright, Tristram, old mate,' Tom leaned toward Randolph to comfort him, his wattles altering in hue, 'I'm glad I'm turning into an actual turkey. Makes a nice change, you know. Now they'll have to put me in the mental hospital.' He reached out to take Randolph's hand but Tom's turkey's claw was sharp with curved nails.

Concomitantly, the voice of Anomaly Zoran boomed over a loudspeaker, 'The turkey shall not dare set its scaly foot in this blessed land!'

Randolph screamed in his sleep and woke with a start. He opened his eyes in the half light of dawn, and observed a figure sitting across the aisle from him, huddled in a blanket. He gasped in fear and thought, 'Dear God, let it be human!'

Tom's lank, long uncut prisoner's hair and scruffy beard peeped out from the folds of the blanket. He still looked like one of the Irish hunger strikers Randolph had watched on television with morbid fascination during his teens.

'It's alright, Tristram, it's me, Tom.'

'Tom? Tom, how did you get here?'

'The fella in the bowler hat came back for me after he took you away. He told me how you'd insisted on takin' me back to England with you.'

'Did he?' Randolph asked, doing his best to conceal his shock.

'Yeah, he said you said you wouldn't go unless I went too. I tell ya, it restored me faith in humanity after the business with me fiancée and me best mate. Prison guards put me in manacles though. You know, cos they think I'm a danger to myself and others, like. Anyways, the little fella brought me here sitting on a newspaper in his Bentley. Lovely motor that, eh? He had me driven right out onto the tarmac and one of them rolling stairways put up to the back door of the plane. Flight attendants were getting the cabin in order. He told 'em to let me lie down across the seats. Gave out gold pieces to 'em an' all. Let me have me passport back. Told me to keep it safe by opening it to the middle and hookin' over the elastic of me pants,' Tom opened the blanket and revealed the ingenious arrangement.

'This is wonderful news, Tom, but didn't Mr Sneed think to leave you some clothes?'

'He seemed to be in a hurry, Tristram. Bundled me into that fine motor of his and away we went, like. I asked him take off the manacles when he put me on the plane but he said to ask you. Told me I should tell you to look in your new purse. No clue what he meant by it.'

Randolph reached into his pocket and took out the purse. There amidst the little golden coins were a couple of flashes of silver. The small steel keys to the manacles. He plucked them out, showed them to Tom and returned the purse to his pocket. Tom held out his hands and Randolph tried a key in the manacles. It turned and they snapped open.

'That's a relief!' Tom quipped. Not wanting to get anywhere near Tom's feet, he handed the other key to Tom, who bent over and freed them.

'Now let's see what we can do about your clothes,' Randolph stood up and opened the overhead bin in which he'd seen the stewards stow the smaller of his holdalls. He'd noticed the old yoga wear and black ballet shoes he'd worn only the once in Kebapistan during the tribulation of the ice-breaker games with the, as it turned out, well named Swineforth Hospital International Team. He certainly had no intention of giving Tom any of his proper clothes. They were far too good to waste on such a ragamuffin. He did determine, however, to spare Tom a pair of briefs and of socks, costly though they were. He tossed the things down to him and told him to go to the airplane loo to put them on. 'Give yourself a thorough wash down first and throw away those damned briefs,' he admonished, 'I'll hold onto your passport. Use plenty of soap and don't think twice about splashing water everywhere. Consider it a shower cubicle rather than a toilet.'

Tom was, understandably, away for some time giving Randolph a time to plan what he would do with him on landing. He could lose him in the crowd or tell him to head down the corridor for connecting flights whilst he headed out of the airport. Easy as it could be to separate from him, he finally decided this would be shabby of him and the noble course of action would be to deposit him in the nearest homeless hostel to the airport. It would take him out of his way a fair bit but it was the right thing to do.

After twenty minutes, one of the surly stewards, who'd all been asleep, stood up and asked Randolph, 'Where is crazy man go?'

'Toilet,' Randolph answered sullenly.

The steward walked over to the sole toilet showing 'Occupied' on the door, banged it hard twice with his fist and bawled, 'Get out! Landings time!'

Tom emerged from the toilet looking rather better, more like someone fresh out of an ashram in India, as opposed to a prison Kebapistan. After a menacing warning from another of the stewards, they buckled themselves in for landing. On the ground, Tom helped Randolph load his luggage onto a trolley left at the landing gate. When they emerged into the arrivals area among a number of people from a different flight, a horde of journalists rushed forward, flashes blazing and shutters whirring. Randolph looked about him for some celebrity, head down in a pair of dark glasses, but no, the journalists were waiting for *him*, calling *his* name, in a fashion... 'Christian! Winston, over here! Mr

Gandalf Himoff! William Randolph!'"

Had news of his remarkable performance last night preceded him? A woman with a microphone followed by a man with a camera on his shoulder were suddenly in front of him, other reporters swarming round.

'What's the present situation in Kebapistan, Sir? Is President Anomaly Zoran going to step down?'

Randolph paused to stand and deliver, 'Anomaly Zoran is, for better or for worse, not the stepping down type.' He thought it best to add 'for better or worse' to paraphrase Sneed's comment to him in order to play it safe and not be seen as taking sides. 'I saw the President and his family at the National Theatre of Kebapistan at the pantomime in which, through a series of coincidences, I found myself in a cameo role that stole the show,' Randolph beamed.

'Pantomime?' asked a journalist, confused. 'Are you referring to the ridiculous claims by Kebapi government that the revolution in progress is only a transient, minor civil disruption?'

Randolph was the one who was confused now, 'No, my friend here is not a transient. He has been through a terrible ordeal in Diskebapisbad prison, which is where I came to know him.'

'Amnesty International are calling you a hero of the negotiating table for getting him out, how do you feel about that?'

'Pretty good,' was all Randolph could think to answer...*What on Earth was all this about?* he wondered.

Then they all turned to Tom, who was trying to hide behind Randolph, peering over his shoulder, overwhelmed by suddenly having so many people around him after his years of isolation. 'What's it like to be free again, Tom?'

Tom searched for the right words and came out with, 'It's that refreshing!' reading aloud the slogan of a canned drink that a journalist had in her hand.

'What are your plans for tonight? How will you be celebrating?'

Tom turned to Randolph for some help with answering this one as he had no idea about tonight, he didn't even have any idea about the next few minutes, and clearly viewed Randolph in loco parentis. Randolph looked into his sad, needy face and it dawned on him that dropping the man off at the closest homeless hostel might not make him look too good in eyes of the press. 'He's coming home with me,' Randolph said heroically, 'Tom will have a quiet few days while he starts to recover from his ordeal and will then consider various options on how to move forward.'

'And will you be seeing your ex-fiancée, Tom?'

'I can't even remember her name right now, to be honest,' Tom grinned, 'I'm content to hang around with me mate, Tristram for the time being.'

A pair of representatives from Amnesty International popped up and called out, 'Sorry, Mr Randolph, but Mr Thomas will need an overnight stay in the hospital tonight for checks, after which we need to debrief him and gage the extent of human rights abuses in Kebapi prisons for our next annual report.'

Randolph found himself much obliged to hear this but masked his joy with a stoical nod of acceptance.

They whisked Tom off, the media in hot pursuit. Randolph was relieved they'd neglected to ask for an address at which to deliver Tom tomorrow. He watched them all trot off and then pushed his overladen trolley of luggage out to the taxi stand for the 5 mile hop to Twickenham. He had no money other than Sneed's gold pieces but that was alright. His parents were almost certain to be in and they could pay. In the cab, he tried to make sense of what had happened...Sneed must've leaked a false announcement that he, Randolph, had somehow rescued not only himself but Tom. He'd ask his parents about it so that his story would be consistent. He instructed the cabby to bring his luggage into the porch and he knocked at his parents' door. His father opened it and smiled broadly. 'You're the hero of the Christmas hour, my boy,' he laughed, 'I always knew you had it in you...however deep down.'

'Thanks, Dad,' Randolph responded, 'You couldn't spot me a twenty, could you, old man, along with a tip to the cabby for bringing out the luggage? I had to catch a cab here with all this stuff and all I've got on me, in typical pantomime style, is a few gold pieces.'

Giles did what was asked of him and Randolph strolled into the sitting room where Barnaby Glibly was glued to a daytime soap with an oversized bag of cheese and onion crisps. He didn't seem to be cinnabar-coloured anymore and his hair had been shorn back tidily. He was dressed in some of Randolph's clothes, which didn't thrill his erstwhile elder sibling. Barnaby jumped up and took his hand, greeting him with, 'Hello brother!'

Randolph freed his hand, 'I think 'Hello, very distant cousin!' will suffice. Look Barney, why don't you be a good little chap and bring my cases up to my room? I'm bushed.'

Jocelyn appeared from the kitchen, burst into tears and rushed forward to hug Randolph, leaving, he sensed, an impression of off-kilter lipstick upon his weary cheek.

Later in the day, once Randolph had had a good kip, they all sat together sipping hot chocolate and sampling the contents of a Walker's shortbread selection tin Barnaby had picked out at Marks & Spencer.

'Giles is making progress with sorting out the viscountcy for Barney. We think there may even be a property near Merthyr-Tydfil he's entitled to,' Jocelyn revealed.

'Well, that will be useful if he wants to return to the mine,' Randolph quipped.

'And what will you do now, Tristram? I don't suppose you'll be going back over there,' Giles enquired.

'Oh, no, no, definitely not. I rather thought I'd try

my luck treading the boards again, but haven't given much thought to how I'll fund the actor's life. I imagine the Silligator has been shelved?'

'I'm afraid it has,' Giles lamented, 'The Major hasn't spoken to us since that episode out in the desert, but your mother has had a bit of a windfall that'll tide us all over until my next great invention...'

'Yes, Tristram, do you remember I told you I'd been penning some children's books? They were taken up by a top agent who sold them to a leading published and I got an advance to write a collection!'

'You mean the book with the ridiculous title?' Randolph was stunned.

'Yes!' Jocelyn smiled, '*The Canine Jamboree*, and the rest of the trilogy, *The Feline Jamboree* and *The Gerbil Jamboree*.'

'Erm, shouldn't the last one be *The Rodent Jamboree*...for zoological consistency?' Randolph suggested.

'Funny you should say that as it was a bone of contention between the publisher and myself,' Jocelyn nodded sagely, 'But I stuck to my guns and kept it as it was to keep the children on their toes...a sort of 'life isn't always as we expect' lesson meant to—'

The doorbell rang, followed almost immediately by insistent sounding knocking. Annoyed, Randolph signalled to his parents to remain seated and rose to deal with whatever it was. It was the press again. It certainly hadn't taken them long to find his parents address. A microphone was thrust toward him and he was asked, 'Dr Randolph how exactly did you bring off your and Tom Thomas's escape from Diskebapisbad prison. The place is meant to be a fortress, isn't it?'

Randolph was instantly in his métier. 'Yes, it truly is a fortress, originally built during the Timurid Empire, I believe.' He still didn't have his story straight and played for time, 'Look, it's a convoluted tale, which I really should hold off telling until such time as Tom and

I are reunited and can relate it together. Nevertheless, I will reveal that it involved my having to become a pantomime dame and to perform at the National Theatre of Kebapistan in that role. Let me show you something...Barney, come out and hold the fort a moment.'

Barnaby Glibly stood in the doorway looking befuddled, as if he were one of the gerbils from Jocelyn's fictive jamboree, while Randolph went to fetch his wig box. He opened it with a flourish, removed the flamboyant hair piece, thrust the box into Barnaby's hands, set it on his head and struck a vintage bathing beauty pose, left hip out, three quarters to the cameras, and hands above his head with palms upturned. He was in the limelight and was determined to seize the day to relaunch his theatrical career.

It is was also an ideal moment, Randolph realised, to burnish his newfound reputation as a good Samaritan, 'May I introduce my adoptive little brother, Barnaby Glibly. My parents and I met this exceptional young man in Kebapistan only a few weeks ago, after discovering that the daughter of my great, great grandfather from a second marriage in Kebapistan, where he served as a British diplomat at the height of The Great Game, married the son of this chap's great, great, great, great grandfather, a fellow Victorian diplomat, likewise caught up in The Great Game, and the last known Viscount Glibly. At the time we found this poor lad, he was working in a mercury mine in conditions similar to those endured by British miners during the darkest days of the Industrial Revolution. Through my efforts, we were, thank goodness, able to bring him back here to London, where it is my hope that we shall be seeing him take up his family's long vacant seat in the House of Lords when he turns 21.'

Several photo ops followed, in which Barnaby Glibly wore the blue wig, in which Randolph chuckled as he handed it over, in which Barnaby was handing it back, in which they engaged in a cautious mock tussle over it. Randolph resumed his oratory, 'But what we'd both really love to find mentioned in your articles are the names of those two forgotten, brave Englishmen, my great-great grandfather Sir Gannet Vainglory and Barnaby's great, great, great, great grandad, Barnaby Glibly, who, like me, found themselves imprisoned, in Kebapistan, then known as the Sultanate of Mish Lope. I had the good fortune to escape and to be able to take Barney here, and my friend Tom Thomas, with me. My Victorian forebears, however, did not get off so lightly. Following a major miscarriage of diplomacy involving a gold-plated bidet, which I will leave it to you gentleman and ladies of the press to look up for yourselves in the official records of the Foreign Office for 1886, they were left for dead and lived out the remainder of their lives as hostages in a barbaric land. It really is the stuff of a BBC period drama if any producer wishes to call on me to discuss the project. Thank you, that will be all for now.'

At breakfast the next morning, Giles brought home from the corner shop, whither he had gone to replenish the household milk supply, an armful of newspapers featuring his son, mainly on the front page among a range of headlines from 'Clear-Headed Headmaster Escapes Revolution with Political Prisoner' in *The Times* to 'Tom Thom the Turkey Man Stolen by the Head and Away he Ran!' in *The Sun*. The family favourite, however, was a longer piece in *The Financial Times* Sunday Supplement entitled, 'Second Act of Silk Road Victorian Melodrama Unfolds 130 Years Later'.

As Randolph sat at the breakfast table about midday devouring every word, who should call around but Tom. He still had his mad, darting Turkey's eye, but he was properly clean now with a hipsterish haircut and beard trim and improved winter clothing, including an Amnesty International hoodie, jogging bottoms and pair of trainers that were too big for him. Jocelyn sat him at the table and rushed off to bring him some fresh tea as he made a start on a plateful of scones. Hoping he'd be on his way soon, Randolph asked him what his plans were.

'I haven't given that much thought, Tristram, but I thought I'd hang on here a while. Your mum rang up Amnesty HQ. They wanted me to stay there longer but she told 'em you were missing me, like, and that I could share your old room with yous.'

'Did she now?'

'Just 'til I get meself together, you know? It'll be like sharing the cell again, only without the bucket! I tell you, Tristram, I'm enjoying using a toilet again, not usually missing on the old Number 1s either. And did you see how I ate them scones? I'm totally overcoming the impulse to break things into crumbs and throw in the air to catch in my beak. I'm getting right over me turkey persona and back into me person persona.'

Giles strolled in and recommended the five of them go out for a drive to get Tom familiar with the local area. Tristram, regretting his decision to tag along, sat cramped on the back seat of his parents' 15 year old Rover estate, wedged in between the two foundlings, with Giles and Jocelyn up at the front.

'Oh, Giles, it's like we've got three sons in the back!' Jocelyn clucked.

Randolph writhed. Giles pointed out the Stoop, as if this weren't already glaringly obvious with its being the largest rugby stadium in the country, Strawberry Hill House, Orleans House, his former preparatory school, his former secondary school, their favorite ice cream parlour. 'Why don't you three boys get out at the Green and play a little footie together?' Giles suggested, as if they were respectively 7, 9 and 11 years old.

'I'll just get out here on my own and have a walk, thanks Dad,' Randolph offered, doing his best to keep calm, 'I fancy some fresh air.' Tom and Barney were eager to accompany him but he insisted they stay with his parents and start to get to know one another.

'I think Tristram needs a little alone time,' Jocelyn smiled.

As they drove off, he walked onto Twickenham Green fuming. Entering the park, he looked heavenward and shouted 'Damn and Blast! What did I do to deserve this?' at his inane shambles of a life.

26

Four and a half years later, Randolph was in attendance at the annual Retired Headmasters and Headmistresses Dinner at the Drapers' Hall on Throgmorton Street. He was admiring the Gobelin silk tapestries depicting Jason's trials and tribulations in pursuit of the golden fleece and ran his fingers through his own golden fleece which had been restored to something above and beyond its former glory. He had insisted that the hair transplant clinic overcompensate for his loss when he'd first returned from Kebapistan. He was want to stay celibate since the traumatic incident when his hair was plucked out before his eyes by that nymphomaniac wild cat.

The room was packed out with silver-haired sages, clattering and clinking their tableware, guffawing and holding forth over their *confit de canard*. Randolph's eye, on the other hand, had now wandered up to the magnificent ceiling mural, a lofty depiction of Titania and her fairies, naked in aerial feats amidst clouds and swathes of gossamer. To his consternation, his thoughts turned forthwith to Zina Zoran up in the gods strapped into her harness in that fetching Peter Pan outfit. How much more splendid would that have been if she had been unclad like Titania above?

'Randolph? Tristram Randolph?' a voice brought him out of his revelry and he looked down to see a familiar face...it was Roger Swainson.

'Good lord, Roger! I was wondering if I'd bump into you here along with a few of my other old colleagues.'

'I always meant to catch up with you after the Kebapistan shambles, Randolph, but I never managed to get round to it.'

'Ha! I was well out of that one!'

'Quite the experience you had out there! You should write a novel about it.'

'Hmm, I've toyed with that idea, Roger, or a one-man show even.'

'Yes, it's certainly not short on the drama and possibly, in your hands, high comedy! You could call it...'

'*Randolph in the Underworld,*' Randolph proclaimed, striking a pose.

'Or *Let the Swine Go Forth!*' Swainson added, 'And that's no comment on your good self, naturally.'

'I like the way you're thinking, Roger, I'll properly sit down and have a go at writing something in the not-too-distant future.'

'Whatever became of those young fellows you got out of Kebapistan?... I read about it in the newspapers: you were quite the hero! How's that turkey chap doing?'

'Tom? Oh, we did all we could for him but he just couldn't fully shuffle off his turkey coil when faced with the challenges of modern life. Took to scratching up the carpets and started being terribly defensive about the house, menacing the postman and suchlike. We had to have him assessed, just to be on the safe side. Social services found him a place in a very nice group home full of similar types. I believe he shares a room with an unassuming fellow who seems to think he's a wren. Always hiding in hedges apparently.'

'And what about the Kebapi chap, your distant relation, who was in line for a peerage?'

'Well, that turned out to be a long and rather squiggly line. The Lord Chancellor in the Crown Office wouldn't accept the documentation he'd brought over with him from Kebapistan so all that was a fool's errand, as I'd warned my parents from the outset.

Believe it or not, he's gone back down the mine. He confessed to my parents that he was missing it terribly so they took him to a mining museum in Wales and they got talking to a fellow there who set our very own Viscount Barnaby up in a little miners' cooperative. He's digging for copper now so he's turned greenish, looks like a leprechaun, but totally happy and earning a damn sight more than he did in Jizbizisbad.'

'And I hear things are *justasbad* in Jizbizisbad and the rest of 'Zoranistan'. The attempt to overthrow the dictator came to nothing, as expected. Shame...that Preyn fellow seemed quite decent but he ended up fleeing for his life... lives in exile somewhere in Scandinavia with that niece of his, I believe. His deputies are dead or rotting in jail in Diskebapisbad, serving as examples to anyone who thinks to embark on the gargantuan undertaking of unseating the tyrant. Providing the electorate is hampered by ill education, the Zoran regime will remain indefinitely, voted in by those scant of reasoning.'

'And that is why we are here today,' Randolph proclaimed, 'To champion education!'

'Hear, hear,' everyone around the table called out and raised their glasses.

'And what is it you are doing with yourself these days, Randolph?' Swainson smiled up at him.

'Well, other than the occasional spot of relief catering, which brings me here with you today - actually, may I take that empty glass?-'

'I know! I almost didn't recognise you in your waiter's livery!'

'-I'm doing some work as an extra here and there and...drum roll for this *tour de force*... I have worked in panto *every season* since returning from Kebapistan!'

'Jolly good show, Randolph! I was having a giggle about that in the papers with Nigel just after you got back - you play the Dame, correct?'

'Yes, I am widely regarded as one of the finest

Dames of my generation. I've been called upon by theatres the length and breadth of the British Isles... Aspatria, Pontardawe, Fife to name but a few. Last year I played in a prominent London theatre, the Croydon Empire, perhaps you know it?... *Advancing steadily toward the West End*, I hear you thinking.'

'So, your modicum of fame after Kebapistan came in handy - that's the first step into getting panto roles, isn't it, the modicum of fame?'

'Well, it was a bit of door opener but in my case it was mainly down to raw talent.'

'Well, I'm so pleased for you, Randolph. In your twilight years you have found satisfaction in this unusual path. The prodigal swine went forth, but returned to find happiness in his own backyard. A classic tale, albeit a curly one.'

Printed in Great Britain
by Amazon